MORTAL REMAINS

STERLING TEEN
New York

An Imprint of Sterling Publishing Co., Inc
122 Fifth Avenue
New York, NY 10011

ISBN 978-1-4549-3948-1
978-1-4549-3949-8 (e-book)

Distributed in Canada by Sterling Publishing Co., Inc.
C/o Canadian Manda Group, 664 Annette Street
Toronto, Ontario M6S 2C8, Canada
Distributed in the United Kingdom by GMC Distribution Services
Castle Place, 166 High Street, Lewes, East Sussex BN7 1XU, England
Distributed in Australia by NewSouth Books
University of New South Wales, Sydney, NSW 2052, Australia

For information about custom editions, special sales, and premium and corporate
purchases, please contact Sterling Special Sales at
800-805-5489 or specialsales@sterlingpublishing.com.

Manufactured in the United States of America

Lot #:
2 4 6 8 10 9 7 5 3 1
12/20

sterlingpublishing.com

Cover design by Elizabeth Mihaltse Lindy
Interior design by Julie Robine

Cover credit:
Shutterstock.com: FOX IN THE BOX (rose); jessicahyde (background);
KaoStock (ivy)

MORTAL REMAINS

MARY ANN FRASER

STERLING TEEN

To my husband, Todd.

And to my father, Noel.

Not all heroes make it to the end of the story.

Death sets a Thing significant
The Eye had hurried by,
Except a perished Creature
Entreat us tenderly

To ponder little Workmanships
In Crayon or in Wool,
With "This was last her fingers did"
Industrious until

The Thimble weighed too heavy,
The stitches stopped themselves,
And then 'twas put among the dust
Upon the Closet shelves.

A Book I have, a friend gave,
Whose Pencil, here and there,
Had notched the place that pleased him,—
At rest his fingers are.

Now, when I read, I read not,
For interrupting Tears
Obliterate the Etchings
Too costly for repairs.

—Emily Dickinson, "Death Sets a Thing Significant"

LILY McCRAE'S
RULES OF CONDUCT

RULE #1
ONLY LET THE DEAD SEE YOU CRY.

No one listens like the dead. Not in my house, anyway.

Take Helen Delaney. She arrived a week into summer, and after two days I was confessing things to her—the dark private things, the self-incriminating fragments of my life that I'd never told another living soul. But, like most people who entered through our back doors, her time with us was coming to a swift end. With organ music as our soundtrack and converted gas lamps to light our way, we caromed down the hall to the cold room for the last time. The warped flooring my great-grandfather had salvaged from the town's infamous hanging tree at the edge of our property creaked rhythmically. It was the house's way of reminding me that it still breathed with the echoes of my ancestors' footsteps.

"Hang on," I told Helen. The shimmying gurney collided against the chair rail with a *bonk* that jolted her arm over the side. I was running late, but what were a few minutes to put things right? Helen was in no rush.

I placed her fallen limb back across her midsection and rearranged the plastic strand of pearls caught on a button, all while noting how the Caribbean Coral lip stain I selected perfectly framed Helen's unwavering smile and complemented her peachy complexion.

People often ask, "Doesn't it gross you out to work on cadavers? What if a corpse comes back to life? Aren't you afraid of ghosts?" None of that frightened me. Truth is only the living can hurt you, but I also knew dead isn't necessarily gone. That day six years earlier, when I somersaulted out of a tree, proved as much.

So no, corpses didn't bother me. Never had. I accept that bodies come with expiration dates. It's their stories that haunt me, and there's no end to stories when your family owns a funeral home. Helen's story was like too many—seventy-one, living out of her car, and, if the trash in the back seat was any indication, surviving on Spudnuts and Big Macs. A whole day had gone by before someone found her slumped over her steering wheel at the far end of a Walmart parking lot, a crumpled wad of photos in her hand. It was the many images of a scruffy little boy that convinced me at least one person would come to her viewing to say goodbye. I was wrong. That's how Helen became one more in a growing tally of people I've washed and dressed in preparation for the grave, and in the end, it changed nothing.

I straightened the oil painting of Eilean Donan Castle—the gurney nearly knocked it from its hook—and noted the trail of scuffs and gouges I'd added to the wainscoting behind me. "Dad's going to take that out of my pay for sure." It wouldn't have happened at all if I'd been upstairs changing instead of keeping Helen company. Mallory would be here any minute, and I was still dressed as if I were on my way to one of my parents' Rotary Club luncheons instead of to a party.

Party? More like an intervention. It was all part of Mal's summer plan to reinvent herself—and me, too, while she was at it. But

Mal had stuck by me when I was a broken mess, so if she wanted to go to this party, then I needed to go to this party. Ugh. I would rather chill in the cold room with Helen.

I popped into the office only long enough to unpin my name tag, which read LILY McCRAE, McCRAE FAMILY FUNERAL HOME, and drop it with a *clink* into my *Life Is Good, It's Death That Sucks* mug—a birthday gift from my stepbrother, Evan. Back in the hall with Helen I undid the top button of my blouse and finger-combed my hair. It was the most I was willing to do.

A lean to the right got the gurney running straight again, but I still managed to clip the doorjamb on the way into the prep room. I looked to the regulator clock to bolster my courage. My stepmother, Rachel, claimed the old timekeeper had the steady beat of a dependable heart. "Something we don't hear enough around here," she liked to say. That always used to make Dad laugh. Now, when I needed it most, the ailing mechanism hung ominously mute—probably because no one bothered to wind it.

"I can't do it," I told Helen. "I can't face the loneliness of another crowded party, not even for Mal." I pulled out my phone and started texting.

> ME: Go without me.

> MAL: R U sure?

> ME: Very.

> MAL: But everyone's going to be there.

> ME: Exactly.

I pocketed my phone, hoping she'd forgive me one more time. Then I gave Helen's stiff hand a gentle squeeze. "That's what I like about you, Helen. You aren't going to waste your breath telling me to lighten up and go have a good time when it'll be more of the same." After all, I was the "mortician's daughter," a title that had made me the target of more sick jokes and lame pranks than there were thorns on a briar rose.

The cold-room door seal made a sucking sound as I pulled open the latch. I pushed in the gurney and parked it. With each lock of a wheel, Helen's salt-and-pepper curls bounced lightly over the pillow I'd stitched for her. I pulled out my embroidery snips, the pride of my scissor collection, and clipped a loose thread. Now the pillow was perfect. Of course in cases like Helen's, the county covered the basic costs. According to my parents, anything above and beyond was something we couldn't afford. But life is humbling enough. As the resident apprentice and makeup artist, the least I could do is dignify the departure.

And wasn't the family motto "Take care of the dead and they'll take care of you"? Okay, maybe sometimes I took it too far. Like arranging a viewing for Helen. And so what if I commandeered one of our rental caskets or "borrowed" flowers from a prior service? So what if I stitched angel wings onto Helen's headrest and picked out a cheery little ensemble from the nearest thrift shop? It was my money, my way of letting her know at least one person cared.

But helping the grieving? Nope. Not my job. I'd felt the vacuum the departed left in their wake. That was one vortex of misery I refused to get pulled into, especially when my father already insisted I was too sensitive. It's not like I didn't try to check my emotions. I just sucked at it. Even more reason, I liked to point out, why Evan was the better candidate for taking over the family business when my father retired. And with my dad's hypertension being what it was, that day was coming sooner than any of us was willing to accept—that was, of course, if the McCrae Family Funeral Home didn't go belly-up first.

As much as I appreciated Helen's company, it was time to let her go. I adjusted her body bag, pulled up the sides, and patted her hand one last time. It was the same hand that had held the fistful of photos now waiting in our safe for someone—anyone—to claim. It took all my effort to swallow back my sorrow for yet another forgotten soul. "It's not professional," Dad would have said—had been saying since the day I first toddled into a memorial service. "Look it up," he'd add, "page twenty-one in your grandpa Ted's book, *The Funeral Director's Rules of Conduct.* Twenty thousand copies sold." I loved my grandpa Ted, but damn that book. I'd write my own rules, thank you very much.

For Helen's sake, I bowed my head and offered a moment of silence marred by only a few stifled sniffles. Then, bending close to her ear, I whispered, "I know you had people you loved. And what did that get you? A pine box." I took Helen's smile to mean she agreed, but it was small consolation since I was the one who put it there. "Goodbye, Helen Delaney. Rest in peace. I won't forget you. I promise."

Zipper teeth ground together as I sealed the bag over Helen's stiff, upturned lips. That's as far as I got when an enormous concussive blast slammed the house, pitching me into the gurney. I scrabbled for the door and flung it open. Outside, brakes squealed. Car alarms blared. Dogs howled.

I turned back to the cold room. "Wait here, Helen."

RULE #2
DEATH DOES NOT KEEP HOURS.
NEITHER SHOULD YOU.

Charging from the cold room, I collided with Evan in the hall and stumbled backward, landing on my butt. He jerked me onto my feet and dragged me along behind him.

"What the hell was that?" Nana Jo intercepted us by the front parlor, waving hands stained terra-cotta from sculpting class earlier in the day.

Sirens pealed through the sultry night air.

"Sounds like incoming business to me," quipped Evan. Nana and I exchanged eye rolls, knowing any scolding would be a waste of time. Evan was Evan.

A second later Dad and Rachel joined us on the front porch, and together we gaped, trancelike, at the firestorm funneling skyward only a few blocks away. Huge, billowing black clouds smudged out the waxing moon as sparks rained on neighboring wood-shingle roofs dry as kindling, making the scene both mesmerizing and threatening.

Evan joined the parade of onlookers marching toward the inferno while Rachel, Dad, and Nana Jo collected with neighbors by the weedy, trash-strewn parkway to speculate in hushed voices over possible causes. News vans crowded the streets, and a helicopter circled overhead, the *chop chop* of its rotors adding to the already frenzied pulse of activity.

I didn't budge from the porch. I couldn't. My feet were glued to its knotty planks as one thought crowded out all others: *Please, oh please, don't be the Lassiter house.* But my gut already told me it was. A fire needs a lot of dry wood to burn that hot, that high.

It had been years since I last visited the Lassiter property. In all that time my guilty conscience had struggled to wipe that place, that family, from memory. Some things had been easier to erase—the walnut-shell boats with twigs for masts and leaves for sails that we raced in the irrigation ditch, the baby owlet returned to its nest, the tree hollows stuffed with small gifts for me to find. But it was those somber eyes—deep brown with gold flecks—that I could not forget.

His name was Adam—the boy at the heart of my darkest secret. Deserting him was certainly not for my benefit, and since then his memory had become like the phantom pain after an amputation. In my defense, I deserted him for his own sake. My desperate hope, my prayer, if I were the praying kind, was that he moved away years ago. I'd seen what fire does to flesh.

Two hours later the flames had abandoned the sky and everyone had retreated indoors but me. I lingered on the front steps, waiting for the inevitable. Then the thing I'd been dreading turned the corner: the county coroner's white van. I shuddered. Someone was dead. What if it was Adam? His father's words still haunted me: "Say anything to anyone, or come here again, and it will be Adam who pays."

❊ ❊ ❊

Within days of the explosion, my night terrors returned with a vengeance. In them I was falling, always falling, until I heard the crack of bone and woke screaming, my hair plastered to my sweat-drenched cheeks. I knew I'd only find peace when I put the question of Adam's fate to rest once and for all. It became my obsession. For the next two weeks I scoured the paper and the internet, but the police weren't releasing any information about the blast, its cause, or the names of victims. Sooner than seemed right, the entire event vanished from the news, as though it had never happened. I'd have to find answers somewhere else. I'd have to call in a favor.

Alone in the office, I gave our county coroner, Marty, a ring.

"Hey, Lily. What's up?" he said, in a voice that sounded much too chipper considering what he did for a living.

"Marty, you remember that fire at the old Lassiter place a couple weeks back? What can you tell me about the deceased?"

"Not much. We recovered a body. Male."

I gulped. "How old?"

"Not enough left to determine age or identity, I'm afraid. No matching dental records, either. Why you askin'?"

"I used to know someone who lived there, is all. A friend."

I thanked Marty, hung up, and dropped my head onto my desk, aware that I might never know whether Adam was there the night that old shack of a house blew sky-high. And whose fault was that? Mine.

"Sleeping on the job?"

I jumped half out of my skin.

"Sorry. Didn't mean to startle you." Mallory squinted at me. "You all right? You look like you haven't slept in days."

"I haven't. Not much, anyway." I left it at that. Mal knew me well enough not to bother pushing for anything more.

We met at a funeral. Surprise. Seven-year-old Mallory had taken one look at her aunt Aurelia lying in a coffin and bolted for the garden. My dad sent me to track her down. I found her huddled behind a hydrangea, her black-velvet dress pulled up to her chin to keep it out of the mud. To coax her back inside, I'd explained how each flower in the memorial wreath had a special meaning, like a secret code you could read. In the end, it worked. After that Mal began sitting with me during lunch at school, and she took a lot of crap for it, too.

"You didn't answer my text," I said, sounding needier than I intended.

"Yeah, been busy."

Right. Except, according to Evan, she had plenty of time for her other friends. But she was here now. That gave me hope. "Does this mean you forgive me for bailing on the party?"

"Don't I always? But seriously, Lils, you need to escape this place once in a while. It's so depressing."

Not to me. "Next time," I promised. How many times had I said that before?

Mal shrugged. "Okay then, come to the mall with me."

It was a test. I hated the mall, and she knew it. "I can't. Really. I'm supposed to clean the display room today."

"Then I'll help and we'll go after." She'd cornered me.

❋ ❋ ❋

We'd been polishing smudgy urns and dusting coffin cutaway samples for the better part of an hour when Evan poked his head through the open window, all sly-eyed. "Feel like doing a little treasure hunting?"

Mallory lit up like a candle. "Where?"

"The Lassiter place. Free pickings until the bulldozers come."

Mal snatched up her dust rag and lobbed it into the bucket of cleaning supplies. "Beats doing this. Unless you'd rather go to the mall, Lily?"

I knew I should question Evan more about this supposed treasure hunt, but this was probably my last shot at finding out the fate of the boy with the gold-flecked eyes—the one who brought me back to life when I was good as dead. The one I abandoned.

I raised my hands in false surrender. "All right, I'm in."

RULE #3
MAKE EACH PERSON'S LAST DAY
ABOVE GROUND MEMORABLE.

DEAD END read the sign. Dead end was right. A life was recently lost not far from where the asphalt met the weeds. My stomach churned as I took in the pall of ash smothering the ravaged lot with its stubble of charred stumps. A few scattered clusters of tortured trees were all that remained of the sprawling orchard that was once my refuge from school—my Sherwood Forest, my Terabithia, my Neverland. Yellow crime-scene tape hung in loose swags: CAUTION CAUTION CAUTION. Dread seized me by the throat.

"This place gives me the creeps," said Mal. "Always has."

Most people in Smith's Hollow felt that way about the old Lassiter house, which is saying a lot in a town founded on the site of a mob lynching back during the Quicksilver Rush.

Mal swatted at a persistent fly. "Anyone figure out what caused the explosion?"

"Oh, someone probably forgot to turn off the gas on the oven. KABOOM! Do-it-yourself cremation." Evan did an exploding-star thing with his hands.

Mallory pretended to be offended, but her coy grin betrayed her. "You're sick, you know that?"

"What? Can't handle a little funeral home humor?" Evan's dimples deepened. "Come on. Let's go see what we can scrounge up." He stepped over the caution tape and ploughed through the gate strung between stone walls crowned in shards of glass. Marching up the long gravel drive, he aimed straight for the rise where the old Lassiter house once stood, so derelict and feeble that a strong gust would have brought it down. It never stood a chance against detonation.

Mallory followed right behind, a puff of soot rising with her every step. She stopped once to slap the dust from her legs. Dirt was not her thing. Black, sooty dirt was even less her thing.

I was having second thoughts of my own. What exactly was I expecting to find here? Certainly not the remnants of a pathetic old sand dollar wrapped in a brown paper bag. That was long gone. Grandpa Ted had given it to me in the hospital following my accident, explaining that every sand dollar holds the wings of three guardian angels. One of those guardian angels was there the day I fell out of the walnut tree. I'd asked why he thought the angel saved *me*. In the funeral home, I'd seen so many my age who should have survived but didn't. He was sure it was because I was meant to leave my mark on the world—something more than the divot I'd left in the dirt. That day I swore I'd find the reason I was spared. I cherished that sand dollar, but I brought it here to give to Adam, believing he needed the protection of an angel more than I did.

"Lils? Are you coming?" called Mal. "Let's go see what we can dig up."

I took a shaky breath and ducked under the police tape. Let her think what she wanted. I hadn't come for treasure. I'd come to clear my conscience.

From the random holes, scattered debris, and fresh prints, it was clear scavengers had already picked the lot clean. Hadn't Evan told me the previous day that he'd seen the next-door neighbor, Mr. Zmira, nosing around with a metal detector?

A meandering trail of paw prints—a cadaver dog's would be my guess—led me through the minefield of broken glass, twisted pipes, and jagged timbers that two weeks ago had been a house. I searched for any evidence of the boy whose memory still haunted me.

Several feet away, Mal poked at a pile of rubble with a length of galvanized pipe. I hoped she was up-to-date on her tetanus vaccine. True to form, Evan had even less concern for safety. On the other side of the yard, he high-stepped over what remained of the threshold as if passing from the actual world into some postapocalyptic video-game world. Check off another reason why he was better suited to taking over the business. Nothing fazed him.

I continued wading through scorched drifts of debris until I came to the spot where I once lay in pieces. The ache in my hip turned to a throb in my chest. It had been six years and my body still wouldn't let me forget. If only life offered do-overs. (Of course, if that were the case, we'd have been out of business.) I would have taken one in an instant, and this time I'd keep my feet on the ground instead of following some boy up a tree, no matter how many times he promised to keep me safe. An immense satisfaction warmed me to the bone to see that damn spiteful tree had been obliterated. Only a smear of harmless ash remained. Sometimes life *was* fair.

As I circled back toward where the house had stood, I stumbled upon a die-cast toy truck, evidence that a child once lived and played here. I kicked ash over this unwelcome reminder, then stumbled back. Beyond it, several pairs of arms reached up out of the earth, as if clawing at the sky. A few were melted.

Melted?

I realized my mistake and broke down in nervous laughter. The dismembered body parts were all cast fiberglass pulled from the shattered molds half-buried beside them. Remnant mannequin parts? The discards of a budding sculptor? Could any of this explain the suspicious bundle I took to be a corpse the day Adam's father chased me from the property?

I arranged several limbs atop a nearby stump and stepped back to admire my impromptu sculpture. A second later, Mallory craned her neck around the side of the house and shrieked.

"Mal, they're fake," I said, trying to calm her before she alerted the whole neighborhood. We were trespassing on a possible crime scene, after all.

"Well, stop messin' around. You're creeping me out."

Evan abandoned what was once the house and wandered over to examine a blackened contraption beside a pile of rocks. "Hey, get a load of this."

"Please, not another body part," moaned Mallory as we went to take a look.

"It's part of an old walnut sheller. There used to be a shelling shed, too," I explained, realizing my mistake too late.

"And how would you know all that?" asked Evan.

I'd told no one about my visits here—no one living, anyway—and didn't intend to start now. "A guess. It was a walnut orchard, after all."

Evan glared at me suspiciously.

They spread out to hunt for whatever was left of the shed, figuring investigators might not have given it much thought and hoping they'd find a few tools worth scavenging. I knew exactly where it used to be—in the far west corner of the three-acre property, hidden behind a wall of blackberry brambles about one hundred yards from the house. Adam had warned me to stay clear of the shed because it was infested with black widows. Today I had other reasons for keeping my distance.

I headed to the north corner of the property, toward a section of the orchard that had somehow escaped most of the fire damage. I came upon the Lassiter burial grounds beneath a canopy of leafless branches. An ornate wrought iron fence bounded the family cemetery, which was as old as the homestead and just as neglected. Lichen-encrusted headstones teetered among the encroaching weeds and twisted nightshade vines. At the base of a nearby tree that appeared to have been split by lightning lay a flat granite stone. It struck me as oddly out of place. I was about to examine it more closely when Evan called out.

"Hey, Lily, over here!"

Crap. They found the shed.

"Coming." I couldn't help it. I had to see, although whatever I thought his father stowed in the shed that day had to be long gone by now. I shuffled across the property to where Evan and Mallory stood examining a tree shaker half-buried in scorched nut hulls, bricks, pottery shards, and the heads of gardening tools, their handles turned to ash. I let out a sigh of relief. No bones.

Mallory gave the tree shaker a kick. "So how did this thing work?" Evan, king of fake it till you make it, launched into a totally bogus explanation. Like he knew the first thing about harvesting walnuts.

A few feet away on the other side of some rubble, a pair of garden snips poked up out of a tattered sack of bonemeal. Like Grandpa Ted, I was a collector, but instead of padlocks, I collected scissors. Eager to add to my stash, I scrambled over the mound of bags and bricks. The whole lot shifted under my feet and I went down hard, landing on an object that jabbed into the back of my thigh. Tipping sideways, I discovered it was the spine of a large hinge.

I flung aside the remaining bricks to reveal a metal lid held fast by an iron bolt and embellished with a flowery design consisting of six interlocking circles surrounded by a seventh circle. A manhole cover? If so it was the fanciest one I'd ever seen. What if it was a door to a safe? But why would someone hide a safe in a shelling shed?

Then again, what better place?

"Can we leave now?" pleaded Mallory, her voice shrill and whiny.

"Might as well," said Evan. "Lily?"

"Hold on," I said, brushing away the last of the dirt from the hatch. "Look what I found."

"Treasure?" he asks.

"Not treasure. A vault, I think."

"Sounds like treasure to me." Evan inspected the lid. "What are you waiting for, an invitation? Open it."

I recalled the crazed look in Adam's father's eyes. If there was a body stashed below, I was in no hurry to find it. "You're right. We should go. This is private property. We have no business here."

"At least give it a try," coaxed Mallory.

To satisfy her, I gave the bolt a half-hearted yank. "See. Stuck."

"Here, let me." Evan picked up a brick and dislodged the bolt with two swift whacks. He grabbed hold of the hatch handle and heaved. The hinge keened against its rusted pin as the hatch swung up and away, releasing a blast of cool, dank air.

Evan gave the swirling dust a moment to settle, then leaned into the opening, eager for his reward—a cache of jewelry, a stack of bills, a hoard of rare antiques. Instead a bare bulb illuminated the damp walls of a seemingly bottomless stairwell. "Nothing but an old mine shaft," he said. "Let's go. I'm starving."

"Me too," said Mal.

"Wait," I said. "Why is a light on? And where's it getting power?"

"Probably runs on a generator," said Evan. "Whoever was here last must have forgot to shut it down."

I pointed to the tracks leading down the dusty steps. "Look. No footprints coming back up. What if your 'whoever' is still down there?"

Evan cupped his hands around his mouth and bellowed into the hole. "Hello-o-o-o?" A ghostly echo answered, and now his curiosity was peaked. "I'm going to check it out. You two stay here and keep a—"

"We should stick together," I said, but not because I was worried for Evan's safety. My own curiosity was hard at play now.

Clinging to the rickety railing with Evan in the lead and me at the back, we descended step by slippery step. The damp and musty air drew us down into the cool depths like an anchor. Spindly tree roots fingered through gaping fissures in the ceiling to claw at our hair and clothes. I listened for the flutter of wings, imagining a swarm of bats might rise up through the shaft at any moment, but there was only the intermittent *drip-drip* of water and our labored breathing to splinter the silence.

The stairs led down to a long and narrow tunnel ribbed with wooden beams. We passed a pair of gas masks hanging beside two hazmat suits, each bearing the brand name Aftermath. "Hey, I bet I know what this is," announced Evan.

"A torture chamber?" whispered Mal.

"No, a fallout shelter."

Mal stared at him blankly.

"You know," he said, in that way he does that makes you feel like a total idiot. "To escape the radiation fallout of a nuclear blast. Probably built into one of those mine tunnels left behind after the quicksilver ran out."

"No wonder it survived the explosion," she said.

"Don't be so sure." I rattled the railing where it was detached from the wall.

"Maybe this wasn't such a good idea," murmured Mal.

Ya think?

Evan shushed us and waved us on.

Mal took my arm, and together we shuffled along until we came to a small utility closet containing several electrical panels and a generator. The contraption rumbled and wheezed as though struggling to catch its breath. Evan was right about that much at least, but who left it running? Was there another exit, or were they still trapped down here—alive?

Around a corner we came to a partially open door welded in place by years of corrosion. A barely legible sign read THIS DOOR TO REMAIN LOCKED AT ALL TIMES. By then even I was beginning to shake, but not Evan. With effort, he squeezed through.

Mal gave me a gentle shove from behind. "Your turn."

I slipped through and emerged into an octagonal, concrete chamber with seven adjoining rooms, each to a side like spokes on a wheel. We saw and heard no one. Again Evan called out a hello, but there was no response.

The ceiling sagged between the hodgepodge of wood and steel supports, making me question how much dirt was suspended over my head. The real creep factor lay in the details: strobing fluorescent lights, a jumble of stainless steel tables, abandoned lab equipment, and everything shrouded in a dense blanket of grit.

I peered into a bucket of hardened plaster perched on a medical scale, counted the test tubes in a wooden rack, examined a pair of gloves stained with what I imagined to be rust, but could have been anything. The most unnerving thing of all was a large copper capsule, maybe four feet in diameter and nine feet long, suspended from the center of the ceiling by eight cables connected across the vessel's top. It was clear from the popped bolts and fractured casing that this machine had suffered some catastrophe. More disturbing still was a glass porthole at the far end of the thing, its inner surface clouded by fine scratches.

I shuddered. "This is more than an old mine shaft or fallout shelter, isn't it?"

Mallory raised a flask to examine the yellow substance crystallized at the bottom. "Maybe it's a meth lab?" She sounded strangely excited by the prospect. "You don't suppose there'd be a reward for reporting it, do you?"

"Could be," said Evan. "Can't hurt to look around."

"That's what you think," I mumbled, eyeing a particularly large crack in the strut overhead.

In the first room to the right, a droopy canvas cot was jammed between the wall and a waist-high cupboard filled with corroded tin cans and mason jars with bulging lids. The cans' labels had all disintegrated into powdery pulp, and several tins had burst their seams. Opposite the cupboard an iron collar, shackles, and chains were bolted to the wall. It was like a scene out of a horror movie, but this was no set.

I lifted an open Bible from a bed of dust thick as felt and turned to where a faded red ribbon marked a page. *Psalms 30:9: What profit is there in my blood, when I go down to the pit? Shall the dust praise thee? Shall it declare thy truth?*

The truth? The truth was Adam's father hid this place for a reason—a real reason, not some lame movie reason. "Guys, this whole place could collapse at any moment. We need to get out of here. Now."

"As soon as we check out these last six rooms," insisted Evan.

The sooner he was convinced there was nothing of value to be found, the sooner we could escape this crumbling catacomb. Mal and Evan each took a room. Resigned, I hitched up my pack and picked my way between the instrument-laden tables, past a wall papered in tattered star charts, to the room farthest from the exit. More than once I tripped over the snarled electrical cables that snaked across the dusty floor. But this wasn't ordinary dust. It was a rainbow of earthy colors: iron red, yellow ochre, chalk white, and charcoal, all leading to a storage area crammed with crates and barrels of every shape and size. "Nothing but provisions," I announced only loud enough to be heard for fear of bringing down the roof. "Satisfied?"

"What kind of provisions?" called Evan.

I checked the label on the nearest barrel: BARRINGER CRATER, ARIZONA, 1975. I moved to the next: KANAPOI, KENYA, 1981. And the one beside it: DEAD SEA, EIN GEDI, ISRAEL, 1968. One barrel had burst, its iron-rich soil bleeding onto the floor. I ran a finger through it. "Dirt," I choked out. "The barrels all contain dirt."

"Hey, Lily," shouted Mallory. Her voice rocked the chamber, causing a soft rain of dust from overhead. "You were right. Someone's been here recently. There's a whole mess of empty cans in here—green beans and SpaghettiOs."

"Let me see," shouted Evan from the far side of the chamber. He plowed between two tables, knocking one into a center support. Chunks of ceiling tumbled down, barely missing his head and putting two large dents in one of the tables.

"That's it," I cried above the straining metal. "I don't care if there's gold bullion stashed down here. I'm leaving!"

"Me too," shouted Mal. "Evan?"

"Right behind you."

Shielding my eyes against the falling dust, I wove between the barrels. Midway I stumbled over something lying on the floor. I reached out to feel what it was, expecting the rough burlap of a sack or a tangle of cords. My hand found neither. Instead it touched skin—the skin of an arm made of flesh and bone.

RULE #4
BE PREPARED FOR THE
UNEXPECTED REMOVAL.

The shouts coming from the other room sounded as if they were sifting through sand.

"Where's Lily?"

"She was right behind me."

"I'm here . . . over here," I stammered. "B-b-by the barrels."

Evan trudged toward me. "Quit screwing around. We've got— Holy Mother of—!" He twisted the swinging light fixture overhead to illuminate the space where I crouched between four barrels. The dull arc of light exposed a figure sprawled in front of me, facedown in the debris.

Mallory appeared a second later at Evan's shoulder and shrieked. "Is it . . . he . . . alive?"

"Don't know," I said.

"How can you not know?" said Mal. "It's what you do."

Evan nudged me in the back with his knee. "Check his pulse."

I glared up at him. "Why me?" Seriously, why me? This was all his idea. But someone had to check. My trembling hand reached toward the limp wrist. I was used to touching dead people, right?

No big deal. But it couldn't have been a bigger deal. I told myself not to jump to conclusions. The dead guy could be anybody. I mean, the maybe-not-so-dead guy. My fingertips pressed into the stone-cold flesh. No pulse. *Oh god oh god oh god . . .* I pressed more firmly.

A deep, throaty moan erupted.

I flung myself backward, crashing into a tray of instruments and sending everything clattering to the ground. He was alive.

"Good one," said Evan. He stepped over me and rolled the man with the heel of his foot. "Looks like one of those dumpster divers you see behind the Speedy Mart. Smells like it, too."

Mallory inched away. "If you say so."

Whoever he was, he was in a pitiful state: cracked and swollen lips, matted hair, ribs that jutted out from beneath ragged clothes like those of a stray dog. It was no one I'd seen around this part of town lately. No one from school, that's for sure. So then who? It couldn't be Adam Lassiter. I would have run into him, wouldn't I?

The ugly truth was no. I made a point not to.

I looked as closely as I dared. He was about the right age—one or two years older than me—but his hair was darker brown than I remembered, as was his complexion (what I could make of it through the grunge and grime). No. Not him. Not my Adam.

"How long do you s'pose he's been trapped down here?" asked Mallory.

"From those empty tin cans and the looks of things, I'd guess a couple weeks," said Evan. "Now let's go. We'll call the police from up top."

Evan tried to pull me away, but I wrenched my arm free. "Stop! We can't leave him. What if the roof caves in?"

"More reason to get out of here, and *now*," he said.

I came here for answers. If this not-so-dead guy *was* the kid who saved me when I lay shattered in the dirt all those years ago, I'd be an even bigger sack of crap for leaving him behind. For leaving *anyone* behind. And even if it wasn't him, this guy might still hold the answers I was seeking. "You go. I'm not leaving without him."

"Sometimes you can be a real pain in the ass, you know that?" said Evan. But to my surprise, my stepbrother with the heart of lead lifted one of the guy's rag doll arms. "Well, come on, you two. Help me."

Mallory backed off, so I took up the other arm. Together Evan and I muscled the guy out into the corridor and toward the stairs. From there it was too narrow for the three of us to pass all at once, so while cussing and muttering that I was going to owe him big time, Evan grudgingly shifted the full weight of the still-unconscious guy onto his back. "Why do I always have to carry the stiffs?" he grumbled.

"Because dragging them is not an option," I snapped. "Now get going."

Mal and I hurried ahead to clear a space up top so Evan could lay him out.

"Evan, stop shaking him like that," I scolded. "He's coming to."

Like Lazarus rising from the dead, the mystery guy sat up and opened his eyes, shielding them against the sun with a hand. I waited to see if he recognized me. Nothing. I dug out a water bottle from my pack, unscrewed the cap, and tipped it to his mouth. He gulped greedily. "Slow down," I told him. "You'll make yourself sick."

He squinted up at me against the sun's glare through shaded irises the color of dull molasses. Not the color I'd hoped for.

"Who are you?" Evan asked.

The answer we got was more like the harsh cackle of a crow than a name. He guzzled down another mouthful of water and tried again. "A-a-dam."

He wiped the grime from his forehead and exposed a patch of light brown skin. Still unconvinced, I stepped aside to let the sun bathe his face, and gold glints like flakes of mica danced in his umber eyes. My every nerve tingled. Square jar, long limbs, tussled dark brown hair. It had to be him, and it was both everything I'd hoped for and everything I'd feared.

Rule #5
Before proceeding, examine
the condition of the body.

Adam Lassiter and I never should have met. He was a homeschooled wild child forbidden from leaving the family property. His only escape from his parents' watchful eyes was among the trees. I was a gangly kid already more comfortable with the dead than the living who had been warned never to go anywhere near the Lassiter place. If not for the relentless pursuit of bullies after school, I never would've cut through the orchard that first afternoon. After that I couldn't keep away.

My last day with Adam started not so different from the first: I came zigzagging through the orchard chased by three boys with better aim than sense. Sticks, rocks, walnuts, and cutting words pelted me as I ran.

Adam called to me, "Lily, up here." I leaped for his extended hand, and he pulled me into the canopy of the largest tree in the grove—*our* tree. "Climb to the top. You'll be safe there."

He never lied to me, but we'd never climbed so high before. Mystified by how I'd escaped them yet again, the pack moved on, careful to avoid the house. It had a reputation even bullies respected.

"Were you waiting for me?" I asked.

"Of course not." That's what he always said. "My mom sent me to pick walnuts. She's making banana bread. My dad hates the stuff, though."

We remained high in the old walnut tree for a good hour, talking. (Guess his mother wasn't in a big rush for those walnuts.) I knew from past conversations that his mother was well educated, did light bookkeeping for a few local businesses, and liked her wine early in the day. His father was a scientist with a fondness for black licorice, rare books, and cheap watches. He was also a very private person who trusted no one when it came to his son's welfare—especially not doctors. Lately he'd been acting strange—well, stranger—pacing the halls at night, losing his temper over the littlest things, disappearing for hours at a time. His parents had been arguing a lot as well. Adam couldn't wait until the day he could leave it all behind.

"To do what?" I asked.

"I want to have an orchard of my own someday," he replied.

I told him it didn't matter what I wanted to do when I got older. My father had decided for me the day I was born. He had it all planned out. I would intern under his watchful eye, study mortuary science at our local college to become a licensed funeral director, and take over the business when he retired.

The sun had started to dip below the distant hills, flattening the light. "I should be getting home. Do you think it's safe?"

"I'll go down first to make sure." Adam swung down to the next branch, and the next. "All clear," he called when his feet hit the ground.

I shifted my weight and let myself down to the closest limb but couldn't see where to go from there. "Adam, I'm stuck!"

"You're going to have to jump and catch that branch with the knothole, but no worries. I've got you."

"Promise?"

"Always."

I leaped and lost my footing, crashing head over heels through the tree. The next thing I remembered was looking up into Adam's deep brown, gold-flecked eyes and hearing, "Breathe, dammit, breathe." He inhaled and then pressed his lips to mine.

So yeah, I owed him my life, but months passed before I was well enough to leave the house on my own. By then going to see him was about more than gratitude; I needed to know he was okay.

My timing was all wrong. Sand dollar in hand, I wrestled my way over the wall—no easy feat when your legs don't want to bend. I'd only crossed a few rows of trees when I spied Adam's father lugging a large bundle on a hand truck through the grove, toward the shelling shed. The size and shape of the load looked exactly like a full body bag. Had Adam's father murdered someone? Or had I simply seen one too many body bags pass through our home?

He unloaded the bundle into the shed, pulled out a hefty ring of keys, and locked the doors. By time I turned to run, it was already too late. Adam's father caught me by my shirt collar as I was leaping for the wall. "What are you doing here?"

With a shaky hand, I held up the crumpled brown paper bag containing my gift. "I brought this for Adam. As a thank-you."

Adam's father snatched the paper bag from my hand. Thrusting it toward my face, he tightened his hands around it until his knuckles turned bone white. Then, tipping the sack, he let the fragments sift through his fingers and to the ground. "You think

I didn't see you lurking behind that tree? I don't know what you think you saw, but you say anything to anyone or come back here again," he hissed, "and it will be Adam who pays. Now get off *my* property!"

Terrified, I hobbled away as fast as my pinned hips and legs would allow. Secretly I hoped Adam would sneak away and come find me. When he didn't, I did everything I could to avoid that horrid man, that place, and Adam.

Adam saved my life, and I'd just saved *his*. I'd pulled him up out of a hole in the earth.

"So I'm Evan, that's Mallory, and . . ."

But Adam wasn't listening. All his attention was directed at me. "And you?"

I was too rattled to answer.

"Her name is Lily," blurted Evan.

"*Li-ly*," Adam repeated, pronouncing each syllable so mechanically that I hardly recognized my own name. No one had ever said it like that—like it held meaning.

Again I looked for any sign that he remembered me.

"Hmm." He grunted and looked away.

Guess not. I was both hurt and relieved. It was a lifetime ago. We were just dumb kids, after all, right? Why would he remember?

How could he forget?

He took in the total devastation that surrounded us. "The . . . orchard. The house." Panic rose in his voice. "Neil! Where's Neil?"

"Who's Neil?" demanded Evan.

"My . . ." He didn't seem to know how to finish the sentence.

"Brother, father, stepfather?" Mallory volunteered.

"Father," he confirmed.

I scrabbled to my feet. "Don't tell me he's still down there!"

Adam glared at the hole. "No, there was only me."

The body found in the rubble. It must have been his father, but I said nothing.

Adam pulled himself slowly to his feet. He was a good head taller than Evan and scalpel-thin. He turned a full circle unsteadily, surveying the lot and muttering gibberish.

Mallory corkscrewed her index finger beside her temple. "There's a nut loose in that one. What language is that, anyway?"

"Pretty sure it's Latin," said Evan.

"Latin?" she repeated. "S'pose he's a priest?"

Evan and I ignored that one.

Before we could stop him, Adam lurched and pitched his way back toward the ruins of his home, to an area that might have been a library. He began tossing armloads of torched books aside as if searching for something.

"Hold on! You're in no shape to—"

It was no use. He lifted a twisted metal picture frame from the rubble, its contents turned to ash. "How?"

"There was an accident," explained Evan. "An explosion."

"Not an accident!"

Of that he seemed certain. He tugged at a fallen water heater, but it refused to budge, leaving him defeated and breathless.

"Looking for something?" asked Mal.

"A box, like . . ." He pointed to a galvanized pipe.

"Even if it's here," said Evan, "you'll never find it."

"Must"—he weaved and rubbed the side of his head—"have it."

I knew that look. I'd seen it at viewings, especially on blisteringly hot days. He was about to keel over. Small wonder. He probably hadn't eaten in days. "We can deal with that later. Right now, we need to get you to a hospital."

"No! No hospital! All I need is food." He retreated to the far side of a still-standing stone fireplace.

"Okay, okay," I said in my most soothing voice. "No hospital."

He seemed unsure whether to trust me. Then again, why would he trust anyone after what he'd been through? I pictured the shackles bolted to the walls. Was it possible he'd been chained down there all these years? Someone must have known he was there. *I* should have known.

"There's always animal control," Evan mumbled to Mal from behind a hand.

"You're the dog," she said, and gave him a playful swat.

"Guys, seriously?" I scolded. "How can you be so insensitive? Adam, where's your mom?"

"I do not know. She left five years ago."

I could relate. "Is there someone else we can call?"

"I think we should call the police," said Evan.

"No. Call Neil," said Adam.

"They found a body, Adam," blurted Evan with all the sensitivity of a wooden mallet.

At first nothing registered, but then Adam began to slowly melt before our eyes. His shoulders drooped. His arms fell limply to his sides. His legs accordioned toward the earth.

I rushed to catch him, but he swatted me away. "*Discede.*" When I didn't let go, he snapped, "I said leave me!"

"I'm not going to leave you," I said. "We're going to take you home. Give you something to eat. Then we'll figure out what comes next—"

"Uh, Lily," interrupted Evan. "Is that such a—"

"We'll call the police from there, all right?" I glared at Evan, daring him to argue with me. For the moment it did the trick.

Adam looked back toward where the shed had stood as if still tethered to it in some way.

I knelt beside him. "Come with us. It'll be all right, I promise." Quite a bold promise, I realized, when I already knew from experience that it would never be all right again. Different, maybe, but not all right. "Let us help you."

He didn't say no.

At Adam's insistence, we closed the hatch and disguised it with bricks, debris, and dirt. We didn't need someone else getting trapped down there. He continued to insist he was fine, that all he needed was a meal or two. But when he stood, it was clear he'd never make it the five blocks to our house. I convinced Evan to run and fetch the hearse. With Mal on one side and me on the other, we helped Adam down the drive to wait in the weedy shade of an overgrown juniper.

Mallory lit a cigarette and rolled it nervously between her fingers. She'd been flirting with smoking since school let out—part of her plan to reinvent herself into one of the more popular girls. "You know those can kill you, right?" I said.

"Who made you surgeon general? Besides, my father's been smoking his whole life and he's fine."

"So you're going to gamble on genetics. Good luck with that." What was with her, anyway, and this whole reinvention kick? Did it have something to do with my dropping out last year to get my GED and that I wouldn't be there to hold her back her senior year? The only reason we were in the same class at all was that I had to make up a year of school after my accident.

Time clicked by to the incessant chirring of cicadas. "What's taking so long?" I grumbled. "Any minute, someone's going to catch us loitering and tell us to beat it."

"He'll be here," Mal assured me.

I paced up and down the sidewalk as she kept a faithful watch for Evan from the curb. A few feet away Adam stared at the ground, using his hands as blinders and muttering Neil's name over and over.

Out of the corner of my eye I caught movement through the tinted windshield of an SUV parked across the street and a few houses down. Who would sit in a car in this heat? Had they been watching us this whole time? My skin prickled. *Hurry up, Evan. Hurry up.*

Finally the hearse swung into view. "Come on, Adam. Let's get you outta here."

"Where are you taking me?"

"To our house," I answered. I left out the part about it being a mortuary. In his state, I was hoping he wouldn't notice.

Mal and I convinced him to climb into the hearse. As soon as the back doors shut, he curled into the far corner of the casket tray like some feral animal, his sooty face and palms pressed to the window for a last glimpse at what was once the sum total of his world.

RULE #6
A BLUSH SHOULD BE SUBTLE.

Adam tugged at his shirt neckline as if it were a noose about his neck. The investigating officers had been peppering him with questions for the last hour and a half. They told him it would be best if he simply accepted that his father was dead, but whatever he was feeling looked nothing like acceptance.

Everyone in the room was staring at him—the officers, Evan, Nana Jo, Dad, and Rachel. The dozen or so grim photos of my ancestors hanging above the sofa formed a more silent jury, but they seemed to judge all the same. I couldn't look at him. Instead I stood back from the others, propped up by an armature of guilt beside the brass umbrella stand. My fingers rolled the hem of my shirt up, then down, then up again, over and over, until my annoyed father sent me to the kitchen to fetch coffee. I left the door ajar so I could listen in.

"Mr. Lassiter?" said Officer Wells.

Adam didn't respond immediately, probably because no one had ever addressed him that way before. "My name is Adam," he reminded the officers.

"Okay, Adam, let me get this straight. You never left the property? Is that right? Not to go to school, to a store, to see a doctor?"

"Never," said Adam, for the third time.

"So you're telling us that your father held you prisoner."

"I wasn't a prisoner. I promised him I wouldn't leave. There's a difference."

What about the shelter, the chains and shackles? I wanted to ask. What was that laboratory all about, and why didn't he remember me like I remembered him? Questions flooded my head, but he offered few answers.

"And you never once thought to break that promise?" asked Officer Rodriguez.

"That's what it means to promise," Adam answered. Score one for him.

"I understand." But even from the kitchen, I could hear in the officer's voice that he understood no more than I did how a father could shut his son away from the world and deny him proper medical care, a formal education, and friends. Why did no one do anything about it? Why didn't I?

The father Adam talked about in the early days of our friendship was nothing like the man I later encountered in the orchard. Adam often boasted that his father knew how to do the most amazing and, to my mind, useless things. He could name more than ninety stars, speak multiple languages, recite the periodic table—forward and backward—and grill the perfect Bunsen burner burgers. Sure, he was overprotective and had little time for his family or maintaining their home, but that describes a lot of parents. As time went by, though, I heard more and more about instances of paranoia, unwarranted accusations, and wild threats. Adam always defended him, explaining that it was the stress and long hours of his work—whatever that was—but I witnessed firsthand the frightening changes in his father. Did I say anything to anyone? No. I was too afraid of what he might do to Adam in his increasingly erratic state.

Well, if the reporters outside had their way, the world would soon know all about Neil Lassiter. A battalion of news vans waited at the ready, their satellite dishes like shields all pointed skyward, their crews like so many foot soldiers prepared to pick off the first person to leave the house.

"And then the night of the explosion," Officer Wells continued, "he locked you underground?"

"Yes."

Officer Rodriguez drummed his pen against a notebook. "Did you and your father have an argument that night, son?"

"I am not your son."

"Yes, of course you're not," interjected Rachel. "It's an expression."

"Please answer the question," said Wells.

I peered through the kitchen door to see Adam sinking back into the sofa. "Yes, we argued, but—"

"What about?"

"The usual. My studies, me wanting more freedom."

It was Rodriguez's turn to pitch. "Did you lose your temper? Is that why he shut you down there?"

"No!" Adam's outburst did little to convince them, but he'd lost his family, his home, everything that could have mattered to him. I couldn't listen anymore. I took up the tray loaded with coffee and marched back into the room. "Can't you see—"

Adam held up a hand that stopped me mid-step. "You all want to know why Neil Lassiter locked me in the . . ."

He was searching for a word. Maybe *shelter*? But that was the wrong word. What had it sheltered him *from*? An intruder? The world beyond the orchard? This inquisition?

"The answer is he did it to protect me. He promised to return when it was safe."

"Protect you from what?" asked Wells.

"Not what. Whom."

"Okay, from whom?" pushed Wells.

"*Nescio.*" Adam cleared his throat, stared at the hole in the rug. "I mean, I don't know."

"Did your father ever physically harm you?"

Adam shook his head almost imperceptibly. He was obviously covering for Neil. I didn't get it. If my father locked me in a hole in the ground, I'd want everyone to know. I'd wear my bitterness like a badge. Not him.

"And your mother?" Wells continued. "How can we contact her?"

Adam dissolved into the upholstery a bit more and mumbled something in Latin.

"Come again?" said Wells. "We didn't catch that."

He gave it another go, this time in English. "She left."

Wells readied his pen. "And her name?"

"I don't remember."

"You don't remember your own mother's name?"

"I have memory issues."

"Memory issues? Hmm," said Rodriguez.

"There was . . . an incident. It left my memory impaired."

So maybe I hadn't been so easily forgotten. I'd say this for him: impaired memory or not, he was no dummy. All his answers so far had been carefully measured. No obvious lies, only spare truths. But couldn't he see how that made him appear less credible? And it didn't help that he was worming deeper and deeper into the corner of the sofa with every question.

There was a pounding at the front door. Startled, Adam bolted to his feet. When he saw that no one else had moved, he eased back down but didn't fully settle. I wondered when he had last heard someone knock at a door.

"I'll get it," offered Evan.

"Better if I handle this," said Dad. A moment later there was a harsh exchange of words, followed by "Can't you leave the boy alone?" and the slamming of the door. "Damn reporters," swore my father.

Hoping to deflate the mounting tension in the room, I cleared my throat. "Coffee?" I offered a cup and saucer to my father.

"Guests first," he corrected.

Why did he always have to point out my failings in front of people? I gave a napkin and a cup to each of the officers, my embarrassment as plain as the hitch in my step. Adam blinked mechanically as he took a cup. "Careful, it's hot," I warned.

He gulped down a mouthful, then spewed the scalding liquid into the saucer. It was his turn to be embarrassed, but if he was, he hid it well.

I could take a lesson from this guy.

The officers allowed Adam a brief moment to recover, and then it was back to the grilling. Mostly he shrugged, nodded, or gazed vacantly at the stained-glass transom above the door to the display room.

Dad and Evan stood shoulder to shoulder, both clearly baffled by this stranger wedged into our sofa but also hanging on his every word. At least Nana Jo was a bit subtler, although not by much. She pret-ended to read her *Fine Woodworking* magazine, her head gophering up from behind the pages at every interesting scrap of new information.

Meanwhile Rachel fussed over Adam. "Another snickerdoodle? How about a pillow for your back? Is the glare from the window too much?" She always did have a soft spot for strays, which is why, Dad says, she swooped into our lives. According to him, she put the "home" in McCrae Family Funeral Home.

I still wondered why Adam's father made him promise never to leave the property. More puzzling was why Adam would keep such a promise. When we were kids he often talked about leaving, so once he was old enough to legally be on his own, what possessed him to stay? If it were me, I'd have gone over the wall at the first chance.

"Nervous, Mr. Lassiter?" Wells indicated the shredded napkin in Adam's hand.

"Of course he's nervous," I said, offering Adam a fresh napkin. "You're interrogating him like he's done something wrong. He's the victim here."

"Lily, please," said Rachel with a pacifying smile. "The officers are just doing their job. Why don't you bring over that plate of cookies from the buffet?"

As if that's all I was good for.

"No need," Wells said, slapping his notebook closed. "I think we have enough for now." He rose from his chair and shook hands with my parents. When he came to Adam, he said, "I gotta say, you're lucky these folks found you when they did. It's a bit of a miracle. I'm going to ask you again: Are you sure you don't want us to take you to the hospital?"

Adam ignored Wells's offered hand. "No hospital." He could not have said it more firmly.

"Well, you're over eighteen. It's not like we can make you go. Can you at least tell us where we can drop you off?"

Adam had no answer.

Rachel placed a hand on his shoulder. He flinched and she quickly retracted it. "Sorry. I only meant to ask if you have any other family. Grandparents? An aunt? An uncle?"

He shook his head.

"Then you'll stay here," declared Nana Jo, hammering her fist like a gavel on the chair arm, as if the decision was never Adam's to make. From what I'd heard so far, I imagined that was nothing new to him. Dad looked skeptical but wasn't willing to throw the boy onto the street—not in front of the cops, anyway—and no one says no to Nana Jo.

The detectives were at the door when Adam stopped them. "When can I see him?"

"Your father?" asked Wells.

Adam nodded.

"The coroner will be contacting you to make arrangements. Again, we're sorry for your loss, Mr. Lassiter. Mr. McCrae, Mrs. McCrae. We'll be in touch." The two officers squared their shoulders, stepped outside, and were immediately besieged by the press.

Dad rushed to turn the dead bolt, waited for Nana Jo and Evan to step out of the room, and gave a final glance at Adam, who had burrowed back into the sofa. "He can stay until other arrangements can be made. No more than a couple days, hear me?" Rachel and I nodded. He retreated to the office.

As I gathered the coffee cups, assorted spoons, and tray, another neighbor from down the way called inquiring about all the commotion this afternoon. Nana Jo gave her the now stock abbreviated version. Meanwhile, Rachel unfolded the sofa much to Adam's bewilderment. "You can sleep here," she said, then sent me upstairs to fetch fresh linens and toiletries.

By the time I returned, Adam was spread eagle across the sleeper sofa, counting z's. I set my armload onto the coffee table, careful not to wake him. It was a wasted effort. He was out cold.

Alone with him for the first time, I couldn't resist a long, hard look. I studied his hands, his bony hips and ribs. It was not often that a body made me blush, but his did. Still, something about him nagged at me, something I couldn't put a finger on. Having worked intimately on so many bodies these past couple months, I'd learned to spot the details that made each person distinctive, because it was often my job to decide what got covered and what got preserved. There was the crooked nose of the barfly brawler, the model's signature mole, the tipped shoulders of a professional bowler. So what was it about Adam that had me so unsettled? It was not the dirt caked under his nails, nor his ratty hair and thread-bare clothes. I'd seen worse. No, it was something more subtle.

It took me a moment more and then I had it—symmetry. His right side was a perfect mirror to his left, something I'd never seen before.

Satisfied that I'd solved at least one mystery out of so many, I headed up to my room to finish a shroud for the Nguyen family service tomorrow before turning in. It took much longer than expected because Mal called, insisting on a status report. I shared what little more I'd learned about Adam: he'd never stepped foot beyond the orchard before today—that he remembered—and his father supposedly locked him in the shelter the night of the fire to protect him from someone, though *who* he couldn't, or wouldn't, say.

"But that laboratory was set up so someone could live down there," she pointed out. "At least for a while."

"Good thing, too, because without those provisions, Adam wouldn't have survived as long as he did."

"I thought I'd bring Aslyn and Vega by tomorrow. They really want meet him."

"You told them about Adam?"

"Yeah. Why not?"

"Mal, you saw what he's been through, and with the press and the police here all day, the last thing he needs is more people drilling him with questions." Besides, they were her friends—not mine. Not that I was jealous. She'd always been the social one. "I'll talk to you tomorrow."

I returned to my stitching, but the floss knotted and twisted along with the thoughts weaving through my head. I gave up and shoved the shroud aside. Hours later, in the dark, I was staring at the macabre dance of moon shadows across my bedroom walls. The ceiling fan wobbled ominously overhead. Or was it the world around it that spun off-kilter? When a parent could lock away his child and no one noticed, it was hard to say. But fate had a way of evening the score. Neil Lassiter certainly got what he deserved—in spades. And if Adam hadn't been holed up fifty feet underground, he'd probably have ended up in the morgue, laid out in a drawer right beside his father instead of asleep in our living room. I tried to fool myself into believing that my silence all those years ultimately saved him. It was a tough sell.

I rolled onto my stomach, punched my pillow, and told myself to forget him and go to sleep. It was no use. My mind was stitched to thoughts of Adam Lassiter. A glass of milk was the cure, and, for all my trouble, I planned to make it chocolate with an ice-cream cone chaser.

I tiptoed down the back stairs, keeping to the outside edges of the treads to avoid any creaks that might wake our guest. Muffled voices spilled from the kitchen.

" . . . rumors the boy died," Rachel was saying. "No one had seen him in years. Child Protective Services investigated but was told he was visiting relatives."

It wasn't an unusual discussion for our house, or a particularly private one. I was just glad they weren't ripping into each other. Lately even their Hallmark marriage had felt the stress of keeping a failing business afloat.

"Any chance you could be mistaken?" asked my father. "I mean, Lassiter's a common enough name."

Did he say Lassiter? I pushed open the door. My parents were on opposing sides of the kitchen island, picking at roast chicken leftovers.

"Who are you talking about?" I asked. I'd never told them about meeting Adam in the orchard after school. Like everyone else in town, Dad heard all the dark rumors surrounding the old Lassiter place and forbade me from going anywhere near it. So, after the accident, I pretended I had amnesia, told them I had no idea how I'd ended up broken and bleeding amid row upon row of walnut trees.

"Oh, Rachel remembers a neighbor telling her something about a boy who went missing a few years back. She thinks the last name was Lassiter," Dad explained.

Adam told me he was an only child, and his parents would never have sent him to visit relatives, not when he wasn't even allowed to leave the property. Maybe he'd been restricted to the house, or worse, locked in the fallout shelter, for much of that time. Or maybe he'd run away for a spell? He'd certainly talked enough about wanting to. "I don't remember hearing anything about a missing kid," I said.

"It was that summer we sent you to camp," said Rachel. "Right after your father and I got married."

That I remembered. I was thirteen, fresh out of leg braces, and someone thought it would be a riot to push me into a patch of poison oak during a scavenger hunt. It worked. They all got a good laugh. Me? Not so much. I spent the rest of my summer alone in a bunkhouse, caked in calamine lotion. The camp had wanted to ship me home, but my parents insisted I stay. They said I would itch no matter where I was, and I could use the time to make a few friends. Instead I made more scars.

"If the rumor was true, wouldn't the police who were here today have known something about it?" I asked.

"You'd think so, wouldn't you? No, most likely it's just more neighborhood gossip," grumbled Dad. He waved his piece of chicken at me. "Care for a drumstick?"

"Thanks, but I prefer the ice cream variety." I pried the freezer open and stuck in my face to fill my lungs with frosty air before grabbing a frozen cone.

"Can't sleep?" asked Rachel.

"Too hot." I peeled the paper from the cone and nipped off the bottom, as usual. "Dad, I thought you said you were going to get the air conditioner fixed."

"Can't afford it. I'll take another look at it tomorrow, right after I pull together the papers for the bank."

"The bank?" I repeated, fearing the worst.

"For preapproval. Crenshaw and Madsen Crematorium might be coming up for sale. Bill mentioned to me at Rotary last week that he and his partner are thinking of retiring soon. I ran through the numbers, and if we can get an offer in before the news becomes public, we might have a shot at buying them out, assuming we get the right price . . . and a loan."

A deal like that was exactly what we needed to resuscitate our business. Ever since our biggest competitor, Eternal Memorial Services, Inc., had metastasized its way into town, it had been a cancer to our business with no sign of remission. As it was, Jim Sturbridge, owner of EMS, had already bought out the other family-owned mortuaries and tried more than once to do the same to us.

Rachel huffed and shoved what was left of the chicken carcass into the trash. "Cameron, how can we possibly afford to buy a crematorium when we're already struggling?" She dropped the trash lid and stomped from the room.

"Heat's gotten to her," Dad said, and chased after her.

"Goodnight," I said to no one.

I switched off all the lights, save the one over the range, and plunked down on a chair beside the open window to nurse my ice-cream cone and throw back a tall, cold glass of chocolate nirvana. The sudden revving of distant engines and screeching of tires announced that street racers were at it again. I set down my glass and waited to hear a squeal of brakes and crunching of metal, but it thankfully never came. The night settled back into the cadenced lullaby of crickets and swamp coolers.

❊ ❊ ❊

The next thing I knew, someone was whispering in my ear. "Lily?"

I lifted my head and opened my eyes. "Adam. Wha—what are you—?"

He shrank back. "I was thirsty and saw the light on. Is this where you sleep?"

I thought he was joking until I realized there was no smile behind it. "No, no. I just dozed off." I shook my head to clear it. "Here, have a seat. Let me get you something."

I poured him a glass of chocolate milk. The whole time he

watched me with the scrutiny of an anthropologist. *Come on, remember me. You must remember me.* Not a glimmer of recognition, but it had been a long and difficult day, and then there was the amnesia. With time his memory might return. Still, it stung to be so forgettable.

He dipped a finger into the milk, the earlier coffee scalding obviously still fresh in his mind, took a cautious sip, then gulped down the rest. "That's good," he said, a frothy brown mustache across his full upper lip.

I grinned like an idiot. "Well, if you didn't like chocolate milk, I was going to have to ask you to leave."

"So it was a test?" he asked seriously.

"No, that was a joke." And a very feeble attempt at conversation. "So I'm guessing your sleep schedule must be pretty messed up after all those weeks in the dark."

He nodded. "Day, night. It was all the same."

I tried to imagine what that was like for him. Probably close to being buried alive and not so different from the stuff of my night terrors. "Can I get you anything else?"

"Yes. There is something."

"Name it."

"My father's lockbox. It has important papers in it. I have to get it back."

I'd been expecting something along the lines of a comb or a pair of socks. "Let's worry about that later, okay? You've been through a lot. You're going to need at least a few days to recover." I held up the milk as if it were a remedy. "More?" Without waiting for an answer,

I refilled his glass and tossed the empty carton, but I couldn't stop thinking about my parents' conversation. "Adam, are you sure you never left the property, maybe to visit relatives?"

"Yes, I'm sure."

"It makes no sense," I said, more to myself than to him.

"You don't believe me? You should know I can't lie."

"Can't? That seems like something a liar would say."

"It does," he admitted, "except in this case it happens to be true. Why the questions?"

"It's something Rachel mentioned. Forget it." Either he didn't remember, or his parents lied to child services. Either way, he hadn't died. Otherwise he wouldn't be here, gulping down chocolate milk at our kitchen table.

Nana Jo shuffled into the kitchen to raid her box of nuts and chews. "Pay no attention to the old lady by the cupboard."

"Nana, we all know about your secret stash of See's Candies," I said.

With a look of alarm she stuffed the white box under her arm and scurried from the room.

"So," I continued, "what was that place where we found you?"

"Neil's laboratory."

"Yeah, but for what?"

Adam hesitated. "He conducted experiments with soils to grow . . . things."

"Things? You mean plants and trees." Well, that accounted for the garden tools in the shelling shed and the barrels of dirt below. And they did live in the middle of an orchard. "Did you help him with his experiments?"

"You could say that. And he was teaching me so I could do more."

I detected some resentment in his voice. Maybe being chained to our fathers' expectations was one more thing we had in common. "Is that why you speak Latin?"

"And Ancient Greek," he added with pride.

"Okay. I hate to break it to you, but people don't exactly go around conversing in Latin or Ancient Greek every day—unless, of course, you work at the Vatican."

"Those languages have other uses . . . or did." He wiped the chocolate milk from his upper lip with the back of his hand.

Those lips. His time locked in the shelter had not been kind to them. They were pale, cracked, and peeling, but they made me think back to the day of my accident and to what I'd always considered my first kiss.

Okay, so it was really mouth-to-mouth resuscitation. But it was sort of one of those whole Snow White scenarios, saved by the kiss of a true love. A ridiculous romantic notion, I knew, but I was young then and had bought into the whole fairy-tale version of how life was supposed to be. I could not have had it more wrong. The memory, though, as painful as it was, made me suspect that dead languages weren't the only useful thing Neil had taught his son.

"Was your father also the one who taught you mouth-to-mouth resuscitation?" *Oh, shut up shut up shut up, stupid girl!*

Adam spluttered, the milk apparently having gone down the wrong way, then plunked the half-empty glass onto the kitchen counter, the ending punctuation to our conversation.

I rose from my stool. "I'm sorry. You must be exhausted."

He cocked his head oddly and narrowed his eyes.

I swiped at my nose. "What? Do I have fudge on my face?"

"No. I want to see what sorry looks like."

Okay . . . so that's weird.

I switched off the range light, but we reached the doorway at the same time. I twisted sideways to let him pass. "Thank you," he said, his cool breath more soothing than any freezer.

"For letting you through the door first?"

"For bringing me into your . . . home . . . and everything."

"No problem." But I was thinking it *was* a problem—a big problem, because I had the feeling that if we'd pulled anyone else from that hole, I'd have played it smart and called the police before hauling him here.

I heard the *twang* of sleeper-sofa springs. "Goodnight, Adam," I whispered, not intending him to hear. Certainly not expecting a reply.

"Goodnight, Lily."

RULE #7
GET OUT OF THE WAY
WHEN PEOPLE ARE GRIEVING.

The sagging lead glass of the dormer window gave a warped view of the street below. The media minions were still there. Some of the faces had changed along with the vehicles, but the scene was much the same as it had been all week. Our home, our place of business, had become our prison.

At first Evan was more than eager to talk to them and did a great job of painting himself the hero. He even went so far as to suggest we try capitalizing on the situation until I reminded him how he felt when his face made front page of the local rag last year after a certain game-betting scandal.

Dad thought all the media hype would help business—*Good Samaritan Funeral Home Rescues Homeless Fire Victim* and all that— but the reality had become something entirely different. Sure, lots of people were cruising by, hoping to catch a glimpse or snap a photo of "the boy unearthed," as one journalist coined Adam. But for the most part business had stayed away, or gone to EMS no doubt. Certainly none of us ever imagined the media's interest in Adam would last this long, and with each day I expected Dad to announce it was time for Adam to move on. Just last night he reminded me "This is not a boardinghouse."

Of course Evan was quick to make a joke out of it. "Sure it is. This is where you check in when you've checked out."

I swear.

Drawing my bedroom curtains to the chaos below, I started down-stairs but pulled up short at the first step. Adam was hunkered in the darkest corner of the family room, an atlas splayed across his lap. The constant scrutiny by police and the public had put a strain on all of us, but none more than him. He rarely spoke, clung to the dark recesses of the house, and ate alone if at all. My parents thought he should see a therapist to help him adjust to life on the outside before he left to live on his own. "He probably should see a therapist," I told them. "But he also just needs to see what daily life is like in the real world."

Until he came here, his entire universe was confined to a weedy patch of land where he knew every irrigation ditch, every low-hanging branch, every exposed root. Here, the hazards were all new, from the sleeper sofa that tried to swallow him whole on his second night to Specter, the suspicious, ghostlike cat with teeth and claws always at the ready. Never mind the swarms of strangers all clamoring for the lurid details of his captivity.

"Besides, who's going to pay for a therapist?" I asked. "Us?"

That killed *that* discussion.

With my head poking between the banister rails, I tried to guess what might be going through Adam's mind. His memory of us as kids had not returned, so we were starting over as strangers. Part of me, the more sensible part, thought that was as far as it should go. But sometimes loneliness won out.

Like four nights ago when a lightning strike took out a trans-former. Maybe it was the intensity of the storm or maybe that was merely an excuse, but I'd crept downstairs with my sewing and an offer to share some candlelight. When Adam didn't object, I took a seat in the wing chair opposite the sleeper sofa. Utility wires whipped and crackled beyond the nearby window. I wanted to say something, anything, to distract us from the approaching storm, but all my words were logjammed in my head.

Flash.

One one thousand. Two one thousand. Three one thousand . . .

Boom.

At this rate the house would soon be reduced to matchsticks. I snuck a nervous glance at Adam. Back during our days in the orchard, he always knew what to say to get my mind off my worries and troubles.

As if he had read my thoughts, he set aside his untouched dinner. "Want to talk?"

I nodded a little too desperately.

"Hmm. Well, did you know lightning produces heat three times hotter than the surface of the sun but has no temperature of its own?"

Not exactly comforting or what I had in mind, but it was a start. "Did you know," I said in reply, "lightning kills more men than women?"

Flash.

One one thousand. Two one thousand . . .

BOOM.

The center of the storm was drawing closer, as was Adam, who had shifted to the edge of his seat. Our knees were now nearly touching.

"More men than women, you say. Fascinating—and a little threatening."

I smiled and held up my hands in defense. "Just stating a fact."

FLASH. The room lit up for a sliver of a second—

BOOM!

The loudest yet. I jumped, losing the thread from my needle—and my composure.

Adam leaned in. "And did you know the word for an irrational fear of thunder and lightning is *ceraunophobia,* from the Greek word *cerauno*?"

"Are you saying I'm irrational?" I pretended to be offended.

His held up his hands. "Just stating a fact."

"Fine. Did you know lightning kills more than two thousand people a year?"

"You're a bit obsessed with death, aren't you?'

I laughed for the first time that evening. "Well, duh, my home is a mortuary."

He turned serious. "At least you have a place to call home."

"Adam, I'm sorry.

"It's okay. Not your fault."

True, I didn't cause the fire, but I'd let him down in other ways.

Flash.

Our eyes found each other. Silently we counted off the seconds, and with each I wished this could be his home for a little longer. That sort of thinking frightened me more than the storm. Ten long seconds passed before the faint rumble of thunder found its way to our waiting ears. The storm was retreating. It was time for me to do the same. I gathered my needlework and bounded up the stairs. Adam was right. I was being irrational, but I had been struck before. Not by lightning, but by a desire just as likely to stop a heart. Never again.

After that stormy night I was more careful to keep my distance, but that didn't mean I'd lost interest in learning everything I could about him. I wasn't alone. Adam was all Nana and Mal talked about, and Rachel was determined to find something he would eat. The first items ruled out were SpaghettiOs and green beans. He'd eaten enough of those while holed up in the shelter to last a lifetime. Dad kept probing for more information, too. All he'd gathered so far was that Adam's days were filled with studying, house chores, and futile efforts to revive the aging walnut grove. Even Evan, who was usually too wrapped up in his own affairs to pay much attention to anyone else's, made it his personal mission to get Adam computer literate before the week was out. That was fine until Adam's face appeared on a news feed and freaked him out. But we all agreed Adam was an enigma that had defied explanation—so far.

During his time here, I'd spied him picking up the most peculiar objects, things I usually took for granted—a TV remote, a stapler, a pair of forceps. He would turn them over and over in his hands, shake them, sniff them. I caught him binge-reading my father's old college

textbooks one day and flipping through Rachel's stack of *Family Circle* and *Good Housekeeping* on another. You'd think he was cramming for a test on survival in the modern world. Maybe he was.

As I continued watching him from the safety of the stairs, Adam exchanged the atlas in his lap for one of Nana's old gardening books and began reciting the plants' scientific names aloud as if the very sound of them was a comfort. According to what little he'd told us, his father use to drill him daily not only in Ancient Greek and Latin but also in such subjects as antiquities, horticulture, and astronomy. And yet the boy could barely boil water. "*Zantedeschia. Zantedeschia. Zantedeschia,*" he practically sang, and I wondered what the word could mean.

I rested my head against the staircase spindle, mesmerized by his mindless chant, but my traitorous earring clinked against the rail. Adam's head whipped up. Quickly I pretended to adjust the strap on my sandal, then darted past him toward the kitchen. Neither of us managed so much as a "good morning" to the other. Economy of words. In that we had always been alike.

As I passed the front window on my way to the kitchen, I noticed a stranger outside our house crouched over a rusted bike, his helmet and shades shielding his face from view. I watched as he fiddled with the chain. Pathetic. A five-year-old would have been done and gone by now. He didn't appear to be a reporter—no voice recorder, phone, or camera that I could see—but he was definitely scouting the house. Chances were good that he was another one of Sturbridge's stooges. We'd already caught one fronting as a meter reader when he was really scouting for code violations.

When the stranger caught me watching him, he mounted his bike and pedaled away.

I scraped together breakfast, then went out back to tell Dad about the suspicious bicyclist and help him load the hearse. He didn't think much of it. I figured he was too tired to care. He and Tony had been up much of the night on a call. When you own a funeral home, you work all hours.

With Evan still out on his morning run, it was up to me to deliver one of our recent arrivals—or I should say departures—Mr. Pranav Singh, to the crematorium so my dad could get some shut-eye. Driving was definitely not my forte, but what it came down to was this: I was eighteen, Evan was college-bound in the fall, and now that I had formally begun my apprenticeship under Dad, he was counting on me to pick up the slack by helping with ship-out paperwork, graveside deliveries, and general errands. It was all part of his master plan for me to take over one day, and the only reason I'd agreed to it was that it legally allowed me to work directly with the dead. It had required dropping out of school, busting my butt to get my GED, and skipping out on my senior year. I was fine with that if it meant no longer having to endure the cruel pranks and taunts of fellow classmates. And it made my dad happy.

I snatched up the keys and braced myself to run the gauntlet of news vans.

"Why don't you take Adam with you?" suggested Rachel. "It'll do him good to get out of the house for a spell."

"Sure," I said feeling anything but. "Come on, Adam." I climbed in behind the steering wheel of the hearse and unlocked

the passenger side. Cautiously he slid in. He ran his hands across the glove compartment, accidentally elbowed the window button, and jumped, hitting his head on the roof as the glass slid down and then back up again.

"Automatic window," I explained. He angled away from it nonetheless. "Ready?"

He blinked.

I instructed Adam to slouch down in his seat and then pulled around to the front of the house. A reporter rushed at us, cameraman at his heels. I sped up but hit the large pothole at the end of the drive and the hearse bucked. "Okay back there, Mr. Singh?" I called, driving off in a plume of exhaust. No complaints.

It was a short ride to Crenshaw & Madsen Crematorium—one more reason we needed to convince the owners to sell to us. Why wouldn't they? They'd been a family business for nearly as many years as we had. We'd need a sizable loan to swing it, but pulling off the purchase would allow us to put profits into our pocket for a change, instead of into the middleman's.

I kept to the side streets to avoid crossing the train tracks. No need for more unnecessary jostling. Still, every time we took a corner Adam gripped the armrests like he was trying to wring blood from them. Hey, it's not like I was taking turns at warp speed. Far from it. In fact, Mallory and Evan were always teasing me about how I drive like an old granny. (I assume that by "granny" they didn't mean Nana Jo, who had a bit of a lead foot.) It was all so easy for them. They weren't the ones who'd dabbed face powder and mascara onto countless car crash victims. So yeah, maybe I

was a tad overcautious. It wasn't as if it did our patrons any good to be tossed around like a shoe in a dryer.

Neither of us said a word, and it was okay. Apparently, with the exception of violent thunderstorms, we were each content with the simple comfort of a ready listener if anyone bothered to say anything. Again, talk for either of us had always been more burden than necessity. What we needed was each other's company.

Across from me, Adam had his nose pressed to the glass. Honestly this part of town was nothing much to look at—abandoned cars, boarded-up houses with dry weeds to the sills, sun-bleached For Sale signs. But to Adam it was the new frontier. He glanced over his shoulder. "What's in the box?"

"You mean who. Say hello to Mr. Singh," I said.

"Hello?" said Adam, as if expecting an answer. He frowned. "Doesn't he need air holes?"

I laughed. "Nope. He hasn't needed them for about a week now."

Adam thought about this a minute before saying, "So he is dead then."

"Yup. He's passed on, is in a better place, has climbed the stairway to heaven, crossed over, cashed in his chips, shuffled off the mortal coil. You okay with that?"

Adam was too confused to know if he was or wasn't, but it didn't matter. We'd arrived.

I escorted Mr. Singh into the crematorium to get him settled in, crossed all the *t*'s and dotted all the *i*'s on his paperwork, and then Adam and I loaded into the hearse.

"Do we have to go back so soon?" he said.

"What do you have in mind?"

"Home."

I gulped, trying to swallow down my disappointment. "Has staying with us been so bad?"

"No. Not at all. What I meant is I want to go look for my father's lockbox." He squinted at me. "What does that face you're making mean?"

His accident had clearly affected more than his memory. "It's called doubt. You do realize it would take an act of God to find that box, right?"

"I'm not above praying."

"All right then, but we can't stay long, and if there's anyone hanging around the place, we'll turn around and keep on driving."

He agreed by giving me a thumbs-up and wagging it side to side, a sure sign he'd been spending too much time around Evan.

We turned onto the road that led to his house—or what used to be his house. There were no trolling news vans around, but there was someone far worse: Mr. Sal Zmira. The street was too narrow for us to make a U-turn, so I veered the car toward the curb, solidly hitting it before shifting into park to wait out Zmira. "Don't let him see you."

Adam ducked low in his seat. "News people?"

"No. See that guy yelling over there?"

He peeked out his window. "The one waving his middle finger in the air?"

"No, the other guy."

"You know him?"

"Had him last year for history class. I didn't realize he was your neighbor."

"Neither did I," said Adam, sounding as if he thought I meant it as a good thing. So not.

I cracked open the windows. Even from several houses away I could hear Zmira bellowing something to the driver of a tractor trailer about blocking the driveway and it being about time that rubbish heap next door was carted away. I squirmed in my seat, my arms already beginning to tingle and itch.

Hives. That's what Zmira did to me.

Early last year I made the mistake of dozing off in his class after staying up all night assisting Dad as he put a face back together for an open casket the next morning. Did Zmira care? No. He made me explain to the whole class why I found it impossible to stay awake. I told the truth, perhaps with too much detail, and as a reward Zmira moved me to the front of the class. From then on he got his jollies by calling on me any time my head dropped. By the end of the term, the mention of his name was enough to make me break out in a rash. I dropped out shortly after that.

For the moment we were hidden by the trailer, but if we left now, he would surely see us. There was nothing more conspicuous than a big black hearse with a silk calla lily wired to the antenna, blue-velvet curtains, and vanity plates front and back that read XPIRED—Evan's not-so-brilliant idea.

I sat up slightly to assess the situation and was just in time to see Zmira tromp back inside, his mop dog at his heels. "See," I said as I shifted into drive. "It's not only me. Zmira intimidates every-one."

But Adam wasn't listening. All of a sudden he flung open his door, leaped out of the rolling car, and sprinted up the drive toward the ruins of his old house, where a mustard-yellow, smoke-spewing bulldozer was tearing up the remnants and dumping them into the bed of a monstrous truck. The sound was deafening but not loud enough to block out Adam's screams. "Stop! Stop!"

I put the hearse in park, cut the engine, and chased after him. "Adam, wait, come back!"

A foreman halted him at the gates, allowing me to catch up. "If you two agree to stay back, I'll let you watch," the man said, as if we were four-year-olds.

"You can't clear this lot," I yelled over the roar of the dozer. "The estate hasn't been settled!"

"Not my problem. Just following orders."

"Whose orders?" I pointed to Adam. "He's the owner." Or would be once the bureaucratic dust settled.

"Don't know nothin' about no new owner," answered the foreman.

Together Adam and I watched in disbelief as the dregs of his former life tumbled into the truck bed, load after load. With each crash of concrete, dirt, and debris, Adam's head jerked back like he was being slapped across the face. When the hauler was full, it rumbled off, belching thick diesel fumes, heading for the local landfill and most likely taking Neil Lassiter's lockbox right along with it.

The bulldozer mounted the tractor trailer, which then backed its way down the street, its incessant beeping piercing my every nerve. Left behind were only a corner of the house's foundation, an acre or less of dead and dying walnut trees, and a plot of weed-smothered grave markers. But somewhere buried deep beneath the far side of the ramshackle estate was the fallout shelter, unmarked but certainly not forgotten, at least not by us.

The foreman wadded up the last of the caution tape, pulled the gates closed behind him, and drove off in his pickup.

"I shouldn't have brought you here," I said. "It was a mistake."

I strolled back to where the gravel drive met asphalt to give Adam the time and privacy he needed to mourn, or to celebrate—I'm not sure, maybe a bit of both—the obliteration of what was once his prison. He took it all in, not moving so much as an eyelid. Then, out of the blue, he plucked a length of railing from the tortured earth, reared back, and swung at the nearest gatepost, beheading its stone cap. Not even Evan could do that. He pitched a fistful of rocks over the wall, ranting in Latin. No translation needed.

I did nothing. Better he get it all out than hold it in. I knew.

Fifteen minutes later, when he was done vanquishing whatever demon had possessed him, he joined me by the hearse, his chest heaving from the effort, a faint madness still sparking in his eyes. "Better?" I asked.

"A little," he admitted. "I think I needed that."

"I bet you did. Feel like getting lunch?"

"Yes. I'm famished."

"About time."

RULE #8
You're only as good as your gear.

I read the five possible questions for my college admission essay and, by process of elimination, narrowed them down to two:

1. Recount an incident or time when you experienced failure. (Plenty of options there.)

2. Describe a background, identity, or talent that is so meaningful, you believe your application would be incomplete without it. (Makeup artist to the dead? Too obvious?)

Last year I took a career aptitude test. The results were laughable. They suggested I'd be good at working with people. Yeah, so long as they weren't breathing. Instead I settled on a business degree. Who knows? Maybe someday I'd have my own company specializing in cosmetics for the departed. One thing was for sure: if I attended a college near home, Dad would do everything he could to pressure me into changing my mind. But if I went away, he'd be forced to consider Evan as his replacement.

Three obstacles stood in my way. First, I had to get accepted, and it wasn't like my grades and GED score were anything to brag about. Second, my savings fell far short of what I'd need for tuition, room, and board. Evan was lucky. His father left him a trust fund tagged for education. Third—and this was a biggie—I had to break the news to Dad.

I was still waffling between essay topics when St. Margarita's Transport rolled up to the delivery door out back. I unlocked the double-wide door. The mechanism, which my great-great-grandfather installed when he first opened for business, clanked and rattled like a drawbridge, reciting its own piece of our history. To my right was a dent in the wall from the time Great-Grandma Hazel pitched an urn at her cheating husband and missed. That urn was now his permanent residence. To my left was an ice chute that my aunt Agnes used to send her broken dolls down to the basement. And directly below the chute was an old wooden table where her father, my grandpa Ted, would prep the dolls before laying them to rest in a discarded cigar box. To this day we can't dig in the garden without exhuming one of those dolls. Aunt Agnes must have had a dozen of them—a sign of better times for the family. I had never owned a doll, but I made do. When I was little, I secretly set up my father's work cart with reception china and held tea parties with dead girls in the prep room.

No one in my family had ever truly escaped this funeral home. Their bodies may have been buried elsewhere, but slivers of their souls remained. They jabbed at me from every floorboard, lathe, and shingle of this old house, not as ghosts but as memories hammered into place. And with each prod or prick they pleaded for me to stay, to honor what they slaved so hard to preserve. But I refused to be nailed down. Unlike Adam, I would not be making any promises to my father.

The screeching halt of the delivery door cleared my thoughts, and I immediately recognized the transport driver, José. In his late twenties, built like a bear and about as hairy, and one of the few people who could pry a conversation out of me. I rolled out our sturdiest gurney. "*Jo-o-sé, can you see?*" I sang out.

And as usual, he responded with an "Eh, beautiful" and gave me a flirty wink. "Been a while."

"Yeah, work's been slow."

"Not at EMS. Jim Sturbridge tells me they've got more than they can handle."

"Figures," I grumbled. "So did you get the house?"

"Yup, moved in and everything. Now all I have to do is pop the question to Lonnie."

I envied Lonnie for the way José beamed when he said her name.

He pulled out the dead pan and transferred the body bag from the van to the gurney. Then he unlocked the wheels and together we escorted our newest guest inside. "Is your old man here? I'm supposed to pick up a check." He handed me an invoice stamped PAST DUE.

I grimaced and shoved the invoice into my back pocket. "My dad had a meeting at the bank, but I'll make sure he takes care of it today."

Jose cleared his throat and lowered his voice as he leaned

across the body bag. "Hey, I, uh, heard you guys might be a little strapped."

"Who said that? We're totally fine. In fact, we're thinking of expanding."

"You are?" He looked surprised.

"Sure. Dad's there right now about a loan to buy a crematorium. You know, so we can be more competitive."

"A crematorium? Didn't know there were any up for sale."

I felt a pinch of pride. For once I knew something José didn't. "That's because technically there aren't any, but we heard Crenshaw and Madsen might be soon."

"Well, glad to hear the rumors are wrong. Your family is our oldest customer. I'd hate to see you go."

That made two of us. Even though I couldn't see myself as the future funeral director, that didn't mean I didn't care what happened to our family's legacy. It wasn't about preserving history; it was about dignity for the departed and those they left behind, as well as service to the community. Lofty ideals aside, I'd hate losing everything my family had worked for to someone like Sturbridge.

I nodded toward the gurney. "So who do we have here?"

José knew the drill. "Christian Tomopolo, fifty-three, stockbroker, father of sixteen."

"Sixteen?"

"Yup. He was on his fifth wife when he died. Literally."

"Let me guess: heart attack."

"Hah. You're good."

I didn't hear that enough and beamed.

"His wife insisted on dressing him, which reminds me." José reached into his breast pocket, pulled out a gold pendant along with a length of chain, and placed them in my hand. "It broke when we were bagging him."

"I've never seen a medallion like this before."

"It's *chai*, the Jewish symbol for life. Kind of ironic if you think about it. His name is Christian, according to his wife he's an atheist, and he bit the big one while wearing the Hebrew word for 'life.'"

"Yeah, ironic." More like tragic if you ask me. "I'll see if I can fix it." I signed the necessary paperwork, and José was on his way.

Mr. Tomopolo's ride to the prep room was less than smooth sailing, but somehow I managed to leave only one small dent and a few wheel scuffs on the baseboards to mark our passing. It was a good day.

Since Dad was at the bank and Tony, our other mortician, had called in sick *again*, getting Christian checked in was up to me. I slipped on a pair of gloves, unzipped the body bag, and got to work listing information on an ankle band before securing it to his leg. Next I documented all his personal effects, including the necklace. His Rolex, one of those self-winding types, had to be brand-new. In the back pocket of his chinos I found a couple casino chips, a receipt from Victoria's Secret, and a ticket to tonight's doubleheader. Each item told his story.

Everything went into a Ziploc labeled with his name and a shelf number. "Well, Christian, can't say you didn't make the most of your time here on Earth." The design for his pillow was already gelling in my head: a diamond-shaped border in gold floss.

My thoughts were interrupted by impatient pounding at the prep-room door. Irritated that whoever it was couldn't be bothered to put in the code, I opened it.

Adam stood there with a pained expression. "A woman is at the front door."

"That would be Mrs. Tomopolo number five. Can't Rachel or Nana Jo talk to her?"

"Rachel left to get kitten formula?" he said, obviously unsure he got the message right. "And Jo is at yogurt."

"That's yoga. Well, let Mrs. Tomopolo in, give her one of those pamphlets we keep in the entry, and I'll be right up as soon as I finish here." I wouldn't be right up. I figured if I stalled long enough, someone else would have to handle things.

By the time I was done tucking Christian in for his stay, I'd given him a full report on my essay dilemma, a review on the two books I'd recently read, and more than one apology for the lack of air-conditioning. I had no way of knowing if Christian Tomopolo was much of a listener in life, but he got top ratings in death.

I placed a head block into position, rolled him to the cooler to wait for Tony's return, and then checked the hall to make sure the coast was clear before sneaking up to my room.

"Go away!" Adam was shouting. "Just go away!"

What the hell was he doing? That was no way to treat the bereaved. I ripped off my apron and raced to the parlor, where a woman dressed in an unfortunate pantsuit had him pinned against the fireplace. She had a cell phone shoved in his face. A reporter.

Adam clutched the mantle's candelabra in one hand, waving it to ward her off, and shielded his face with his other hand, but her rapid-fire questioning was relentless. "What was life like for you? Was your father a cruel man? Did he beat you? Why didn't you try to escape? Did you ever think to ask a neighbor for help?"

Adam's eyes narrowed and his lips curled into a snarl, but the reporter either didn't recognize the signs that she'd crossed a line or was ignoring them. "We did a little research. Did you know there are no records of you or your family? No birth certificates, no school records? Explain why that is. Are you part of a federal protection plan? What are you hiding?"

"Stop!" I cried, barely processing her accusations. "Who are you?"

"Mae Wu with the *National Examiner*," she said, flashing a badge. "And you are?"

"Never mind who I am. How dare you come into our home and harass him."

"Not only a home but a place of business," she reminded me. "I merely wanted to ask him a few questions. People have a right to know."

"No—they—don't. Now get out before I call the police."

Unruffled, she lowered the phone but was obviously still recording the conversation. "Fine, but the truth will eventually come out. Someone will talk, and I'm going to be there when they do." With a flip of her hair she turned for the door, but not before getting off one last shot. "Adam, did you have anything to do with your father's death?"

"Get out now!" I shouted. I was about to slam the door on her skinny ass when I saw another woman stepping up to the porch. She had a fireplug figure, overplucked brows crowning weepy eyes, and a bad case of hiccups. *This* was Mrs. Tomopolo number five, I guessed.

"Um, please come in," I said, awkwardly extending a shaky hand. "I'm Lily McCrae."

She pulled a face like I'd offered her a wormy apple. Then I saw why. In all the commotion, I'd forgotten to remove my latex gloves. She had to be wondering where they'd been. Anyone would. "Excuse me," I blustered.

Mortified, mouth dry as face powder, I retreated down the hall, snapping off the gloves and shoving them into the bathroom wastebasket until I could dispose of them properly. In the kitchen I threw back a glass of water, collected myself, and then filled a pitcher for our guest.

Traces of laughter spilled from the parlor. That couldn't be good.

I returned to find Mrs. Tomopolo seated by the window, peering through teary eyes at one of our many florist brochures. Adam stood stiffly by her side. Confused, I poured her a glass of water.

Hiccup. "Thank you," she said, trying to mask a giggle.

"Something funny?" I asked, shooting Adam a puzzled glance. He shrugged.

"This young man"—*hiccup*—"was explaining to me that every flower has its own meaning." *Hiccup, hiccup.* "Some of them struck me as so amusing, considering how Christian died and all." Her golden brown cheeks flushed a rosy russet. "What was that one you were telling me about, not the tuberose, the other one?"

"Red carnation. It means 'my heart breaks.'" Adam studied her face as if decoding it.

Mrs. Tomopolo chuckled. "Yes, that was it. I know I shouldn't be laughing. I mean, he did die of a heart attack, but my husband always had a wicked sense of humor and a soft spot for irony."

No kidding, I think, remembering the necklace pendant.

I took over from there, clumsily walking Ledah Tomopolo, step-by-step, through the many decisions she now faced, because of course Christian had put off making any kind of prearrangements. She shared some stories about her husband, including one about her gifting him the *chai* pendant necklace before discovering he was an atheist. "He wore it anyway, for me."

I thought she might break down in tears again, but one look at Adam and the pamphlet's picture of red carnations had her smiling again. It was a pained smile, but it got her through.

❀ ❀ ❀

After dinner Mal called wanting to know how it was going with Adam. "Strangely okay," I said. I didn't know what else to tell her. He was nothing like I remembered or like anyone else I'd ever met. Naive in so many ways yet wickedly wise in others; recklessly candid one moment, cagey the next.

"Find out anything more about his past?"

"They had no phone, television, or computer in his house." But I'd already known that.

"So what did they do in their free time?"

"Um, read?"

"Boring. Hey, how about I come over? We could watch *Night of the Living Dead*."

We'd already seen it a million times. I wasn't stupid. It was nothing but an excuse to see Evan.

"Sorry, not tonight. It's been a wild day. Tomorrow, maybe. Okay?"

"Sure," she replied, obviously disappointed. "Tomorrow."

I told myself I was doing her a favor; I'd be lousy company. Instead I buddied up to Christian. Asked him whether he thought Neil Lassiter truly loved his son, and how was it there were no records of Adam or his family?

I could almost hear Christian's reply. *"You want answers? Go find them."* I knew he was right, but if the press couldn't dig them up, how could I?

Between the formaldehyde and the heat, my head was pounding. I stuffed my cosmetics kit back under the counter and went in search of Adam. I found him laid out across the weed patch we called a lawn. Dressed in the drabbest of clothes, he could have been mistaken for a grave marker if not for his shallow breathing. I tipped my head back to see what had him so entranced. A fingernail clipping of the moon set against an ocean of stars so deep you could drown in it.

"Lie with me?" He gestured toward a patch of turf an arm's length away. We were going to have to work on how he phrased things, but I got the gist of what he wanted. I picked a spot and lay back, grateful for the earth at my back and the shelter of the dark, but my cowardice earlier this afternoon still needled me. "Sorry about the reporter. If I'd known—"

"But you didn't know."

I should have. Ever since his arrival, I'd been hopelessly distracted. It was affecting my work, my sleep, and my relationship with Mal. Maybe Dad was right; the sooner Adam was settled somewhere else, the better. And yet I continued searching for a reason to keep him here—one my parents would accept. So far I'd used the crush of reporters as an excuse, but that wouldn't last forever. The world had a short attention span.

"By the way, nice job with Mrs. Tomopolo," I offered. He shrugged, as if to say *no big deal*. But it was a big deal. He'd smoothed over a situation that could have been embarrassing and costly. "We could use someone like you around here." *I could use someone like you.*

As we stared heavenward, the silence between us pulled as taut as Orion's bowstring. So many unasked questions notched and ready to fly. I took aim. "Adam," I began, but he'd already anticipated my arrow.

"If you're still wondering, my father did not physically abuse me. Knowing I failed him was always punishment enough."

"I get that." Boy, did I. "You've seen what my father's like." Oddly, there was an ounce of comfort in knowing Adam and I shared the same weakness: a need to please.

I found myself desperately wanting to reach out, to bridge the distance between us, to run a finger across his palm where his lifeline should be. How strange it would be to touch warm skin. We'd come close the night of the storm but were still too unsure of each other to seal the deal.

His fingers twitched, egging on mine. I slid my hand an inch closer in a counter-dare. He extended his arm an inch more. I smiled to myself at this game of chicken we were playing. How close could our hands get without touching? Who would be first to close the gap, to pull back? Why did the stakes feel so high?

The porch light flicked on, the screen door swung open, and out bounded Specter, ending the game. I sat up as Dad stepped onto the back stoop, dressed in his grungiest tee and his *How the Grinch Stole Christmas* pajama bottoms. "Lily, what are you doing out here? I've been looking for you everywhere."

"Needed some fresh air," I answered. "What's up?"

"Ledah Tomopolo called. She wants you to trim Christian's nose hairs. Guess she's got a thing about that."

"You could have left me a note."

"Need it done tonight. And, Adam, I think tomorrow we should discuss what's next for you." It was his way of saying the time had come for Adam to move on. I'd known this was coming, but I still couldn't bear the thought of losing Adam again—certainly not so soon.

Dad went back inside but kept us in his line of sight. He didn't trust us. If he only knew what a waste of worry *that* was.

I stood and brushed off my butt. "Seriously, you should think about staying on."

"Nobody's asked me to."

"I am."

Now all I had to do was sell my parents on the idea.

RULE #9
TO AVOID UNRAVELING, MAKE YOUR STITCHES TIGHT, YOUR KNOTS TIGHTER.

From downstairs came the familiar staccato of sobbing followed by the *click* of the front door and the smell of something baking in the oven. Another typical morning.

According to my clock, it was well past the time my alarm should have sounded—if I'd remembered to set it the night before. I'd missed the morning appointment I promised to take so my parents could sleep in.

I showered, dressed, and crept downstairs, where Nana Jo's latest project, a bust of Grandpa Ted, greeted me from its makeshift pedestal—an upturned bucket. Its eerie, hollowed eyes tracked me as I stole into the kitchen.

"Sale on mixers," Dad announced from behind his newspaper barricade. "Tried mixing rye dough with that old one of ours and it started smoking."

"We need a new gurney more," said Rachel, pulling a tray of what she called "morning glory" bagels from the oven. Fourth batch this week. She was perfecting her recipe.

Head down and counting on my superpowers of invisibility, I pulled up a stool. I thought I'd escaped detection until Dad plunked down his mug. "Lily, what have I told you? Death waits for no one, so—"

"You might as well get used to it," I finished. "Sorry. I overslept."

"And then there's the pair of gloves I found in the bathroom trash. I'm guessing they're yours?"

I hung my head a little lower. "I forgot. I'll take care of them first thing."

Rachel served me a bagel with a dollop of marmalade on the side, the way I liked it. I propped my chin on my hands and stared at it, wishing it were a lifesaver, because I was drowning here.

What right did Dad have to assume I'd follow in his footsteps—in *all* their footsteps, five generations' worth? But I didn't have the heart—or the courage—to tell him that. Like my mother, who walked out on us two days after I was born, I didn't want the business or the responsibility that came with it. The difference was that she didn't want me, either.

That's when Evan lumbered into the kitchen. "What's the matter with you?" he asked, knowing it was easier to irritate me when I was already in a mood.

"Nothing," I grouched, because in my father's eyes that's about all I had done right lately.

Rachel mopped her brow with a pot holder. "Going to be another scorcher. Good day for cleaning the cold room."

"Evan, consider that one of your jobs today," piped in Dad.

"Speaking of jobs, I've been thinking—"

"Uh-oh, Lil's been thinking again," joked Evan.

I snatched a damp dish towel from the counter and whipped it at him.

"Hey!" He laughed.

"Like I was saying . . . I've been thinking Adam's going to need a place to stay."

"What he's going to need is a way to support himself," said Dad.

"That's what I mean. He could work for us." Dad walked right into that one. "He could have the room behind Nana's workshop, the one we've been using for storage. It'll need cleaning out, but I don't mind."

Dad eyed me suspiciously, obviously questioning my motives. Maybe I should have been doing the same. "And you should have seen how he handled Mrs. Tomopolo yesterday."

"Yes, she told me all about it last night when she called."

"Don't forget I'll be leaving for school in a few weeks, too," added Evan. "You're going to need the extra help, especially with moving the bigger ones."

"The bigger ones?" I repeated.

"You know what I mean."

Sadly, I did. (Someone seriously needed some sensitivity training.)

"And if the crematorium deal goes through, we're going to be even busier," said Rachel. "Besides, I don't like how tired you've been looking lately. You make that appointment for a physical yet? It's long overdue."

"I've got a business to run. I don't have time for doctor appointments."

"Even more reason to take on extra help," I argued.

"Okay. Okay. I hear you all, except . . . what do we really know about him?"

Yes, what do *we really know about him?* my thoughts echoed. Not much more than when I found him. I knew he still didn't remember me, he had not been able or willing to tell us much about his past, and he was obsessed with getting some old tin box back. I knew he was the one person outside of Mal who didn't see me as *that* girl, the one who lived in a creepy old house with dead people. And I knew this was my chance to make up for abandoning him. I intended to make the most of it.

Evan cleared his throat and signaled with a whirl of his finger. We all spun around, and there was Adam, towering over me, fresh from the shower and as ill at ease as ever. "You smell . . ." *like fresh-turned earth*, I wanted to finish, but that would have been too weird. Weirder still was that I liked it on him.

"I smell?" he said.

"Ignore her, Adam," said Evan. "Everybody does."

Thankfully the phone rang. We all looked to see who would answer, the usual question on our minds: Who died? Rachel was closest to the phone so lost by default. "McCrae Family Funeral Home," she said. "How may I help you? Why, yes, he's right here. One moment." Eyes wide, she covered the mouthpiece with her hand. "It's for you, Adam. It's the police."

Adam shook his head. "You take it. Please."

Rachel returned the phone to her ear. "He's asked me to speak to you on his behalf." There were several "No, you don't say?" and "Have they figured out . . . ?" before Rachel ended the call. "That was Officer Wells calling to say the FBI has closed the case."

Adam's expression hardened. "F-B-I? What does that mean?"

"It means," she explained, "that the government agency who took over the investigation from state and local agencies has determined that the explosion was the result of a gas leak. They're ending the investigation. It is odd, though, that it went all the way to the national level. I would've thought this was a local issue or of interest to the California's Bureau of Investigation at the most."

"Very odd," Dad agreed.

Evan nudged my shoulder. "Told ya it was a gas leak."

"But we never used the oven," insisted Adam. "We microwaved everything."

"Then it was probably a faulty water heater," offered my father. "It happens."

I was with Adam on this one. The explosion was more than a gas leak. The federal government would not have taken over the investigation otherwise. "What about the fallout shelter?"

Adam shifted his weight from one foot to the other, the mention of it making him uncomfortable.

"Officer Wells said they conducted a thorough search to ensure that no one else was down there and then sealed it. He also said that you all were lucky the whole place didn't collapse on you." Rachel knotted her arms over her chest and gave both Evan and me one of those piercing *What were you thinking?* looks.

At the time I thought we were out of our minds for going down into the fallout shelter, and now I was thinking there was something very suspicious about this whole investigation. If Neil's death was an accident, then why were the feds involved? And why the rush to seal up the shelter and clear the lot? It was like someone wanted this whole case buried and forgotten.

Not Adam. "So they're not going to do a thing about Neil's murder?"

"Trust me," said Dad, reaching for the business section of the paper. "If they had any reason at all to suspect foul play, the case would still be open."

"He's right," agreed Rachel. "The best thing now is to find a way to accept what's happened and begin putting your life in order. It won't be easy, but we're here to help."

"Thank you, but if the police or this FBI refuse to find the murderer, then I will." He straightened, as though gathering together the fragments of himself. "Before I go, I . . . I would like to ask a favor. Would you handle the arrangements for my father? I can't pay you anything now but will send money as I can. You have my word."

"We'd be happy to," I interjected, afraid my father would turn him away. "But you don't have to leave. Dad, tell him."

"Cam?" pleaded Rachel in that voice she reserved for him alone.

Dad sighed, knowing he'd lost the battle before it had even begun. "Adam, I don't suppose you'd consider staying on and working for us? What you earn could be put toward the cost of handling your father's arrangements plus your room and board."

I braced myself for a no. It was one thing to share a house with

the dead—although, strangely, it had not been an issue for him so far—but it was quite another to hands-on work with them. I was born to it. He was not.

Adam's eyes narrowed. "What kind of work?"

"You could be an attendant," said Rachel. "Help with pickups, setup, and takedown."

"If you like, I could care for the yard, too," he offered. "I used to tend the orchard."

"Oh, that would be wonderful!" Rachel clapped. "We could use a new gardener." She heaped a plate with bagels and shoved it into Adam's hand. "It's all settled then."

Settled hardly seemed the right word, but it was a start.

The spring of the screen door twanged. It was Nana Jo back from her morning walk. She yanked out her earplugs and plopped her pedometer onto the counter. "Three thousand steps!" she declared, in case anyone was keeping track.

Dad set aside the paper. "Gone a long time this morning, Mom."

"Oh, I got to talking to Fran Ullman. You know what a gossip she is. She was telling me all about how she caught Sal Zmira in her front yard the other night with a metal detector. Says he's found all kinds of stuff with it. You can imagine where she told him to go."

I recalled what Evan said about seeing someone combing the Lassiter property with a metal detector. Adam must have been thinking the same thing. "Did he mention anything about a lockbox?" he asked.

"Well, Fran did say something about a keepsake box Zmira found recently."

"Could have been a jewelry case, Adam—from anywhere," I was quick to point out.

"My suggestion," said Dad, "is to go ask Zmira if it matters all that much."

Easy for him to say. He'd never met the old buzzard.

For the moment, though, we had more pressing matters. If Adam was going to start work right away, he would need something other than the ratty hand-me-downs he'd been wearing for the past six days. He needed an entirely new wardrobe.

Time to call in reinforcements.

Rule #10
The clothes make the corpse.

Mal arrived half an hour later and sweet-talked Evan into driving us. Not much of a challenge considering he'd do anything to get out of cleaning the cold room.

While we waited for Evan to rustle up a more appropriate pair of shoes for our newest employee—something other than flip flops, Mal shouldered up to me. "So whose idea was it to hire Adam full time? As if I couldn't guess."

"Um, it might have been mine?" I admitted.

She pulled out a toothpick and stuck it between her lips. "Hmph."

"He has nowhere else to go, and I figure a job will help get him on his feet." Who was I kidding? She saw right through me. "Since when do you carry toothpicks?"

"Since you talked me out of cigarettes."

"Well, put that away when you're in the car. If we have to make a sudden stop—"

"Like for a fire hydrant?" piped in Evan, sneaking up from behind.

"Hey, that was an accident, and I did manage to avoid the squirrel." (Not that Evan cared about a rodent. We still couldn't pass a fire hydrant without him shouting, "Thar she blows!") "Anyway, if we stop suddenly, you could choke on the toothpick. Just saying."

She snapped the toothpick in two and dropped it in the waste-basket beside the coatrack. "You know, Lils, bad shit happens. Lighten up and take a chance once in a while. Be bold." With that she commandeered the front passenger seat, leaving Adam and me stuck in the back. "Oh, I almost forgot." She whipped out a folded piece of paper from her purse and handed it to Evan.

"What's this?" he asked.

"It's a flyer for the End-O'-Summer Beach Bash. Look, com-mercial sponsorship, an all-night bonfire, and, wait for it . . . they're bringing back the beach challenge!"

It was a total setup, but Evan was either oblivious or playing stupid. He excelled at both. "Whoa!" he exclaimed. "That's some prize money."

I met his hazel eyes in the rearview mirror. "Tell me you aren't seriously thinking of competing again after what happened last year."

"You kidding? This time I'm ready for Kyle Mumford. He's gonna eat my sand."

Well, Evan might have been able to put his disgraceful display behind him, but I was not. While he was getting cheated out of a trophy, I'd been wading around a cove, trying to find a seal pup a bunch of kids from school said they saw stranded in the rocks there. No one mentioned it was dead—a deliberate omission, I'm sure. I had to wait hours until the tide went back out to rejoin the group. Of course the girls all apologized, saying they had no idea I couldn't swim. Yeah right. Mallory had eventually returned to fetch me, but that hardly made me want a repeat. But what had she said about being bold?

"Okay," I said. "I guess I'm in, too."

"Well, don't get too excited about going." Mal's voice dripped with sarcasm. "You come too, Adam."

Before I could lodge a protest, Evan launched the van out of the drive and onto the street, causing a reporter loitering by the streetlight to drop his box of doughnuts. It was good for a laugh until a dark SUV pulled away from the curb and started shadowing us.

"Looks like we've got reporters on our tail," said Evan. "Watch this." He whipped a right turn into an alley, pitching me into the door.

"It's an Astro, not a Maserati," I reminded him.

He drove two more blocks and pulled behind an abandoned filling station, where we all held our breath until the SUV rolled by. Adam was pretty shaken—we all were. Not so funny now.

"That was some slick driving," said Mal.

"Yeah, but did you notice there was no satellite dish on that car and no plates?" I said. "That was not a news van." And I'd swear it was the same SUV I saw parked across the street the day we found Adam.

"Probably some sleazebag hoping to snag a photo to sell," said Evan. "But hey, if you ever want to make a few bucks, Adam—"

"Don't even think about it," I warned.

"I'm kidding!"

Sure he was.

Evan waited a few more minutes to be sure we were in the clear before pulling back onto the road. To distract Adam, Mallory swung into full tour guide mode. "Oh! Oh! Look! There's Manny's Pizza Shack. They have the most outrageous Hawaiian pizza. Tons of cheese and the pineapple is totally fresh, not the canned stuff. And over there, that's CyberZone, where the hard-core gamers go, and . . ."

Her tour babble trailed off as we all saw a billboard of Jim Sturbridge's giant mug plastered top to bottom with the words: A VOTE FOR JIM STURBRIDGE FOR CITY COUNCIL IS A VOTE FOR GROWTH AND PROSPERITY.

I groaned. "Since when is *he* running for city council?"

"Since he realized he could buy his way into politics," answered Evan, meeting my eyes in the rearview mirror. "I heard he wants to rename the town."

"To what? Sturbridge Hollow? You know if he wins the election, he'll rezone us right out of business, not to mention what he'll do to all the other mom-and-pop shops in town."

"Who is Jim Sturbridge?" asked Adam.

"A big business developer from the city," I grumbled. "He owns Eternal Memorial Services, and would like nothing more than to see us close our doors for good—if he can't buy us out first. I'd rather see our mortuary sold to almost anyone else than see a hundred and fifty years of my family's blood, sweat, and tears end up in his greedy hands. He'd have the McCrae Family Funeral Home on the auction block before you could say rigor mortis." *Damn Sturbridge. He's the kudzu to all those who put down roots in this town long ago.* "There she goes again," said Evan, shaking his head. "Most of the time you can hardly get her to talk, but bring up Sturbridge and you can't shut her up. But does she do anything about it? No. She would rather dump that on someone else."

I threw up my hands. "Like you're any better. The way you talk, it sounds as if you'd like nothing more than for us to lose the business."

"So not true. I just don't want to spend the rest of my life hauling stiffs. Besides, the pay sucks. You know that."

"Not everything is about money. What we do matters to people."

"Not if they're dead, it doesn't, but hey, I forget who I'm talking to. Or I should say I forget who *you* talk to."

"We help those left behind, too, you know."

"You don't, not if you can help it. Sometimes I think you'd spend your whole life locked away in the prep room if you could avoid having to deal with people. But as far as I'm concerned, you can have it all. Besides, it's what Dad wants."

"What about what I want?" I said under my breath.

"What *do* you want?" asked Adam.

"A way out." Not that I didn't care about the business. I did. But I couldn't expect him to understand. When his father demanded he stay, Adam obeyed.

"So, Evan, you declare a major yet?" asked Mallory.

"Sure did. Game design."

"That's so cool," she gushed. "You'd be great at it, too. Those sketches for your senior project last year blew me away. And that whole dungeon model. Too cool for school."

"Game design?" I couldn't believe what I was hearing. "You told Dad you were going into marketing."

"I changed my mind. It's my money. I ought to be able to choose my own major. And don't you say anything, either," Evan warned. "I'll tell them when I'm good and ready."

And leave me to break my father's heart.

The Way We Wore thrift shop occupied what used to be the library before the new one was built on the east side of town. The owner claimed he carried vintage clothing, but it was more of a catchall for clothes no one wanted anymore—plaid skorts, gamy hunting vests, bibbed overalls. There was a rack of ghoulish costumes even though Halloween was three months away. The women's clothes were sorted by color, but the men's looked as if they'd been shot onto the racks with a cannon. We dug in.

"How 'bout these?" I held up a pair of black pants and a dark gray button-down.

"Seriously," huffed Mal. "Just because you dress corpses for a living doesn't mean you always have to go with dark and dismal."

She had a point. Outside of my usual black attire, I usually opted for faded denims and what Mal labeled my "downer shirts"—the ones that said things like *Nothing Sweet about Diabetes, Click It or Ticket,* and *Don't Let Cancer Steal Second Base.* Most I got from various volunteer gigs, but at least that beat the free corporate advertising disguised as cutesy logos that she plastered across her butt and chest. It was exploitive, I told her. Mallory took that to mean she should be paid for contributing to their brand recognition.

"Now this is what I'm talking about," said Mal, and she

shoved a pair of bright paisley board shorts into Adam's hands. "Try these."

Adam had unbuttoned his fly and was about to drop trou right in the middle of the aisle when Evan intervened with a "Whoa, dude, let's save it for the floor show" and directed him to a dressing room.

"Have you forgotten that we run a funeral home?" I said to Mal. "He doesn't need swim shorts."

"No, but they're perfect for the beach now that he's going to stick around a bit longer." She gave me a wink.

I rolled my eyes.

"Don't give me that," she scolded. "He's not my type, but he's clearly yours."

"What do you mean, 'my type'?"

"You know."

"You mean weird."

"I didn't say that. More like . . . brooding."

"You've been reading your mother's romance novels again, haven't you?"

"The point is he's a viable option."

"I don't need an option. I don't need anyone."

"Right. You keep telling yourself that." Her phone rang, and she took the call outside.

Evan and I managed to scrape together a suitable wardrobe for Adam along with a couple of casual items. Adam then accompanied me to the register while Evan rooted through the Halloween costumes in search of a mask to scare Mal.

"Hey, I saw you on the news this morning," announced the

cashier loudly. "You're the boy they found down in that mine shaft, aren't you?"

"Fallout shelter," he corrected.

Several heads popped up from behind clothes racks. I dropped the money onto the counter and quickly dragged Adam and Evan from the store.

"Who was on the phone?" I asked Mallory once we were safely back in the van.

She checked to make sure she had Evan's attention. "Only Hayden Jornet, a friend of Aslyn's. He's having a small party on Friday to show off his new loft downtown, no big deal." She paused for effect. "Oh, and I think he said something about members of the Jaded Corpses dropping by for a bit of jamming."

"For real?" Evan snorted. "*You're* hangin' with Hayden Jornet and the Jaded Corpses?"

I crossed my arms. "Why do you sound so surprised?"

"It's Hayden Jornet. He's so, so . . ."

"Out of her league?" I said.

"Well, yeah. That's one way of putting it." This from the guy who was parading around the thrift shop in a *Creature from the Black Lagoon* mask not ten minutes earlier.

Mallory looked crushed. "Fine, don't come. He's only the most up-and-coming badass music agent in town. At twenty he's already repping two of the hottest teen bands."

"Hold on. We're invited, too?" said Evan.

Mal shrugged. "He said to bring a few friends, but if you don't—"

"I was just messin' with you, Mal," Evan backpedaled. "You know me. I'm always up for a party. When is it?"

"A week from Friday. How 'bout you, Lils?"

First the beach bash and now this. She was really testing my limits. But I still owed her for bailing on the last party. "Fine. I'll go. It'll be fun."

Like sticking yourself with a needle is fun.

RULE #11
DON'T MASK THE FACE; GIVE IT LIFE.

"It used to be the caretaker's cottage," I explained to Adam. "It's a bit primitive, and you'll have to put up with Nana banging around the shop in the next room, but it beats the bunker in the fallout shelter and the sleeper sofa, don't you think?"

Adam flopped onto the bare mattress and spread out his arms like an albatross's wings. The old springs complained loudly. "Yes, much better," he agreed.

"And it has a nice-size window. See." I pulled back the curtains, and the late-afternoon sun bathed the dingy walls in a wash of golden light, making them appear much cheerier than they deserved. If only I could pull back the curtain keeping him from seeing me, the girl he once befriended. Then again, maybe starting over was better.

He watched me with an intensity I should have found unnerving but didn't. Probably because I didn't sense any judgment attached, only curiosity. It wasn't the first time I'd caught him studying me. Usually I was in the midst of the most mundane task imaginable—threading a needle, removing an earring, filing my nails. That was the thing about Adam; he made me feel utterly visible . . . just not memorable.

The vague look of contentment faded from Adam's face as his eyes drifted up, toward the open rafters. I searched the ceiling for spiderwebs or signs of water damage. "Something wrong?"

"In my old room there were stars on the ceiling. They glowed at night."

"The kind that stick on?"

"That's right. I would stare up at them and try to imagine a night sky without branches or walls. I never could. Silly, I know."

"Not at all. You were a hostage in your own home. But prison cells come in all shapes and sizes," I reminded him, thinking of my own situation. "It's about freedom, really, isn't it? Freedom to choose where to go and who to hang out with?"

"Hmm. I suppose," he said, but he seemed consumed by some bigger worry.

"Did you ever wish you had someone to talk to, someone besides Neil?" I fished, hoping to stir some lost memory of me.

"I did, but it was like wishing for wide-open skies. Since coming here, though, I've begun to see what I was missing."

Same here. I'd thought the company of the dead was enough until he arrived. It wasn't anymore.

He rolled onto his side. "Can I ask you something?"

I took a seat at the end of the bed. "Sure, shoot."

"Why would I want to shoot?"

I sometimes forgot how literal he could be. "That means say what you want to say."

"Oh, I'll make a note of that." Blink. Blink. "Do I look . . . different to you?"

Different? If he was asking whether he was anything like the boy he once was, the boy who taught me how to crack a walnut with the well-aimed thwack of a rock, who once shook a spring tree to shower me in blossoms, then I would have to say he looked the same and different. It had been six years. But if he was asking whether he'd changed since I found him in the shelter, then the answer was no. I mean, sure, he was stronger now and didn't tire as easily, but there was still an "otherness" about him. It was in the way he had to decode people's expressions, the way he marveled at items I take for granted—organ, laptop, cell phone—and the way he clung to the dark as if it were a security blanket but shirked tight spaces. "I'm not sure exactly what you're asking?"

"I mean compared to other people."

"Other people? Well, yeah. No two people are exactly alike—unless they're twins, of course, and even then there are always subtle differences. Take the Swain brothers: They died within a week of each other. One had ground his teeth smooth, but the other twin's teeth were still sharp—less stress, I guess. Why do you ask?"

"I wonder if I fit in. Is that odd?"

"No. I wonder the same thing all the time," I confessed, shocked that I would so willingly break one of my hard-and-fast rules. He did that to me: opened me up and made me spill thoughts I rarely shared outside the prep room. "I'll leave you to get settled in," I said, rising and reaching for the door. "If there's anything else you need, let me know."

"Wait." He slid his feet to the floor and stood, blocking my exit. "There is something."

He was standing so close—too close. I inched away and, to cover my unease, said, "I'm not doing your laundry, if that's what you want."

He cocked his head in that way he did when I'd lost him. "I wasn't going to ask you to."

"Smile, Adam. It was a joke. You're so serious all the time."

"I will have to work on that," he said so gravely that I couldn't help but laugh. "See," he said, "it's working already. No, I wondered if you would take me to Sal Zmira's house to ask him about his metal detector and my father's lockbox."

"You can ask him yourself."

"You're better with people than I am."

That's like saying a grenade is better than a missile; they're both going to bomb. So I made an excuse. "I can't. I told Nana I'd take in a pair of pants for her so she can wear them to the senior center tomorrow."

"Can't you do it for her in the morning?"

"I would, but I promised I'd do it tonight," I lied. "You wouldn't want me to break a promise, would you?" It wouldn't be the first time, but thankfully he'd forgotten that we once promised to always be there for each other. I waited six long years to return to him and had been nearly too late.

"No, of course not."

"Besides, you don't need me. It's only a few blocks away. Ask Mr. Zmira if he has the box, and if he does . . . I don't know, tell him you want it as a keepsake, something to remind you of your father." Although, knowing Zmira, I seriously doubted he had a sentimental bone in his body. "It'll be fine." With that settled, I skirted around him and out the door.

"Tomorrow, then," he called after me.

"Busy," I yelled back.

Later that evening Adam was a no-show for dinner. I asked if anyone had seen him, but they all shook their heads. He was probably sulking in his room because I wouldn't drop everything to go with him to Zmira's. Besides, if Zmira *had* found the box, it'd probably been cleaned out and trashed by now.

By the time I finished altering Nana's pants, everyone else had turned in for the evening. Still no sign of Adam. He hadn't struck me as the sort to hold a grudge. Maybe I'd underestimated how important that box was to him. I'd see about getting Evan to drive him over tomorrow.

I went out back to tell him my idea, but all the lights in the cottage were out. No point waking him. It could wait. I retreated to the main house, drew the shades, and checked and double-checked all the doors. Satisfied that I'd secured the house, I stopped in the kitchen for a drink. As I reached for a glass, I heard the creak of the screen door's hinges. The door handle twisted left, right, and then rattled violently. Someone was trying to break in. Everyone here was in bed or had a key.

Hands trembling and heart galloping, I slid open the knife

drawer and fished out the largest cleaver I could find. "Leave now or I'm calling the police," I threatened, my face inches from where the door met the jamb.

"Lily?" answered Adam's strangled whisper. "Let me in!"

I turned the lock and was nearly bowled over as Adam shoved past me, slammed the door, and flipped the dead bolt. I switched on the light. He saw the raised cleaver and shouted, "It's me! It's me!" That startled me into dropping the knife. It clanged onto the countertop and fell to the floor, where the blade stuck into the linoleum inches from my foot.

"Adam, you scared me half to death! I thought you were a burglar."

He fell back against the sink, holding his arms up around his neck and panting as if he'd run a mile. "I lost my key."

I pried the cleaver from the floor and slipped it back into the drawer. "You can lower your arms now."

His right arm dropped to his side, but his left elbow remained wrapped over his chin. There was a bright orange stain where a piece of flesh the size and shape of a pencil eraser was missing from his forearm. "Adam, what's that on your arm? And why are you hiding your neck?" I wrenched his hand away, exposing an angry red mark around his throat.

He jerked away. "I don't want to talk about it."

"But if you—"

"Please. It's nothing. Really."

"If you're sure."

"I'm sure. Can I sleep on the couch one more night?" Without waiting for me to answer, he went to the family room.

"Of course," I said to his back. "I'll let my parents know." But if he thought the conversation was over, he was sadly mistaken. I'd seen enough suicide victims to know the mark circling his throat was not from any chafing collar or dull shaver.

That was a rope burn.

RULE #12
TREAD LIGHTLY ON
HALLOWED GROUND.

Brianna Marshall lay beneath a crisp white sheet—weak chin, college dropout, naked except for chipped black nail polish and a Harley-Davidson tattoo on her left breast. My job was to erase all traces of the twenty-year-old who arrived from the coroner's the day before and replace her with the girl her mother wished to remember: an angelic vision dressed in a simple lilac frock. But Brianna was not that girl—not even close. A brain clot from some sort of trauma killed her, but traces of cigarette burns, old bruises, and a missing chunk of hair told a darker story. And if re-creating her mother's distorted image of her daughter wasn't challenge enough, she was a "post"—aka fresh from autopsy. I had my work cut out for me.

"Dad, you're hovering," I said. "I've got this."

"Fine, I need to make a few phone calls anyway. I'll be back in a while to check on your progress. And don't forget to fill out your work log this time." With that he left me alone with Brianna.

"My father's a bit of a micromanager," I explained.

I spread out my kit, which once belonged to my grandfather, its leather still surprisingly supple thanks to decades of exposure to skin preservatives. "So this guy, Adam, he's been avoiding me all day," I told her.

I removed the tub of "peanut butter"—a hardening compound filler—from the lower cupboard and slathered the creamy beige-brown paste over the incision on the side of Brianna's head. "All I want to know is where he was last night and how he got that rope burn around his neck. Is that unreasonable? At first I thought a suicide attempt. But then there's that hole in his arm—a piece of his skin was missing! Like a punch biopsy, only it looked like he'd put antiseptic on it—that orange Mercurochrome crap Nana used on scratches before she found out it had mercury in it. Too weird."

I continued obsessing over the rope burn as I smoothed and blended, covering the sutures. "Don't you think he at least owes me an explanation? I mean, if it weren't for me tripping over him, he'd probably still be down in that hole. Fly fodder."

I stepped back to assess my work. The application was too heavy-handed, too amateurish. Instead of reconstructing a face, you'd think I was frosting a cake. Normally this *was* a piece of cake, but not today. Today I'd lost my focus. Clearly.

"Sorry," I said to Brianna. "Totally off my game today."

Gritting my teeth, I scraped away the paste to give it another go, but my usual steadiness was gone. By the time I finished, she was as overdone as one of those pageant contestants you see on TV. I grabbed a towel to wipe off the mess but scrubbed too hard and loosened a stitch near her temple. "Aagh!" I pitched aside the towel in disgust, removed the headband holding back her hair, and slingshot it across the room.

My frustration boiled over. I took a deep breath and brought it back to a simmer. "Tell me what I should do, Brianna. Do I confront him?" I wasn't sure why I was asking her. She had no more answer than I did.

My cell chimed from my back pocket. "Hey, Mal," I answered flatly.

"You sound funny. Everything all right?"

"Just living the dream." I could confide in a corpse, but telling Mal about Adam? Not going to happen. She'd confirm what I already knew—I should tell my parents. "What's up?"

"You and Evan free tonight?"

I glanced at the block of wood temporarily supporting Brianna's head. "Nah. I don't know about Evan, but I've got a pillow to finish."

"A pillow? Okay, as your only friend, I'm not about to let you stay home on a Friday night to embroider a pillow. We'll go do something."

"Like what?"

"I'll figure something out. Let Evan know, okay?"

There was a click. "Mal?" She'd hung up on me—but at least she hadn't *given* up on me. Lately she'd been spending most of her time with her other friends, but maybe things between us weren't as shaky as I imagined.

I finished Brianna's face, then went to my room to work on her headrest. Around nine o'clock Mal texted.

> MAL: Pick you all up around 10:30.
> Wear dark clothing.

> ME: Pick me up? You don't drive.
> And when DON'T I wear dark clothing?

She never responded. I left a note for my dad telling him I was going out with Mal and went downstairs to wait. As usual, she was late.

"Where's Evan?" were the first words out of her mouth when I opened the door.

"Upstairs teaching Adam how to slaughter alien hordes. On the computer," I added, in case there was any confusion.

"Oh," she said with a shrug, but her fallen expression made it clear she was bummed Evan wouldn't be joining us. I'd have called her on it, but she'd deny it.

She escorted me out front, where three girls waited in a gleaming new four-door. *Those* girls. The ones who painted lipstick and nail polish on a dead rat, stuffed it in my gym bag, and pretended it was a joke. Mal's omission felt like a betrayal, and I wondered what she'd bribed them with to include me, her social ball and chain.

"You didn't tell me we were going with anyone else, and besides, the car is full." I said, hoping to finagle my way out of what was sure to be a night of me shadowing Mal.

"It'll be fine." She motioned for me to crawl in the back. "It's just Aslyn, Melissa, and Vega," she said, as if that made a difference.

It did. It made it worse.

Melissa, sulky and looking good in green (though her nails could use some reshaping), grudgingly scooted to the middle of the back seat to make room for me.

The first stop was a drive-through, where they all ordered fries with lots of ketchup, followed by a cruise around town to kill time—why, they didn't say. I played along as if I were in on the secret, but a tense knot was growing in my stomach. The whole time they blathered on in banshee voices about shopping sprees, new cars, dating, and other things I couldn't begin to relate to. It wasn't like Mallory's family was any better off than mine. They owned a small, struggling dry cleaner in one of the local strip malls. She was just better at faking it.

We ended up back in my neighborhood, I assumed to drop me off. I assumed wrong.

"It's midnight," announced Aslyn. "We're late."

I turned to Melissa. "For what?"

"It's a surprise," said Vega.

Surprises never bode well. The dead rat was a surprise. So was switching out my flask of hydrochloric acid for formaldehyde in chemistry class. And all in the name of good humor, only I was never the one laughing.

We passed my house and kept on going. I had a sinking feeling I knew where we were headed. The car slowed and drifted to a stop on an unlit road beside a familiar stone wall smothered in ivy. Ahead sat three more parked cars, all empty. The girls' voices fell to a guarded hush. My hunch was right. We were at the far end of the Lassiter property. This had to have been Mal's idea.

"Everybody out," ordered Vega.

"Mal, why are we here?" I whispered.

"Because if we go in this way, we won't alert the neighbors," she said. That's not what I meant and she knew it.

She took my hand and gave me a toothy smile. "It's the perfect setting. It'll be fun." Translation: *You're so screwed.* It wasn't like I could stay in the car while they all went to do whatever it was they were here to do, and I wasn't about to walk home by myself this late at night. So, against my better judgment, I let Mal lead me through a gap in the wall where the stacked stones had fallen. We pushed through a thicket of oleanders crowding the other side and emerged into what was left of the walnut grove. The smell of ash still lingered in the leaden night air.

My blood turned cold. The twenty or so figures gathered in the gloom were the same people who'd made my life a living nightmare all last year. Some stood shoulder to shoulder, hands in their pockets. They could have been mistaken for grave statuaries if not for their hushed whispers. Others perched on a toppled tree like gargoyles, heads bowed and knees bent. They all thought they were so cool, but I knew better. Up until a few weeks ago not one of them would have ventured here on their own.

Most wore ripped T-shirts smeared with what I assumed was ketchup; flattened tomato-red packets littered much of the ground at my feet. "Here," said Aslyn, tossing me one. I shoved it in my pocket, now understanding the reason they ordered fries.

"You're late," crooned a voice I'd learned to loathe.

Dana Blackwell.

Back in sixth grade she was this skinny girl with knock-knees and buckteeth, but thanks to her parents' ample bank account and the miracles of modern dentistry, she was now a model for a minor fashion agency and a "total smoke show," according to Evan. Rachel was forever pointing her out to me in the online

JCPenney catalog, saying, "See what the right clothes and a touch of makeup can do?"

I always wanted to respond with "And see what dressing down stiffs can do?" No one gives a crap what you look like when that's your job description.

I elbowed Mal. "Okay, now can you tell me why we're here?"

"Zombie tag," said Vega. "Right up your alley."

"Zombie tag?"

"It's only a game," said Mal. "Relax, okay?"

Relax? Yeah, that's going to happen.

They gathered around the entrance to the Lassiter family cemetery. Adam and I had seldom ventured near here, not because of the graves but because of the rat and snake-infested woodpile just beyond it.

I nodded toward the iron-girdled graveyard. "Out of respect, wouldn't a park be better?"

"Hey, Morticia, what's the problem?" taunted Jake Najarian. "Aren't graveyards your regular stomping grounds?" This from the genius who copied off my geometry exams all last year. The problem was he'd nailed the truth. I'd spent as many hours in cemeteries and graveyards as most of them had spent glued to their games—not that I had anything against video games. I just had the reflexes of a sloth.

Vega, who was apparently the ringmaster for tonight's festivities, went on to explain that first we had to select who would be *it*. Someone suggested we draw straws, but Aslyn dragged me from the back of the pack. "I say we pick Lily. She was made for the role!" This solicited a wheezy chortle from a short, nerdy guy dressed in what I guessed was supposed to be an undertaker's suit, although I couldn't recall anyone in my family ever dressing in tails.

Of course they all agreed I was the perfect candidate. *I'm so sorry,* Mal mouthed at me. I told myself to be a good sport. It could be worse. I could be getting a root canal. But I also wasn't stupid; they were mocking me as much as including me. "What do I have to do?"

Mal beamed and flipped me a thumbs-up.

"Close your eyes," said Vega, "count to one hundred, and then come find us. Home base is . . ." She spun around. "We need something small. Jake, give me that pack of condoms in your back pocket. Come on, I know you've got 'em."

With a proud smirk, he slipped the plastic-wrapped rubbers onto a nearby tree stump, and several whoops went up accompanied by a few awkward snickers and snorts.

"Your goal, Lily, is to tag each of us before we can tag the condoms and shout 'safe.' Anyone you catch before they reach home base becomes a zombie and has to help you hunt down the others. But if you don't manage to tag anyone before they call 'safe,' then you're it again."

"Yeah," said nerd-with-tails, "and don't forget to moan and groan and walk all stiff-like, you know, like . . . like the living dead." His eyes bugged out, channeling his inner Boris Karloff.

"*Da-da-da-doom,*" sang Jake, very melodramatically.

I should have walked away, but I didn't have the courage—the *gumption,* to use Nana's word—to say no. Reluctantly I leaned against the tree stump, buried my head in my arms, and began counting out loud. I wanted to get this over with.

"Slower and louder," called one of the girls.

Behind me, feet swished through dried grass. Guarded whispers and ghostly murmurs filled the air. I imagined it was the Lassiter dead, begging me to stop this charade, this treason. I asked for their forgiveness, but it wasn't them I feared. It was the ones skulking in the shrubbery and tramping through the bone-dry irrigation channels. I knew what the living were capable of.

" . . . ninety-eight, ninety-nine, one hundred." My eyes opened. I was alone in the stillness of the orchard. Everyone else had vanished into the moonless night. For a moment I wished it could stay that way, but then the panic set in. What if this was another joke? What if they ditched me to go off partying somewhere else? Mal wouldn't do that to me, would she?

"Moan!" commanded a deep voice from the far-off oleander bushes. They did know oleander leaves and blossoms were poisonous, right?

I refused to moan, but as a concession, I stuck my arms out in front of me. Muscle memory from months of wearing braces took over, and soon I was swinging my legs all lock-kneed and looking like something out of a B-rated horror flick. My bleached-flour skin nearly glowed, making the whole act even more convincing.

I swayed and lurched toward the rustling oleanders, but then had a brain flash. They wanted the base. If I stuck close to it, I'd have a better chance of tagging someone.

"We can't he-e-a-r you," shouted Vega from the opposite direction. There were giggles, followed by "Stop that!"

I stalked a twenty-foot perimeter, never letting the tree stump leave my sight. More voices baited me, but I'd devised a strategy to lure them out. Crouching beside the tree split by lightning, I waited.

There was a patter of running feet; someone was making a break for the Trojans. I leaped up, but my foot snagged on a vine and I was down for the count.

"Safe!" Another pair of feet dashed through the grass, followed by another shout-out. Soon it was a stampede. If I didn't get up and tag someone, I'd be the diseased, flesh-eating zombie all over again.

I pushed up onto my bruised knees and discovered I was an arm's length from the odd granite stone I'd seen lying at the foot of the tree the day Evan, Mal, and I had snuck onto the property. Its edges were too sharp, its face too free of lichen, for it to have been here more than a few years. More than that, its placement was too deliberate. Ignoring the shouts and pounding feet, the taunts and laughter, I flipped the stone over.

No. That can't be right. It can't. But the deeply chiseled words were unmistakable: Our Beloved Son, Adam N. Lassiter, followed by birth and death dates. The name could have been a coincidence, but not the dates. Trusting that my memory of Roman numerals was correct, the deceased would be almost nineteen today—if he hadn't died five years ago.

Still not convinced, I dug into the soft earth and let it sift through my hand. Bits of black ash and bone clung to my skin. If this was the grave of my childhood friend, then who did I unearth from the fallout shelter?

RULE #13
TAG, BAG, AND DOCUMENT EVERYTHING.

The next morning I found a note taped to my stapler. It was from Adam.

Please call again about my father's remains.

I ripped it off, shoved it into the shredder, and savored the grinding of the blades. *Let him call the coroner himself.*

I'd been a fool for listening to my bleeding heart; Adam couldn't possibly be the boy who once breathed me back to life.

It wasn't as if we hadn't tried to have Neil Lassiter's body brought here. Rachel called the coroner's office at least three times, and each time she received the same answer: the release had been delayed. It wasn't all that unusual in a criminal case, but now I was convinced there was more to Neil Lassiter's death than the police officers let on. More importantly, who *did* I find trapped in the shelter, and why did he care so much about retrieving a body?

There was one way to find out. I dialed Marty at the coroner's office, and a man answered on the fourth ring. I didn't recognize his voice. He must have been new. I gave him Neil's name, and he put me on hold immediately. The rapid *click click* of my pen exposed my impatience.

A woman finally came on the line. "This is Racine. How can I help you?"

"Hi, Racine. This is Lily McCrae with the McCrae Family Funeral Home. Is Marty there?"

"Marty no longer works here."

Odd. "Well, I'm calling to arrange a pickup for Neil Lassiter." There was an awkward pause on the other end. "Racine?"

"I'm afraid the deceased made very specific arrangements with Eternal Memorial prior to his death."

Through gritted teeth I explained that there'd been a mistake and that his son wished to have him brought here. She insisted that no relatives were listed. More proof Adam was lying. There was another very pregnant pause, and at that point I knew something else was up. "So EMS picked up the body."

"Um, not exactly."

"What does 'not exactly' mean . . . exactly?"

She cleared her throat. "There was a break-in."

"Someone stole the remains?!" I shouted into the receiver.

"The police are investigating the situation. That's all I know." The line went dead.

I didn't dare bring this up with Dad or Rachel, at least not until I knew more. They had enough to deal with already, with credit companies breathing down our necks and a damaged custom-made coffin. But I was far from letting this one go.

Hoping Mae Wu, the reporter who accosted Adam in the parlor, was mistaken—or at the very least incompetent—I did an online search of my own for anyone named Lassiter. I didn't find a single listing. Not for Neil, his former wife, nor a son. It was as if every trace of the family had been erased, and yet I knew from the grave markers in the family cemetery that the family was nearly as old as the town. It's not like you can remove public records. Regardless, it was obvious I wasn't going to get anywhere this way. Maybe one of the Lassiter's nosy neighbors knew something, but hearsay and gossip weren't exactly what I was after. It looked like the best I was going to get was already in my phone.

I rocked back in my chair. How could he do this to us, to me, after everything we did for him? What could he possibly hope to gain from such a scam? Sympathy? An inheritance?

Another possibility occurred to me. Maybe Adam had forgotten who he was and had adopted a mistaken identity. If that were the case, he needed professional help. At the very least I needed to tell my parents, but first I had to confront Adam—or the boy who claimed to be Adam—and the sooner, the better.

❊ ❊ ❊

When I asked Nana Jo if she'd seen Adam, she directed me to the basement. "He's hunting for a jacket to wear for the Marshall viewing. I've sent him back down four times. I swear that boy doesn't know the difference between a windbreaker and a housecoat."

Or between a truth and a lie.

The wooden treads leading down to the basement creaked ominously. The furnace was silent this time of year, but the water pipes trailing across the ceiling pinged and moaned. I heard shuffling coming from the basement's far side.

"Adam?" I called, my voice cracking with nerves. The clothes rack swayed. "Adam?" I repeated. Why didn't he answer?

Irritated, I wove through the maze of broken coffee urns, spare chairs, and forgotten easels to where I expected to find him rummaging through the racks of spare clothes. Specter scurried out. No Adam.

The basement door creaked open. His angular silhouette loomed at the top of the stairs. "But I like this coat," Adam explained to someone out of sight.

Maybe this was a mistake, confronting him here, alone. Who knew how he might react? I tried to duck farther back into the shadows but bumped into a samovar, sending it crashing to the floor in a glorious symphony of clanging metal.

"Lily? Is that you?"

Defeated, I stepped into the light.

"What are you doing down there?"

"Looking for you."

"Oh." He held out his arms. "What do you think of this jacket?"

"I'm not here to do a fashion consult." I took a bold step closer. "Just how long did you think you could pull off this charade?"

"What are you talking about?"

I waved my cell phone. "I have proof that you can't possibly be Adam Lassiter."

"Of course I'm—"

"Come look for yourself."

He slowly picked his way down the stairs. He had no sense of personal space and stopped not twenty inches from me. I brought the screen to life and pulled up the first photo: the grave marker bearing Adam's name. He snatched the phone from my outthrust hand and stared at the image. "Where'd you take this?"

"By a tree beside the Lassiter family cemetery." I scrolled through the remaining pictures. "Did you know about this?"

"No! What does this mean?"

With a confidence I seldom possessed, I stabbed him in the breast pocket with my finger. "Let me break it down for you. It means the real Adam Lassiter died five years ago. His body was cremated until all that remained were fragments of bone and ash. Those were ground bit by bit into dust, scattered beneath a dead tree, and marked by a chunk of granite. So, you see, *you* can't be Adam. Adam is about six pounds of dust."

"It's a mistake."

Hot tears threatened to spill, but in my rage I fought them off. "Yes, and I made it. I believed you, and I probably still would if not for that marker. But wait. It gets better. This afternoon, after I found your note, I called the coroner's office. They said Neil Lassiter's body is supposed to be delivered to EMS and that there is no listing for next of kin."

"EMS? But he's to be brought here. The officer said so."

"Well apparently Neil Lassiter made his own arrangements."

"If that's true, it's news to me. And what do you mean, 'supposed to be delivered'?"

"Seems there was a break-in and his remains were stolen."

"What?! My father's body was taken?"

"Oh, but there's more. I did a search online. Not only could I not find a record of you; I couldn't find a single trace of your parents ever living in this town. But whoever erased all the records either didn't know about the gravestone or forgot it." I tapped the sleeping screen on my phone and resurrected it.

"I don't care what that marker says. I am Adam Lassiter. I couldn't lie if I wanted to."

"Everyone lies."

"Everyone but me."

"Okay, then explain it to me. Make me believe, because I want to. I really want to." *Come on, Adam. Convince me that bringing you home wasn't a huge mistake.*

He couldn't.

I reached for my phone. "That's what I thought."

He yanked it back. "Wait." He screwed his eyes shut, like it pained him to think that hard. When he opened them, he said, "Your . . ." He pointed to my left hip, where my pelvis jutted out more than it should.

My daily reminder of that afternoon in the orchard, when I thought I was as good as gone. My hand drifted to the seam of puckered skin. "What about my hip?"

"It was broken." He indicated a spot on my side, below my waist. "There."

"You've seen me limp." But he never asked me about it. Was that because he already knew the story?

"You fell from a tree," he said, sounding surprised by his own statement. "Our tree. You were wearing a light blue blouse the color of your eyes."

Goose bumps prickled along my arms. That blouse was my

favorite. I wore it all the time back then. And how did he know about our tree? Still, it wasn't enough to explain the gravestone. "Do you remember why I climbed that tree?" I asked, my voice trembling.

He massaged his temples in his struggle to come up with something to satisfy me. I wanted him to know the answer but knew it was an impossibility. How could he? It wasn't him, *couldn't* be him, and all my wishing wasn't going to make it so.

"You were running from. . . someone . . . no—from *someones*."

"Lucky guess. Besides, you said you lost your memory in an accident. If that's true, you couldn't know that. So which is it? Do you have amnesia or not?"

He was pacing now, tearing at his hair. "I . . . I swear there's this picture in my head. A girl."

"Well, there's a simple answer to that: you saw my photo on the mantel."

"No, before that. A memory, I think. I never understood where it came from or who it was. Until now." He turned, his face a perfect picture of bewilderment. "You're that girl—the one in the orchard, the one my father told me died. He said it was my fault. *My* fault."

"He told you I died? Well, I'm not dead."

"No, I can see that. Obviously this broken memory of mine has jumbled the facts."

I wanted so badly to believe him. Everything—the tone of his voice, the way he met my eyes without blinking, the way his forehead wrinkled like a washboard above those pitched brows—everything was begging me to trust him. "Can you tell me why I fell?"

He tapped his head with his fist as if to knock another nugget of memory loose.

"So you're saying you're the Adam who was there the day I fell, but you don't remember the circumstances. You know what I think? I think you're a liar."

He shook his head. "What possible reason would I have to lie?"

"I can name several, but let's start with the will. And let's not forget a piece of land like that must be worth a sizable chunk of change."

"Will?"

"Oh, quit with the act. You know what a will is. It's a document stating you are entitled to your father's estate."

"If something like that even exists, it's in my father's lockbox and I've never seen it."

"Is that why you're so desperate to find the lockbox?"

"NO! I've explained that already."

"What about your mother? Give me her name. We'll look it up. Oh, wait, that's right—you don't remember that, either. And yet I'm supposed to believe you remember a girl who fell out of a tree, a girl you haven't seen in years, a girl who died."

"It's the truth."

"The truth? What about that mark around your neck, the one you're hiding under that ridiculous starched collar? And the hole in your arm? How do you explain those?"

"*Mehercle!* It was your fault!"

"My fault? How was it my fault?"

"If you had come with me to Zmira's like I asked"—he held up his bandaged arm—"this would not have happened."

I knew my old teacher was cantankerous, but to physically attack someone? "You're telling me Mr. Zmira did that to you?"

"No, not him!" His hand tightened around my phone. "I never made it that far. On my way to Zmira's, two men followed me."

"Reporters?"

"I don't know. Could have been. I ran into an alley, but they caught me from behind and knocked me to the ground. The next thing I knew one of them slipped a bag over my head and tied it with a cord around my neck. That's when I felt the bite in my arm."

"A bite?"

"Not with teeth, but that's how it felt."

"How would you know? Did your father ever bite you?"

"No! Ground squirrels. The orchard was full of them."

The more Adam talked, the less sense he made. And it all sounded so bizarre—two mysterious men, ground squirrels, sacks over heads. "Why would someone do that?"

"That is the question."

Whatever the answer, it was something far more sinister than overzealous reporters. "Adam, you have to talk to the police."

"And say what? The police didn't believe me when I told them an intruder came to the house the night of the fire. Why would they believe me now? No, I gave them the truth and they did nothing, and now my father's remains are missing."

"How do you know whoever jumped you won't be back?"

"I don't."

"Well, even if what you say is true, it still doesn't explain the gravestone with your name on it. Now give me back my phone."

Adam held it defiantly over my head.

"I have copies of those pictures, you know. And even if I didn't, it wouldn't change the fact that Adam Lassiter is dead."

"Fine." He let me have my phone. "Lily, I've never lied to you, but there are things about me I can't explain—not yet. That's why I need to find my father's lockbox. Please. Say you'll help me."

My brain was telling me to do the safe and easy thing: go to my parents with my suspicions and let them deal with him. My heart was telling me to trust him—at least until we found the box. But apparently my mouth was on autopilot because what did I say?

"Fine. Tomorrow I'll take you to see Zmira."

"Tomorrow," he agreed.

I hobbled up the stairs before I dug myself in any deeper but halted at the top, my finger hovering over the light switch. *I should leave him in the dark. That's what he did to me.* Instead my hand fell limp to my side. The guy had been left to rot in a shelter by his own father. I hollered down to him, "And, Adam!"

"Yes?"

"The jacket you have on looks fine."

RULE #14
LEATHER HAS NO PLACE IN A
MORTICIAN'S WARDROBE.

I'd been on the phone with Mallory for an hour. She was a one-note song, and the tune was all about tomorrow night at Hayden's. Apparently she'd blabbed about it to everyone. Fame through association, I guessed.

"You sure you wouldn't rather go cosmic bowling?" I asked. "I hear they use black lights and the balls glow in the dark."

"Yeah, as fun as that sounds . . . I'm sure."

"But you used to love bowling."

"When I was ten. Next year is my senior year. I want it to be epic, hence 'the summer of reinvention.'"

"Stop with the air quotes. I can hear them through the phone. And you don't need to reinvent yourself. You're perfect the way you are."

"It's not you I'm trying to impress."

I made the fatal error of mentioning I had nothing to wear to the house party, and an hour later she hauled over a half dozen outfits for me to try. I told her I didn't think I could pull off the dominatrix look, and since when did she go for black leather, laces, and buckles? I reminded her that my idea of a party was a laid-back get-together with a few friends—not a costume parade. It was almost a relief when Adam showed up later that afternoon.

"Ready?" he asked.

"Where are you guys going?" asked Mal, ever the opportunist.

"To—"

I quickly cut him off. I wanted to keep this between the two of us for now. "To the morgue to sign some papers," I lied. Normally Mal wouldn't come within twenty feet of the prep room, and in her book, the morgue was nothing but a prep room on steroids.

"I'd go with you, but I've got a load of chores to do. Leverage for going out tomorrow night," she said.

"Good strategy." It was all I could do to hide my relief.

She packed up all the rejected clothing except for a short black leather skirt she'd coerced me into wearing, and I escorted her to the door.

"See you tomorrow night." She was almost giddy with anticipation.

"Yeah, tomorrow night." I felt the acidic burn of a nervous stomach.

I waited to be sure she was long gone before I signaled to Adam that I was ready to take him to Zmira's—although I used the term *ready* loosely. I was still hoping the Lassiter grave marker discovery was all a big coincidence. And the only reason I agreed to go at all was because Zmira was the one person who might know something about Adam's true identity.

We scaled the chain-link fence and cut through the property of my old elementary school, now a collection of condemned buildings. It seemed a safer option than sticking to public streets. For all I knew someone could be out there looking for another piece of Adam—literally.

With each step closer to Zmira's house, I felt my bravado slip a bit more. Whatever possessed me to agree to this? Already my arms tingled like they were buried up to the elbow in anthills. The itching would come next. And for what? The unlikely chance that Zmira knew something about a boy who supposedly died? A box that was either long gone or buried so deep we'd never exhume it?

The mailbox with ZMIRA painted in red did me in. "I'll wait here. It's probably better if only one of us talks to him."

"And that one of us is me?"

"Uh-huh."

"You're scared."

"Like, clinically." I showed him my forearms, which were already decorated in angry raised spots. "If I get any closer, I might faint," I threatened.

"I didn't realize." He looked genuinely apologetic.

"Yeah, major case of Zmiraphobia."

"Is that even a real word?"

"Whatever. We're here. Let's get this over with."

Adam marched up the front stoop and pounded on the door. There was no answer. I indicated the driveway. "Look, no car. I don't think he's home."

Adam ignored me and stepped into the shrubbery lining the front of the house. He cupped his hands around his face and pressed his nose to the front window, leaving a smudgy impression of his face on the glass. Then, to my horror, he returned to the stoop and tested the door handle. The door swung open.

"Adam, what the hell are you doing?!" I called in a raspy whisper.

"Nobody's home," he said, and disappeared inside.

The drapes on the house next door parted and a woman's craggy face appeared in the window. I smiled all friendly-like and waved. The woman whipped the curtains closed. Adam was going to get us both arrested if I didn't get him out of there. I rushed up the walkway and slipped inside Zmira's open door.

Other than smelling like Bengay and fried onions, the inside was nothing like I expected. Who would have guessed that my crabby, Janis Joplin–obsessed, ex-marine history teacher would be into mid-century modern decor? I expected the floor-to-ceiling wall of books—he was a reader—but the macaroni menorah on the mantle and the leopard-print doggy bed beside his recliner? Who was this man?

"Adam," I whispered, "where are you? We've got to get out of here. I think the neighbor next door is calling the police."

Adam emerged from the dining room. "I'm the neighbor next door."

"The *other* neighbor next door!"

He opened the linen closet. "I'm not leaving until I find that box."

"We don't even know if it's here!"

"That's why we're looking for it. Now help me search."

"How big is this thing?"

"About the size of two chocolate-milk cartons."

With that he vanished down the hall. *I swear that boy does not know the meaning of fear.*

The most obvious places—cupboards, closets, under beds—yielded no box. "I bet he tossed it," I said. "Did it have a lock?"

"Yes. But Neil always kept the key on him. There used to be a spare, but I don't know what happened to it."

That meant Zmira would need a tool to open it, and most people kept their tools in a garage. "This way," I said, pointing to a door off the kitchen.

The garage was dark and reeked of gasoline. I felt for a light switch, but Adam managed to kick over a trash bag of aluminum cans before I could locate it. "Watch where you're going," I hissed. But he was already squeezing past the car and toward the workbench, where a battered and beaten gunmetal box sat.

Wait. A car? That couldn't be good.

On cue, a dog began barking in the side yard. "Adam, he's home!"

Adam grabbed the box from the workbench. A lawnmower blocked the side exit, and opening the garage door would give us away for sure. We had no choice but to return the way we came. Adam was one step ahead of me.

He opened the door and ran, nose to muzzle, into a shotgun held by Zmira, who was dressed in a *Skillz on Grillz* apron. All I could do was duck behind an oil drum and pray I hadn't been spotted.

Mr. Zmira's pupils were dilated. His hands trembled. If he didn't shoot Adam on purpose, he was going to shoot him on accident. "Slowly now, set the box down and step back. You thief," Zmira growled.

Don't be an idiot. Do as he says, Adam.

As if he could hear my thoughts, Adam obeyed, but not without a mouth full of back talk. "I'm not the thief here. You took that from my property. It belongs to me."

Smooth move, Adam. Poke the viper with a short stick, why don't ya?

"Your property? Don't tell me you're that kid I used to see playing in the dirt in the orchard, the same one who liked to trap ground squirrels and chuck walnuts at my bathroom window whenever I was on the pot. What's your name?"

"Adam."

"Adam what?"

"Lassiter."

"Not possible. That boy's been gone for years."

I inhaled sharply, nearly giving myself away.

"And yet here I am," said Adam coolly.

"I have to admit you do look a bit like him. You alone? I thought I heard a girl's voice."

Adam didn't answer.

Zmira kicked open the door wider. "Okay, I know you're in there. Come on out."

Chin to chest and hands in the air, I stepped out from behind the drum and into view, praying to the patron saint of morons that Zmira didn't recognize me. "You could have lied," I said to Adam out of the corner of my mouth.

"I can't, remember?"

Who does he think he is, George Washington?

"Lily McCrae," exclaimed Zmira, swinging the barrel of the shotgun toward the kitchen ceiling. "Is that you?"

So much for saints. I nodded but was shaking badly.

"Well, I never expected you to be the sort to break into a man's house."

Yeah, that makes two of us.

"We didn't break in," corrected Adam, who didn't seem to comprehend the seriousness of our situation. "The door was unlocked. Now if you'll let me take the box, we'll leave and never bother you again."

"Hold on. That box must contain something pretty valuable to go through all this trouble."

"It belonged to his father," I volunteered, since apparently all my coaching had been a waste of time. "He wants it as a keepsake."

"That may be so, but—"

Beyond him through the kitchen window a cloud of dense black smoke billowed skyward.

"*Ardes!*" Adam yelled alongside my "Fire! Fire!"

"My tri tip!" Shotgun in hand, Zmira grabbed the lockbox, sprinted through the house, and elbowed open the glass slider. It was our chance to escape, but no sooner did we reach the family room than mop dog bolted from out of nowhere and clamped onto my sandal. The harder Adam pulled at the demon dog's collar, the more it growled and writhed like a Tasmanian devil.

Outside, curses filled the air as Zmira yanked the meat from the grill and dropped it on the patio table behind him. He batted at the flaming steak with a pot holder, but couldn't see the tongues of fire licking his backside. Adam grabbed the hose just outside the door, aimed it at Zmira and the grill, and turned on the faucet full force.

"Shut it off! Shut it off!" roared Zmira.

Adam panicked and cranked the spigot handle the wrong way. The hose whipped about, spraying water everywhere, including through the open slider. Adam repeatedly lunged for it, but the hose stayed out of reach. Finally, with mop dog in tow, I managed to shut the water off. The soggy mutt released his hold on my wet shoe and belly-crawled under the deck. Zmira streaked into the house to fetch a stack of towels. We all did our best to soak up the water that had soaked the flooring and drenched his sofa, but the damage was done.

"Sorry," I said. "We were trying to—"

"Save it. That couch is leather. It's ruined. And the gun's going to need a cleaning. But don't think it doesn't still work," he added quickly.

"At least let us repay you for the damages," offered Adam, forgetting we'd be lucky to have a dime between us.

"Tell you what. I'll keep the box, and we'll call it even. And to ensure that you and your girlfriend don't try any more stunts, I think I'll lock it in my gun safe."

Before we could argue with him, he tottered down the hall with the lockbox tucked beneath his bony arm. I took one slow step in the direction of the front door. The mop dog snarled, and I reconsidered.

Adam nodded toward the backyard where there were several bags of cement, a stack of flagstones, and an orange circle spray-painted onto the patchy grass. "What is that for?"

"A minute ago you nearly got shot for attempted burglary and now you're wondering about some unfinished landscaping project?"

"Are you angry with me? You're doing that thing with your forehead, squishing it all together like this." Adam made this ridiculous face, and despite our present circumstances and our failed mission, I had to laugh.

"You think this is funny?" said Zmira, returning from down the hall.

I bit my lip and hung my head. "No, sir."

Again Adam asked about the orange markings on the lawn. "I'm putting in a pond," answered Zmira. "Or *was*, till my back gave out a week ago."

"I could dig the hole," volunteered Adam.

Zmira squinted thoughtfully, paying particular attention to Adam's arms. "Maybe you could at that. But what would it cost me? As if I can't guess."

"The box—which is rightfully mine," Adam hastened to add.

Mr. Zmira gave a snort. "We'll see. Come back next week and I'll put you to work, only this time don't let yourself in. I'd hate to shoot you and then have to pay someone else to do the job."

"Yes, that would be a crime," said Adam, so straight-faced that I nearly busted up again.

Zmira frowned. "Did you crack a joke?"

"Did I?"

"Guess not, if you have to ask."

He walked us to the front door, but I was still puzzled about what he'd said earlier. "Mr. Zmira, you said you haven't seen the boy next door in years. What did you mean?"

Adam pulled up short.

"Just that. One day the funeral home came to pick up a body. Too small for an adult," said Zmira. "Didn't see the boy after that—well, not till now—so I assumed it was him. Obviously I was mistaken."

That made no sense. If there's a sudden death at home, an autopsy is required by law, and a death certificate is mandatory for cremation. I found no record of either. "Which funeral home was it? Not us."

"No. It was that other one. UPS."

"You mean EMS?"

"Yeah. That one. They've been by a few times before."

"To do what?"

"How would I know? Maybe the Lassiters had friends at EMS. Now if you two don't mind, I've got a poker game waiting for me."

And we have a party.

"See you next week," said Adam.

"Good." Mr. Zmira pointed to the doorbell. "And see this? Use it next time."

Adam gave it five presses before Zmira lifted his finger from the button. "Okay. Okay. That's enough." He shot me a look as if to ask, *What's with this guy?*

I shrugged. *I wish I knew.*

RULE #15
ALWAYS SET THE BRAKES
ON THE GURNEY.

"Will you hurry up!" shouted Evan from downstairs. "I'm not getting any younger, you know."

Or any more patient. "Hold your hearses," I hollered back. "I'll be right there."

I sucked in my breath to pull up the zipper on my skirt, then added one more coat of mascara and refined the arch of my left brow. This was as good as it was going to get. I took a deep breath and wobbled down the stairs in the ridiculously high shoes Mal dropped off earlier in the day. This was what friends did for each other, risk life and limb, right? I wished the skirt weren't so tight. I felt like a bratwurst.

"Finally," said Evan. "If we don't get a move on, the traffic's going to be impossible."

Adam stepped out from the hall shadows. His tussled hair looked as if it had never seen a comb. We weren't exactly on the best of terms, not since I reminded him on the way back from Zmira's that nothing was resolved between us. He had one week to prove himself to me. One. And if that entailed going back to Zmira's for the lockbox, then he was on his own. He called me unreasonable. I called him a liar.

But tonight was not about Adam. It was about getting my friendship with Mal back on track. I sensed she was outgrowing me. Why else would she spend so much time with Aslyn, Vega, and Melissa?

Adam was having his own doubts about the party. "Maybe I should stay here tonight."

"You kidding? Girls, music . . . Trust me, Adam, you're going to thank me tomorrow," said Evan. "Besides, it's time you got out and experienced a bit of the real world."

"It's just a house party, Evan," I reminded him.

"If that's so, then what's with the duffel bag?"

"It's not a duffel bag, it's my purse. I like to be prepared."

"This isn't a scouting expedition." Evan turned and gave Adam a wink. "Then again . . ."

"That is such a totally sexist thing to say!" I snapped. "Adam, don't listen to him."

A newly minted Mallory pranced in, and of course she looked amazing in her clingy knit skirt and camisole. Next, it was time for my inspection. "Give us a spin," she directed. I extended my arms and did the kind of twirl you might expect from a super-stoned ballerina. "See. I told you that skirt would look amazing on you. Adam, am I right?"

Adam looked to Evan like a seaman to his captain. "It does not make her look fat," he said stiffly.

Evan slapped his forehead. "That wasn't what I told you to say." I rolled my eyes.

"Dickwads," said Mal with a chuckle. "Lils, what do they know?"

"It's not too much?"

"Trust me, with that outfit you'll get noticed."

Since when was attention a good thing? I gave the sides of the skirt a tug. "Can we go?"

Evan cleared his throat. "So, I have good news and bad news." This usually meant there was mostly bad news. "The good news is Mom and Dad went to see a show. They won't be back till late. The bad news is they took the van. We'll have to take the stiffmobile."

"But there aren't enough seats for all of us," complained Mal. "And I'm not sitting on the rollers!"

"Then sit up front with me," offered Evan. "The other two can sit in the back."

We could argue all night, but Hayden Jornet's loft was near the downtown theater district. The later we left, the less likely we'd find parking, and I didn't feel like walking any farther than I had to in these torture devices. I locked the house and we loaded up.

Evan barreled through every yellow light and weaved from lane to lane through traffic like he was navigating an obstacle course. Twice he came to an abrupt stop, and both times Adam and I rode the casket rollers and slammed into the front seats. It was all I could do to keep down my dinner.

"Are you okay?" Adam asked. He pointed to the red crescent marks on my arms where my nails had dug into my flesh.

"Oh, I'm great," I said. "I love bouncing around the back of a hearse like a pinball."

He had to think about that a minute, his sarcasm radar not yet fully calibrated.

Evan took a sharp left. Adam braced his legs across the width of the van, stopping me mid-slide. I had enough momentum that I nearly ended up in his lap. "Awkward," I said, and squirmed away. In the process my skirt rode up my thigh, exposing one of many jagged scars. It was a hideous thing, white and puckered. Totally gag-worthy. But if Adam saw, he was careful not to react.

I yanked the skirt down and punched the back of Evan's seat. "Take it easy on the turns, will ya? This thing's an eight-thousand-pound weapon. You're going to kill someone."

At the next light I took a peek between the drawn blue-velvet curtains. We were a few blocks from downtown. Here buildings crowded out the sky, and the few trees lining the sidewalks were stunted and girded by metal bands. Large signs with missing lights advertised liquor or GI LS! G RLS! GIR S! Trash clogged gutters and vacant lots.

As expected, all the public parking lots were full, so we had to keep circling the knot of one-way streets. By the time Evan found a spot, I was queasy from a mixed cocktail of anxiety and motion sickness. I couldn't get out of the car fast enough. I checked myself in the side-view mirror, then indicated where the front tire met the curb. "Evan, you're too close to the fire hydrant."

"Thar she blows!" he shouted, throwing his arms into the air.

He was always forgetting I knew where he slept.

"Lils, it'll be fine," said Mallory, reining in a smile and patting my back in sympathy. "You worry too much."

I wonder why.

A six-pack of young girls—each looking like she should be babysitting instead of wandering the streets on a Friday night—turned down the nearest alley. "Must be that way," said Evan.

Steam rose through grates in the sidewalk, bringing a smell of sewage with it.

"Nice painting," praised Adam.

"That's graffiti," Mallory corrected.

"Graffiti? I don't know the word."

"Unsanctioned art," she explained. "The kind that can get you arrested."

I hadn't considered how new and overwhelming this might be to him. I wondered if, after so many years of longing for his freedom, it wasn't all a bit disappointing.

"Here we are," announced Evan, stopping in front of a large brick building. The distressed paint on the wall read HEARTLAND BREAD COMPANY. A cacophony of loud voices and blaring music leaked from a broken window several floors above.

The back door swung open, and a blast of screeching guitars assaulted us. I experienced a moment of panic. My arms and chest started to itch. "Mal, I thought you said this was going to be a small affair, not a full-on rave!"

"A rave?" asked Adam. "That's a good thing, isn't it?"

"It's a great thing!" cheered Mallory. "Dancing, techno. What's not to love?"

"The crowd," I said. "And if a fire breaks out, how will everyone escape in time?"

Mal and Evan shut me down with condescending glares. Evan I understood. He fed on this kind of stuff—music loud enough to make your ears bleed, raucous hordes of potential DUIs. Mallory not so much, or at least she didn't used to.

"If you don't want to go in," Adam said to me, "I'll stay and keep you company."

It was a tempting offer, but this was my chance to show Mal that I could step out of my skin and prove to them all that I was more than *that* girl.

"No, I'm fine."

"All right Lils!" cheered Mal. She led us up a loading ramp to the door, where a large, barrel-chested man—a double-wide, in my profession—checked his clipboard and waved us in. Together we passed through the converted delivery door and emerged into a swirling vortex of people, light, and music. Instant sensory burnout. It reminded me of this ride at the county fair called the Spinout. It spun so fast that when the floor dropped away, you stuck to the wall.

Well, my floor just dropped.

I motioned toward where it was less crowded, but Evan was fixated on a tall blond who'd emerged from a back room. It was Dana Blackwell, and she was weaving like the drink in her hand was not her first, or even her second. She motioned for Evan to join her and, like a good dog, he obeyed.

Mallory's upper lip curled. "What's he see in her, anyway?"

Then it hit me: For Mal this night was never about hanging with Hayden's crowd, or even about the studio. It was about getting

Evan to notice *her*. Leave it to Dana to knock Mal off her horse, but, true to form, Mal got right back on.

"Come on," she said, linking arms with Adam and me. "There's someone I want you to meet."

We waded through the vast room hazy with grape- and tobacco-scented smoke. Hookah, Mallory explained to Adam. Sure enough, a cluster of people was tethered to a water pipe perched on the edge of a glass table the size of Manhattan. Around a bar, half a dozen more revelers hovered beneath a mural of a guitarist touching fingers with Carlos Santana à la the Sistine Chapel's *Creation of Adam*. "How can Hayden even afford this place?" I asked.

"I heard he's renting it from his uncle," said Mal. She glanced at Evan, who was at the far end of the bar throwing back a brew and getting all chummy with Dana, and ordered a couple Long Island iced teas—one for her and one for Adam. I passed, figuring someone needed to keep their wits about them tonight.

Adam mistook the drink for the stuff we serve at home. He took one gulp and made a face like he'd swallowed lighter fluid. "Want it?"

"Thanks, but I think I'll pass."

When Mal wasn't looking, he "lost" his glass behind a fake ficus.

"Hey, Mal the gal!" boomed a voice. Hayden Jornet swaggered out of the crowd, waving a highball glass as though it was his scepter. "Well, look at you," he said. His green eyes started where her skirt met her thighs and moved upward. They never reached her face. Scan complete, he said, "Glad you made it. Let me give you the tour."

Mal eagerly accepted Hayden's offer with instructions for him to lead on, but not before she ordered a second drink from the bar. *Who is this girl tonight?*

I spotted Aslyn and Vega in the crowd at the exact same moment they spotted Adam. Immediately they made a beeline for him, and Adam tipped his head toward the back of the loft. I nodded, and together we threaded our way through the throng and ducked into a secluded corner. Two girls had already taken up residence and were heavily into a make-out session. Adam stared at them, analyzing the scene as if he were Jane Goodall and they a pair of chimpanzees.

"Hey, freakazoid, buy a ticket," swore the one with braces.

"*Verba tua intellegere non possum,*" Adam replied. "*Filone ferreo maxillae tuae iunctae sunt?*"

"Ignore him," I told the girls. "He's not from around here." I directed him toward the emergency exit door. He leaned up against it, arms folded and looking rather pleased with himself.

"What did you say to those girls?"

"I said, 'I can't understand what you're saying. Are your jaws wired together?'"

I laughed. "I thought you called her mother a . . . Oh, never mind." For an instant, I forgot I was supposed to be angry at him. But it had done the trick. Maybe if Adam could lighten up, I could, too.

A tall guy dressed all in black and with shoulder-length brown hair to match stumbled into Adam. "Mind your space," Adam warned.

"Who yous talkin' to?" his assailant slurred.

That voice was worse than nails on a chalkboard. It was deeper now, but it was still the same voice that had plagued me for most of my life. It belonged to Shep Bramstead, the jerk who made a sport out of tormenting me on the playground, ridiculing me in class, and leading the pack that chased me into the orchard on my way home from school.

Adam held his ground. No pithy Latin phrases this time—only clenched hands itching to hit something. If Adam knew any better, he'd back down. Shep was a bully, a brawler, and a bassist, with mad skills in all three. Adam would be a smear on the floor if he started anything here.

"Ignore him, Adam," I warned.

There was no need. Shep was already so wrecked that when he reached for the edge of a nearby table to steady himself, he missed. Two people rushed in to right him. One said something about him being so wasted that he wouldn't be able to tell the difference between his axe and his ass. A guy who could have been his double lugged him away for the band's sound check and the promise of another cold one. His brother, Grant, I assumed.

It took a long time for the fury in Adam's eyes to fade, longer than I would have expected, but he eventually settled. I told him he was free to mingle, but I couldn't make it sound convincing, so we made a game of people watching. He totally sucked at what I dubbed Name That Expression.

Adam tried for, like, the fourth time. "Depressed?" he said, indicating a redhead with a scrunched-up face.

"More like pissed," I corrected. "How 'bout the guy looking at that girl's backside?"

"Awed," he answered rather proudly, sure that this time, he had it right.

Maybe he did, but I refused to concede the point. "More like horn-gry."

We were so wrapped up in our little game that I almost forgot about Mallory. Last time I saw her, she was hanging on Hayden like a superhero cape. If she thought that was going to make Evan jealous, she was delusional. He was too oblivious to notice. I scanned the room but didn't see her anywhere. "I need some air," I said, pushing open the emergency exit door.

"Me too," admitted Adam. We emerged into a narrow alley lined with dumpsters, a stained mattress, and innumerable piles of boxes and pallets. Adam pulled up a couple crates for us to sit on beneath a fire escape, and I couldn't take my shoes off fast enough. Free of them at last, I leaned back against the crumbling brick building and took in the starless strip of heaven wedged between the rooflines.

"So what do you think of your first party?" I asked.

"Too . . . everything."

"Yeah, same. I had to get out of there. Escape, you know."

But we'd escaped nothing. From an open window above us we heard a girl scream.

"Let go of me! I said stop!"

Mallory.

RULE #16
Handle all fluids with care.

Adam leaped for the bottom rung of the fire escape. He scaled the ladder, swung over the railing, bounded up the stairs two at a time, and slipped through the open window. I heard shouts. A voice cut off sharply.

The fire escape was too high for me to reach, and the emergency door was locked from the inside. Snatching my bag but leaving my shoes behind, I tore through the alley to the back entrance of the building.

The bouncer refused to let me in, but someone flung open the back door and shouted, "Fight!" The bouncer dropped his clipboard and charged inside with me hot on his heels as he cut a wide swath through the crowd. He had no idea where to go, but I did, and once inside, I barefooted it to the stairwell.

Exiting on the second floor, I followed the sounds of grunts and muffled threats. Something or someone slammed into a nearby wall. I opened the door to find Mallory tangled in a pile of sheets on the floor beside a bed, shrieking, "Stop! You're killing him! You have to stop!"

Adam's hands were clamped around Hayden's neck like an iron collar. Hayden flailed his legs and arms as his face turned from crimson to a sickly shade of purple.

"Let him go, Adam," I cried. "You have to let him go!"

Somehow my voice filtered through, and Adam's hands relaxed, letting Hayden fall back against a nightstand in a gasping, wheezing heap.

"Get out, Adam," ordered Mallory. "I'll handle this."

Before Adam could respond, two guys built like linebackers burst through the bedroom door. Hayden wiped spittle from the corner of his mouth and leveled a condemning finger at Adam. "That animal tried to kill me."

The two bruisers lunged for Adam, pinning him to the floor. One dug a sharp knee into his back while the other twisted his arms up and behind. Adam broke free, but a sharp punch to the ribs knocked him back, and then they were on him once again, like stray dogs on a scrap of meat.

"Damn, he's strong," complained one of Hayden's henchmen, giving Adam's arm a sharp twist. "Where's Bramstead?"

On cue, Shep's brother, Grant, appeared at the door, a guitar pick clamped between his teeth and looking seriously sober. Faces crowded behind him, some curious, others out for blood. At their encouragement—as if he needed any—Grant dove into the fray. It took the three of them to force Adam into submission.

Hayden found his legs and pulled himself up. He cracked his neck from side to side and brushed lint from his jeans. It was a warm-up for his swift kick to Adam's ribs, which was followed by a cheer from Grant. Adam didn't flinch.

Hayden prepared to give him a second punt but noted the crowd of witnesses pressed to the door and reconsidered. "Grant, see to it that he's escorted outside, will you?"

"My pleasure." Together, the three men pushed Adam out of Hayden's bedroom. He threw one last elbow to free himself. It caught Bramstead square in the jaw. His repayment was a slug to the kidneys.

"Adam, don't fight," I begged. He surrendered and let them drag him away. The bedroom emptied, and a moment later, I was unraveling Mallory from the jumbled sheets. "What happened? Are you all right? If he hurt you, we need to—"

"We need to nothing. I'm okay—physically, at least. One thing led to another, but then I realized where we were headed and it wasn't what I wanted. He wasn't what I wanted. I told him to stop, but he wouldn't listen. If Adam . . ." Mallory wiped an eye, then shook her head and forced a faint smile.

"I know. Come on. Let's get out of here." I helped adjust her torn blouse, then took her hand and pulled her along, gently guiding her down the stairs and out the emergency exit. *How appropriately named*, I thought.

We found Adam sitting on a delivery platform in the alley, and although *modesty* was not generally a word in Adam's vocabulary, he assumed it was part of Mal's and averted his eyes.

"I'm so sorry," she said. "I don't know what got into me."

"Stop trying to take all the blame," I said, realizing she'd nearly joined one of those statistics parents cite from the evening news. "Seems to me Hayden deserves his fair share."

"Yeah, well, my little scheme sort of backfired. I don't think he even noticed I was gone."

I didn't bother asking who she meant. Evan.

"Well, Hayden's still a giant sleaze." Adam was rubbing his side. "You took quite a beating back there. Maybe I should check for broken ribs. Lift your shirt."

He shifted away from me. "I'm fine."

"Are you sure?"

He nodded.

"Then keep an eye on her for me, will you? I'm going to find that idiot stepbrother of mine."

It took the better part of an hour to locate him. He was too busy schmoozing with the Jaded Corpses' lead vocalist in a back room to notice that his sister, her best friend, and their second-string escort had left the party. I dragged him outside, where he took one look at Mallory and said, "What happened to you? You been fighting again?" Like it was all some kind of joke.

Not wanting any more trouble, I answered, "No. She got a little carried away on the dance floor, that's all."

"Yeah, you missed it," said Mallory with a withered smile. "I was spinning on my head and bumpin' booty."

"There's a picture I didn't need," said Evan, blinking like there was something in his eyes. But, to his credit, on the long walk to the car he apologized for not keeping better tabs on her.

"Not your job," she said, then thanked Adam and me for coming to her rescue.

"What are best friends for?" I replied.

She threw her arms around my shoulders and squeezed. I stiffened, and she released me. Mal, my childhood friend—my only friend—still needed me, and as much as I hated to admit it, maybe sometimes I needed her, too. Counting on someone like that? Total rule breaker.

Lagging behind with head down and hands jammed into his front pockets, Adam shuffled his feet along the littered sidewalk. I should have insisted he stay home, but I'd been selfish. I wanted him to come with us tonight, not to keep tabs on him but because I craved his company. I knew I was walking a shaky tightrope.

I dropped back and padded barefoot beside him, my shoes long gone along with a charm bracelet Nana Jo had given me on my first day of school. "That was a noble thing you did for her."

"Not so noble. If you hadn't stopped me, I would have strangled him."

"But you didn't," I said, and wondered if what he said was true. I kicked a wad of newspaper that was lodged in a gap between two buildings, freeing it. "Do me a favor."

"Anything."

"No more rescuing."

The corner of his mouth curled the tiniest bit, but it was still far from the smile I longed to see. "Even if you fall out of another tree?"

I slowed, trying to reconcile the bundle of conflicted emotions I was packing. How much could I trust this guy? If I wasn't careful, I could set myself up for the biggest fall of my life. "I'll think about it."

We walked a couple blocks before he hit me with another confession. "I have a history of losing control. It was so bad at first that Neil had to restrain me."

I stopped. "At first?"

He looked away. "You know."

"No, I don't."

"After . . . my accident. While I was recovering."

"The one where you lost your memory." Could that have been what all those shackles and chains were about?

"Like I said before, I don't remember any of it. All I know is that my father told me there was an *erraum*. A malfunction in the laboratory."

The condition of the copper capsule was certainly hard evidence of that, and I'd read once that head injuries could cause extreme reactions and mood swings. But his accident took place years ago. What happened in the loft tonight was different. He was different. The Adam I used to know was also very protective, but he used his wits, not his fists.

We resumed walking, the trailing laces of his right shoe slapping out with each footfall. Annoyed, he stopped under a lamplight to retie them, and I realized that no matter who he was, beneath all that awkwardness and pent-up anger and bitterness was someone as equally out of step with the world as I.

We caught up to Evan and Mal a few feet away from where we'd parked the hearse. Of course it had been towed. The moment begged for a big, fat "I told you so," but I didn't have the stomach for it.

It was a ten-block hike on blistered feet to the police station, where the clerk at the front desk explained that impound had already closed for the night. My parents would have to come on Monday morning to pay the fine before the hearse could be released. In the end we scrounged up enough bills and loose change between us to cover the cost of a ride home and took a seat on the curb to wait.

I was pinning Mal's blouse back together with a safety pin I'd dredged up from the depths of my bag when two headlights on high beam whipped around the corner, blinding us. We all stood, assuming it was our Lyft. Not until it pulled even with us did we realize it was a small pickup truck. A stream of four-letter words bearing Shep's earmark poured from the open passenger window. A cup flew toward us, hit the asphalt, and exploded, showering Adam's new shoes with what smelled like piss.

I threw up my arms. "For real?!"

Adam was more willing to accept this as his due for coming close to murdering a guy. He whipped off his Vans and flung them over an adjacent wall. "They pinched anyway."

Yeah, tonight sucked big-time for all of us, but especially for Adam. In the time since Adam had come to live with us, he learned that he'd lost not only his father but also his home. I'd threatened to expose him when he clearly had no better understanding of the situation than I did. And if that weren't enough, he now had to live with the fact that he almost throttled Hayden Jornet to death while defending Mal's virtue, a virtue she was nearly ready to throw away to make Evan jealous.

None of that meant I was willing to surrender my suspicions about him, but considering he'd put himself on the line for a friend . . . maybe I could at least give him the benefit of the doubt. But until I had proof of his identity, one way or the other, I vowed to temper any feelings for him. That would be the real challenge. If this small bit of leniency made me a raging fool, then at least I was a generous one.

I sacrificed my best handkerchief to wipe the piss from his hands, balled it into a wad, and sent it over the wall to join his shoes.

The rideshare finally arrived, and by time we dropped off Mal and made it to the house, it was close to midnight. Evan headed in, leaving Adam and me alone on the front porch, both of us still too keyed up to call it a night.

I sat on the bottom step and ran my bare, bruised feet over the soft tufts of weeds poking up through the crumbling walkway. The step was so narrow that when Adam dropped down beside me, our shoulders nearly brushed. He raked his fingers through his hair, but there was no taming it, so he tipped his head back and searched the heavens. For what, I don't know. An explanation? A cosmic apology?

"You miss your old life?"

"A little," he said. "You probably find that hard to believe. I do."

"You seem awfully willing to forgive your father, that's all. I'm not sure I could."

"He had his reasons for doing what he did."

"That's what all parents say."

"I know he loved me in his own way, sometimes too much. He was so afraid to allow me any freedoms. I told him I wanted to be like other people my age—not that I knew what that meant. You know what he said to me?"

I shook my head, aware that this all sounded a bit too familiar.

"He told me I wasn't ready for the world and that the world

wasn't ready for me. After tonight I think he may have been right. I never should have gone to that party."

"No, Adam, he was wrong. No one can hide from the world. Not really. One way or another, the world always finds you."

"Like you found me?" He dropped his gaze from the heavens and turned to look at me, our faces unexpectedly close.

"S-something like that," I stuttered, hypocrite that I was. I made a career out of dodging life. I put my heart on a diet so strict that it was starving. If Adam tried to kiss me right then, I would abandon every ounce of resolve and hungrily kiss him back until my heart was full to bursting.

But he didn't. So I didn't. I knew what was stopping me, but what was stopping him?

"If, as you say, the world always finds you," he said, still wrestling with the ways of the universe, "then do you think the trick is to go out and find the world first?"

"Maybe," I replied. "Then again, maybe the trick is to do a better job of hiding."

I tucked my hands between my knees, looked up, and sighed. A single dark cloud had drifted in to cloak the stars.

RULE #17
KEEP THE DEAD'S SECRETS,
AND THEY'LL KEEP YOURS.

I sat at my computer, Adam leaning over my shoulder. "See? Click, drag, drop. Don't overthink it," I told him, referring as much to the computer program as to the other night. I was wasting my breath.

Dad arrived with the day's mail. "Looks like you got another parking ticket," he said, tossing an envelope onto Evan's desk. Evan shoved it into a drawer and went back to flicking a folded paper football over an imaginary goal post. "And here's something for you, Lily." Dad handed over an envelope and dumped the rest into his inbox, grouching, "Bills, bills, and more bills."

The envelope contained a thank-you from Brianna Marshall's family, praising my work and thanking me for respecting the family's privacy. In a town like ours, where rumors spread like influenza, secrets could become a heavy load to bear. They were a burden I was used to carrying, but it was nice to know my discretion was appreciated.

Feeling slightly empowered, I slipped the note under my keyboard. "Dad, I can set it up so you can pay those bills online, if you like."

"My method works just fine." Dad was not into change, especially when it came to technology.

"It's easy. And look here—I made us a new website. It's loading right now. I even redesigned our logo." I pointed at the image on the website: a simple white calla lily on a field of muted green. "It was Adam's idea."

"You think we can up and print new business cards and stationery? Come on, Lily, those things cost money we don't have. Adam I can understand, but you? You'll have to get that into your head if you're going to keep this all afloat someday. The old logo's fine."

As if he did any better. Well, that was a responsibility I didn't need. With a click, I deleted the logo from the page.

"What's this nonsense?" My father flipped open the glossy pamphlet I'd left on his desk. "Hawg Heaven Hearse? 'Take your final ride, biker-style.' This your idea, too?"

"It's the newest fad."

"If your grandfather could see this, he'd be rolling over in his grave. You know that, right? Adam, am I out of touch or is this just wrong?"

As if Adam knew the first thing about the latest funeral trends.

Adam glanced at the photo of a motorcycle pulling a glass-sided coach and shrugged. "I think it's—what's the word?—*cool.*"

"Guess that makes me out of touch then." My father tossed the pamphlet into his out-box. "Your job is to honor the dead," he quoted. "Page sixty-four in your grandpa Ted's book, *The Funeral Director's Rules of Conduct.*"

"Twenty thousand copies sold," Evan and I said in chorus.

"Then you know," said Dad.

He slit open the envelopes like he was slitting throats and chucked the empties at his wastebasket. Half ended up at my feet. "Well, hallelujah! Finally some good news. The bank approved our loan for the crematorium."

"That's great!" I said, relieved to see his face fading to its usual ruddy color.

Rachel poked her head in through the open door. "Have any of you seen a Tupperware container with a green lid? It was sitting on the table in the parlor. I can't find it anywhere."

"I put it in the dishwasher," said Evan.

"Oh, dear. That was supposed to be for Bud Velman's cremains. They're being delivered this afternoon."

"I thought it was from lunch yesterday. How was I supposed to know?"

"Fine time to start picking up, Evan," she scolded. "And, Lily, enough with the new website already. I asked you to work on the garden this morning. It's the least you can do after the stunt you and your brother pulled the other night. Do you know what it cost to get that hearse back?"

Yup, she was still pissed.

"I'll get to the garden as soon as this finishes loading, I promise."

"Well, an acre of performance is worth a world of promise," Rachel replied. Right, because why say what you mean when a cliché will do? She stomped from the office to retrieve the missing container.

"Cremains?" asked Adam once she was out of earshot.

"It's what we call the bits of bones and carbon left over after cremation," explained Dad. "Technically it's not ashes, like most people think. A machine pulverizes it all and then it's sealed in a bag and placed in a container of some sort. Could be an urn, or anything, really."

"Could be Tupperware," I said.

"Tupperware?" asked Adam.

"Plastic storage containers," I clarified. I guess his father didn't host many kitchenware parties.

"Yeah," says Evan. "People come up with all kinds of wild ideas."

"They're not wild," I said. "They want something personal. Remember Agnes Shreve?"

"No."

"Tina Turner's doppelgänger, pigeon-toed, appendectomy scar? The woman loved hats. She had more than two hundred in her collection when she died. Her grandchildren wanted her cremains placed in a hatbox. I had them draw pictures of special memories and then I pasted them all around the outside. And there was that bull rider, Malcolm Flisk. He left instructions for his cremains to be placed in his best boot. I had to figure out a way to stitch a leather lid on it. My hands had blisters for days after that one. People get very creative."

There was a beep and my monitor went black. "What? No!" I pressed every button on my keyboard as if that were the answer to resuscitating a hard drive. "No, no, no!" An error message having something to do with a backup battery flashed briefly before the entire office plunged into darkness for the third time that week.

"Three solid days of work, gone!" I wailed.

"I'd better go call an electrician," groaned Dad. "That loan can't come through soon enough." The creak of a chair and the dragging of feet over the worn carpeting marked his passage through the office and into the hall.

"Well, no point putting off the garden now," I said.

"I'll help," offered Adam.

Together we followed the gravel path that led to the back of the property. It wound past the chapel, which used to be a carriage house when horse-drawn caissons were in vogue. Adam read aloud the small sign tucked between a pair of hibiscuses. "*This way to Paradise.* That's a big promise for such a small sign."

"You have no idea how big," I grumbled.

"I can fix that." He gave the sign a twist until the arrow was pointed heavenward.

I applauded. "Much better."

We passed the caretaker's cottage, where Nana was prying nails out of recycled barn siding, and ducked beneath the apple tree she had planted as a child. Its barren branches stretched over the stone wall surrounding the garden. A second hand-painted sign swung from a lopsided post. WELCOME. MAY YOU FIND PEACE AND COMFORT WITHIN THESE WALLS. I swung open the creaky wooden gate and a slat fell to the ground. Some Paradise. Purgatory, more like. Neglected rose canes arced over weedy flowerbeds, their river-rock borders lying scattered beneath a blanket of dropped leaves.

"My grandma Daisy and her sister Violet built all this after the caretaker left," I explained. "They stacked the stones for the walls, laid out the paths, and planted the beds. They especially loved calla lilies, but all that's left now are those sad, droopy things."

"Is that how you got your name?"

"That and my lily-white skin. Anyway," I continued, now feeling totally self-conscious, thank you very much. "After Daisy and Violet passed, Nana reluctantly took up the baton—or should say I spade? It was never her thing, so Rachel hired a gardener. It looked better for a while, or at least greener, until Dad discovered that the gardener was using the back beds to grow pot."

"You're mocking me now. Even I know you can't grow a pot."

"Honestly, Adam. He was growing marijuana."

"Oh, you mean *Cannabis sativa*. Did you know *sativa* means 'useful'?"

"Yeah, well, he was using it, all right."

The garden paths converged where a white-marble angel balanced on a pedestal in the center of a fountain. Algae-green water dribbled from the angel's mouth and into the basin below, forming the perfect mosquito nursery. At least the pump still worked—barely.

"I'll tackle these," I announced, and snapped off a withered rose hip. "Did you know that in ancient times the rose represented respect for the dead? They're also masters of self-preservation and are unbelievably resilient."

"Sounds like someone I know."

"Really—ouch!" I plucked a thorn from my thumb and held it up. "See what I mean?"

"Are you sure you know what you're doing?"

"How hard can it be? Snip snip." I made cutting motions with my fingers. "Why don't you see if you can resuscitate that fountain-turned-cesspool."

Adam went in search of something he could use to scoop out the water while I dove into clipping and pruning, pinching and deadheading. Within an hour my arms were scratched and my hair had become so entangled in the briar that I risked tearing it from my scalp if I turned my head.

Adam returned to check on my progress just in time. "Hmm." He flipped over a metal tag wired to the nearest rose and read, "*Rosa* 'Queen Elizabeth.' Seems the queen has taken a prisoner of war."

"Don't just stand there. Do something!"

He kicked at the pile of hacked canes littering the ground. "Haven't you done enough?"

"I was trying to reshape it, but I think I may have killed it."

"Fortunately, like you said, roses are very resilient. As long as the rootstock still has life in it, the rose can come back. Now hold still while I free you."

He pulled a cane aside with one hand while reaching over my back with the other to retrieve my clippers from the ground. Our bodies were close, both warm from the sun and dewy with perspiration. I could almost imagine the sensation of his touch. The mere thought of his skin meeting mine made me light-headed. "Hurry up," I said. "The blood is rushing to my head."

With a couple quick snips I was freed of the butchered queen's thorny grasp. I stepped away with a new respect for my captor. "Thanks." I wiped my forehead, stalling while I pulled myself together. Adam seemed equally off-balance. He couldn't look me in the eye and ground the soil under a foot. I cleared my parched throat. "So what next?"

"You could divide that agapanthus over there. You'll need a shovel."

"Aga-what? Never mind. I think there's a shovel in the shed. I'll get it." I made a hasty retreat. I couldn't let him see how flustered he'd made me. This was Adam, after all, the "boy unearthed" who wasn't even the guy I'd dreamed him to be. I had no business getting all swoony over him.

From the shed I could see him straddling a desiccated lavender bush, its bare branches thrusting out of the cracked ground in a way that reminded me of the fiberglass arms I'd found in the Lassiter house ruins. He grabbed the shrub at its base and plucked it from the soil as easily as an errant blade of grass, then pitched it onto the compost pile. Dirt flew everywhere. Cursing in Latin, he brushed it from his hair and face, stripped off his tee, and hung it on the bough of the apple tree. His back, still mottled with oddly colored bruising from the incident at Hayden's, glistened in the sun like a battle-worn bronze shield. "I see you watching me," he said.

I quickly averted my eyes. "Don't be so vain. I'm looking for a rake—I mean shovel." *Damn, he has eyes in the back of his head, too.*

Once I'd scrounged up one, he pointed out my target—a sword-leafed, clumpy mass. First he had me dig around its tangled roots so it could be pulled free. I took hold and heaved. The slick leaves slid through my hands, and my ass landed on a little stub of a plant that sadly will never be the same. I tried again and this time came away with a handful of leaves. I'd had enough and flung the shovel at the demonic thing.

"You okay?" Adam asked coolly.

"We're never going to get this garden back to what it was. It's nothing but hard-packed dirt and weeds and more weeds and dead things."

"Not dead. Waiting."

"For what?"

"Opportunity." He picked up a shriveled bulb lying in the dirt. "See this?" He dropped it into the loose soil where a lilac once grew. "With the littlest care, that'll grow into something *glori-ficus.*"

He had me brush enough dirt into the hole to cover the bulb, pat it down, and water it. I stared at the mound. *Not so different from a mini burial mound*, I thought. How ironic that new life could rise from such a thing. "It's sort of magical, isn't it? I mean, a bulb can grow and bloom again and again. An acorn takes in air, water, and sunlight and goes from a little lump to an oak."

"Not magic. Science. I don't believe in magic."

"Oh, I do. There are too many things in this world that can't be explained by science."

"Name one."

"Hmm." I scrunched up my face. "Can't right now, but I will."

"Let me know when you do."

"Uh-huh." I wasn't really listening.

"You're staring again," he said.

"Oh, am I? It's that tattoo."

"Tattoo?"

"The inked characters on your chest."

"What about them?"

"What do they mean?"

"*Emet.* It's Hebrew for 'truth.' A birthday gift from Neil."

"I didn't know your family was Jewish."

"We're not."

"Well, regardless, that's a strange gift for a father to give his son."

"Much of what Neil did was strange, I'm finding."

"But why *truth*?"

"Because Neil valued truth above all else."

"Is that why you can't lie? Because honesty meant that much to him?"

"Something like that." He plucked his shirt from the bough and pulled it over his head. "I think I'll remove that dead branch from the apple tree." Guess it was his turn to be self-conscious.

I plopped down on an old stump, propped my head in my hands, and watched him snap off the split limb as if it were a twig. "You sure know a lot about plants, especially trees. Ever consider becoming a professional gardener? Or, hey, how about an arborist?"

"I've never thought much about my career options. When Neil was alive, there weren't any."

"I know how that feels, but I think you'd be great at it. Look at all you've accomplished in a couple hours."

"You mean *we*."

"Yeah, we. *We* make a good team."

"Like we did on the website?"

"That too. We should call it a *we*-site."

"We-site. That's funny." Not funny enough to make him crack a smile, though. "What about you? What are your . . . options?"

I sighed. "My father wants me to stay here and study mortuary science at the local college, then take over the mortuary as director so he can retire."

"And you don't want to."

"What if I run the business into the ground?" *Like it isn't already six feet under.* "And, I mean, I'm fine taking care of the dead, you know, doing the cosmetics and office work, and I think I'd be a good mortician, but a big part of running a funeral home is working with the people left behind. I don't know if I can handle that."

"You handled Mrs. Tomopolo."

"Only because you were there."

"Is that true?"

"I value truth above all else," I mocked playfully.

Adam saw right through me. "So you're afraid?"

I stared at the ground. "Yeah."

"Of the dead?"

This was all uncharted territory. I didn't talk about this stuff with anyone, not even Mal. "Not of the dead. Of the living."

"Why the living?"

I thought about all the broken hearts and lives I'd seen stumble through our front door. Of Nana Jo, who still cried every time she pulled Grandpa Ted's tobacco tin from her dresser drawer or found one of his padlocks. Of Mallory, who had the power to crush me with a few misspoken words. I remembered the look on my father's face the day I found a photo of my mother between the pages of a book and had to ask who she was. And I recalled the boy in the orchard, the boy who gave me my first kiss and then vanished from my life—because I let him. "I'm afraid of the living because I find it so easy to disappoint them and so hard to lose them."

A shadow passed over Adam's face. He took on an air of gravity I hadn't seen since the day he learned his father perished in the fire. "I understand."

And I believed him. Like me, his mother abandoned him. I could guess at the reasons she left his father, but to leave a child? Unforgivable, or so it had been for me. I changed the subject. "So how's it going over at Zmira's? Are you any closer to getting that lockbox back?"

"No. I finished digging the pond two days ago, but now he wants me to clean out his flower beds and dig him a vegetable garden."

"I don't like how he's taking advantage of the situation."

Adam shrugged. "I don't mind. He's nice enough."

"Zmira? Nice?"

"In his own way. I think he likes my company."

That makes two of us.

"We should get back to work," I said, passing him a bucket and brush. Together we scrubbed down the fountain and cleaned out the leaf trap. Adam refilled the basin using a garden hose, then gave me the honor of turning on the pump.

"Oh my god, look at that!" I cheered at the first gurgles. And although I was covered in muck, sunburned, and scratched, I felt as though we'd taken a solid step toward resurrecting the garden. To celebrate, I flipped off my sneakers and tiptoed into the cool, clear fountain. "Ahh . . . This feels so good. Try it."

"No thanks." He turned his back to me as he coiled the hose. I couldn't resist and kicked up the water, dousing him. It was an invitation for trouble—an invitation he was more than willing to accept. He stuck his hand in and flicked water back, but I was ready.

I grabbed him by the shirt and dragged him in. He looped the hose around me and together we went down in a tangle of limbs and spraying water.

I sat up, and my laughter stopped so abruptly that I found myself short of breath. Our faces were a slip, a tip, a lean apart. That's all it took to trigger the craving I'd sworn off for good. I wouldn't need much. The tickle of an eyelash, an accidental brush of skin against skin, a heartbeat, whatever it took to get me through until tomorrow and the next day and the day after that. But isn't that what an addict says just before the last, lethal dose?

I pressed my face forward. A summons to meet me halfway.

Adam's lips parted. And then retreated. And just like that the inches between us became miles again. "Lily, I'm not . . ."

"Not what?"

"Good enough for you." He rose from the fountain and wrung out his shirt, wringing me out with it.

I floundered for words. As far as I knew, no boy had ever paid me any attention—at least, not the good kind—since those days in the walnut orchard. By time I thought to shout, "Let me be the judge of that," he was long gone.

"Lily?" Rachel called from the yard. "Is that you?"

I slithered out of the water and into the mud like some primordial amphibian. "In Paradise," I hollered. *Not.*

Rachel pushed through the gate. "I just saw Adam, and . . ." She crossed her arms at the sight of me. "You two were supposed to be working in the garden, not wallowing in it."

I scooped up the spade at my feet. "Yeah, well, we got distracted." That was probably a bad choice of words.

She eyed me suspiciously. "So what happened between you two? Adam flew by me like he had a plane to catch."

"I'm not sure," I told her honestly.

Her face grew somber. "Well, you'd better get inside and clean up. The Sandovals called. They lost another one."

The spade slid from my hand. Not again. This made three.

"They're on their way over right now. And, Lily . . ."

"Yeah?"

"Maria asked for you. She only wants to talk to you."

Christ.

RULE #18
DON'T GET RUN OVER AT THE CROSSROADS OF LIFE AND DEATH.

A white dove cooed softly from its cage to the rhythm of "Tears in Heaven," which was playing quietly in the background when the Sandovals arrived for the brief service. Adam was covering for Tony, whose car had decided today was the day to throw a rod or piston or some such. I knew Adam was worried that Zmira wouldn't keep his word, and to be honest, so was I, but he was needed here more.

The coffin was not much bigger than a dresser drawer and sat in a cloud of baby's breath. Inside, the lifeless newborn lay swaddled in the blanket I finished that morning. Unlike the previous two babies, who'd died before birth, the Sandovals had held this little girl in their arms, making it that much harder for them to let go and for me to do my job. The handcrafted guest books and swaddling blankets I'd made twice before had made an impression, which is why, according to Rachel, Maria asked to work with me. I didn't have the heart to refuse.

Maria kept her focus on the mother-of-pearl rosary clutched in her hands, her heavily tinted glasses unable to conceal the dark circles beneath her eyes, her empire-waist dress unable to disguise the post-pregnancy bulge around her middle, and her stoic recitation of the Lord's Prayer unable to mask her grief. But I had to mask mine. It's what was expected of me.

It was on days like this that I hated my job.

A late guest arrived, toddler in tow. I handed her a prayer sheet and walked her to the end of the first pew. Maria looked up at the child and broke into wracking sobs. Across the room, Dad's glower warned me to check my tears. Quickly I retraced my steps to the back of the room, desperately trying to hold it together.

From his post at the door, Adam watched me, no doubt puzzling over my emotional display and trying to put a name to it. He didn't shed a tear when his father died. I found strength in his example, took a deep breath, and was back in control.

After the procession to the cemetery, a dove was released, and the Sandovals' little girl was laid to rest beside her siblings.

I gave Mal a call to see how she was doing and if she wanted to go get a frozen yogurt. Last time we talked, she was still dealing with what happened at Hayden's. I hadn't known what to say at the time. Now wasn't much better, but it didn't matter. She was out shopping at a chic new boutique with Vega. It was Mal's way of getting her mind off things.

An ache settled in my chest that I couldn't explain. It wasn't jealousy. I was glad Vega had taken her shopping. God knows I'd be useless in a boutique. But after the other night I'd hoped we could get back to the way things used be, when I was her go-to.

By the time I finished gathering all the spent candles, tissues, withered petals, and crackly leaves from the cushions and floorboards of the chapel, I was half starved and wallowing in a big fat vat of self-pity. I headed back to the house to self-medicate with a pint of Moose Tracks and a can of whipped cream. I was the last one to lunch, and not one person said so much as a thank-you for taking care of all the cleanup. Not Evan, who was perched on a stool at the kitchen island, playing with his half-eaten sandwich. Not Adam, who didn't even look up when I entered the room. Not Dad, who was ripping the cufflinks from his sleeves and probably revving up to lecture me on my lack of professionalism. Not even Rachel, who was huddled over the sink, scrubbing the griddle so hard it seemed she might wear a hole through it.

"You're all welcome," I said.

"I don't want to hear it," snapped Dad. "The world doesn't always revolve around you, you know."

"Your father doesn't mean that," said Rachel, running interference between us as usual, but this time her voice lacked conviction. "Cam, tell her."

"Tell her what?" demanded Nana Jo, coming in through the door. She made a beeline for the cupboard. "Are we out of baking soda again?" Baking soda was her solution to everything, from scouring saucepans to cleaning the carpet after Specter gagged up a fur ball.

Silence.

"Something happen?" she asked. "You all look like somebody else died."

My father stripped off his tie and chucked it onto the table. "EMS stole the crematorium right out from under us, that's what's happened!"

"*What?*" I was certain I'd heard wrong. EMS had its own crematorium. Why would it need another one—unless it was to put the screw on us?

"After the Sandoval service I went over to make a final offer and was told Bill Crenshaw and his partner signed papers yesterday afternoon with Jim Sturbridge."

"But I thought it was a done deal?" asked Nana Jo.

"So did I, but while I was waiting for the loan approval, Jim Sturbridge stepped in with a cash offer. Someone tipped him off. Probably Tony."

"Cam, stop. You don't honestly think Tony would . . . ?" Rachel couldn't even say it.

"What? Betray us? Who else? He's the only person outside this family who knew what we were planning. All those sick days. And where is he today? I suspected he was up to something, but—"

The whipped-cream can slipped through my fingers and clattered to the floor, releasing a foamy spray across the checkered linoleum. Everyone turned. "It wasn't Tony," I said. "I didn't mean to . . . I was, you know, making conversation."

My father glared at me. "With whom?"

"José. I might have mentioned to him that we were thinking of buying Crenshaw and Madsen."

Dad's hands formed fists tighter than a hangman's knot. "José with St. Margarita's Transport?"

I bobbed my head, my eyes focused on the splotches of cream splattered across the floor.

"Now, Cameron," soothed Rachel, "settle down. You know what the doctor said."

From somewhere outside came the rhythmic *shht-shht-shht* of the sprinkler striking the side of the house. The sound echoed my thoughts. Why didn't I keep my mouth shut like I normally did?

"How could you be so stupid?" demanded my father.

I was asking myself the same question. "I . . . I . . ." I stammered. Tears threatened to spill. Not now. They would only make him angrier. "I'm so sorry, Dad . . . everyone. I . . . We were talking . . . We've known him for years. I never thought—"

"You did this on purpose," accused Evan with a malice I'd never seen in him before.

"I didn't!" I insisted, but it was plain that no one believed me.

But Evan wasn't done. "You could have been honest and admitted you don't want to take over the mortuary. You didn't have to sabotage the entire business."

"Is that true, Lily?" Dad asked, his expression the same as when I showed him the found photo of my mother. "But it's all we've ever talked about. You taking over someday, carrying on the family tradition. What about the college catalog I gave you? You said you were going to apply."

I was no better than my mother. All I wanted to do was run. I hung my head, the weight of my shame and the depth of my betrayal more than I could bear.

"Look at me!" he shouted. "And don't you dare cry."

Tears blurred my vision as I met his eyes.

"Cam," said Rachel, "she didn't mean any harm by telling José. It was a simple slip of the tongue, I'm sure."

Suddenly Dad staggered back against the pantry, clawing at his collar. His legs buckled and he slid to the floor.

"Cam! Cam, honey?" Rachel dropped to his side.

"My chest," my father gasped, his face red. "I can't breathe."

"Oh my god," Rachel shouted. "He's having a heart attack. Call 911!"

I snatched the phone from the counter and punched in the numbers. An operator answered, and I gave her the situation and verified our address. I raced back to Dad, the operator still on the phone. "I didn't know he would say anything to anyone. I swear, I didn't know."

Rachel was yelling at me to step back and give him room. Evan was clearing away the furniture. And now Adam was pulling me to the far end of the kitchen, but I was still calling to my dad. His eyes were pinched shut, his mouth clamped against the pain. Nana supported his head, wiped the sweat from his brow, and comforted him in soothing tones. She was scared like me, but she was also determined. She wouldn't lose her son.

The last thing I ever wanted was to hurt my father.

Distant sirens grew louder.

"Dad, don't leave me," I begged over and over. "Please don't leave me."

RULE #19
EYES ARE BEST GLUED SHUT.

I was numb, so numb that Rachel and Nana had to tell me we were home. If only they could tell me what day it was. In a hospital, hours are not marked by the rise and fall of the sun; they're marked by a smattering of progress reports, some bad, some not so bad, and all you can do is brace for the next one.

I stumbled from the car.

Adam met us at the front door. "Well?"

The others would have to fill him in. At the hospital I'd been able to keep all my emotions stitched up inside. But if I had to face Adam, say the words out loud, then all the tiny knots holding me together would slip, opening a seam so wide, everything would come spilling out, raw and messy. That is not how a proper mortician behaves. I was supposed to be the one to comfort. I was supposed to be the stoic one, the selfless one.

I shuffled past Adam, silent in my disgrace.

Only Nana had it together enough to answer him. "We won't know the extent of his heart damage for a few more days."

"But he will live?"

"Yes," she answered, "assuming there are no more setbacks."

"And Lily? How is she?"

I didn't hear her reply. Rupert Baker was waiting for me. I retrieved the photos I needed from my desk's bottom drawer and retreated to the cold room, where the chill would hopefully steal away any feeling I had left.

I pulled the sheet back from Rupert's face. It was etched with the road map of his life, and from the looks of it, it had been a road well-traveled. I did my best not to think about the brothers, wife, children, grandchildren, and friends he was leaving behind on this next journey, or how close in age he was to my father, but my best was not enough. Not today. I sank to the floor as the strings holding me together unraveled. I made pathetic, mousy sounds, my shoulders jerking with each one.

From behind me, I heard the *click* of the lock and the *swoosh* of the door's rubber seal as it scraped across the floor. The sound was followed by two tentative steps. I didn't need to turn around to know who it was.

"Are you crying?" Adam asked, sounding more curious than concerned.

"No."

He walked around to face me. "You are a terrible liar. Your eyes are red and swollen."

"You're not supposed to be in here when there's a body present," I reminded him.

"You're right. I should go." He started to leave.

"No. Wait. Stay—please?"

Adam hesitated, then swept the door closed and joined me on

the floor, cross-legged and stiff-lipped. I saw how he struggled to find words he thought I needed to hear. But I didn't want his words right now. I wanted his ear.

"You should have seen him," I said, voice cracking, traitorous fluids leaking from my nose and my eyes, running down the hollows of my cheeks. "They had him hooked up to all these tubes and machines. He didn't look so different from . . ." With a hiccup, I nodded my head toward Rupert on the gurney. "If only I'd kept my mouth shut. But no, I had to go and blab to José. I know what a gossip he is." I wiped my brimming eyes. "Dammit, I don't want to cry."

"Go ahead and cry."

And just like that, I began to sob.

He reached up, pulled a tissue box from the counter, and placed it in my hands.

"*Noli desperare. Noli desperare.* Don't despair. Don't despair. *Vita eundo vires acquirimus.* In life we gather strength as we go."

I snorted. Only Adam could say something like that and make it sound wise and true. "I'm such a fool."

"My father had a saying. *Semel in anno licet operari stultus.* One can act the fool once a year." He plucked a tissue from the box and dabbed at my leaky eyes and runny nose.

"Then I'm way over my limit." A timid smile. Another snort. "That crematorium was our last hope for saving the business, and now, because of me, the deal is ruined. We're ruined. How will I ever make this up to my father?"

"You'll think of a way. I know you will."

"I wish I had your confidence."

"Lily, you are not to blame. You thought you could trust José.

What we need to do now is find a way to stay in business until a more permanent solution can be found."

He said we. "But how? That's going to take cash."

"I'll find a way, I promise."

And I believed him. He did not make promises lightly.

"For the next few weeks your mother will be busy caring for your father. Evan and I will have to handle all the removals and deliveries, and Tony will manage the—what do you call it—embalming. Your job will be to keep everything else running until your father recovers."

I started to protest, but he didn't give me the chance. "You can do it. I'll help you."

There was hope in his words. I took a deep, ragged breath and then squared my shoulders.

"Okay." I felt anything but okay. So much had been lost—my father's health, the crematorium, my faith in my ability to fix the damage I'd done. But if I surrendered now, it meant handing my entire family legacy over to Sturbridge. I couldn't live with myself if I let that happen.

I blew my nose and gave it one last dab. Adam extended a hand to pull me up from the floor, but I was afraid that if I took it, I'd never let go. So I pushed myself up and put on my apron and a pair of latex gloves, ready to work.

"Can I stay?" he asked, to my surprise.

"You don't have to if you don't want to."

"I want to. Mr. Baker, is that okay with you?"

Rupert Baker did not object, so I handed Adam one of Evan's aprons, then told him that the man lying on the gurney had been cleansed, embalmed, and dressed. All that remained was the cosmeticizing, which was my job.

We rolled Mr. Baker into the prep room where I opened a drawer crammed with assorted jars, tubes, and applicators and withdrew two plastic half circles. "They have little nubs on one side to keep the eyelids closed," I explained. "See?" I placed one over each of Mr. Baker's eyeballs, pulled over the lids, and sealed them top to bottom with glue. "You okay so far?"

Adam nodded. "He could be sleeping."

"That's the idea." I held up a razor. "Now we shave him." That's when it dawned on me that I'd never seen so much as a hint of stubble on Adam's face. Born lucky, I guessed.

Next I demonstrated how to apply a thick cream to the skin to keep it from forming deep creases—or, in Rupert's case, deeper creases. "Now we need foundation to tone down the age spots. Can you hand me my makeup case?" I pointed to the well-worn leather satchel on the counter, which contained my best brushes and mineral powders.

"The trick with makeup is to make it look natural. You should've seen some of my first attempts. One woman looked like I gave her a pair of those big wax lips. And then there was our dentist's father. By the time I was done with him, he looked like a drag queen."

"Like royalty?"

I laughed. "No, like a person who dresses up as a woman for entertainment."

"I'm glad my ignorance amuses you."

I had him push over the compressor. I selected the paint that best matched Mr. Baker's complexion, placed five drops into the airbrush reservoir, and flipped on the power. Adam watched in rapt attention. I couldn't tell whether he was intrigued or completely mortified that I was painting a dead man's face, but when I was done, he proclaimed me an *artifex*.

"You're different in here," he conceded. "Confident."

That's because *here* was safe. No one can leave you if they're already gone. But he was right. Cosmeticizing was what I did best. I belonged here. I knew it like I knew my name. And, for the first time, someone else knew this about me, too.

"Adam."

"Yes?"

"You *are* good enough for me. More than good enough."

RULE # 20
MEASURE TWICE, BOX ONCE.

I jabbed the flashing playback button on the answering machine. It was West Hill Linens, informing us that they were suspending our service due to nonpayment. Rachel, who had snuck down to the office to catch up on bills, overheard. "Probably better not to mention this to your father."

She didn't need to tell me. I hardly recognized the man who'd returned home from the ICU two weeks ago. It wasn't only his appearance, which was like a pencil point worn to the wood; it was his worn spirit. To make matters worse, his life had been whittled down to a monotonous routine of bed rest, doctor visits, and trips to the pharmacy.

To break the tedium, Rachel sometimes walked him out to Paradise to read or doze beneath the apple tree, which was showing signs of life again. Once I caught him sitting with Adam, who was discussing the merits of the new compost bin he and Nana Jo were building beside the shed. "Nothing improves soil like decaying organic material," Adam had boasted. Later I teased that I would get him a T-shirt that said GOT ROT?

Despite the garden's improvements, though, Dad still griped about the dead lilac bush I yanked out of the garden a while ago. Never mind that it had been leafless; it was a gift from a former client. Who knew my father could be so sentimental? Must have been all those defibrillations. I tried explaining to him that the bush was never going to bloom again, but he didn't care. Rachel said to give him time, that he'd get over it. But if my father could hold a grudge over a dead shrub, how would he ever forgive me for killing the family business to impress a transport driver? How would I ever forgive myself?

Since Dad was not allowed to drive, Rachel and Evan took turns carting him back and forth between doctors, leaving me to cover the business. The phone and doorbell rarely rang these days, so I filled the time searching for a way to salvage the mess I'd made. I looked into what it would cost to build our own crematorium. I explored ways to advertise our services by reaching out to local senior centers and florists. But hiring an architect, acquiring permits, and printing brochures all took money we didn't have.

I watched Rachel shuffle papers and bills at Dad's desk, but the piles weren't getting any smaller. "You mind checking the mail?" she asked, thumbing through a wad of receipts.

"Sure," I said, grateful for an excuse to stretch my legs.

I removed several envelopes from the box beneath the mail slot and opened the door to check for any packages. A man in a tattered windbreaker and duct-taped helmet stood at the far end of the walk, staring up at the bedroom windows. I realized it was the same man who pretended to fix his bike chain in front of our house back when reporters were still hanging about. Sturbridge was certainly determined to dig up something to use against us, but honestly he could have done better than this guy.

"Can I help you?" I asked.

The stranger grinned at me with coffee-stained teeth. "You work here?"

"I do."

"You the girl who found the boy at the old Lassiter place?"

"Yes, but—"

"Is he here?"

Why would Sturbridge be interested in Adam? Maybe this guy wasn't one of his snoops after all. A reporter then? "Look, we've—"

Before I could explain that we'd already told the reporters all there was to tell, Rachel appeared beside me. "Lily, you seen your Dad's readers? I can't find them anywhere."

"He left them on the kitchen table this morning."

"Oh, that's right. Thanks."

When I looked back, the stranger was pedaling away.

"Who was that?" she asked.

"I'm not sure." Not a reporter, but funeral homes do tend to attract less-than-savory characters—especially when said funeral home has been all over the news. A horrible thought occurred to me. What if this was one of the guys who attacked Adam in the alley? If he was, I'd just confirmed where Adam lived.

Back in the office I placed the stack of mail on the corner of Dad's desk. Rachel returned from fetching Dad's glasses and flipped through the bundle. "This one's for you," she said, holding up a large padded envelope.

I read the return address. "Oh, I know what this is! Is Adam around?"

"I think he left early this morning again. Said something about a side job."

"He's been helping out Mr. Zmira." I didn't mention he was doing it to earn back an old lockbox. Let her think it was out of "fiscal responsibility," a term my father was fond of using even though he couldn't keep his own business afloat.

With me holding down the office and Adam working for Mr. Zmira and assisting Evan, we hadn't seen much of each other lately. I told myself it was for the best. I'd misjudged José. I couldn't afford to repeat the same mistake with Adam.

But there's no rulebook for dreamland. There I could freely play out my misguided hopes and desires. In some of my dreams Adam and I were in the dark doing things I couldn't imagine doing in the light. Those were the dreams that made me eager for sleep. But in others we were adrift in deep, churning waters. We clung to each other like human life rafts, taking each rise and fall as they came, while below the surface we kicked wildly to keep our heads above water.

I took the envelope along with the spare key to the cottage. Nana was in her workshop, attacking several planks of cedar with a rotary sander. Sawdust and sound billowed from her open door, so I went around back and knocked loudly on Adam's door. When there was no answer, I unlocked it and entered.

Like Evan, Adam had the habit of leaving on lights when he left a room. The door to the pass-through connecting to the bathroom and workshop beyond was closed, but it was not enough to seal out the brain-numbing racket of Nana hard at work. No wonder Adam spent so little time here.

On the floor beside the bed were a pair of dirty jeans and a ripped tee, a teetering pile of gardening books, and a half-eaten granola bar. His newly minted name tag rested atop the dresser. Other than the few items hanging in the wardrobe, that was it. The sum of his possessions would fill a grocery bag.

I peeled open the envelope and emptied it of its contents—two sheets of glow-in-the-dark stars. Using the enclosed constellation map as a guide, I climbed onto the bed and began pressing the stars, one by one, to the ceiling, smiling smugly to myself as I imagined the look on Adam's face later that night when he turned out the lights. I dragged the rickety ladder-back chair from the corner and, despite visions of falling off and breaking my neck, continued pasting stars until both sheets were empty. In twenty minutes I'd transformed his ceiling into a galaxy.

Adam would be back soon. Time to clean up and clear out. I reached under the bed to retrieve the envelope from where it fell, and my nails clinked against something hard and tinny. I pulled it out. His father's lockbox. How long had he had this?

The door leading to the pass-through creaked open, and in strutted Adam, a towel wrapped loosely about his waist. Nana had been making so much noise in the next room, I hadn't realized he'd been in the bathroom showering this whole time. I leaped to my feet, nudging the box back under the bed with the heel of my foot. "Adam, I thought you were at Zmira's. What are you doing here?"

"I finished up early. And, if I'm not mistaken, this is my room? Why are *you* here?"

"I . . . I . . ." My attention drifted to three water droplets racing down his chest. They coursed over the small tattoo on his upper torso, meandered over his abs, and finally disappeared into the terry-cloth towel, the middle droplet the victor.

"Lily?"

My head snapped up.

"Oh," I said lamely. "I wanted to surprise you."

"Okay. I'm surprised."

"No, I mean . . ." I pointed to the stars on the ceiling. "I know it doesn't look like much now, but tonight—"

"The night sky." Head back, he turned a full circle, reciting the names of each constellation. He sounded pleased, although he noted that Ursa Major had an extra leg.

"Here, I can fix that."

"No need. It'll make me think of you."

"In a good way, I hope."

"In the best way possible."

I smiled, not knowing what else to say but also not wanting to leave. "Oh, by the way, a man came by the house a little while ago asking about you. Weird dude. Were you expecting anyone?"

"No."

"Well, he rode off before I could find out who he was, but I thought I'd mention it. Can't be too careful, you know."

He looked curiously at me. "Right."

The end of his towel slid free. He caught it in time, but the embarrassment was clearly mine. "Give me a minute," he said. He scooped up the jeans from the floor and ducked back into the pass-through.

I wanted a better look at the lockbox, but it had slid farther back than I expected. I scrambled onto my belly to retrieve it.

"Looking for something?" Adam had come back for his shirt.

"I can explain," I said, my voice muffled by mattress and bedding.

"No need. I see now the stars were an excuse to snoop through my things."

I shimmied out from under the bed and held up the box. "Looks to me like neither of us trusts the other."

"I was going to tell you."

"Then you won't mind if we open it together."

From the way he balked, it was obvious he did mind. "Not possible without the key. I've tried."

"That explains the dents. Stay here. I'll be right back."

"Wait. Where are you—?"

I marched into Nana Jo's workshop. She was hunched over a bench, a wadded rag in one hand, steel wool in the other. Walnut-colored stain freckled her face. "Do you still have Grandpa's set of lockpicks?"

She raised an eyebrow. "You planning a heist?"

"No, it's for Adam. He has his father's lockbox but not the key."

"I think they're in that crate with your grandfather's padlock collection. Over beside the planer. You know how to use them?"

"Nope, but that's what the internet's for."

I found the picks, printed a quick set of instructions in the office, and was back in under fifteen minutes. By then Adam had run a comb through his hair and was fully dressed.

Together we knelt at the side of the bed, the lockbox between us. With my finger I traced the strange circle-within-circle design etched into the lid. "Look, it's the same as on the fallout shelter hatch."

Adam crossed his arms. "So?"

"There must be a connection, don't you think?"

"Forget that. How are we going to open it?"

"We're going to pick the lock."

"But there's only one lock. What's to pick?"

"Must you always be so literal?" I unrolled the canvas pouch containing the lockpicks and spread it on the floor along with the printout. "It says here that most locks consist of pairs of pins that, when properly aligned, allow the plug to turn and the lock to open. All we need is the right size pick."

It took several tries, but eventually I found one that fit. "Now, according to the instructions, the trick is in recognizing the sound the pins make when they slip into place." I tried first, but Adam's hearing proved sharper than mine.

"Last one," he said. He twisted the pick. There was a faint *tick* and the lock released. He lifted the lid and, heads together, we peered into the box.

RULE #21
THERE ARE SOME REQUESTS THAT SHOULD NOT AND CANNOT BE HONORED.

A plain white envelope addressed to N. M. Lassiter with an Oakland, California, postmark and no return address rested atop a house deed, a key, and a pink slip for a car long gone. There was no will and not a single birth, marriage, or death certificate to vouch for lives lived or lost. It was as if Adam never existed. The answers I'd hoped for were not there.

Adam shuffled through the papers, setting aside the envelope and pocketing the key, but not before I noted that it had the same engraved emblem as the box and the hatch. The hatch had been bolted, not locked, so it was probably a spare key for the box but not a very useful one if it was locked inside.

"See this," I said, my finger circling my face. "This is what disappointment looks like."

"What were you expecting? Gemstones?"

He knew what I was after—proof he wasn't lying about his identity. But I was not about to admit it. "Maybe. You were acting like whatever was in here was a big deal."

"It is a big deal," he said, holding up the envelope and giving it a wave. "By Fortuna, this letter will tell me who came to the house the night my father died."

"For tuna? What do fish have to do with it?"

He looked at me like I was an imbecile. "The goddess Fortuna."

Man, I'm starting to take things as literally as him. "What makes you think this letter can tell us anything?"

"It arrived the day before the explosion. After he read it, Neil locked it in this box, then went through the house, bolting doors and closing all the shades. At first I assumed it was more of his usual paranoia. But the next night Neil woke me saying there was a man at the gate and that I needed to go. I asked for a few minutes to pack, but he refused. Said there was no time. He took me to the hatch hidden in the shed and told me to climb inside. He promised he would come for me as soon as it was safe. He promised."

If the letter could tell us anything about the man who came to the house that night, it would be well worth the effort it took to retrieve it. "Go on, read it."

Adam removed a single sheet of yellow paper from the envelope, took one look at it, and passed it to me. "I can't."

I could see why. It was in cursive, each rushed word flowing into the next. With stubborn determination, I worked it out.

Neil:

Don't think anything has changed between us. What's done is done, but that doesn't mean I wouldn't warn you if I thought you were in danger. Despite what you think of me, I'm not that vindictive.

Today I received a phone call—the one we've both been dreading. Our conversation was brief. Miles said he'd been released early on good behavior, and he needed to reach you. I explained that you and I had not spoken since the divorce, and I was not sure if you were still living at the old house or even alive. I don't know if he believed me, but it's probably only a matter of time before he comes looking for you. Considering you're the one who wrongly sent him to prison, figure on it being sooner than later. Hopefully you've long since abandoned your lofty ideas and moved to where he can't find you. But knowing you as I do—your ambition, your competitive nature, and, yes, your arrogance—I suspect you proceeded with your plans. I pray I'm wrong.

There. I've cleared my conscience. The rest is up to you and fate. For your sake I hope he can find it within his heart to forgive you. I never could. Because of you, I lost my only son, my dear, sweet Adam.

God save your soul,

Veronica

"Veronica," I repeated. I unfolded my legs and tapped the letter with my finger. "She says right there that she lost her son Adam, so you can't be Adam Lassiter."

"She probably means she lost her son when she and Neil separated. She doesn't mean her son died. What it does prove is that she felt she had to warn Neal against the person he sent to prison."

"*Wrongly* sent to prison," I corrected. "You have to take this to the police."

"Why? She didn't. There must have been a reason."

I considered this. "I think she was afraid."

"I agree."

"Did Neil ever say anything about someone going to prison? Or who Miles is?"

Adam shook his head. "He made a practice of telling me as little as possible about his affairs." He took the letter from my hand and stuffed it back into the lockbox, not even bothering to return it to the envelope. "Well, that's it then." He stood and held the door open for me, his less-than-subtle way of telling me we were done here.

"That's it? If this Veronica is your mother, you have to find her. How else are you going to get any answers?"

"We're not. You yourself said that all traces of any Lassiters were erased. If she wanted me in her life, she knew where to find me. Now let it go."

I couldn't, but he didn't need to know that—or that I'd pocketed the envelope.

RULE #22
EMBALMING CAN BUY
ONLY SO MUCH TIME.

I typed *Veronica Lassiter, Oakland, California* into the search bar and hit ENTER. Nothing came up. No surprise there. She was either divorced and remarried or going by her maiden name.

Sure, I questioned my motivations for so doggedly pursuing this. Was it for Adam, or for my own peace of mind? It didn't matter. If I didn't keep looking, I'd always wonder, always doubt.

I scrolled through screen after screen of birth, marriage, immigration, and death records—all the significant events in a person's life or death that might have found their way into a digital archive. I located no Lassiters and only two Veronicas. One had been dead for three years, and the other moved to Minnesota four months ago. Then I remembered that back when Nana Jo was into genealogy, she subscribed to a newsletter written by a local historian. Sometimes it included records or articles related to the early pioneer families of Smith's Hollow.

I asked to borrow the bundle of newsletters and began the tedious task of thumbing through each issue. I'd about given up hope when I stumbled onto a listing of local marriage records. And there it was: *Family: Lassiter. Veronica Marie Forbes, married June 16, 1984, to Neil Michael Lassiter.* I marked the page with a postcard mailer, snatched up the envelope from Veronica's letter, and raced out to the cottage.

I pounded on the bedroom door. "Adam! Adam, are you in there?" He opened the door. "I found her. I found your mother. Look." I tapped my finger on the page marked with the postcard. "It's her. I can prove it." I held up the envelope and pointed to the address on the outside. "See, this letter was sent to N. M. Lassiter— Neil Michael Lassiter. It's his wife! Well, his ex-wife. Your mother. I'm certain of it."

Instead of the smile I expected, he gave me scowl. "I asked you to let this go."

"I don't understand why you're upset. I did this for you," I lied. "Don't you want to find your mother?"

He didn't answer.

"Adam, I know better than anyone what it's like to have your mother bail on you, but don't you see? This may be the only way to find out who might have killed your father."

"I suppose you're right."

"Of course I am. Now come with me." I dragged him back to the office, where I typed *Veronica Marie Forbes, Oakland, California* into the search bar. We held our breaths, each for our own reasons. The search icon spun and spun. One match appeared: a small newspaper blurb.

Procea Pharmaceuticals, Inc., announced yesterday at their Oakland, California, headquarters that

Veronica Forbes, C.P.A., will step in to replace David Reynolds following his resignation. The spokesperson indicated that although relatively new to the company, Forbes comes with years of experience in the field and is the individual first responsible for alerting auditors of inconsistencies in the company's financial records.

A few more clicks and I had the address and phone number for Procea Pharmaceuticals, Inc. I placed the call and put it on speaker.

A recording answered. "*If you know the extension for your party, you may dial it now. Otherwise please remain on the line and an operator will be with you shortly.*"

Adam nervously toyed with the stapler in rhythm to the looping melody on the other end of the phone. My stomach tightened.

"Procea Pharmaceuticals Incorporated," interrupted a young man. "How may I assist you?"

I cleared my throat. "I'd like to speak with Ms. Veronica Forbes, please."

"May I tell her who's calling?"

"Lily McCrae," I answered, trying to sound like this was a professional matter.

"One moment while I connect you."

There were two more monotonous rounds of Tom Jones's "What's New Pussycat?" before a soft, melodic voice answered. "This is Veronica Forbes."

I couldn't find any words. We should've thought this through more.

"Hello?" asked the woman, now sounding annoyed.

"Uh . . . hello. My name is Lily McCrae. I'm calling about your son, Adam Lassiter?"

There was a long pause on the other end. "Who is this?" she said curtly. "What do you want?"

This was not exactly the reaction I'd expected. "I told you, my name is Lily McCrae. I'm an acquaintance of your son's."

"Listen, I don't know what kind of sick joke this is, but . . ." Her voice trailed off. The line went dead. We stared at the receiver.

"Nothing more we can do," Adam said, sounding too much like my father.

"We can't give up," I said. "We're close. I can feel it. If you quit now, you might never know what happened the night your father died or who's responsible for his death." And if we didn't find his mother, I would never know for certain how much of what Adam told me was truth and how much was lies. She held answers for both of us.

"Whoever it was," I added, "he's still out there." Adam's hand involuntarily drifted to his throat. The harsh red marks had disappeared, but the memory of the assault had not. "Adam, your father's dead. You could be next. We have to go to Oakland and speak to her."

"You heard her. She doesn't want to talk to me."

"We won't give her a choice. We'll take the train, then catch BART to Oakland."

"Who's Bart?"

"BART is not a who. It's a what. Bay Area Rapid Transit. Don't worry. I'm going with you."

He pushed his chair away from the desk. "That's not necessary. I'll go on my own."

I couldn't believe he was fighting me on this. He knew he'd never find her without my help. I doubted he'd ever used a map before, let alone public transit. "Tell you what: I'll get you there and back. The rest is up to you."

He considered my offer, then reluctantly accepted. We made plans to go the next morning. I talked Evan into covering for me in case any calls came in, which, considering how slow business had been lately, was unlikely. In exchange Evan made Adam ride along with him on a pickup—an elderly man had broken his neck tumbling down a flight of stairs. That left me to catch up on various calls: one to the US Social Security Administration, another to the Department of Veterans Affairs, and one to the County Recorder's Office. As usual, that meant leaving lots of messages and waiting for people to return my calls.

I was jotting down notes when the phone rang. "McCrae Family Funeral Home," I answered.

"Lily McCrae, please," said a vaguely familiar voice, but I was having trouble placing the vendor. Then again, it was a terrible connection, and we dealt with so many sales people that it was hard to keep track of them all, especially since the turnover rate was so high.

"Speaking. How may I help you?"

"Actually I'm hoping we can help each other."

I sat up straight. "How so?"

"I need your assistance with a matter. It's nothing illegal, mind you, and I'm willing to reward you substantially for your time and effort." Something in the tone of his voice kept the receiver to my ear. "Interested?"

"I still don't understand why you need my help."

"Well, one could say you have a reputation for being both resourceful and discrete."

It was true; we did get the occasional referral from past clients who appreciated the extra care I'd given to a loved one, but resourceful and discrete? Sounded like false flattery to me. "What's the catch?"

"No catch."

"I don't know . . ."

"Think about it." He had me write down his number, which I scribbled onto my napkin from breakfast. "If you want to save your business, give me a call. If not, well, your choice."

"Excuse me, but I didn't catch your name."

There was a click and the call ended. How did he know our business was in trouble?

RULE #23
TRUST THE DEAD.
THEY NEVER LIE.

Morning arrived veiled in a thick, ghostly fog. In swirling breaths, I told Adam it was two miles to the station. We'd have to pick up our pace if we were going to reach it in time. We walked without speaking, Adam's silence no more readable than the corner street signs. I had my own worries—like whether I was leading us down a rabbit hole that was better left ignored.

We had barely stepped onto the platform when the train to Millbrae pulled into the station. Commuters swarmed aboard like angry worker bees, sweeping us along. We made it into the last car and ended up honeycombed between a toothless woman who smelled like egg salad and a man whose briefcase swung into my leg each time he shifted his weight.

Twice Adam nearly exited at the wrong station. Each time I reminded him how lucky he was to have me along. It was a hard sell made harder after I missed our stop and we had to double back, costing us at least a half-hour delay. Oddly we were not the only ones; briefcase man and another guy made the same mistake. I might not have noticed the other man except his hair was much too dark for his complexion. It was the kind of DIY dye job I'd be all over fixing given half the chance.

At last we reached the correct station. We transferred to a BART train. This time we clung close to an exit, our backs pressed hard against the metal paneling of the car. With a lurch the train left the station. Adam grabbed hold of the nearest stanchion as though to yank it from its moorings and spike it through a window.

"You all right?" What a stupid question. Of course he wasn't.

"Can't breathe."

The people closest to us took a step back. One woman murmured a bit too loudly to her husband, "I think he's on something."

"Ignore her," I said and pointed to the map overhead, hoping to distract him. I explained that the green route was ours and began tracing it with a finger. Without warning, the train tunnel plunged beneath the bay. The daylight vanished, and the view became a stream of concrete rippling past, faster and faster.

Wide-eyed and frantic, Adam clawed at the door. "Let me out! Neil, let me out!"

"Adam. Adam!" I tugged at his jacket. The strangers penning us in drew back as far as was possible. "What are you staring at?" I snapped at them. "Adam, don't look out the window. Look at me." He turned to face me, and I gazed into his beautiful, terror-filled eyes and smiled. It worked. His shoulders relaxed ever so slightly. "Good. Now take slow, even breaths. That's it. We're almost clear."

A moment later the train resurfaced. The cool light of a dull day filled the car.

"*Twelfth Street*," announced a disembodied voice. The train slowed. The doors opened, and Adam leaped for the platform and kept on going. It was all I could do to keep up with him. He didn't stop until we were out of the station and on the street.

"Hold up," I panted. "I need to catch my breath." I guided him toward the alcove of a dress shop, where we took a moment to collect ourselves and get our bearings. "So what happened back there? A little claustrophobic, are we?"

"Maybe a little," he admitted. "But I'm better now. Thank you."

"No problem." I checked my watch. "All right then. It's nearly noon, and we've got about eight blocks to go. We have to hurry if we want to catch Veronica before she goes to lunch."

The streets were bustling with coffee-chugging, phone-chatting, laptop-lugging workers, all scurrying like lemmings to who knows where. After three blocks my left leg began to ache, and I was noticeably limping. Adam offered to stop, but I insisted we keep going.

At last we saw it: a gleaming tower like some obsidian mono-lith. Corporate intimidation honed to its finest. We scaled a broad stone staircase to the glass entry and went inside, where a half dozen boxed palms surrounded a grand fountain. A guard in a well-pressed blue suit sat behind a massive desk. Behind him, brushed-chrome letters spelled out PROCEA PHARMACEUTICALS, INC., WHERE LIFE MATTERS.

I approached the desk. "Could you direct us to the office of Veronica Forbes, please?"

"Do you have an appointment?"

"No," I admitted, "but I believe she'll want to talk to us."

"Your name?"

"Tell her Adam Lassiter," I said. I figured that would get her attention.

"One moment."

He called up to her office as Adam's fingers drummed out a jittery beat on the desktop. The guard glared in irritation, and I nudged Adam's foot to stop. We looked suspicious enough without him tapping it out for all to hear. But I understood his nervousness. What if she wouldn't see us? Would she recognize him? Would meeting her jog Adam's memories?

He dug his hands into his front pockets. "I want to see her alone."

"But—"

"I'm sorry," interrupted the guard, who did not appear at all apologetic. "She's not answering. Would you like to leave a message?"

"No, thank you. Well, Adam, looks like we came all this way for nothing."

"I told you it was a waste of time."

"Okay, you were right. Happy? I know this was a dumb idea, but I was trying . . ."

There was a *ping*, and an elevator opened to the left of the guard's desk. Three men and a woman all dressed in tailored suits emerged.

"That's her," said Adam.

"Are you sure? I thought you had no memory of her."

"I don't. I mean, I didn't think I did." He rubbed his head, confused. "But that's definitely . . . her."

"Ms. Forbes," called the guard. "These two young people are here to see you."

She kept walking but cast a token glance over her shoulder. "Do I know you?"

"This is Adam Lassiter?" I volunteered.

She stumbled forward like she'd suddenly caught a heel. One of her colleagues caught her by the arm. "You okay?" he asked.

"Yes, I'm fine. Go on without me. I'll catch you later," she answered, her nails digging into her leather clutch as she examined Adam's face more carefully. She scanned the lobby, waiting for the three men to leave, then tipped her head toward a side exit. "There's a boulangerie down the street. We can talk there."

If possible, Adam seemed even more tense now. He tried persuading me into meeting him in the Procea lobby in an hour, but I had sunk my teeth too deep to let go now. He was hiding something, and had been since I first laid eyes on him, half-dead from starvation. It was the one thing standing between us, the one thing I couldn't ignore.

Veronica checked her watch. "I have a meeting in forty-five minutes. I'm leaving now whether you two are coming or not."

"We're both coming," I said, with an emphasis on "both." Adam clearly was not happy about it.

It was the lunch-hour peak, and the restaurant was packed with people dressed as though they were all on their way to an internment: drab-colored slacks and pleated skirts, stiff black-leather shoes, crisp-pressed shirts with pointy collars. Veronica secured a booth toward the back, and as soon as we were seated a server plunked a basket of bread on the table. Veronica asked for a glass of wine and a side salad. I ordered two iced teas and a ham and cheese to share.

"Okay," Veronica said before either of us could explain why we were there. "Cut the crap. You two are working for Devlin, aren't you?"

"Who?" Adam asked, confused.

"Admit it, because if he sent you . . ."

"I have no idea who Devlin is," insisted Adam. "And—"

"And it's nothing like that," I added.

Veronica very deliberately set her reading glasses aside. "Then who are you? Because we both know you can't be Adam Lassiter. My son is dead."

I'd seen the grave, traced the letters engraved in the marker, and read her letter. This was exactly what I'd expected her to say. That didn't mean I hadn't left the door open to the possibility that it was some weird coincidence. That door had slammed shut.

What I did not expect was for Adam to be so crushed by her response. He was doing his best to mask it, but I knew him well enough by now to see beyond his blank stare and calm demeanor. I could sense the hope draining from him as he let out a long breath. He'd never lied to me. He simply didn't know his circumstances— and he still didn't. Worst of all, he'd been hoping this woman was his mother.

I slid out of the booth. "I'm so sorry. When we found your letter we thought, maybe . . . but I see now that we have the wrong person. Come on, Adam. We've taken enough of her time."

Adam rose from his seat, but Veronica's French-manicured

nails darted out and latched onto his wrist. "Letter? Tell me, who was it addressed to?"

"His father. Neil Lassiter," I said. "Again, we're sorry."

"Sit," she ordered, releasing Adam's hand. We hesitated a moment, nodded to each other, and retook our seats. "So Neil sent you."

"No. He's . . ." I stared at my fork.

"Deceased," Adam finished for me.

She bit her lip and gave a nod. "I was too late, then."

"No," said Adam, more calmly than I would have believed possible. "Your letter arrived in time to warn him."

"Then how . . . ?"

"I don't know exactly," he answered. "That's why we're here. One of the reasons. A month and a half ago, Neil received a letter we believe you sent. He . . . well, let's say he found a safer place for me to stay. There was an explosion, and he was killed. Investigators claim it was an accident. I have my doubts."

"What do you believe happened?"

"I believe he was murdered, but I can't prove it—not without your help. They said someone left the oven on. But Neil and I never used the oven."

"I don't doubt that. Neil was a brilliant chemist, but the worst cook imaginable."

"Yes," Adam agreed. "He once tried to convince me that the eggshells in my omelet were good for me. He said they were loaded with calcium for strong bones."

"I remember those omelets. Like leather. Awful." She paused. "Go on."

The server interrupted with our drinks. Veronica went straight for her glass of wine, downing at least a third before Adam could continue. "Like I said, there was a letter, and Lily—"

"Lily? The girl on the phone yesterday. That was you?"

"Yes," I answered.

Veronica Forbes eyed me knowingly. "And what's your connection to all this?"

"She's my . . ." Adam looked to me to finish the sentence for him, but I was hesitant to commit to a word.

When she realized she wasn't going to get an answer, Veronica asked, "So how did you find me?"

"Your name was in a local ancestry newsletter," I explained, grateful for the change of subject. "That led us to an announcement regarding your promotion at Procea. We looked up the number and called."

"When you hung up on us yesterday," added Adam, "we decided to come in person."

"And you used my son's name to get my attention. Well, it worked."

"But my name *is* Adam. Neil raised me as his . . . son. He never told me there was another Adam."

"I see. So you're saying that, when he adopted you, he gave you our son's name? Or was it a coincidence—?" Her voice caught. She pulled at the collar of her jacket, moisture pooling in her gold-flecked, brown eyes.

I offered her my napkin, but she refused it, saying, "This isn't easy for me, you know."

"I know." Boy, did I know.

It took her a moment to collect herself. "Five years ago there was an accident in my husband's laboratory. I'd cautioned our son repeatedly about sneaking into his father's lab, but he was nearly fifteen and well past listening to any of my warnings. I was at work, and Neil was slaving on one of his many projects. He stepped away and neglected to lock the door. Adam went down there, probably looking for his father. He idolized him, you know. Thought the sun rose and set at Neil's whim . . . Something went wrong. Neil did everything he could to save Adam, but it was too late. In the process Neil's hands were terribly burned. He nearly lost the use of them."

"He told me the scars were from playing with a campfire when he was a boy," said Adam.

"It was no campfire." She shook her head. "Neil always did have a tenuous relationship with the truth—and yet he demanded nothing else from others."

Adam touched his shirt as if verifying the inscription beneath. "Yes, he did."

"Was the accident ever reported?" I asked, still trying to account for the missing death certificate.

"Because of the nature of his work, Neil refused. He told the authorities we sent Adam to stay with relatives. After he buried Adam in the orchard, he buried himself in research. He changed. We both did. I shut myself off from the pain of my loss, from him, and from the world. I was as close to dead as a person can be and still have a breath in their body. Without Adam to keep us together, our marriage dissolved. It's taken me years to pull myself back from that dark place, but you never fully recover from the loss of a child. You learn to endure." She reached for her wine. "I'm not sure why

I'm telling you all of this. I've told no one before now. It's just, you look so much like him—or how I imagine he would have looked if he'd . . ."

Veronica drank her glass dry, and waved down the server for another, which quickly arrived along with her salad and our sandwich. She immediately lifted the glass to her lips and threw it back.

Watching her, I realized my own mouth was dry. I reached for my iced tea and noticed how the ice cubes distorted the view. This conversation was not so different. Everything I thought I knew about Adam and about Neil Lassiter's death was turning out to be a warped version of the truth. And how odd that Neil never mentioned to Veronica that he adopted a son. Maybe he wanted Adam all to himself. Adam had warned me that his father was unusually possessive. Strangest of all was that Adam recognized this woman the moment he saw her. None of it added up. Someone was lying.

"So what do you want from me? Money?" she asked.

Adam looked up from his folded hands. "No. I don't want money. The police closed the case. Federal investigators are calling it an accident. I want to know who is responsible for Neil's death. You're my only hope."

"The feds are involved in this?" She shoved an avocado slice across her plate, then stabbed a tomato wedge with her fork. "That's not good."

"Give me a name," said Adam. "Is it this Miles person you mentioned in your letter?"

"You don't know what you're asking."

"Actually he does," I said, recalling the night he was jumped on the way to Zmira's. "We have reason to believe that whoever killed Neil may be looking for Adam. We need to know who and why."

She glanced about the room. "Look, I've spent years in hiding thanks to what Neil did, and now you've put us all in danger."

Adam was losing his patience. His fist hit the table "I—want—his—name!"

The people nearest us gawked and whispered at the sudden outburst.

"All right. Keep your voice down." Veronica didn't speak again until the guests at the surrounding tables returned to their conversations. "I'll tell you what I can, but it isn't much." Her voice went so soft, Adam and I had to lean across the table to hear her. "A couple months ago, I received a phone call. The caller didn't give me his name, but I knew it was Miles." She sighed. "The name you want is Miles Devlin." She downed the rest of the wine and pushed the glass to the edge of the table for a server to collect.

"Who is Miles Devlin?" I asked.

She studied Adam. "You swear he didn't send you to find me?"

"We swear," Adam assured her. "I've never heard of him before."

"I suppose that's no surprise. Neil kept his secrets for a good reason. Years ago, Neil, Miles, and I worked for Arman Research. Technically it's an independent government defense contractor, but Neil, Miles, and another man were hired to work on what was referred to as the Seed of Life Project. Or so we thought."

I looked up from the twisted napkin in my hands. "The Seed of Life Project?"

"It had to do with soil."

I felt Adam tense beside me. "Oh, like, for growing things," I said, recalling his earlier words.

"That's right. They . . ." She hesitated. "Well, the truth is I was never privy to the specifics other than the project had to do with soil properties."

I think she knew more than she was telling us. I remembered all those barrels of dirt stored in the fallout shelter. Maybe Neil was conducting studies independently. The orchard could very easily have been a natural extension of his research. "But what does dirt have to do with defense other than bulwarks and trenches?"

Again her attention fell to Adam. There was something in her stare. She rocked back in her seat, wary. "Look, you asked for a name and the reason why. I've given you the name. The why is what Neil did to Miles. Neil was lead scientist, but then there was talk of handing the project over to Miles, who was not only Neil's subordinate but also his closest friend. Neil was incensed. He felt he'd been betrayed by the corporation, by Miles, by . . . well, by me."

"Why you?" asked Adam.

She took a deep breath and briefly closed her eyes. "Miles and I had a . . ."

"Relationship?" I guessed.

She nodded. "It was before Neil and I were married."

"So what happened to the Seed of Life Project?" I asked.

"Shortly after Miles took over, some important research documents went missing. Evidence pointed to Miles because he was the only person authorized to work on the project at that point. When news of the scandal broke, Arman attempted damage control. The stolen documents were never found. Funding was diverted, Miles went to prison, and the program was scrapped."

"Is it true what you said in the letter about Neil framing Miles?" asked Adam.

"I'm afraid so."

"So Neil stole the documents," I guessed.

She shrugged but didn't deny it.

"Did you have to testify?"

"No. I refused. I wanted my son to have a father. As a result, Devlin got ten years. Then, three months ago, my lawyer called to tell me Miles had been released early for good behavior. Naturally I was nervous. Miles had more-than-good reason to hold a grudge against Neil and me, and I was afraid of how far he'd take it. Shortly after that he called me. He said he forgave me for what I did, but I didn't believe him. How does someone forgive something like that? But he was looking for Neil. They had business to settle. I felt I should warn Neil. I couldn't bring myself to speak to him directly, so I wrote the letter."

Veronica jabbed her fork at Adam's face. "Now. I've answered your questions. Time for you to answer mine."

At that precise moment, Adam knocked over his glass. A stream of iced tea cascaded off the edge of the table and into my lap. "Ahh!" I screeched as liquid and ice met skin.

A server rushed over with a towel to sop up the mess. Adam kept repeating, "I'm sorry, so sorry."

"Excuse me." I wound my way through the restaurant to the ladies' room, as much to dry off as to collect myself. Veronica had more or less confirmed my suspicions: Adam was not Neil's son. He wasn't even a Lassiter. I wasn't convinced he'd been adopted, either. There should have been records, but I'd found nothing. If he wasn't Adam Lassiter, then who was he and how was it that he remembered Veronica and the day I fell from the walnut tree?

After a few minutes under the hand dryer, my skirt was still damp, but if I stood there any longer, my thighs would blister. I left the restroom just as two city inspectors entered the restaurant through a back door. The taller of the two turned slightly as he scouted the place, and a chill passed through me that had nothing to do with my damp clothing. It was the briefcase man from the train, only he'd changed clothes and ditched the case. And his cohort was none other than bad-dye-job guy, who was now sporting a cap.

Head lowered, I took a roundabout route back to the booth. Veronica and Adam were so deep in conversation, neither heard me approach.

" . . . that my suspicions are wrong," Veronica was saying, her voice stern, her tone grave. "But if I'm right, God save us all, and if you care anything for that girl, which I see you do, then you will get as far away from her as you can."

Adam's eyes gave me away, and Veronica abruptly fell silent and began searching for her clutch, which had fallen to the floor.

I slumped into my seat, still processing her words but with one eye on the two supposed city inspectors, who were still sizing up the restaurant.

"You've gone pale. Well, paler," observed Adam. "Something wrong?"

"See those two men by the condiments?" I said. "They were

on the train with us. The one's briefcase kept swinging into my leg. Could they be the men from the alley?"

"I didn't get a good look that night, but they could be."

Veronica snuck a peek, then masked her face with a handy dessert menu.

"You know them, don't you?" I accused.

"Not personally. Neil used to have drinks with them occasionally when we were both at Arman. They were with the FBI back then."

"Suppose they're investigating Neil's death?"

"Hardly. They both left the bureau not long after the scandal broke. I must warn you—soon after Miles was arrested, the one other researcher working on the project was found strung up in his apartment. It was ruled a suicide, but I've always had my doubts. Then, during his trial, Miles slipped me a note via his lawyer telling me to watch my back. I never knew if the note was a threat or a warning. Looks like they followed you here. I want to know why."

Veronica and I both turned to Adam. "Don't look at me!" he said. "I don't know—"

"They're coming this way," hissed Veronica. She dropped a wad of cash next to her salad plate, then gestured with her head toward a chorus of servers delivering a birthday sundae to the booth behind us. The moment the servers burst into song, she scooted out of the booth and motioned for us to follow.

We walked casually through the restaurant, avoiding any undue attention and keeping our backs to the two men. We didn't stop until we'd made it to the corner half a block away. By then my heart was pounding.

"Veronica, where are you taking us?" Adam asked.

"I'm not taking you anywhere. By coming here, you put me at risk now, too. You're going back to wherever you came from and never contacting me again. Understand?"

We both nodded.

The signal to cross the street turned green just as the two men appeared outside the restaurant. "Go," she ordered with a sharp wave of her hand. Adam and I needed no more encouragement. We merged into the crowd of pedestrians surging across the street. Halfway across, I glanced back. Veronica had vanished.

I led us the long way back to the station on the off chance the ex-feds spotted us crossing the street. The throbbing in my hip grew sharper with every jog, but I didn't dare slow down. We jumped aboard the next BART train, and to our relief our only company was an old woman seated across from us, her *Reader's Digest* rising and falling with each snore.

We'd lost our pursuers—unless they knew where we lived.

RULE #24
WHEN ALL ELSE FAILS,
WASH THE HEARSE.

"It's impossible," I told Adam. "I've tried."

"But you found Veronica Forbes," he argued.

I plunked the bucket down. Liquid sloshed over the rim, making a sudsy mess. "She wasn't a murder suspect. For all we know Miles Devlin is miles away by now and using an assumed name. I don't know what else I can do. Maybe it's time to move on."

I expected him to yell back or hit something. That's what the Adam I found in the fallout shelter two months ago might have done. Instead he retreated to the garden to weed whack away his frustration while I finished washing the hearse.

Later that afternoon I found a set of gold teeth in a plastic bag on my desk, accompanied by a note from Tony asking me to log them (welcome to my world), and a potted pansy from Adam. A pansy, to mean "think of me." As if I didn't already do that 24-7. I viewed his pathetic offering as a plea to continue the search for Miles Devlin. He was obsessed with finding the man he blamed for his father's death, and nothing I said could convince him he was asking the impossible.

Still, the plant with its perky green leaves and crimson-and-gold blossoms was a cheery thing, full of vigor and optimism, so I carried the pot up to my room and placed it on my dresser, beneath my window. I gave it a healthy drink, accidentally dripping some water on the napkin holding the mystery caller's number. Some of the ink blurred, but whatever. The guy was either hoping to worm some tabloid-worthy info on Adam out of me or was working for Sturbridge. With all that had happened recently, I wasn't about to trust anyone right now—not even Adam.

Dad called for me. "Be right there," I hollered back. I wadded up the napkin and tossed it in the trash.

Dad was propped up in his bed, surrounded by a half dozen pillows and nearly as many remotes. The room smelled of stale coffee and ointments, furniture polish and Rachel's favorite body spray—something called Patience. He muted the cooking show on the small flatscreen we brought up from the office. "If you're not busy, would you mind bringing up the paper?" He was probably the last person on our block who still got his news the old-fashioned way.

"Sure." I trudged downstairs, where Nana was pinching clay onto a small human-shaped armature. "That for your sculpture class?" I asked.

"Yes. I need it for tonight, but I can't get the head right. It's either too big or too small. I asked Adam to model for me, but you'd think I asked him to pose nude by the way he raced out of here."

That was odd. Adam never struck me as being particularly modest. "Did you try Evan? Oh wait, his head's too big." I laughed at my own joke all the way to the porch, where I spied Mr. Zmira on the sidewalk. He was wrestling with his snarling, soggy mop dog and cursing our broken sprinkler.

Immediately I felt the familiar prickling up and down my arms but was determined to override my fear. In that singsong voice I reserved for teachers, I said, "Hello, Mr. Zmira."

He grumbled a stream of obscenities and stormed off.

With the all clear, I went curbside to fetch the damp paper. Nana Jo intercepted me on my way back in and offered an exchange— today's mail for the entertainment section.

"Done," I said, and hustled upstairs, arms loaded.

I handed Dad the stack. "Nana hijacked the entertainment section. Sorry."

"Al Pacino?"

"Yup. A whole retrospective piece on his career." Nana had a thing for Al Pacino. It went back to the first time she saw *The Godfather*. She watched *Scent of a Woman* so many times, she wore out the DVD.

Dad fished out the classifieds.

"Looking for anything in particular?" I poured him a glass of water from the pitcher on the bureau.

"I want to see if our ad ran."

I set down the pitcher with a *clunk*. "What ad?"

"Our ad for the business. We've decided the time has come to sell."

We? I stood there, my jaw slack. I didn't bother arguing that we could find new vendors. I didn't suggest we build our own crematorium, advertise more, or try any of the ideas I'd come up with on my own. It was too late for that.

"Don't feel too bad," said Dad, misreading my stunned silence. "Although I'll never understand why you refuse to take over the reins. Our profession is an honorable one, and you may not see it, but you have a gift for it, more than I ever did."

"But you always say I'm too sensitive for this line of work. You never like my ideas."

"I know I can be a bit hard on you, but it's because I want you to be better than me. Believe it or not, when I first started out, I struggled to hold myself together, too. My father's solution was to knock me upside the head. Be grateful times have changed."

"I never knew that," I said, unable to picture my grim-faced father with so much as a moist eye. All this time I thought I was letting him down. "You can't sell, Dad. You've worked too hard for so long."

"Rachel, the doctors . . . they all tell me it's time I retire, and, much as I hate to admit it, I'm done. I don't have it in me anymore. Holding it together takes a lot out of you."

Don't I know.

"I only hung in there this long because I hoped you'd stay on." Dad's voice softened. "Truth is I don't want to lose you, kiddo."

So much for not letting him down. "I'm not Mom. You're not going to lose me. I just want to lead my own life and do what suits me best. I know I've said it before, but what about Evan?"

"I love that boy, but he's about as compassionate as a watermelon. Besides, he's decided on game design. Not my choice for him, but I guess it isn't mine to make. So we're selling. Nana Jo's a bit disappointed, of course, but she'll get over it. And as she's always said, life is short. I've seen that firsthand." He patted his chest and cast a weak smile I couldn't return. "Oh, cheer up. This is what you wanted, isn't it? To get out of the mortuary business?" Dad rubbed his eyes. "Of course, it's going to be a challenge finding a buyer in this market, but with any luck, Sturbridge is still interested."

"Please tell me you won't sell to that sleaze."

"Let him have it. He can deal with the headaches. Would serve him right."

"But he doesn't care about people. It's all about business to him."

"I can't worry about that. I can only do what's best for our family. Rachel and I want to open that bakery we've always talked about." He flapped a hand weakly. "Yes, I know what you're thinking, the 'dismal trade' is all I've ever known, but I'm ready for a new adventure. And if we don't do it now, we might miss our chance. I even have a business name: Dawn of the Bread."

Kill me now. "What about Tony? Have you told him?"

"Tony's going to be fine." He screwed up his face, pretending to have a mouth full of cotton, and said, "EMS made him an offer he couldn't refuse."

"That isn't funny."

"Oh, come on, smile. I thought that was a great *Godfather* imitation."

I couldn't smile, not when I was trying so hard not to scream or, worse yet, cry.

"The point is we all know I can't afford to pay Tony what they can or to match the benefits. Of course he said he'd rather stay with us, but he has a family of his own now. He gave us a month's notice. By then I should be back on my feet or, better yet, we'll have our buyer."

I said nothing. After all, I was the one who screwed up the crematorium deal. If I'd followed my own rules and kept my mouth shut, none of this would have happened. Even if I agreed to take over for Dad and Rachel, running a funeral home was a team effort, and I had no team.

Rachel poked her head through the doorway. "How we doing in here? Can I get you anything, Cam?"

"No, I'm good."

"Did you tell her?"

"Yeah, I told her."

What am I? Invisible?

Neither one noticed me shuffle back to my room. They had every right to pursue other ambitions, and I supposed that if I told them I made a huge mistake, changed my mind, and now wanted to earn my mortician certification, they'd support that, too. But if the sale went through, it would mean working elsewhere. I didn't know if I could do that. *Here* had history—our history. It was where my ancestors carved out a living shortly after coming to this country. Grandpa Ted proposed to Nana Jo on the front porch. There was still a crack in the ceiling from the 1906 earthquake and a cradle stashed in the attic that had rocked four generations of McCraes. It deserved a fifth. To abandon this house, this business, would be to throw that all away.

If we'd bought the crematorium, gotten out of debt, and paid off our bills, then maybe Dad wouldn't be considering selling and I could have a do-over. I'd learn how to better deal with people without taking it all so personally. I could study mortuary science *and* business at the local college and talk Tony into staying on. I'd do whatever it took to make us the best funeral home in town—the way it used to be.

But the opportunity for the crematorium was gone. There was only one thing left to try.

I removed the scrunched and soggy napkin from the trash, did my best to decipher the blurred number, and dialed, hoping I got it right. Maybe I was that desperate.

"Hello, Lily." There was no hint of surprise in the raspy voice on the other end. "I knew you'd call."

RULE #25
A BIT OF BLING IS THE PERFECT DISTRACTION FROM AN IMPERFECTION.

I made a final check to make sure I hadn't been followed. With a book tucked under my arm, I entered Hole-in-the-Wall Bagels, where the mystery caller and I had agreed to meet. After the incident in Oakland with the two ex-feds, I couldn't be too careful.

Inside the shop bustled with people seeking a carb-and-caffeine fix to start their day. No one hailed me, so I grabbed a seat in the corner and pretended to read *DOWN UNDER: Diary of an Aussie Mortician.*

This was absurd. I wasn't even sure what the guy looked like. He claimed he knew me by my reputation, but if he was a previous client, why not say so? Or maybe this was all part of some screwy sales tactic. He probably wanted to talk me into a new line of caskets or brand of cosmetics. That was a pitch for Rachel or Dad—not me. There was still a possibility that he worked for Sturbridge. But if there was even the slightest chance he had a way for me to save the business, I was all ears.

I should have been home packing. The annual beach party

marking the end of summer was tomorrow. The only reason I'd agreed to go was because it would be Adam's first trip to the shore . . . and, okay, because I had visions of us strolling through the sand, scouting tide pools, and wading in the surf. Maybe there would even be a moment of hand-holding. A kiss.

Whoa, girl! Take it easy. I shook myself back to reality. What had gotten into me? I took a deep gulp of ice water, then gave each of my burning cheeks a brisk pat.

"Hot Mayan cocoa with an everything bagel, walnut-and-honey cream cheese," called the girl behind the counter. I liked the sound of an everything bagel. I was up to here with "not enough." Not enough business, not enough money, not enough courage to order what I wanted—a chance to be more than a makeup artist to the dead.

A cyclist coasted up to the shop and dragged his foot, bringing his bike to a stop. It was the same man I spotted outside our house fixing his bike, the one who asked if I'd found the boy at the Lassiter place, the guy possibly connected to Adam's assault. I untangled my legs beneath the table, ready to make a run for it.

He chained his bike to a scraggly gingko at the curb, came inside, and scouted the shop. His glasses were the sort that darkened in the sun, but the film had worn off around the edges, giving the lenses a halo effect. He was a scarecrow of a man, with sallow skin that nearly hung off his bones. Thin wisps of gray hair were plastered across his sweaty forehead. There were bruises on his arms.

I'd seen these same traits too many times not to recognize the signs. Chemo.

He spotted me staring and sidled up to the table. "We've met before," I said. "You're not one of those stalker types, are you?" That was a stupid question. What was he going to say?

"No. It's nothing like that, I assure you." He indicated the seat opposite mine—"May I?"—and took it without waiting for an answer. He had to be the man I'd called.

"Sorry," I said, "but who are you?"

"Where are my manners? Miles Devlin." He extended his hand.

"M-Miles Devlin?" I said, nearly choking on my own tongue. The man Veronica suggested was responsible for Neil Lassiter's death? I rose from the edge of my seat. "I'm sorry. I think—"

He gently placed his gnarled hand on mine. "Please. Sit. Hear me out."

"Why should I?"

"Because I'm here to help. And because"—he waved a hand at the crowded restaurant—"it's not as if we're meeting in a back alley somewhere, now is it?"

It did seem safe here, or safe enough for me to at least listen to what he had to say. (Yes, I was that desperate.) "Okay, but I can't stay long. I'm meeting a friend."

From the way he twitched one brow, I could tell he wasn't even close to believing me. "No worries. I plan to keep this short for both our sakes. If at any time you're uncomfortable, all you have to do is ask me to leave. Fair enough?"

By now the server was giving us the stink eye, so we each ordered a bagel, mine everything, his plain. He waited for the server to leave before continuing. "As I believe I mentioned over the phone, I need your assistance with a small matter. I used to work with Neil Lassiter. I believe you know who he is?"

I made a sound like something was caught in my throat. "No, I—"

His rubber band lips stretched tight across his gaunt face, stopping me in the midst of yet another lie. "Please." He leaned in. "I happen to know that you and two others were nosing around the Lassiter property a couple weeks after that tragic explosion."

There was a hint of sarcasm in the way he said "tragic" that raised goose bumps along my arms. "How do you know that?"

"It was all over the news. You and your friends are quite the heroes," he said, but his tone suggested he suspected otherwise. "What I'm wondering is why you were there in the first place."

I shrank back into the vinyl upholstery. "We didn't mean any harm. We were exploring, you know—looking for things. We would've turned anything valuable over to the police."

"Naturally. But you didn't, did you? Turn over anything, that is?"

I shook my head.

"If this is going to work, we'll need to trust each other." He waited as the server delivered our order, then took a bite and, with a full mouth, said, "Let me tell you a story, Lily." He swallowed. "You like a good story? Silly question. Of course you do. Who doesn't? The thing is *you* can give this one a good ending. You see, years ago Neil Lassiter stole some valuable research from the government. Research he and I developed together."

So you say.

"He framed me for the theft and sent me to prison."

So far everything he was saying jived with Veronica's story, but I still didn't see what this had to do with me. And if this *was* Miles Devlin, the man Veronica referred to in her letter to Neil, then I was sitting with a possible murderer. At the very least I was talking to someone who knew much more about me than I did about him, placing me at a frightening disadvantage.

I got right to the point. "Did you have anything to do with the explosion that killed Neil Lassiter?"

He considered me carefully. "Would you believe me if I told you no?"

"Probably not."

"Honest answer. I like that."

He wasn't exactly denying responsibility. "My friend will be here any minute," I reminded him.

"Yes, you mentioned that before. You're referring to the Lassiter boy, aren't you?"

"Maybe." I squirmed in my seat.

"Yes. You saved his life. And so now you're friends. Good friends?"

"I guess. Yeah."

"Well, friends are good, but they aren't always who they appear to be. There was a time when I considered Neil Lassiter a friend. That assumption cost me eight years of my life."

"Adam is nothing like Neil Lassiter," I said.

"And how do you know that? He tell you about his . . . upbringing?"

"Enough. He doesn't remember much."

"You don't say." Devlin grinned in a way that made me uncomfortable.

"You talk like you know something more about Adam."

"How could I know more? Adam and I have never met."

"I see." But not really. I was flying in the dark here, everyone with their secrets—Veronica, Devlin, Adam, and now me. "What do you want from me exactly?"

"Ah. Right. What I want from you is a small thing. Should you know or learn from a certain someone—a certain friend, perhaps—as to where I might find those research documents, I would be most grateful. I know better than some that gratitude won't put food on the table or save a failing business, so I'm prepared to reward you substantially for your assistance."

If those research documents existed at all, they could be stashed anywhere—a storage locker, or an abandoned building maybe. My money was on the fallout shelter, although I saw no sign of them on the day we explored it. Besides, I'd have to be insane to go back into that death trap. Who's to say they didn't burn in the fire?

"Why don't you ask this *certain someone* yourself?"

He gazed out the window toward a dilapidated warehouse across the street. "I think you and I both know why."

If he's afraid of Adam, he has a right to be. I've seen what Adam's capable of. "And how is it that you know so much about me and my family's business?"

"I told you: I'm a researcher by trade."

"Then why can't you find the documents yourself?"

"My probation officer might not approve, so, you see, the less I nose around the neighborhood, the better. As it is, I took a big risk meeting you here, but I have reason to believe you're the sort to help an old man in need of a second chance to make things right. All I'm asking is for you to call me if you know where I can find the documents."

"Not that I'm agreeing . . . but if I were to agree to this, how will I recognize the documents?"

"That's a good question, and it makes me think I'm right about you. You're a bright girl. You remind me of myself when I was your age—a loner, a bit ill at ease in the world, but smart."

No one had ever called me smart before, but I knew enough not to trust his flattery.

"You'll know the documents by this symbol." He made a small sketch of interlocking rings on the corner of a takeout menu. "I see from your expression that it's not completely unfamiliar."

"I think I saw it once, in one of my biology books," I said, trying to sound convincing.

"Then you know it represents the Seed of Life?"

"Sure. But why don't you tell me what you know about it."

"Okay." He smiled at the game we were both playing. "As you know, it's a universal symbol for creation."

"Creation? Adam said his father was working with soils, like for gardening."

"Hmm. Yes, well, gardening is a form of creation, isn't it?"

"So these documents you're looking for, they have to do with the Seed of Life Project?"

"Precisely."

"And that's it?"

"That's it."

There had to be more to it than he was letting on. "I don't know. Say I do find these papers. What do you plan to do with them?"

"Ensure that they never fall into the wrong hands." He pulled a billfold from his back pocket and laid a hundred-dollar bill in front of me. "Take it."

"I can't." I pushed it back toward him, but he folded the bill in half lengthwise and slipped it between the pages of my book. "This"—he patted the book jacket—"is a token of my faith in you to do the right thing."

"I don't want your money," I said, looking once more out the window. "I haven't done anything to earn it."

"You came here, didn't you? Your time is worth something. Besides, you need it more than me. I have no family and, according to the doctors, not much time, either. Liver cancer. I don't mind telling you, it's a shitty way to die."

I recalled Anna Pendlebury and George Davies. "One of the shittiest."

"All I'm asking is for you to help me locate some papers. If you do that for me, I promise the last thing I do in this life will be to make sure your family's financial problems go away for good."

This man knew way too much about me, and yet the obvious signs of his illness made me want to believe him. One thing still nagged at me. "How can you afford to pay me if you can't afford a decent bike or a car?"

"Call me sentimental. The bike was a gift from a dear, sweet lady; I haven't been able to part with it. But your question is a reasonable one. Some years ago I bought stock in a little upstart dotcom enterprise, and, as you know, I can't take it with me, now can I?"

I leaned back in my seat. "No, but you'd be surprised how many try. There's a fortune buried in the ground: wedding rings, priceless heirlooms, cash. I think some people are under the impression they can buy their way into heaven."

He laughed hoarsely. "No, I'm afraid bribery only works when we're alive, and even then, it's a risky proposition."

"Honestly, though, I have no idea where the research notes might be."

"Maybe not, but with a little resourcefulness and the right incentive, I think you have a far better shot at finding them without drawing unnecessary attention than I do. I'm gambling on you. I don't have a choice; they're watching me."

"Who's watching you? Your probation officer?"

He inhaled deep and let out a long, drawn-out breath. "Look. I'm doing my best here, to protect you. Like I said, the less you know, the better. Even so, be careful."

"I gotta go."

"I'll be waiting to hear from you," he said, "but remember, it's crucial that we keep this strictly between us. No one—and I mean *no one*—can know about our little arrangement, including your young . . . friend. It might get back to the wrong people—people who aren't afraid to kill for what they want. Understand? Bad for me, bad for you."

I nodded, blinking a little too rapidly, and slid from my seat. "I'll think about it, Mr. Devlin."

"Please do. And watch your back."

I rushed out the door, my book clutched tight to my chest, the hundred-dollar bill still tucked inside.

I'd either made a pact with the devil or found a way to save the mortuary.

RULE #26
Even endings have ends.
Learn to say goodbye with grace.

On the way home, I resolved not to tell Adam about my meeting with Miles Devlin. I was afraid to, since all he'd talked about after our trip to Oakland was what he would do to Devlin when he found him. I felt like a traitor.

I put off packing for the beach trip again and dug into my list of chores. I was the only person my age that I knew of whose family responsibilities included folding body bags and polishing caskets.

My duffel was still sitting empty on my bedroom floor when Mallory arrived in the late afternoon. "Tell me you're not backing out on me."

A loud slap on my door saved me from answering. "Hey, you two," crowed Evan. He was in a pair of running shorts with a towel draped around his neck.

"Evan, you're still going tomorrow, aren't you?" asked Mal.

"Yup, all ready." He flexed what he referred to as his "guns" as in "loaded and ready for action." Mallory beamed at him, and I swore he puffed out his chest a little more. The rooster. "I'm gonna jump in the shower and then make a run to the store to pick up some drinks for tomorrow. You two wanna come?"

"I'll go!" Mal cheered like she was one number from winning the lottery. "You don't mind, do you, Lils? It'll give you more time to pack."

"No, course not. Go without me."

"If you're sure." Mallory tugged the hem of her shirt down to reveal more bronzer-enhanced cleavage and did a hair-flip thing. "I'm going to get a bottle of water. You want any, Evan?"

"Nah, I'm good," he said.

I noticed she didn't ask me. Once she was out of hearing range, I laid it all out for my brother. "You know she's totally crushin' on you, right?"

"Mallory? Okay, yeah, so that's too weird and potentially very messy. Ugh." He shuddered. "Why'd you have to tell me that?"

"Because I don't want her to get hurt."

"O ye of little faith. By the way, did you hear? Adam quit this morning."

"He quit? Why?"

"Ask him. He's in his room packing right now."

He must have found out about my meeting with Devlin, but how?

I hobbled back to the cottage and knocked on the door. When there was no answer, I shouted, "Adam. Adam, open up!" I raised a fist to pound again when the door flew open.

Adam held a stuffed pillowcase in one hand. "Lily, what—?"

"Evan told me you quit." I barged past him and into the room.

"Were you even going to tell me?" I wore my hurt like a suit of armor.

"I did tell you."

"No, you didn't. I think I would remember."

"The pansy? Think of me, as in when I'm gone?"

"Is that what that meant?"

"I thought it was obvious."

"Well, it wasn't. And where exactly do you think you'll go?"

He shrugged. "Home?"

"And what, sleep in the dirt? Are you serious? Adam, this is your home. I thought you liked it here. I thought . . ."

I couldn't bring myself to say any more because I saw now that I thought wrong. He didn't care for me, not in the way I imagined. But at least here he had a roof over his head, a few dollars in his pocket, and people who cared. "Why would you leave us?" *Why would you leave me?*

"I thought it's what you wanted when you said it was time for me to move on."

I released the breath I hadn't realized I was holding. This had nothing to do with my meeting Devlin. "Oh, Adam, it never occurred to me you'd take it literally." Although knowing him, it should have. "All I meant was that you need to look past all that's happened and toward your future."

He dropped onto the edge of the bed and wouldn't look me in the eye. If this were a game of Name That Expression, I'd have called it regret. "It's more than that, isn't it?"

He nodded. "My father died protecting me, and you heard

what Veronica said. Those two men who followed us to Oakland won't give up until they have what they want. As long as I'm here, I pose a risk to your family."

"How do you know?"

"I know."

"You're safer here than out on the streets somewhere, and with Dad out of commission, we need you. I need you."

He lifted his eyes to meet mine. "It's you I'm thinking of."

"But you promised to help me find a way to save the mortuary." I saw from the way his face fell that he'd been hoping I forgot.

"I will, but not from here."

"How 'bout this: you stay until the issues with the funeral home are resolved. I overheard Dad tell Evan this morning that he expected to hear something within a week or so. Deal?"

"No deal."

"At least give us the weekend to work something out. You've never been to the ocean, and no one will bother us there. We'll be safe. If you still want to move out when we get back, I'll help you find somewhere to go."

He considered this for a moment, then upended the pillowcase, dumping its few items onto the bed. "Okay."

I'd take what I could get. Besides, if we lost the mortuary, we'd all be looking for a new place to live.

❋ ❋ ❋

Life was really weird. The family business was tanking. I was supposed to find and deliver papers to an ex-con. There was a good chance we had a pair of rogue ex-FBI agents on our tail. Adam wanted to leave.

And yet here we were, crammed in the van with all our gear, winding our way through the Santa Cruz Mountains toward the coast, and all wearing matching flip-flops. Mallory's big idea.

Totally weird.

Up front, Mal channel surfed the radio while Evan surfed the highway and rattled on about league standings. Beside me, Adam stared out the window, counting off memorial markers. One was surrounded by stuffed animals: Easter bunnies, reindeer, bears with flannel hearts—all tokens of holidays missed. Another wore wreaths of faded silk flowers. The third was a simple white cross. "Place markers or hazard warnings?" he wondered aloud.

Once we exited the highway, we cruised past produce stands and artichoke fields to join a parade of cars heading to the state beach. Evan was lucky to snag a space in the parking lot next to the fenced-off revegetation zone. He cut the engine and we unloaded. Swarms of beachgoers trudged up the dunes, their pilgrimage to this mecca of sand and surf nearly complete. Soon they would all gather on the wind-swept shore, bow to the hovering sun, and crack open the ice chests. No parents, no work, no worries—well, almost. For some there were still the competitions. My worry was devising a way to save our family's livelihood while convincing Adam to stay.

Mallory flung out her arms and took a long drag of the briny breeze. "Yeah, baby, bring on the negative ions."

I did the same, hoping the ocean air would lift my spirits. "Yeah, this is the best," I said, but I wasn't feeling it. The day was warming up fast. I unzipped my hoodie and tossed it into the car.

"What's that loop thing on your shirt mean?" asked Adam.

"The pink bow? Breast cancer awareness," I explained.

"Not very sexy," noted Mallory, barging between us to retrieve a Sunbrella.

"Neither is a mastectomy," I pointed out, and handed Adam a towel.

"That's what I love about you, Lils," said Evan with a fake punch to my shoulder. "Always a ray of sunshine."

Maybe so, but it's hard to be sunny when you're losing everything you care about.

An El Camino squeezed into the sliver of space beside our van. Justin Blackwell climbed out from behind the wheel, followed by his sister, Dana, who was wearing these ridiculous rhinestone sandals and had a vibrant paisley scarf tied low on her hips. "Hey, guys," she said with her signature fluttery hyper wave.

"Oh, joy," mumbled Mallory. "Look who's here."

Dana sauntered over to Evan, doing this runway thing with her shoulders and hips. When Mal gave her the evil eye, Dana's attention shifted to Adam. "And who do we have here?" she cooed, rummaging through her bag. Now *I* was the one wishing she'd take a long walk off a short pier.

"*This* is Adam," Mallory volunteered in a perfect imitation of Dana's skanky warble.

"Hey, Adam, do me a favor, will you? Rub some sunblock on my back." She passed him a tube and peeled off her cover-up. Adam squeezed out much more lotion than he needed and began slathering it all over her pumpkin-colored, spray-tanned skin. She was too busy flaunting the Italian she'd picked up during her semester in Florence to notice. I swore if she giggled or said, "*Oh, le tue mani sono così fredde, Adam, sono così fredde!*" ("Oh, your hands are cold, Adam, your hands are cold!") one more time, *my* cold hands would be around her scrawny neck.

Adam stepped back to assess the results. Intentional or not, Dana looked battered and ready for the deep fryer. I suppressed a smile and gave him a thumbs-up.

With gear loaded and van locked, everyone began the long slog over the dunes toward the beach—everyone except Adam. He was too busy testing the sand at the edge of the boardwalk with his toes to notice the others were leaving without us.

"Come on," I said. "There's plenty more on the other side."

Together we started up the first set of dunes with only the sound of sifting sand under our bare feet to break the stilted silence. With his long, steady strides, he quickly outpaced me. Three-quarters of the way up, I stopped to catch my breath beside a patch of icicle plants. Hands on knees, huffing and puffing, I searched for our van to see how far I'd come. A familiar-looking SUV with no plates cruised through the parking lot.

Did they follow us here? Or did they just assume we'd be at the beach bash like every other teen in town?

I sank to the ground behind my beach chair and prayed we hadn't been spotted. Most likely they were searching for Adam. Why, I still didn't know. Luckily he was already on the other side of the dune.

The SUV trolled slowly up one row and down another. It passed the last two open parking spots and coasted to a stop at the base of the dune. I sighed a moment later when the vehicle moved on, leaving the lot. By time I caught up to Adam, he was already starting up the second and final set of dunes. I said nothing about the car. Why give him one more reason to leave if the danger had passed?

"Beautiful," he said from the crest of the second rise. Below us a carpet of sand rolled down the hill to meet the sea where breakers thundered through the arched rocks. Gulls reeled overhead, and colorful kites fluttered like confetti in the steady breeze.

"It's even better up close. Race you."

There was a twitch at the corner of his mouth—my only warning—and then he was off in a mad sprint down the dune. "Hey, not fair," I shouted and gave chase, careening over clumps of sea grass and dodging the catawampus fence posts that dotted the slope. He sailed across the rock-and-shell-cobbled sand and bounded straight into the foaming brine. Teeter-tottering his arms to keep his balance, he waded in up to his chest, oblivious to the wave surging toward him. Did he know how to swim? How could he?

The swell crested, curled up and over his tawny head, and swallowed him whole.

Galloping toward the water, I left a trail of clothes, towels, and sunblock in my wake. I leaped in up to my thighs and scanned for any sign of Adam. I was about to hail a lifeguard when he rose from the sea like Neptune.

Amazing what a few weeks of healthy eating and digging dirt can do for a body, I thought as he splashed toward me. I was so mesmerized that I was completely unprepared for the force of the next incoming wave. It swept my legs out from beneath me and took me under. Turning and rolling, I couldn't tell which way was up. Finally my head broke the surface. I gulped in air and struggled to my feet.

Those onshore gawked and pointed at the spectacle. Nearby in the surf, Evan cupped his hands to his mouth. "Hey, Lily, I'd think twice about thrashing around like that. You're liable to attract sharks." Dana burst into spastic laughter and together they swam off.

Ouch.

Adam flipped back his dripping hair and strode right past me as I limped onshore, briny and bedraggled. "I thought you were in trouble," I explained.

"Do you even know how to swim?"

I didn't appreciate his condescending tone. "It's more like a flounder. I missed swim lessons at summer camp. It's a long, sad story not worth repeating." He turned away to face the seemingly endless Pacific. "Wait. Are you mad at me because I embarrassed you?"

He looked at me sideways. "What do I care what people think? Why do you? I don't understand why you let him bully you."

"It was a joke."

"You let Evan make *you* the joke."

"It's what brothers do. No big deal. It's that whole 'sticks and stones' thing." He stared back blankly. "You know, *sticks and stones may break my bones, but words will never hurt me.*"

"But they do hurt you."

"Okay, yeah, sometimes they do. So? I'm a big girl. I can handle it."

"You deserve better."

"Thanks." But it wasn't gratitude I felt; it was failure. Already this day seemed doomed.

Despite my warnings about treacherous kelp beds and red tides, the undertow and great whites, Adam went back into the water. I gathered the items I'd littered across the beach and plopped onto my towel beside Mallory to brush off the sand now plastered to my legs and arms. Mal wasn't faring much better. She twisted and fretted at a loose thread dangling from her swim top as she watched Evan instruct Dana on the finer points of bodysurfing. Apparently a lot of hands-on help was required.

"How does she do it?" Mal asked.

"What, bodysurf?"

"No, monopolize his attention like that." She pulled her hat down over her ears and jammed her sunglasses onto her nose. "I'm going to get a corn dog, maybe three. You want one?"

"It's not even eleven."

"Yeah, well, I need a carb fix." She flung her beach bag over her shoulder and marched to the snack shack, kicking up sand the whole way.

I buried my head in a book, while Adam took the ocean head-on, distracting a lifeguard cruising by on her ATV. She bowled over a Styrofoam ice chest, squashing it like a bug.

She wasn't the only person watching him; he'd managed to catch the eyes of girls up and down the beach. But I knew his weaknesses. He may have been fearless out there, where the walls are made of water and sky, but ask him to fetch a vase from the confines of a dark closet and he melted to mush. Strange boy for a strange girl?

Up the beach a gaggle of tweens erupted into squeals. My eyes followed to where they pointed. Strolling down the dune with guitars, coolers, and a posse of blonds in tow were several members of the Jaded Corpses. And there in the middle of the pack strutted the golden boy with the Midas touch, Hayden Jornet. Thankfully Mallory was off at the snack shack, tripping on carbs with Melissa and Vega. They were laughing so hard that Mallory was wiping her eyes.

I couldn't remember the last time we laughed like that. Had we ever? Did we call ourselves friends because that's how others defined us? Lily and Mal. Like Jefferson and Adams, Simon and Garfunkel, Lassiter and Devlin. None of those ended well, I noted.

Three long shadows passed over my legs. I squinted up toward the sun to find Shep Bramstead peering down at me. He was in the company of two girls I didn't recognize, but between the pair they had more curves than a BMX raceway. Shep was wearing his usual smug mug with the addition of a spectacular black eye that even his Ray-Ban rip-offs couldn't hide.

"Well, well, look who crawled up from the crypt," he drawled.

Normally I'd have ignored him, but Adam was right. I didn't deserve to be the joke. "Nice shiner. Your brother give you that?"

His escorts laughed off my pathetic attempt at a comeback, but Shep looked stricken. It was a horribly mean thing to say. I'd heard Grant had a temper. I figured it probably explained Shep's bullying me all those years, but if I'd struck a blow, it was purely by accident—and it was short-lived.

"Yeah, well, I heard the crematorium deal went up in smoke. Get it?" he snorted.

A slap would have stung less. "How do you know that?"

"You kidding, Mort? Sturbridge told Jornet, who told me."

"Jim Sturbridge knows Hayden?"

"Yeah, Sturbridge is his uncle. Who do you think is renting Hayden his new studio?"

Someone ran up to announce that the skimboard contest was getting underway.

"Now for some real sport," said Shep, and he escorted his arm candy toward the judges table.

The reminder of my failure was too much. My lower lip began to quiver, and my eyes were threatening to release an ocean's worth of salty tears when Dana and Evan, along with several of Evan's teammates, returned to dry off. I pretended to wipe sand from my face so I could borrow a few seconds to regain my composure.

"Hold my keys for me, will ya?" said Evan, tossing them at me.

"What do I look like, a coat check?" I snapped.

"What's with the serotonin suck?" I heard someone say.

Evan and his buddies passed around a few drinks before migrating to the water's edge to join the others. Mallory had disappeared with Melissa and Vega, and the lifeguard had captured Adam's attention with an up-close-and-personal look at the workings of the ATV. There was no one to see me rise on shaky legs and follow the trail of flotsam that divided land from sea.

I walked past tide pools lined in a rainbow of anemones and starfish, past shuttered lifeguard stations and driftwood lean-tos, until I came to a jetty jutting into the tide. I scaled the closest boulder. A passing couple cast doubtful looks my way. I ignored them and continued inching my way toward the lonely point where waves battered boulders in suits of musseled armor. The shells, I noted, were sealed tight against the pounding; I envied their resilience.

There was a *whoosh*, and all the water drained from between the boulders. The horizon grew noticeably higher. A massive swell was building, and at any moment it would crest and strike the jetty.

I took one step back. The lip of the wave curled. I braced.

They don't call them breakers for nothing.

RULE #27
GET COMFORTABLE WITH DEATH, BUT NOT TOO COMFORTABLE.

I was jammed upside down in a narrow cavity between two of the jetty's boulders, and the water was rising. Another wave surged between the rocks, temporarily submerging me. I squeezed my eyes shut against the briny torrent. When the water retreated and I opened them again, a rock crab the size of my hand was skittering over the anemones not two inches from my nose. I screamed and tried to wriggle free, but only slid deeper in the hole.

I was going to drown, and it was my own fault.

"HELP! He-e-l—" I gurgled. The next wave hit and sucked me down, wedging me even more firmly. The blood ran to my head, my eyes burned from the salt water, and sea foam filled my ears.

Through it all, I imagined I could hear Adam calling my name. "Lily!"

"Adam, I'm here!" I cried through chattering teeth. "D-d-down here!" I listened for the telltale scraping of feet over rock and barnacle, but only the slapping and sloshing of surf made it to my ears. Hope floated out of reach.

Without warning a pair of hands clamped around my ankles. "I'm going to pull you out," shouted Adam from above.

Praise Fortuna. I clenched my teeth against the pain I knew was coming. He pulled, but the craggy stone wouldn't release me. He tried again, harder this time. Barnacles, limpets, and jagged rock grated my skin. I bit down harder, stifling a scream. The next wave crowned the jetty and surged into the space. His hands slipped away.

"Adam?" A dreadful moment passed. "ADAM!"

"I'm still here."

"Get help!"

"There's no time. Hold on. I'm going to try something."

His bare foot appeared beside my left shoulder and his other, the opposite. He was lowering himself down between the boulders. "Go back! You're going to get stuck and then we'll both drown."

Bracing his back against one boulder, his legs against the other, he grabbed me by the waist and heaved. A muffled cry escaped my lips. It was no good. I was stuck tighter than a limpet.

"I'm sorry," he yelled.

"Forget apologies. Just get me out of here!"

"I'm doing my best."

"Do it faster!" I pinched my eyes and mouth shut against a wave rushing in and gasped for breath when it cleared.

"I have another idea. When the next wave hits, wait for my signal and then push all the air from your lungs. *All* of it. Ready?"

I bobbed my head, but inside I was losing hope that either of us would escape this. On cue, the next wave gushed in through the narrow cavity. "Now!" Adam shouted above the torrent. Against my better instincts, I emptied my lungs, allowing my chest to shrink. Water flooded the sliver of space between the slime-covered rocks until I was fully submerged. I fought the urge to breathe. If I held my breath much longer, either I'd lose consciousness or my body would override my brain and my lungs would involuntarily expand to fill with seawater.

Adam placed the ball of his foot against my shoulder and pushed. My whole body twisted sideways, and I was free. Gasping for air, I had less than a minute to shimmy into a wider space before the next onslaught. Then, with Adam's coaching, I righted myself, grabbed hold of a ledge, and scrambled up and out.

Together we limped across the boulders to safety. Once clear of the incoming waves, Adam hopped down onto the sand. "Jump. I'll catch you, I promise."

I hesitated. The last time I heard those words, it ended badly.

"Lily?" he asked, his arms open and ready.

The moment was about more than my safety. Did I trust him or not?

I closed my eyes and leaped. The next thing I knew, I was cradled in his arms. I lassoed my arms around his neck, craving the warmth of his sun-drenched body. His hold on me was awkward and unsure, but full of such unimaginable tenderness, it nearly brought me to tears. A new kind of terror seeped in. What would happen to me when he let go? But he didn't; instead he pulled me closer. The fact that we clung so tightly to each other underscored the depths of our mutual loneliness. Why were we resisting the thing we'd both desperately needed for so long?

Gradually my shivering subsided, and he gently set me on my

feet beside a beached tree stump, its protective bark long gone, leaving its inner layers exposed to the elements. "Thanks" was all I managed. The word was so inadequate, but if I said any more, I would lose it. Dad trained me better than that. "How did you find me?"

"When I asked where you were, that girl with the lotion said she saw you wandering down the beach."

"I needed to be alone." Nothing could be further from the truth. What I needed was him, and he found me—like I found him.

"I've really screwed things up with the funeral home, haven't I?"

He took my pruney blue hands in his. "Sturbridge would have found another way to get what he wants. You know that. But I'm surprised you care."

"You couldn't be more surprised than I am. All this time I thought I wanted out, when what I really wanted was a choice. How can my father sell our family business?"

"Maybe he thinks it's best for everyone."

"Like you wanting to leave."

This, I realized, was the real reason I was so devastated. I lost my mother before I knew her, and now I was close to losing both my future career and Mallory. I was terrified I would lose him, too.

"Don't leave me," I said. Saying the words out loud and opening my heart to him brought me to a whole new level of vulnerable. And vulnerability? It felt a lot like drowning.

I braced myself for the inevitable rejection. Instead he stroked my cheek. "I'm here now. Can't that be enough?"

No. I wanted more.

He folded me into his arms. Warm skin and a steady hold. *Is this what love feels like?* Heavy breathing and a racing heart. *Is this what love sounds like?* There was only one way to know for sure: I had to tell him how I felt. "Adam, I—"

"Lily, wait." The way he said my name sounded nothing like the first time; the meaning was gone. With a single finger he lifted my chin, forcing me to look him in the eyes. I saw no love there—only guilt. "All I want is to do the right thing by you. Please don't make it any more difficult."

I eased away. "What do you mean, 'do the right thing'?"

"Hey, there you guys are!" shouted Mallory, jogging toward us. I wondered how much she'd seen. "Sorry. Didn't mean to interrupt." She pointed to the scratches up and down my legs and shoulders. "What happened to you?"

"I fell between some boulders. Lucky for me, Adam came along." In more ways than one, I realized. "I'll be all right. Where are Melissa and Vega?"

"They're on assignment." She smiled wryly.

"Does that assignment happen to have a name, like—oh, I don't know—*Dana*, perhaps?"

"It might." She waved her hand. "Oh, did Adam tell you? Evan won! He actually won! You have to see the trophy. It's made of gold-sprayed sunblock cans and bike handlebars and is nearly as tall as me." She grabbed me by the hand and started pulling me back toward the party. I signaled for Adam to join us, but he chose to trail behind.

It was a painful slog back along the beach, each step a reminder of how close I'd come to drowning. The three of us circled the public restrooms to find a small crowd gathered around two rows of heads poking out of the sand—today's losers. It was a wonder I wasn't joining them.

A disgruntled Dana was reading them their last rites. She spotted me. "Hey, this should be your job, not mine."

I could feel Adam willing me to reply with some smart remark. I came up empty.

"Dana, you've got this," Mallory said, chuckling. "Carry on." She leaned close and admitted to me that Melissa and Vega's task had been to volunteer Dana for the job.

"Nice one, Mal," I said.

Dana muttered something in Italian, then continued where she'd left off. "And forever more we shall remember your pathetic performance today. May you rest in pieces."

To whoops and hollers, a guy dressed in a black terry-cloth shroud stepped forward and dumped buckets of seawater over their heads while another guy sprinkled them with stale hamburger buns donated by the snack shack. Immediately a seagull circling overhead dive-bombed one of the losers for a piece of soggy bread. Another bird released a foul white stream. Together Mal and I had a good laugh, my first of the day. Adam, I noticed, almost smiled. *I've got to work on that with him.*

When we reached the showers, I asked for a minute to clean up. They gave me time to rinse off the grit, slime, and blood, and then Mal insisted we stop by the lifeguard station for bandages and ointment. Adam held my hand the whole time it took to patch me up, ignoring the ghoulish, puckered scars that railroaded my upper thighs.

"I'm starving," I said, once my wounds were dressed. "Let's check out the barbecue."

"You two go ahead," said Mal with a wink. "The rest of us already ate."

I ignored her insinuation, telling myself nothing happened between Adam and me. But something had happened. I'd opened up to Adam, and he didn't run screaming.

Adam and I wandered over to where they were serving the last of the burgers and dogs. Too late I spied Hayden and his goons schmoozing it up with some of the sponsors.

"Wait here," snarled Adam, "while I wipe that grin off his face."

I reached for his arm. "Knocking out his teeth won't change what he did to you or to Mallory. People like that don't change."

"I'll make him wish he could change."

"No. Then you'll be just like him. Promise me you won't do anything to Hayden."

"I can't make that kind of promise," he said.

"Please," I begged, fully aware that his promises weren't like other people's. "For me."

He wanted to fight me on this, but to my relief he gave in. "All right. I promise I won't touch Hayden Jornet."

"Or anyone else this weekend."

"But I—"

"Or anyone else." I wouldn't budge on this. The last thing I wanted was another incident like the one at Hayden's spoiling the weekend.

"Fine. For you. I promise no fighting."

Hayden strolled over, all false charm, and I felt Adam tense beside me. "You promised," I reminded him under my breath.

"I won't touch him." He squared his shoulders and glared as Hayden passed off his designer shades to a bystander. His fellow sharks smelled blood and circled, ready for a feeding frenzy.

Adam advanced to meet him, hesitated, then, true to his word, backed down.

"Coward," Hayden taunted. As if he would lift a finger against Adam. He'd rather egg someone else into doing his dirty work for him.

Together Adam and I returned to where our towels lay half-buried in the sand, crisis averted—for now. "You're no coward," I reassured him. "It takes guts to walk away."

"No. Only a promise."

RULE #28
PAY SPECIAL ATTENTION TO THE LIPS.

We were clustered around our beach encampment, but unlike this time last year, Evan was in a celebratory mood.

"How did you win?" I asked. "Adam said you didn't even place in the skimboard contest, and that's supposed to be your best event."

"I won't lie," said Evan, "I didn't think I stood a chance at winning, especially after I took third in the Frisbee toss. My only shot to win was the run. What I couldn't figure out was how Mumford's feet weren't burning. Those dunes were blisteringly hot. He's used to racing in track shoes, not barefoot. Then, halfway through the race, I got a peek at the bottom of his feet. He duct-taped his soles." Evan shook his head. "You should've seen his face when I caught up to him. He didn't know I'd been training barefoot all summer to build calluses. By the home stretch, we were running neck and neck. That's when he stuck out a leg to trip me and pulled his groin. I crossed the finish line first, and Mumford had to be carried off the course."

"Serves him right for cheating," said Mallory.

Evan gave a snort. "Actually, I just came from talking to him, and he thanked me."

"Why?" Adam was totally confused.

"Well, for half an hour that hot lifeguard with the ATV held a cool pack to his groin. He's thinking it all worked out for the best."

We all shared a good laugh at that.

The sun gave up the sky as a dense fog slinked inland, driving partiers toward the bonfire. I argued for staying put, but after Justin reported seeing Hayden head for the parking lot, I let Mallory talk me into joining the others.

With Justin, Dana, and Mallory serving as his entourage, Evan waded into the thick of the crowd to bask in the glory of his triumph. Adam, who joined me at the fringe of the gathering, commented that all Evan lacked was a victor's crown of laurel leaves.

In silence we watched sparks and smoke rise to meet the fog while couples bound in blankets beside us did what couples do. New arrivals filled in around us, forcing Adam and me to shift closer and closer to each other. I could hardly breathe. It was not the crowd suffocating me; it was the weight of my own hypocrisy. I'd demanded nothing but honesty from Adam but had failed to give him the same even after he rescued me from the tide.

As if reading my mind, Adam stood and offered a hand. "Walk with me. We need to talk."

It's never a good thing when someone says that.

I let him lead me away from the crowd, but whatever was on his mind, he was in no rush to bring it up. Nor was I. Not when this could be our last evening together. We let the foamy surf washing over our feet do all the scripting. It spoke of change, of rises and falls. It spoke of dark secrets lurking in the wings of our own private theater. But this was Adam's scene to direct, so I waited.

"Pea soup," he said.

Not exactly the opening line I was expecting. "Did you say 'pea soup'?"

He nodded toward our audience: row upon row of black and restless waves beneath a velvet curtain of fog. "I expected the ocean to remind me of pea soup."

"Why?"

"The popular theory is that oceans spawned the first life on Earth from an amalgamation of minerals resembling pea soup. Looking out at the ocean, I wonder how anyone could think that is true."

"Our bodies *are* seventy percent water."

"Good point, except my father had another theory about life's origins. He believed life first emerged from self-replicating clay particles."

I kicked at the surf. "I think I like the pea-soup theory better,"

"I see." He sounded weirdly disappointed.

The curtain of fog closed over us, obliterating the full moon overhead. We continued along the shore, straying farther and farther from the bonfire, and, I suspected, from the point of this walk—owning up to each other.

Clearing my conscience wasn't going to get any easier. "Adam, I have something I need to tell you."

"It can wait, can't it?"

"I guess. Sure." My shoulders dropped in relief. I'd tell him tomorrow.

Something white and crescent-shaped in the sand caught my eye. A sand dollar, half-buried at my feet. I reached down and plucked it from the surf, marveling at my good luck. The ocean here was rough, and few ever made it ashore intact, but this one was whole. "Ever see a sand dollar before?"

"No," he said, sounding unsure, but his bank of knowledge and memories since leaving the shelter often defied explanation. Adam examined the brittle white disk as I pointed out how the markings on top formed a perfect star.

"Shake it," I said. "What do you hear?"

"A rattle. It's broken."

I laughed. "No, it's not broken. What you're hearing are the bones of angel wings."

He cocked his head skeptically.

"When I was little," I said, "I used to lie awake with worry: What if the house caught fire? Or what if I didn't wake up in the morning? Stuff like that."

"Seem like reasonable worries to me."

Considering what he'd been through, he had a point. "Anyway, my grandfather gave me a sand dollar to comfort me after my accident. You see, one day at the beach he told me a story about how we each have three angels: one to bring us into the world, one to watch over us while we sleep, and one to escort us out at the end. Once their jobs are complete, the angels seal their wings inside a white purse in the shape of a moon, mark it with a star, and fling it into the ocean. In time only the bones remain, and that's why it rattles."

"A sand dollar for everyone who has ever lived and died," he mused. "I want to see the angel wing bones." He wrapped his fingers around its edges, preparing to snap it in two.

"No, don't break it! Grandpa Ted said if you find a sand dollar and keep it safe, it will bring you long life."

"Do you still have the one he gave you?"

"No," I said. "It's long gone." And so was the boy I'd intended to give it to.

"And yet here you are."

Thanks to a kiss. I knew he couldn't be the same Adam, yet my eyes found his lips, so full and perfect. I wondered if they tasted salty. Were they warm? Or as cool and damp as the evening air?

"It all sounds like superstition to me," he said.

"Keep it just the same."

Adam slipped the sand dollar into his back pocket.

With our backs to the sea, neither of us noticed the water sneaking up on us until it washed against the backs of our knees. I squealed in surprise, and he scooped me up and carried me to dry sand beyond the ocean's reach. I kicked and fussed—"Put me down. Put me down!"—all while my arms roped more tightly around his shoulders.

He tripped over a chunk of driftwood and together we tumbled into a shallow depression in the sand. "You klutz!" I teased between embarrassed laughter and half-hearted swats. He retaliated by grabbing me by the shoulders and pinning me beneath him. I pretended to call for help.

"Hush, people will think I'm doing something indecent to you," he warned.

"Why don't you?" I said, startling us both with my boldness. "No one can see us in this fog." I placed a hand on each side of his waist, waiting for him to resist. When he didn't, I pulled him closer, in pure defiance of my better judgment.

All my resolve to play it smart, all my common sense, was lost to hot breath, racing pulses, and skin touching skin. Adam's fingers wove into my hair. I could feel his heart beating next to mine, and for an instant, it was as if we shared the one between us.

Adam's whole body tensed, and he pulled away. "Lily, I need to—"

"Shh." I placed a finger to his lips. "It can wait."

He surrendered too easily, and I was too willing to let him.

His fingers smoothed the creases in my worried brow, then traced the swoop of my nose, the curve of that space between lip and chin as though committing each dip and bow to memory. I considered what it might mean, and alarms started going off. *Danger, Will Robinson!* warned what shred of my common sense was still operating.

This is not a movie or a television script with a guaranteed happy ending. Kiss Adam and you've got a whole lot to lose. He's going to dump your sorry ass as soon as you return home, and then where will you be?

I told my common sense to shove it and leaned in.

"LI-LY!" Evan's voice cut through the moment like a foghorn. "LI-LY!"

Adam rolled away from me, and there was a *crunch* from his back pocket. The sand dollar.

I could hear the worry in my stepbrother's voice. "Over here," I called.

Evan emerged from the fog. "Have you seen—? Oh, hey, Adam. Whoa, am I interrupting . . . ?"

"No," I claimed, grateful for the darkness that hid my blush. I stood and brushed off any telltale sand. "We went for a walk and got turned around."

Evan smiled knowingly. "Right. Like you can't follow the shoreline back."

I was not amused. "Evan, what do you want?"

"You seen Mallory?"

"No, not since the bonfire. Why, what's wrong?"

"Oh, I think I might have said some things."

"There's a stunner. Did you try calling her?"

"She hung up on me. I tried again, but it went right to voice mail."

"What about the snack shack? Corn dogs are her usual go-to when she's upset. Or maybe she's with Vega and the others."

"Or maybe she's on the jetty?" Adam added, and got a sharp nudge from my elbow in return.

"I've looked everywhere." Evan shook his head.

"Well, obviously not *everywhere*." My eyes narrowed. "So what did you say to her?"

"That's not important. We need to find her. Party's over. Everyone's leaving."

"Already?" I said, suddenly wanting to stay the weekend, the week, forever, if it could be like this with Adam.

Evan rolled his eyes and sighed. "Yeah, well, back at the celebration for my victory—"

Oh, please.

"—a few of the guys got wasted and tried setting fire to a lifeguard tower. Beach Patrol is closing us down. Look, I'm going to take my trophy and a load to the van and check the parking lot. You two pack up what's left and meet me there. One of us is bound to find her, assuming she didn't leave with someone else."

"Don't worry," I said. "We'll find her."

Evan made a soured-milk face. "She wouldn't do anything stupid, would she?"

No, that would be me, I thought. Mallory knew enough to fold and run. I was the one who kept raising the stakes, and now I was all in with everything to lose.

RULE #29
NEVER UNDERESTIMATE
THE MAGIC OF GOOD LIGHTING.

I bundled together the last of our belongings while Adam combed the beach for Mallory. By time he returned we were the last two people this side of the dunes.

"Any sign of her?" I asked.

He shook his head.

"I'm worried. I know Mal can be a bit melodramatic, but she's never held out this long."

"She'll be at the van. You'll see."

"I hope you're right."

We divvied the goods and began the slow plod back over the dunes, which I could have sworn doubled in size since we last climbed them. More than once Adam had to stop to let me catch up, and it occurred to me that all day we—whatever *we* were—had been like an accordion, drawing together, pulling apart.

By the second set of dunes, the fog had passed us in its race inland. I insisted Adam go ahead, figuring Mal and Evan were probably already waiting for us. I made it to the top and set down my stuff to catch my breath. Below, the lot appeared empty except for our van with Evan's trophy and the pile of gear stacked beside it—until I noticed a dark vehicle skulking through the low-lying fog. It was the same SUV I'd seen that morning.

Praying I was wrong, I hitched up our gear and started down the dune, steadily increasing my pace as I went. The SUV drew closer to our van. I made it to the boardwalk and broke into a run for the pavement. Ahead I could make out Adam seated on the back bumper, impatiently banging out a beat.

I opened my mouth to shout a warning as my feet hit a patch of sand. I skidded and stumbled to within a couple feet of the van's front end, then went down in a flying heap of towels, umbrellas, beach bags, and chairs.

The SUV pulled over, its doors flung open, and two familiar men emerged. Bad-dye-job guy had a tarp over one shoulder and a length of sturdy rope in his hands. Briefcase man, the taller of the two, was armed with a syringe.

"Tie her up," he barked.

His partner stooped to wrap the rope around my outstretched arms, but I kicked out, catching him in the chest. I scrabbled beneath the van and clung to the undercarriage. Cursing, bad-dye-job guy got down on all fours, but I wriggled out of reach.

A pair of bare feet circled the van. "Get away from her!" shouted Adam, and the guy grappling for me was hauled from view.

"It isn't her we want. It's you," rumbled a deep voice. "Alive or dead. Your call."

That's when all hell broke loose. Feet scuffled, tripping over beach gear, flicking bits of asphalt and sand into my eyes. Through flying grit I glimpsed Adam scaling a nearby barbed wire fence. His assailants tried to wrench him back, but the wire tore from the post and all three bodies hit the ground. The syringe skittered across the pavement. Briefcase guy scrambled after it while bad-dye-job guy did his best to subdue Adam with a tarp and a few well-placed kicks.

But unlike at Hayden's, Adam just lay there, taking the blows.

"Get up, Adam!" I shouted. Why wasn't he fighting back? I already knew the answer.

I'd made him promise not to.

"Forget your promise!" I yelled, but it was too late.

A glint behind the van's front tire caught my eye. Evan's keys. They must have slid out of my bag when I fell. Scraping and crawling over loose asphalt, broken glass, and cigarette butts, I inched my way toward them. Snatching the keys, I hoisted myself out from under the van, opened the door, and jumped into the driver's seat.

I'd once referred to the van as a weapon. It was as good a weapon as I was going to get. All I had to do was start the engine, but my shaking hand couldn't find the ignition slot.

Finally the key slid into place. I cranked the engine, glanced into the rearview mirror, and threw the van into gear—the wrong gear. The van lurched forward, and the two thugs leaped aside.

I grabbed the shift and this time shoved it into reverse. The transmission made a terrible grinding sound but obeyed, and the van pulled even with Adam. I leaned across the seat and forced open the passenger door. "Get in!"

Before he could respond, briefcase man seized Adam by the hair and jerked him back. I snatched Evan's half-full water bottle from the cup holder and pitched it at Adam's attacker. It smacked him in the forehead and Adam toppled into the van.

"Hold on!" I shifted into drive and punched the accelerator. With a *THUNK THUNK* we rode up and over the concrete parking chock, flattening Evan's trophy in the process. Now to find Evan and Mallory and get us out of there.

I cranked the steering wheel hard to the left but still managed to take out a row of fencing. We were nearly to the parking-lot exit when two figures waving their arms sprang from behind an information kiosk. I swerved and slammed on the brakes.

A fist pounded the van's hood. "What the hell are you doing?!"

Switching on the headlights, I discovered I'd nearly pancaked Evan and Mallory. Rolling down the driver's-side window, I hollered, "No time to explain. Get in!" Two beams of light struck the side-view mirror. That was all the convincing Evan needed.

He and Mallory slid open the cargo door, Mallory flung her beach tote into the van and they dove in behind it. "Where's all my stuff?" hollered Evan. "Where's my trophy?!"

"I'll make you a new one!" My foot found the accelerator and put it to the floor.

Behind us the SUV cut over an embankment, hot on our tail. Mallory was wigging out. Evan was doing his best to bully me into pulling over. He might've been willing to take them on. I wasn't.

A light flashed on the dash. "Oh god. No gas, Evan!"

"I was going to fill up before we got on the freeway."

"How many miles do I have?"

"I'd say you're running on fumes."

"Dammit!"

The SUV pulled even to the driver side of the van and swerved toward my door. I gave the wheel a hard twist to the right. Instantly the van fishtailed. Recalling the squirrel incident, I turned into it, but that ran us up onto the unpaved shoulder, where I clipped a signpost. Two thumps and a whole lot of four-letter words flew up from the back of the van.

I couldn't worry about that now. Through a flurry of dirt and gravel, I got us back on asphalt, but the road was coming to a T-junction. "Which way?" I shouted.

"Right—no, left!" Evan hollered.

Swerving one way and then the other, we blew through the intersection on what felt like two wheels and merged into traffic. A river of lights filled my rearview mirror. There was no telling if I'd lost our pursuers or not. My only choice was to keep going.

A reflective green freeway sign flashed ahead. I made a multi-lane change that would have caused even Nana Jo to lose her hair and then swung onto the on-ramp, wheels screeching, horns blaring.

"There aren't any stations for miles this way. Go back!" Evan was shouting. "We're going to run out of gas. Pull over, pull over!"

"I will!" I shouted over my shoulder. "As soon as—"

The engine sputtered.

"Oh, great," whined Mallory.

"I think I can make this off-ramp." I spun the wheel. Two more thumps in the back. The van veered over a row of sandbags and across the dirt divide. Hiccupping and lurching, it rolled down the steep freeway exit, drifted along a dark and narrow frontage road, and came to rest in a pullout beside a row of rural mailboxes. I cut the lights and let my head fall onto my hands, which still clutched the wheel.

"You want to explain what the hell is going on?" Evan was rubbing his head and scrambling over the top of the seat like he wanted to throttle me, but I was too scared to be intimidated. I spun around to ward him off.

"While you two were off doing who knows what, two guys tried to kidnap Adam!"

Evan dropped into the middle seat. "Why would someone want to kidnap Adam?"

"No idea." But my guess was they knew something about him we didn't.

"We need to call the police," insisted Mallory, who was holding her stomach as though she might be sick.

Adam was slumped against the passenger door. He'd pulled a towel over himself and had been strangely quiet, even for him. "You okay?" I asked.

"Still . . . here."

But where was here? I peered out the window. Strands of mist twined through dense forest, strangling the bay laurels, oak, and pine until they nearly vanished from view. For the moment we'd lost the SUV, but we were stranded in the middle of nowhere. I pulled out my phone. Nowhere didn't have phone reception.

Rolling down my window, I searched for a way out of our predicament, the one *I* drove us into. No people. No buildings. Nothing but a discarded tire and a half dozen rusty mailboxes. Gradually my eyes adjusted to the dark. Far up a dirt lane to our right, the tiniest light twinkled through the branches of a pine grove. "Is that a house?"

"Looks like," said Evan.

"Why don't you and Mallory go see if you can borrow a phone or bum some gas. Adam and I'll wait here with the van in case someone comes along who can help us." *Like that's going to happen.* The only people likely to come along here were the kidnappers.

Mallory, who was too busy wallowing in self-pity, also hadn't budged, but that didn't stop her griping. "My parents are going to be so pissed if I'm not home by midnight. Why didn't you listen to Evan and go back? Oh, shit. I'm missing an earring."

That's when I lost it. "Will you shut up and try to think about somebody besides yourself for a change?!"

Evan smacked the back of the driver's seat, hard. "Hey! You're out of line. You're the one who got us into this mess. Why are you yelling at her?"

"Because if we hadn't been off hunting for her, this never would have happened," I said. I took a deep breath and slowly deflated. "And because I'm scared. I'm sorry."

"Come on, Evan. If we don't go, we could be here all night," said Mallory, sounding somewhat resigned. "Let's see if we can find a phone."

Still grumbling, she and Evan took off down the lane, but not before Evan pointed out the dents, missing hubcap, and damaged paint where I'd sideswiped the fence and signpost. Dad was going to kill me.

Adam and I sat in stunned silence as the approaching bank of fog engulfed the van. I didn't dare turn on the overhead light in case those two thugs were still out there looking for us. I should have taken a less obvious route home. And it was probably a mistake sending Mal and Evan off into the dark. This whole scene was straight out of a horror movie, the one where the dumb teens lost in the woods are torn to pieces by a serial killer or a swamp thing.

From out of the dark, Adam said, "Some driving." His voice was a weak and ragged whisper.

"Thanks. Yeah, apparently it helps when I have someone trying to run me off the road. How bad are you hurt?"

"It's my ankle. I slammed it in the door trying to get in the van."

Then why was he buried under a towel? It's wasn't that cold. Determined to see for myself, I got out, but not before listening for the telltale snap of a twig or the huff of heavy breathing. The only heavy breathing was my own, so I circled to the other side of the van. Adam held the door fast. "Dammit, Adam, open the door!"

He grudgingly released the handle while pulling the towel clear up to his chin. "Now let me see your ankle." I reached for his leg, but his hand stopped me. His touch was cold, moist, and sticky. I'd helped Tony wash too many bodies not to recognize the sensation. Blood. I reached for the overhead dome light, no longer caring who saw us.

"Don't!"

Too late. The cab filled with a weak amber glow. I sighed in relief. The substance covering his palm was too orange to be blood. But then, through the tatters of his shirt, I saw a wicked gash across his chest. "Adam, you're cut."

"From the barbed-wire fence," he admitted.

I fumbled for the dry towel crammed behind his seat so I could clean the gash, but he warded me off. The sudden movement caused a gush of the same orange, syrupy fluid from the wound.

I stumbled back. "What the—!"

Covering the apparent wound with one hand, Adam slammed the palm of his other against the light, plunging us back into obscurity. But I knew what I'd seen, and it wasn't blood.

My mind reeled for an explanation. Rust? Lotion of some kind. Jam or jelly. Antifreeze. Antifreeze? Coming from an open wound? Pus, then. No way. It hadn't been long enough for an infection to set in. Then what?

My limbs started to shake, my stomach to churn. "Adam, what's that orange stuff? What's wrong with you?"

"That's what I was trying to tell you, back at the beach."

I could think of a thousand possibilities of what he might say, and none of them were anything I wanted to hear. He was going to ruin everything. I could feel it in my bones.

"I'm not who you think I am—*what* you think I am."

Stop talking stop talking stop talking.

"I'm not . . . human."

Adam was delusional. He hit his head during the scuffle in the parking lot. Or maybe that was me, because nothing was making sense.

His hand found my shoulder. "Lily, hear me out." His voice was calm.

Before he could force me to face the reality of that gruesome gash and the peculiar fluid seeping from it, Evan's and Mallory's muffled voices cut through the ensnaring mist. Quickly Adam retracted his arm and rearranged the towel to cover any evidence of his injuries, while I retreated from the van.

I bent over, hands on knees, and took several shallow, shaky breaths. There were two possibilities. Either one of us had lost it, or he was telling the truth.

For once, I wish he could lie.

RULE #30
LEAVE NO TRACE OF BLOOD.

Mal and Evan had returned, hopefully with a means to get us out of here. How would I tell them about Adam? Should I tell them? Evan would simply call me a liar or think it was all a big prank. Mal would flip out. I wanted to flip out.

I straightened and pushed backed my hair, but remained clear of the car. "Did you get it?"

"No one was at the house with the light," answered Evan, "but I found a full gas can in a shed. Left a twenty under the welcome mat in payment."

Mal helped Adam move to the middle seat so she and Evan could take the front, but I was finding it hard to even look at Adam, let alone touch him. Evan drove to the first station off the freeway, filled the tank, and soon we were back on the road with no sign of our pursuers.

"I . . . thirsty," said Adam.

"I've still got a couple drinks still in my bag," said Mallory and passed him a bottle. He gulped it down and took the other. "Guess you've got a thing for cream soda," she teased.

"That's not cream soda," said Evan. "You drank the two bottles we brought, remember? That's beer. I was holding a couple for one of my teammates and put them in your bag to keep them cool. I guess he forgot about them."

"Sorry, Adam," she said. "My bad. But, hey, maybe it'll help you relax after all that's happened tonight."

That, it turned out, was an understatement. Adam closed his eyes, complaining about rolling down the freeway—sideways. He then asked someone unseen to read him the story about jousting knights and unfaithful kings and queens. I couldn't tell if he was drunk out of his mind or suffering from head trauma. At last he settled into a restless sleep, and he remained that way until we were parked in the delivery bay behind the mortuary.

"Adam, wake up. We're here."

His head lolled to the side, but he slowly came to. He adjusted the towel to better conceal his injuries.

The van door slid open, and his body virtually poured out. Body? If what he claimed was true, did he even have bones, muscles, or a heart like ours?

"Man, he is totally sloshed," said Mallory. "And I thought I was a lightweight."

She and Evan assisted a woozy Adam over to one of Nana Jo's benches by the back door to sober up, but it was hard to believe his condition was solely due to a couple brews.

"Come on, Mal. I'd better get you home," said Evan. "Lily, you'll have to get him to his room on your own, and don't let Mom and Dad see him. They'll freak."

"I can't do it," I said.

"Sure you can," said Evan. He and Mallory climbed back into the van and drove off, leaving me standing in the driveway with my arms wrapped about me as if I might fly apart.

With my back to Adam, I said, "You should have told me sooner."

"It's not that bad."

Right, because what's wrong with not being human? "I wasn't referring to your injury."

"Oh. That."

I reeled to face him. "I feel so . . . so . . . I don't know what I feel. I thought . . ." I looked away. There were no words. I was in some kind of denial and wanted to keep it that way, but I was also deeply wounded. He betrayed my trust.

And yet wasn't I doing the same by not telling him about Miles Devlin?

"I tried, but what was I supposed to tell you? That I'm a living, breathing by-product of Neil's thievery and experimentation? How could I possibly expect you to accept such a thing?"

"You give me so little credit. You could have at least given me a chance."

"Is it too late?"

When I didn't answer, he gripped the storm drain and pulled himself to standing, exposing the telltale dark stain as the towel dropped away. "Adam. You've lost a lot of . . ." I didn't know how to finish my sentence, because I had no word for the fluid seeping from his chest. "Can you walk?"

He nodded and stumbled forward as though to prove the point.

"Okay, let's get you to the prep room."

"To prep me for what?"

"I'll know better once I get a good look. Here now, lean on me."

The touch of his cold, clammy skin was unnerving. I was used to corpses, but he felt like something in between living and dead.

I guided him inside and down the hall. We staggered and weaved, occasionally running into a wall. Each time Adam moaned. I was doing no better with him than with that wretched gurney of ours.

I switched on the prep room's overhead lights and immediately averted my eyes from the garish substance that had soaked through his shirt. With a feeble wave, I motioned for him to lie on the table.

"I'd rather have a chair," he said.

"There aren't any. People don't sit much in here."

I snapped on a pair of blue latex gloves, then pulled my shears from a drawer. His eyes grew wide, and he fought to sit up, causing the wound to bleed more. "What are you going to do to me?"

"Relax." I pushed him back down. "I'm going to cut away your shirt."

For most morticians, I imagined it would help that he was stretched out on this cold, metal table. They would be used to distancing themselves from a body in his position. For me, it made matters worse. This was where I best connected.

I took a deep breath, made a snip, and ripped his shirt up the front. The wound was deep and ragged. "Oh, Adam. This is my fault. I should never have forced you to make that promise."

"You didn't force me to do anything. I got what I deserve; I must be breaking at least half a dozen laws of nature. How much did you tell Evan and Mallory?"

"Nothing yet."

"Are you going to?"

"I don't know, but you can't hide something like this forever."

He winced. "That has become painfully clear. Do I frighten you?"

"A little," I confessed. *Okay, a lot.* But as I studied his body—so perfectly molded, a modern-day kouros—I had to admit I was also a bit awestruck. I prodded his flesh. It was cold to the touch but otherwise no different than my own. "Does that hurt?"

"No," he said, flinching.

I thought he couldn't lie. "Well, it's a fairly deep gash, but I see no need for a doctor. Like they'd know what to do with you anyway."

"Is that supposed to be comforting?"

"No, I guess not."

I rooted through the supply cabinets, withdrawing a small packet of gauze, a roll of medical tape, and a bottle of hydrogen peroxide. "Keep in mind I'm a desairologist in training, not a doctor. I do hair, nails, and makeup for the dead. I'm not used to working on . . ."

"Whatever I am," he finished for me. "Do what you have to do. I can take it. Can you?"

"I think so." I assured him I would do my best and repeated that this was totally out of my realm of expertise—anyone's realm of expertise—which was why I'd decided to fix him up myself. "It's a cut, after all. No big deal."

So not true.

"It's a big deal to me," he said, laying an unsteady hand on my arm. Without meaning to, I pulled away. "You don't have to do this," he said.

"Yes, I do."

"Why?"

"Because . . . because it's the humane thing to do."

"Interesting word choice."

"And because you rescued me from the rocks today, and because . . ." I looked away, unable to commit to the truth of the matter: I cared for him—or had. Now I didn't know how I felt. I was running through so many emotions, I couldn't sort them out.

He held his breath as I swabbed the wound, the effects of the beer having nearly worn off. If I could keep him talking, it would distract him from the pain. "So . . . what are you?"

"Not sure exactly. Something like a golem, I think."

"'Something like'? What's that even mean?"

"A golem is molded out of clay and magically brought to life to serve its creator. In my case, Neil used"—he inhaled sharply as I pinched the gash closed—"clay and other organic compounds. The magic was years of scientific research and experimentation. You get the idea."

"But your memories of that day in the orchard? How could you . . . ?"

"I don't know."

I struggled to process this. When I found my voice again, I confessed that I should have suspected something from the beginning, what with the mannequin parts and discarded molds scattered about his family's property, the weird laboratory in the fallout shelter, the supposed accident five years ago, the strangely colored bruising after his beating at Hayden's, his unusual strength. It was quite a list. I tossed a ball of used cotton into the biohazard waste receptacle. "And come to think of it, your hair hasn't grown an inch since you moved in with us. Do you even age?"

"Yes. All *things* wear out eventually," he said.

I couldn't ignore the emphasis he put on the word *things*.

"Well, at least that explains why those two men tried to kidnap you. I imagine a whole lot of people would love to get their hands on some"—I caught myself—"some*one* like you. And that night you were jumped in the alley? It was probably them. They must have already suspected what you were and were looking for confirmation. All of the media attention made it easier for them to find you."

I placed a crisscross of tape across two flaps of skin to hold them together. "Ouch," he said, batting at my hand but missing.

"Then hold still." There was no humor in my voice. I taped a square of gauze over where Neil had marked him with ink, where the cut was deepest. "There. It's not perfect, but you'll live." Then I helped him to the caretaker's cottage and into bed, where he pulled a single sheet up to his chin. The night was too warm for much else. "Now sober up and try to get some sleep." I reached for the light switch. "You know, I've talked to a lot of bodies on that prep table. Of all of them, you're the only one who's talked back."

"Is that supposed to be a compliment or an insult?"

"The highest of compliments."

"Lily?"

"Yeah?"

"There was something you wanted to tell me back on the beach. What was it?"

"Another time." I killed the lights.

RULE #31
LOSS COMES IN STAGES.
DEAL WITH IT.

The full impact of the night's events and revelations didn't hit me right away. It caught me on the second-floor landing, where I withered on the spot. Seeking refuge, I spied the nearby linen closet and crawled into its dark and waiting folds.

When I was a lot younger and the prep room was still off-limits, this cloistered space had been my asylum. It was where I retreated when I felt beaten by the endless taunting at school or needed a good cry free from my father's scolding eyes. Like then, I tucked myself into the bundled quilts and crocheted doilies and drew up my knees. The potpourri of cedar balls and lavender sachets, laundry soap and fabric softener, couldn't calm the shaking that wracked my body.

I had rules—hard-and-fast rules—and still I opened my heart to him. And the punishment for breaking my own code of conduct? I was in love with a lie—a monstrous lie.

I summoned all my usual tricks. I listed the names of my favorite blushes: Love Me Forever, Smitten Kitten, and Nein, Nein, Oh

Mein. I recited Emily Dickinson's "Death Sets a Thing Significant."
I hummed hymns. I tried anything to distract me.

Nothing worked, because none of those things could change
what Adam was or take away the sense that I'd somehow lost the
person I believed him to be. I wasn't even sure he qualified as a person.

Of anyone, I knew how to deal with loss.

First there is denial: I swore it was a mistake. Adam breathed.
He had a pulse. He had feelings. He had to be human.

Then shock: I knew blood, and no human has blood like *that*.

Followed by anger: He should have told me! If he cared for me,
he would have told me.

Replaced by despair: The connection I thought Adam and I
shared was a fantasy conjured up by a girl so pathetic, she poured out
her soul to the dead.

Finally, I am supposed to arrive at acceptance: I wasn't even close.

The next morning, I crept from the closet, picked the lint from my
hair, and tried to pull myself together. I was going to have to explain
the van's condition and the attempted kidnapping to my parents.
Explaining *why* someone would want to kidnap Adam was another
matter altogether and one I planned to avoid for as long as possible.
I mean, what was the good of telling them? So they could call the
authorities? (As if there was someone to call for such a situation.)
And then what? Adam would get hauled off like some alien or
monster or something? To get probed or whatever?

He was not a monster.

Right?

This was nuts. I didn't understand what was true and what was not, and until I figured it out, no way was I saying anything to anybody. Adam deserved whatever protection I could give him. He'd saved me. Twice.

So, no on telling the parents.

I took a tray of food out to Adam's cottage but wasn't up to facing him yet. I eased open the door, averted my eyes from the illusion asleep beneath the crumpled sheet, slid the tray into the room, and skittered away.

I needed answers, anything that could help me come to terms with this new reality. Those two men were after Adam last night for a reason, a knowledge-busting, theory-crushing sort of reason, like maybe Adam was the key to how life on Earth began, or to the process of reanimating the dead, or to eternal life—any one of which would make him worth a mint to the right people or agency. There were plenty of corporations, bullied third-world countries, and zealots with a grudge and a need for expendable manpower who would give anything to have Adam's secret. Small wonder those men tried to kidnap him.

Here we were—about to lose our business and playing Airbnb to a gold mine.

Neil's research alone would be worth a fortune—if it wasn't destroyed in the fire. But what if it was never in the house? What if he hid it? What if Adam knew where he stashed it?

Those were a lot of what-ifs, but I was running out of options.

I turned to my laptop and typed *golem* into the search bar. My search brought up several tales of creatures formed from clay and brought to life through various methods, including incantations and rituals based on the letters of the Hebrew alphabet. In all cases, the golem was never fully human. That was a big *Well, duh.*

The oldest reference to a human conceived from clay was a variation on the creation of Adam and Eve, in which God sculpted the first man out of dust. "Adam," I said aloud. The name of Neil's son. A hint to a lifetime obsession?

There was the tale of Judah Loew ben Bezalel, a rabbi living in the Jewish ghetto of sixteenth-century Prague who shaped a giant figure out of mud he'd gathered from the river Vitava and carved the word *emet* into its forehead. With sacred invocations, he brought that inanimate mass to life. Its purpose? To defend the ghetto from anti-Semitic attacks. Some versions claimed that the golem fell in love, and when rejected, went on a murderous rampage, forcing the rabbi to remove the sacred word from the golem's head, thus rendering it lifeless.

My pulse quickened at the memory of Hayden's party. Adam was nothing if not protective.

I stabbed the power button on my computer, but the words still filled my head. Inhuman. Adam. Overprotective. *Emet.* I wanted to pretend it was all some bizarre coincidence. At some point, though, too many coincidences add up to undeniable fact.

So what was Adam? He was something like a golem. He'd said so himself. What if, buried in all those mystical tales, there was a grain of truth—a grain Neil Lassiter exploited using clay as his medium? This wasn't a question of Adam's humanity.

I mean, okay, maybe his physical makeup had been fudged, and he didn't bleed red blood, and, sure, when he first came to live with us he was (by most standards) emotionally illiterate, but in the short time I'd known him, hadn't I seen firsthand how he adapted and changed? He learned to better manage his anger, to read faces and interpret emotions, and to put others before himself. Could there be anything more human than that?

Nothing about him changed last night. Adam was still, well, Adam. Not the boy from the orchard, but that had always been wishful longing. It was my perception of him that had changed.

Maybe the problem was me. Could I learn to accept him for what he was—someone who skipped over childhood—and not the person I wanted him to be? Even if that were possible, could I convince him to stay? More to the point, *should* I convince him to stay? The two men who assaulted him were still out there, and who knew how many more people had knowledge of his existence?

I heard footsteps down the hall and assumed Rachel and Dad were headed off to church. Dad had never been particularly religious, but ever since his heart attack he'd been letting her drag him to Sunday services. Covering his bases, he called it. I would think an all-knowing god would be able to tell the difference. Then again, maybe there was such a thing as partial credit.

"Evan! Lily!" Dad's voice boomed from the back door of the delivery bay. "Get out here."

Shit. He'd discovered the van. I went right down, knowing the longer I made Dad wait, the angrier he'd get. Evan wasn't far behind. I stood, hands at my back, studying the cracks in the driveway as Dad's fingernail traced a gouge running the length of the car's side panel. He tried to force the taillight's shattered plastic back into position. A big chunk snapped off in his hand.

"You two mind explaining what happened to the van?" he said, waving the plastic at Evan and me. His ruddy face turned nearly purple.

"Now, Cam," warned Rachel. "Stay calm. It does you no good to get all worked up before you even know who's to blame."

"Blame Lily," Evan volunteered. "She was the one driving,"

Thanks, bro.

With a lot of stumbling and verbal self-flagellation, I gave a brief account of what happened, leaving out, of course, the part about Adam's injuries and what they meant.

"Why would someone want to kidnap *him?*" asked my father. "And why did you wait until now to tell me?"

"You were asleep when we got home."

"Did you at least have the sense to call the police?"

"And say what? It was too dark to get a good look at the men, and their SUV didn't have any plates."

Dad checked his anger with a carefully measured breath.

"Maybe Adam got a look at the men," offered Rachel.

"Go fetch him," ordered Dad.

"Uhhhh." I swallowed, imagining the inquisition that would inevitably follow. Rachel would want to get a look at his injuries and might insist he see a doctor. That wouldn't serve anyone, least of all Adam, who couldn't risk any more exposure. "He's asleep. He . . . he had a rough night."

Rachel crossed her arms. "He was drinking. That's why he was too sick for breakfast, isn't it?"

"He only had two," said Evan.

"It was an accident—the drinking, that is," I was quick to add, aware that my credibility was about as intact as the taillight. "Mallory thought it was cream soda."

With all eyes on me, Evan ducked back into the house. The coward.

"I swear it's the truth," I said.

Dad's jaw tensed. "You should have called the police. You could have all been killed. What's wrong with you? Maybe it's a good thing you aren't taking over this place after all. Not that it matters now. You saw to that, didn't you?"

And there it was: the knife to my heart. Traitorous tears clouded my vision; my lower lip quivered uncontrollably. I turned to my stepmother, silently pleading for her to rise to my defense. And did she?

No. She gave him a token pat on the back as he raked his graying hair, questioned where he went wrong as a father, and asked why kids didn't come with manuals like appliances. He ranted until he exhausted himself, then ushered her into the van with orders for me to *goddamn-get-on-the-phone-this-second-and-file-a-report*. And then, to salt the wound, he said, "There's a new arrival in the fridge. Car accident. See if you can handle it without crashing into a wall, will you?"

My shame spilled down my face in fine rivulets, which only added to the sum of my inadequacies, as I watched them drive toward the church, the van rattling down the street like a jar of loose change.

Calling the police wouldn't do any good, but I did it anyway, to appease my father. I couldn't help it. I was a pleaser, just a really lousy one. As expected, the officer who took the report offered little hope of finding last night's perpetrators. She delivered a well-rehearsed "Thank you for calling" and encouraged me to "Keep an eye out for anything suspicious," as if after last night I was too clueless to figure that out on my own.

I retreated to the cold room, where a little numbness would serve me well right about then. With a firm tug on the door handle, I released the pressure seal, and the room inhaled deeply, drawing me in. A black body bag rested on a gurney in the center of the room. Another car accident, Dad had said. We saw too many of those.

I wheeled the gurney to the prep room, slipped on an apron and a fresh pair of gloves, grabbed an ankle band and pen, and, without much thought, pulled down the zipper. The bag yawned open. Staring back was what used to be the face of Shep Bramstead's older brother, Grant.

RULE #32
DEATH IS THE ALMIGHTY LEVELER.

In the prep room, the clock struck three—one for Grant Bramstead, who flew through his windshield; two for the two-lane road that was his racetrack; and three for the brother, mother, and father he left behind.

I gathered myself and made my way to the chapel. Mourners had started to arrive to pay their respects to the grieving. Mr. and Mrs. Bramstead accepted their condolences with tempered hugs and half-hearted handshakes. Shep stood beside them, his swollen eyes safe behind dark glasses. More than once he attempted to catch my attention, but each time I found an excuse to pass someone a prayer card or to direct a mourner to a vacant seat. Half an hour later, the chapel was filled to capacity. Many of those in attendance I recognized from school or from Hayden's party. The body heat alone made heads swoon; men tugged at neckties while women fanned flushed faces with folded memorial brochures.

Despite my loathing for the Bramstead brothers, I had done my best. I'd filled and powdered, stitched and brushed, until the young man on the gurney matched the one now occupying the memory boards surrounding the guest books. Even Dad had to admit that I'd done a decent job. It wasn't easy. More than once I found myself wanting to go off on him for the brutal way he treated Adam the night of Hayden's party, for all the hurt his recklessness caused his family and friends, and, yeah, for wailing on his younger brother until Shep became a shadow of his older sibling. In the end I held my tongue—a rarity for me in the presence of the deceased, but what good would it have done? It's not like he would get a second chance to make it right.

Beside me in the vestibule, Adam fussed with the cuffs and collar of his dress shirt, like usual. He shouldn't have been there. That morning I'd done everything to convince him to take the day off and rest, but he'd insisted on working the funeral. "Then you'd better be on your best behavior," I'd warned. "Dad and Rachel are still fuming over the van."

"I'll explain that it was my fault, say I made you get behind the wheel."

"First, that would be a lie, and you can't lie," I reminded him. "And second, it's sweet of you to offer, but if they believed you, you'd probably lose your job—or worse, your freedom."

He shrugged. "It's only a matter of time, Lily. You said so yourself."

It was a truth I didn't want to hear. Never mind my feelings for him. Neil was right; Adam wasn't ready for the world—and it certainly wasn't ready for him—but he also couldn't stay with us forever, not with those two men searching for him.

I watched him offer an elderly woman his arm. For a monster, he could be incredibly gentle and kind, I noted. She grinned up at him almost flirtatiously. If she only knew. But nothing about him except the deliberate way in which he blinked betrayed that he was an imposter. I knew what he was, though, and it distorted my view of everything. For instance, I knew he could crush that poor woman's arm with a mere squeeze. His gift, though, was that he could just as easily guide her down the aisle like she was made of sugar glass.

If he suffered from his injuries, he masked it well. All the better, since Rachel and Dad were watching our every move. Today Adam had to play the part of the most conscientious employee. Today I couldn't allow myself to shed a single tear.

Our chances of pulling off either dwindled with the arrival of Hayden Jornet.

With a flick of his wrist, Hayden made his mark in the guest book. I shoved a memorial brochure at him. No matter what Mallory said, he was a scumbag, and for her sake I was glad she'd begged off attending the service, although I missed her. From the way Evan kept glancing toward the foyer, I suspected he did, too. Funny, about absence. It has a way of putting things in perspective. Unfortunately it often comes too late.

Beyond the chapel doors, Adam leaned into Hayden's line of sight as he handed a young woman a box of tissues. Hayden sidestepped behind a post, the fear in his eyes hard to miss.

"Yeah, you should be nervous." I said to him. "Adam can be, how shall I put it . . . a little overprotective?"

With a nod from Father Richie, Dad lowered the volume on the sound system until the hymn, "Abide with Me," faded into silence. I swore Hayden waited for that exact moment to make his grand entrance. He sauntered up the aisle like this was the Grammys instead of a funeral for his closest friend, then took a seat behind the Bramsteads. The service began.

Following the eulogy, people were invited forward to speak. Hayden had no qualms about stepping up to the podium. He praised Grant's loyalty and recounted a few of his more colorful antics, making people squirm uncomfortably, before retaking his seat. I'd give Hayden this much: his voice never cracked, he never shed a tear. That explained a lot. You can't have a conscience if you can't feel.

At the conclusion of the service, Shep, Hayden, and two cousins shouldered the gleaming steel-blue casket and walked it down the aisle and out to the hearse, where my father waited behind the wheel, ready to guide the procession to the graveside committal service.

At last the remaining mourners shuffled from the chapel, leaving Adam and me to collect the many wreaths and bouquets for delivery to the internment site. While I wrangled a pair of gladiolus arrangements, he took the largest spray of white roses to the hearse.

Footfalls echoed behind me. Expecting Adam returning for a second load, I did an about-face. It was Shep.

"I can take those," he said, relieving me of the glads. "Can you bring the wreath?"

"Sure." What I really wanted was to wring his neck with it. He'd made sport of me my whole life, but this wasn't the time nor the place for digging up past crimes. I wanted him to see that I took my family's profession seriously, even if he didn't. He would not see me cry, not because of anything my father preached but because he didn't deserve my tears.

I followed him out to his truck and placed the flowers in the cab. Before I could shut the door, he stopped me. "Lily, hold up."

I wheeled on him, certain he was about to slam me with another one of his digs and furious that he had so little respect for the dead—his brother, no less. "No, you hold up! I've put up with your bullying my entire life. You've called me names and harassed me with your childish pranks. I will not stand here and . . . and let you . . ."

Shep toed a chunk of broken sidewalk. "All I wanted to say was thank you." He removed his tinted glasses and stared at me with bloodshot eyes, one of which still showed the greenish tinge of a fading shiner.

"What did you say?"

"I said thank you. I don't know how you did it—how you made my brother look exactly like that photo my mom gave you. That was her favorite picture of him, you know. After the accident, his face . . ."

With that Shep crumpled to the curb, hanging his head between bent knees.

I was stunned beyond words. Never had Shep shown that he cared one spit wad for anyone but himself. Gone was the boy who pelted me with rocks and chased me up trees. Gone was the jerk who couldn't hold his liquor, who thought picking on the weak made him a big man. Gone was his brother, who'd used him as a punching bag. And nothing would bring him back.

Grant had bullied his younger brother, but of course Shep still loved him.

Adam and Rachel were waiting for me in the van. I had no idea how to handle this.

Should I go with the others and leave Shep slumped on the curb to work through his grief in private? That's what Dad would do. Should I pat him on the back and tell him God has a plan for us all? That's what Rachel would do. Or should I point out that the hearse had already left and he needed to pull himself together for his parents' sake? That's what Evan would do.

I raised a finger to Rachel, signaling I needed a minute more. Then I sat down beside Shep and offered him the clean hanky I kept at the ready. He took it but didn't seem to know what to do with it. It became a limp flag of surrender in his lap. "I was there, you know," he said. "At the finish line, when he lost control and plowed into that retaining wall."

"I heard. I'm so sorry."

"Yeah, and that dumbass Hayden didn't even stick around. At the first siren, he split."

Sounded like Hayden.

"I didn't get it until today," Shep continued, running his hands through his shoulder-length hair. "What you do. You're a real artist." That's what Adam had once said only more eloquently. "I bet you're the one who stitched Grant's name into the lining on that pillow, too."

I nodded, embarrassed that someone had noticed, especially him.

"Well, I'm glad it was you who looked after him. You're really good at what you do. You know that?"

I was beginning to.

He tried to hand me back the hanky, but I told him to keep it.

Then he scraped himself off the curb and climbed into his truck to join the procession.

"I'm confused," said Rachel, as I took the seat beside Adam. "Isn't that the same boy who always gave you such a hard time at school?"

"He used to be," I said. *I'm not the same girl I used to be, either. Not anymore.* Too much had happened to me over the summer.

"You all right?" asked Adam, who understood more than Rachel ever could.

"Yeah, I'm fine," I said. Better than fine. If only Grandpa Ted were here. I would tell him I finally figured out the reason I survived that fall from the walnut tree. It wasn't because of some fate waiting for me outside the mortuary. It wasn't because I had something to offer the dead. It was because I had something to offer the loved ones left behind. And, of all people, it was Shep who pointed out the truth.

In a way, it was as if I'd spent my whole life resisting an arranged marriage only to discover I was in love with the groom.

Of course, realizing this now meant squat if we lost the mortuary. Somehow I needed to convince Dad not to sell. There had to be another way out of our financial crisis, but I didn't have a clue what that could be, short of selling out Adam.

RULE #33
NO TIME LIKE MOURNING
FOR DECIDING WHAT REALLY MATTERS.

Nana's gravelly voice was at the door. "Rachel says she can give you a ride over to the high school if you still need one."

I peeked at my tail-swishing cat clock from under the pillow. "Oh hell!" If I didn't get going, I'd miss Mallory. She'd been ignoring my calls and texts ever since the whole beach fiasco. I figured the best time to catch her was during class registration day. I had the perfect excuse for revisiting my old school—my stack of long-overdue library books. I flung back the bedsheets, jumped in the shower for a quick rinse, and raced downstairs.

Rachel traipsed through the back door, her arms loaded with fresh-cut flowers. "You ought to smell these. That boy has such a gift with plants."

Adam is no boy, I wanted to tell her, but she'd take it another way.

"Is he up yet?" she asked. "He might want to enroll in a couple of classes down at the city college. If he gets a move on, I can give him a ride, too. Don't suppose he has a copy of his birth certificate in a safe-deposit box somewhere?"

I'd bet money he doesn't even know what a birth certificate is, let alone have one.

"He left early this morning for Sal Zmira's carrying two jugs of muddy swill," said Nana, who was lacing up her walking shoes.

"Said something about compost tea," added Evan.

He shouldn't be carrying anything, I thought, *not until that wound heals.*

Dad shuffled into the room, newspaper tucked under his arm. "Morning. Heard about the trophy, Evan. You worked hard for that. Proud of you. Shame you didn't get to bring it home."

It was a jumble of gilded sunblock bottles and bicycle parts, for Christ's sake. I shoveled yogurt into my mouth, wondering when I'd finally do something to impress my father. Never mind that while he was convalescing, devising pumpernickel recipes, and ruminating over sourdough starters, I'd been practically running things. There was no trophy for that. Lately there hadn't even been a paycheck.

As soon as I was in the van, Rachel launched into a lecture—twentieth in the series, if I hadn't lost count—on making the most of my time now that I had my high school equivalency diploma. She wanted me to be more like Evan—join some clubs, take up a sport, apply for scholarships. I told her I wasn't Evan. I didn't have his brains or his athleticism, and thanks to a less-than-stellar GED score, it would take all I had to get into a decent college. Forget scholarships.

"You know, not everyone needs a four-year college degree. Have you considered cosmetology? You could work in a salon," she said, because in her mind, now that the mortuary was nearly out of the question, that was my best and only option.

I mentioned that, by the way, putting yourself out there is exactly how Evan got himself into that whole team-betting fiasco last year. That solicited a nasty look, and she said she liked it better when I was silent. Fine. I could do silent.

By the time we arrived, the school was packed with students picking up class schedules, locker assignments, and student IDs. *This was a dumb idea. How am I ever going to find Mal in this circus?*

Walking to the library, I felt so out of place, but then again, I'd always felt that way while at this school. Moving on had definitely been the best choice for me.

I returned my books, paid the hefty over-due fee, and was heading to the office to request a copy of my transcript when I spotted her outside the gym, chatting and laughing with a couple girls from last year's cheer squad. I waved. She pretended not to see me, so I strolled over.

"What are you doing here?" she asked, like this was her arena now and I had no business intruding.

"Oh, Rachel dropped me off so I could return some books and pick up a copy of my transcript." I said casually.

"Uh huh." She turned back to the other girls. "Hey, give me a minute, okay?"

"Coach won't like it if you're late to tryouts," warned one as they disappeared inside.

"You're trying out for the spirit team?" Mal had never struck me as the cheerleader sort.

"I figured I'd give it a shot, try something different. What's the worst that could happen?"

"Besides epic humiliation?"

"Gee, thanks for the vote of confidence, and there are worse things, you know. Where's your sense of adventure?"

"What do you want me to do? Take up skydiving? Share drinks with strangers? Have unprotected sex? And what about the drive home the other night? I thought that was pretty adventurous."

She grimaced at the memory. "That was reckless. There's a difference. I'm talking about being open to meeting new people, trying new things, taking a few risks."

I wanted to point out that I didn't always play it safe. I'd been hanging out with goddamn Edward Scissorhands but without the sharp hardware and zippered leather. Of course, if I was being totally honest, I didn't know that until two nights ago. "Look, I know you're mad at me, and I don't blame you. I've been a real stick-in-the-mud." It was another one of Rachel's go-to clichés, but if the stick stuck, I'd use it. "So if you want me to go to more parties, the mall, whatever, with you, I'll go. And I should never have yelled at you like that, in the car. I'm sorry. I was scared."

"Is that why you think I'm angry? Because you bailed on a couple parties and finally got up the guts to drive faster than ten miles an hour under the speed limit?"

"Speed kills, you know."

"Lily, that's not the point! This is about Evan. The other night at the bonfire, I finally told him how I felt."

"That's good, isn't it?"

"No, it was disastrous. He said he couldn't have a relationship with his stepsister's best friend. It would be too weird. I felt like an idiot, especially after I found out you already knew how he felt. Why didn't you say anything?"

Because you wouldn't have listened to me.

That's what I thought. What I said was "I didn't want to hurt you."

"Well, it would have been a lot less painful coming from you than from him." Mallory sighed. "Lily, friends tell each other things. Personal things."

"I told you I lied about my weight on my driver's license application."

"That isn't a lie; it's a requirement. Everybody lies about that. I'm talking, like, real stuff."

"Like how the bronzer you're using to enhance your cleavage is too dark for your skin tone?"

"What? Seriously?" She glanced down and hiked up the neckline of her tank top. Her face turned Peony Pink. "Yeah, like that. And like stuff about you and Adam."

"Me and Adam?"

"Exactly. I have eyes, you know. I see how you two are—always together, all that whispering, the nervous tension. Adam practically drools when you come into a room. And you're even worse. That thing you do with your lower lip."

"What thing?"

She kneaded her lower lip with her upper teeth.

"Ew. I don't do that, do I?"

She gave me a look like *You gotta be kidding.*

"Nervous habit," I said.

"The thing is you said nothing, shared nothing with me."

I wanted to tell her that it wasn't like I'd said anything to Adam about how I felt, either, but I let her have her say.

"Lily, if we were best friends, you'd have told me you two were a thing."

"*Were* best friends?" I repeated. "Aren't we still?"

Inside the gym the band struck up the school fight song with a head-pounding *boom boom* of drums and a heralding of trumpets. "I've gotta go," Mal said. She gathered her tryout form and stole into the gym.

"Call me!" I said to no one.

I phoned Rachel to tell her I was ready to go home. She replied that I'd have to wait an hour or so while she finished running errands. It was her passive-aggressive way of telling me I needed to think about someone besides myself for a change.

I took my usual seat beneath the blue cedar that graced the front lawn of the school to wait and to do the one thing I usually avoided—think. It was bad enough Dad was selling the mortuary and gutting any hopes of keeping it in the family. I didn't need Mal dumping me, too.

As I mulled over her words, I began to see she was right. I had been keeping my confidences to myself. It was because I feared the day was coming when she'd finally realize I was the one holding her back. And if she left me, would she keep my secrets?

All summer I'd seen signs of her outgrowing me—her whole reinvention campaign, the shopping sprees, the new set of friends. So what did I do in response? I gave her every reason to give up on me. Maybe it was time I gave her a reason to stay. Maybe it was time I trusted her.

I heard the van circling the parking lot long before it pulled up to the curb. Rachel clucked at my red-rimmed eyes and shoved a tissue packet my way before asking what was wrong. I didn't answer, so for the rest of the way home she rattled on about the vacation to Hawaii she and Dad were planning for their anniversary and how they'd been slaves to the business their whole marriage and that no one lived forever, you know.

I knew.

When we got home, the first thing I noticed was that the hearse was gone. "We get a call?"

"No one told you?" said Rachel.

"Told me what?"

"Jim Sturbridge made us an offer on the mortuary. Why'd you think I was going on about Hawaii? It isn't all we hoped for, but it's decent enough and beats filing for bankruptcy. You should have seen how excited your father was. Almost left for the realtor's in his slippers. He's there now, drawing up a counteroffer." She sighed. "What a relief this'll be for everyone."

Not everyone.

I retreated to the prep room to find comfort in my dearest possessions—my basket filled with a painter's palette of embroidery floss, my favorite pair of scissors, and two pampered badger-hair brushes—but what good were they if there was no work? I was alone with no one to listen, not even the dead. Adam would listen. Always Adam. But it was too late for talk. What was done was done.

Or was it?

What if there was a way everyone could get what they wanted? Devlin could get the papers that cost him eight years of his life, Adam could have his independence, and I could have the mortuary. It would be risky. If Devlin double-crossed us or word got out about Adam, more than our funeral home would be at stake. Reporters would swarm him all over again, and chances were good that his entire future would be put on the auction block and sold to the highest bidder. If the truth about him were known . . . well, that would be a total game changer. Those were huge stakes compared to one little family business.

And yet hadn't everyone been telling me all along to take more risks?

I dried my face on a clean towel, brushed the hair from my eyes, and pinched my cheeks to put some color in them. Time to pay my dues to the Cowards Anonymous Club and fess up.

RULE #34
DON'T LOSE YOURSELF IN THE NARRATIVE OF DEATH AND DYING.

I found Adam in Paradise. He was crouched beneath the apple tree, his fingers sifting through a small mound of wood pulp at the base of the tree.

I cleared my throat, and he looked up, not particularly surprised to see me. "Heartwood," he said.

"As in the heart of the tree?"

"Yes, Carpenter ants have moved into the heart of the tree to build their nest."

"Does that mean the tree is dying?"

"Most likely," he said, standing and brushing off his knees.

"But it was starting to come back. Can anything be done to save it?"

"Time will tell, won't it?" He squinted at me and tilted his head. "I would call that look on your face . . . despair."

"Two points to you."

"It's not all bad news. Look." He pointed to a green sprout crowned in red-hued leaves growing out of the otherwise barren *Rosa* 'Queen Elizabeth'.

I sighed. "Starting over is a thorny undertaking."

"That's quite profound. But you aren't talking about the garden, are you?"

"No. Dad got an offer on the mortuary this morning. It's all but sold, and to Jim Sturbridge of all people."

"I'm sorry. For a lot of things."

"Me too."

He held out his hand to me, but as much as his touch tempted me, it felt dishonest to accept it. "Adam, I have a confession. I tried to tell you on the beach, but . . ."

"But I told you it could wait."

"Yeah." I took a deep breath. "But it can't wait, not if I want to stop the sale."

"You're going to fight this. Good. So then . . . ?"

I hesitated but decided it was better just to blurt it out. "I had a meeting with Miles Devlin."

Adam forced a blink. "You what?! How could—? Why didn't you tell me?"

"I was afraid." My trembling voice was proof enough of that. "Look at you. You're freaking out, and I haven't even told you what happened yet."

"Freaking out?" He circled the tree like he wanted to yank it from the ground. "He killed my . . . He killed Neil."

"We don't know that for sure. Please, Adam, let me explain. I think I've found a way for both of us to get what we want, but I need your help."

"How do you know what I want?"

"I know you want to live a life of your own, to go where you please. I know you want to leave and get as far away from here as possible."

"Then you know nothing. You seriously think I want to leave you?"

"Don't you?"

"No! But it's not like I have a choice, not if I want to protect you and your family."

"Then hear me out," I begged.

He planted his feet and crossed his arms. "I'm listening."

"First, know that when Devlin first called me, I had no idea who I was talking to. I figured it was some sort of screwy sales pitch. He said he had a way to help our business, and I didn't see the harm in hearing what he had to say."

"You met with him in secret."

I backed off a step, alarmed by the venom in his voice. "Okay, yeah."

"What did he want?"

I took my time finding the right words. "Your father's research documents. In exchange he'd ensure that we could keep the family business. He claimed he never stole the documents. He said your father framed him and sent him to prison, like Veronica said."

"Lily, the man should be in prison for murder."

"You don't know that, not for sure. Besides, even if he was tried and convicted, he'd never see the inside of a cell. Adam, he's dying."

"So he says."

"You weren't there. You didn't see him."

"You're right. I wasn't there because you went without me. Does he even have the money to pay you?"

"Pay *us*," I corrected. "He says he does."

"And you believe him."

I gave a hesitant nod.

"Then you're a fool. Did he tell you what was in the documents?"

"Only that it had to do with the Seed of Life Project. I think I can guess the rest." My eyes fixed on the bandages faintly visible beneath his white cotton tee.

"I suspect you can. So why are you telling me this now?"

"I hoped you might know where Neil hid his research, if it even exists."

"You want to sell me out to Devlin?"

"No! I think there's a way for us all to get what we want. Devlin wants to prevent the information contained in those documents from falling into the wrong hands. We'll give him only the papers that he and Neil worked on together, and we'll destroy anything else that would compromise your . . . true nature. We'd split the money from Devlin. With your half, you could get a fresh start."

"And with your half, you'd stop the sale of the mortuary."

"Exactly."

"Are you sure this is what you want?"

"More than anything."

He took a couple of turns around the dying apple tree, slower now, careful to mask his emotions but not careful enough to remember to blink. He stopped, leaning against the tree with one shoulder until I couldn't tell which was supporting the other. "He give you a way to reach him?"

"He did. So you'll help me? You'll tell me where the research is hidden?"

"No. I'll take the documents to Devlin myself. It'll be safer that way."

"We do this together or not at all." I braced myself, expecting him to refuse my terms but also hoping he was desperate enough to agree.

"Okay, together."

"You promise?"

"Yes, I promise. Now the phone number."

"Okay, but before I give it to you, I have one more condition. You have to give your word that you'll hear him out. If he's responsible for your father's death in any way, we call the police."

"But I—"

"I'll lose the mortuary before I let you hurt an innocent man."

"You're still assuming he's innocent."

"Innocent until proven guilty."

"*Ei incumbit probatio qui dicit.*" He hesitated. "Okay, I promise."

Knowing he couldn't lie, his word was good enough for me. I pulled out my phone and the rumpled napkin, pressed speaker, and dialed the number. At the first ring, Adam swiped the phone from my hand.

"Clearview Extended Stay, front desk," answered a receptionist.

Adam asked for Miles Devlin. At first the man refused to give him any information until he insisted it was a family emergency. Technically it wasn't, but it must have seemed like one to Adam. How else could he have said it?

"In that case," said the receptionist, "would you like me to put you through to his room?"

"Please."

"Hello?" The deep, coarse voice on the other end was immediately recognizable as Devlin. "Who is this?"

"Adam Lassiter."

There was a long silence. "Your girlfriend doesn't follow instructions very well."

"No, she doesn't." Adam glared at me. "But let's leave her out of this."

"I see," said Devlin with a hint of amusement. "So she doesn't know you're calling me. Interesting."

"I'm the one who has what you want."

"How is that, exactly?"

"I'm Neil Lassiter's son."

There was a loud cough on the other end, loud enough to make me jump. Did he know what Adam was? How could he? He'd been serving time when the lab accident occurred, and for all we knew he had no idea Neil's son had died. But just the remote possibility that Devlin suspected was enough to rattle Adam. He held the phone by the tips of his fingers, as if it might burn him.

"Let me be clear," said Adam, once he'd regained his composure. "I'm prepared to give you Neil's research, but there's a price."

"There always is," Devlin said. "But this is important to me."

"Important enough to kill for it?"

"How much do you want?" The charm in Devlin's voice had evaporated.

I quickly wrote a number in the dirt at the base of the tree.

Adam read it off as if it were a question. "I want one hundred and fifty thousand dollars in unmarked bills?"

Unmarked bills? I didn't write that.

Devlin snorted. "You've been watching too many crime dramas, son. I don't do business with greedy people."

"The money is not for me. It's for Lily—the McCraes," he corrected.

"Ah, how chivalrous. You must care for them a lot to hand over that kind of money so easily."

With our faces hovering over the phone, our eyes met. *I do*, he mouthed to me. To Devlin, he said, "The McCraes took me in when I had nowhere else to go."

"And how do I know you have what I want?"

"Listen. The research documents were part of the Seed of Life Project. Its emblem consists of concentric circles. The overlapping circles form a flower. The precept was that life originated not from a chemical amalgam brought together by the tides, but from clay particles. The notes include multiple volumes of data as well as daily logs written in Greek and Latin. You went to prison for stealing them from Arman Research. Should I continue?"

"No, that's about the gist of it, all except for the part about *Neil* being the one who stole the information from *me*, but I don't suppose he ever mentioned that part, now did he? Nor, I imagine, did he tell you that he was the one who set me up to take the blame."

"And now you want the research. To do what, clear your name?"

"That would only work if I could prove Neil was in possession of it. Most likely they'd say I'd planted the documents. No, I want the research because I intend to destroy it. That was always my intention, which is why Neil misappropriated the documents and pinned it on me. I had learned quite by accident that a particular government agency was interested in obtaining our reanimation process. They wanted to use it to build a super army and were willing to pay an exorbitant amount of money. The one thing holding up the transaction was that we had yet to create a viable prototype."

A prototype? Is that what Adam is supposed to be? He must have been wondering the same, because his free hand drifted to his chest where Neil had inked his skin.

There was a noise on the other end—a knock on a door, perhaps. Devlin's voice was suddenly breathy and lower in volume. "Where and when?"

Adam cut a questioning glance at me.

"Tomorrow night at ten o'clock. Corner of Mason and Fifth, near the old post office," I whispered.

Adam repeated the location and time and added, "Once I see that you have the money, I'll take you to where the notes are stashed. You don't show, I find another buyer. Shouldn't be too difficult based on what you've told me."

With that the call ended, but our heads remained locked over the blacked-out screen, the tension between us palpable.

"Think this is going to work? He'll pay us for the information?"

"It better," he said, eyeing me. I realized I was chewing my lower lip. Curse Mallory for knowing me better than I knew myself.

His answer was not exactly the vote of confidence I was after, but beggars can't be choosers, as Rachel would say, and right then I knew I needed to do a little begging if we were going to see this through together.

He stood so close, I could nearly taste him. "Can you forgive me for not telling you about Devlin?"

"I'm working on it." With an icy finger he traced the curve of my mouth. It made me hunger all the more for his. I should have been focusing on how this was all going to go down with Devlin—not on how to close the distance between us.

My fingers grazed his arms, and he drew me in until we were chest to chest, our lips a hair's breadth apart.

I frowned and pulled away.

"I'm sorry," he blustered, misreading my reaction. "Did I—?"

"No, no, it's . . . You're so cold."

"Am I?"

I slipped my hands beneath his shirt and was rewarded with a sharp inhalation. He closed his eyes as my thumbs traced his waistband, meeting at his navel. I wondered if I should keep going. A contented sigh was my answer. Boldly I let my fingers travel his sides, counting each perfectly rendered rib. Adam's ribs. My hands came together again over his heart.

But something felt wrong, dreadfully wrong. I withdrew my hands. They were smeared with his rust-colored blood.

I backed away, reaching blindly for the gate latch.

"Lily?"

"I have to get—"

"No, stop. Please." He took one step and wilted beside the dying tree.

RULE #35
THERE'S A PERFECT VESSEL
FOR EVERY BODY.

Evan was stone-cold silent, his hand welded to the railing, his eyes fixed on the figure lying so still on the gurney. It was never my plan to tell him, but there was no way I could have hauled Adam to the prep room on my own.

I placed a wad of gauze over the reopened wound. Evan swayed. "I swear, if you pass out . . ."

"I'm good," he said, clutching the counter.

"Then go keep a lookout at the door while I work." To my surprise, he obeyed.

Face to the crack in the door, he mumbled, "How long have you known?"

"Since the night at the beach. He didn't want anyone to know. You can imagine why. So you can't tell a soul, not even Rachel or Dad."

"Like anyone would believe me. I'm not sure *I* believe me. A golem? Holy crap!"

"A golem, yes, but more than—"

In his delirium Adam moaned and lashed out, clobbering me. The blow sent me into a cabinet.

"You okay?" asked Evan.

"Yeah, thanks," I said, rubbing my chin. "He's stronger than he looks."

Adam seemed caught in some night terror, making it nearly impossible for me to finish redressing his wound.

"What's wrong with him, anyway?" asked Evan. "You said it was only a scratch."

"It is, but it isn't healing. If this doesn't work, I don't know what to do."

"I do. You turn him in to the police, and then you call the media and get a bidding war going for the story. With any luck, we'd get enough to stall the sale of the mortuary."

"You can't be serious. I can't do that!"

"Right, because what do you care about the business?"

"It's not that at all. Do you know what would happen if knowledge like this got out, the ability to create life from clay? It would have huge repercussions—in science, in our culture, you name it. We've already seen what people are willing to do for it. And what about Adam? Once people found out what he is, he'd be thrown under a microscope, virtually, if not literally, dissected. His life such as it is would be toast."

"I guess you're right, but what do you care?"

"I just do," I said.

"Oh my god, look at you! You're turning red. My little stepsis has totally fallen for a—a *whatever*. I don't believe it. I knew you were weird, but this!" He gestured at Adam.

"Shut up! Do you hear me? Shut. Up." I threw down the roll of gauze, grabbed Evan by the shoulders, and forcibly wrenched him around to face me. "I have never asked you for anything. I'm asking you to do this for me now. Can you?"

As soon as I released him, he backed as far from me as he could, both hands held high in surrender. "Way to toughen up, buttercup. But all right. I promise. I won't tell a soul."

I had to wonder why I'd never stood up to him before. Probably for the same reason I'd never stood up to Shep or any of the others who took me for easy game: fear that none of them would take me seriously. And why would they, when I didn't take myself seriously?

I refocused on the job at hand. "A couple more pieces of tape and then we have to move him to the cottage without anyone seeing us."

"I have to carry him all the way out there?"

"Evan, you carry bodies all the time, some much heavier."

"Not like his."

"Now who's the buttercup?"

Getting Adam to his room proved no easy feat, but together we managed. Already his temperature had dropped several more degrees. I placed a warm water bottle on his chest and instructed Evan to tell Rachel, Dad, and Nana that Adam and I went to a movie and wouldn't be back until late. To my surprise, he didn't argue.

Rachel had packed away all our electric blankets for the summer, so I sat with Adam, changing out cooled compresses for warm ones to raise his temperature. When that didn't work, I crawled into the bed beside him. Nestled against him, I felt each shiver, heard each syllable of his incoherent ramblings. Most were in Latin or Ancient Greek, but every now and then he spoke to someone he called the girl in pink flip-flops. He told her—twelve-year-old me—that he waited each day, hoping she'd cut through the orchard. I wondered again how he knew any of it. It couldn't be memory. *This* Adam did not exist back then.

I felt his forehead. He easily could be one of the cold ones lying on the prep table. Without thinking I slipped into that comfortable place where I could talk freely, openly, without fear of judgment.

"And then one afternoon in the late fall," I said softly, as if I were telling him a Grimms' fairy tale, "his mother sends him out to pick walnuts so she can bake him a loaf of banana bread, his favorite—or so he tells me. A few nuts remain on the uppermost branches, which is where he is when a girl comes tearing through the orchard, followed by a pack of kids calling her names and pelting her with twigs, walnuts, and rocks. He shouts to her, leans down, and gives her a hand. He promises he'll protect her, and together they climb to the top of the tree. It's a promise he can't keep.

"Eventually, the kids down below grow bored and leave. For a time she's safe. The boy tells her he wants his own orchard someday. The girl says her father is hoping she'll become a funeral director, like her grandfather and her grandfather's father.

"But then it all goes wrong. The boy with the lovely deep brown, gold-flecked eyes lowers to the ground and announces it's safe to climb down. But the girl loses her footing and drops to the earth, breaking a femur and shattering her pelvis. The shock of the fall stops her heart.

"He breathes life back into her, his breath for hers, keeping her alive until someone—his mother, a stranger?—hears his cries for help and comes to see what's the matter. The doctors don't think she'll walk again."

"She's broken . . . broken," Adam muttered.

"No," I say. "Not completely. She endures surgery after surgery, months of physical therapy. One day she takes a step, and then another. By then so much time has gone by. Still, she wants to thank the boy, but she worries. What if he rejects her? Finally she finds an ounce of courage, wraps a sand dollar in a brown paper bag, and brings it to his house. She figures he could use a couple angels."

But her gift never reaches the boy, and he dies.

"And then I found you. So see, I'm not broken. Not anymore. You mended me. You showed me that hiding is worse than facing what frightens me."

Adam calmed after that, falling into a deep but restless slumber, and I resumed my place in the chair beside his bed in case Evan returned.

Later that evening Evan brought me a chicken potpie, still bubbling from the oven. Coincidence, or did he actually remember potpie was my favorite go-to comfort food?

"How's he doing?" he asked, more serious than I was used to.

"Not good," I said.

He tentatively touched Adam's forearm, which was flopped over the mattress. "His skin is really cold—about fifteen-minutes-gone cold."

"Any of the others asking about us?"

He shook his head. "Nope. I told them you two were shacked up at some sleazy hotel."

There was the Evan I knew and loved. "Very funny. What did you really tell them?"

"I said you were sleeping over at Mal's and Adam had gone to Zmira's to play cards."

"Does Adam even know how to play cards?"

"Sure. Tony and I taught him."

And probably took him for every penny he had.

To my amazement, Evan stuck around. We talked about how he was looking forward to school next year and was beginning to wonder if he'd made a mistake with Mal. I told him he could do worse—a lot worse. Yeah, she could be shallow and a bit self-absorbed, but that was exactly why they would make such a great match. That got me a playful elbow jab to the ribs.

"Dad tell you about the offer?" Evan asked.

I nodded.

"Did he tell you it includes the house and the grounds?"

"No, but I guess I shouldn't be surprised." Still, it pained me to think of moving out of this house, of never again hearing the voices of my ancestors in its creaks and rattles, of letting the dust settle on every hand-wrought furnishing without my fingers to run through it, of abandoning all this—everything they'd built from nothing but a dream for a better life. I looked Evan square in the eyes. "I don't want to sell. I changed my mind. Not that I've told Dad, Rachel, or Nana."

"So now you want the business? *You?*" He gave a loud huff, like he thought the idea was totally ridiculous—inconceivable, even.

"Why not?"

"You do makeup."

"That doesn't mean I can't do more."

"Dad failed. What makes you think you can you do any better?"

"Well, for a start, I'd take on a couple additional people to help run the office and rehire Tony with a raise while I get my mortician certification. I also have a whole plan drawn up to do more with our advertising."

"Oh, here we go with that logo stuff again."

"Yes, *that logo stuff again*, plus a lot more. Stop sounding like Dad. Evan, they're good ideas. We have to get out there and advertise."

He shrugged, but at least he shut up and listened.

"We need to make our business stand out from the competition. We could offer premortem packages so people can pay in advance. I think families would go for that. Green burial options are growing in popularity, and there's that new line of caskets coming out called Elements, the size-inclusive ones." We'd seen the brochures from the vendors. "It's more affordable than custom ordering, and honestly, it's about time caskets came in a wider size range. I've also started looking into building our own crematorium. You know, permits, loans, that sort of thing. We have the land—"

Evan held up both hands. "Whoa, hold on, girl. Those are all great ideas. Why haven't you ever said anything before now?"

"I'm *just* a makeup artist," I said, imitating Rachel's honeyed voice. "What do I know about business?"

"You should have said something."

"I did. *That logo stuff*, remember?" He had the decency to look shamefaced. "Standing up and making suggestions has brought me nothing but grief around here. I'm so done with that."

Adam stirred. Had he heard? The way he slipped in and out of consciousness, it was hard to tell. They say hearing's the last sense to go. I couldn't bear to think about it.

"It's not too late," Evan added, giving my shoulder a brotherly fist bump. "I think you should go for it. You'd make a great funeral director. Maybe you could work for someone else and then open your own funeral home down the road."

"It wouldn't be the same."

"Yeah, I guess not."

It wasn't until Evan left and I'd relocked the door that I realized that was probably the most we'd ever talked.

I stayed with Adam, passing the time by mindlessly stitching daisies on a scrap of satin. By two in the morning, his body temperature had steadied and his fits were fewer and further between. It was the first sign that he might survive this after all. Now all I had to do was keep him still long enough for the wound to heal—if that was possible. Did his skin cells even regenerate like mine? I doubted it. In addition to the bruises he received at the hands of the ex-feds, there were still traces of discoloration where Hayden kicked him, and the missing plug of skin on his forearm wasn't any better, either.

I watched him sleep. He was a masterpiece in nearly every regard—*Neil's masterpiece*, I reminded myself—and as human in his actions as anyone I'd ever known, more so than some if you included Jim Sturbridge, Hayden Jornet, or the Bramstead brothers.

I dozed off and didn't wake until long after the first light of dawn had peeked through the gap between the drawn curtains. When I lifted my head, Adam was staring at me, a narrow blade of sunshine falling across his face. "Thirsty?" I asked, handing him the glass of water from the nightstand.

"What happened?"

"Your wound opened. I redid the dressing. If you take it easy for a few days, it should heal."

"But I promised Zmira . . . I'd trim his front hedges today . . . and we're meeting Devlin tonight."

"You and your promises. You're in no condition to do either. You can't even keep your eyes open. Zmira will understand." *Not really.* "And I'll meet with Devlin. You need your rest."

To my relief, he didn't argue. Instead he asked for the mirror on the bureau. I brought it to him, and he had me peel back the edges of the taped gauze to examine where the gash grazed one of the characters inked into his flesh.

"*Met,*" he mumbled.

"Who did you meet?" I asked.

He pointed to the tattoo again. "*Met,*" he repeated.

"Oh, *emet.* Yes, I know. It means 'truth.' I read about it. That's why you can only speak the truth." I was proud I'd figured out that much.

He rolled his head side to side.

"Adam, I don't understand what you're trying to tell me."

But he'd drifted off again. Probably for the best.

I left a plate of food and a note with strict instructions telling him to rest in case he woke while I was out. I'd be back to check on him later. I went to the main house to shower, change, and get a bite to eat. We had a new client, three sisters inquiring for their mother, and I wanted to look my best. Yesterday, to my parents' surprise,

I'd asked to handle the arrangement conference. Rachel assured me she'd be close by in case I ran into any difficulties.

* * *

After going over the various plans we offered, I led the Rhodes sisters to our display room. "Let me show you our options. As you can see, we have several vessels to choose from for a scattering at sea. The pink salt crystal urn has been particularly popular this year."

Lisa, the oldest and most pragmatic of the sisters, frowned. "You drop the whole thing into the water?"

"You can," I say. "In time the vessel dissolves and the ashes scatter with the currents."

"That would be nice," said Hailey. "Mom always did like the ocean."

Lisa shot her a look that could have come right out of Evan's playbook. "Couldn't we leave the ashes in the cardboard box they came in? It would be a lot cheaper, and it's not like she'll know the difference."

"That's such a callous thing to say," sniffed Carla-in-the-middle.

We could be here all day. I checked my watch.

Correction: We'd been here all day, and I was getting worried about Adam.

"May I make a suggestion?" Their heads bobbed in unison. "Your mother was an avid guitarist, am I right?"

Carla blew her nose. "How'd you know that?"

I handed her a fresh box of tissues. "Well, she had long nails on her right hand and short nails on her left. And the calluses on her fingertips? Steel strings." The girls exchanged perplexed glances that slowly gave way to understanding. "So here's my idea. I know a local woman who can make a custom papier-mâché box using some of your mother's favorite sheet music. She's very reasonable, and it would add that personal touch you're all looking for."

They loved the idea, and in my head I was already envisioning what I'd stitch for her viewing: a white-velvet drawstring purse embroidered all around with black music notes. It would be a surprise. We made the final arrangements, and Carla agreed to deliver the sheet music later in the week.

I escorted them to the door, and as they left I overheard Hailey say, "I'm so glad we went with this mortuary over that other one. Lily's young, but I feel like she knows Mom, knows what she would have wanted. That's such a comfort, don't you think?"

The others were quick to agree, and I sensed an inner satisfaction like none I'd experienced before. It wasn't like the dead ever congratulated me on a job well done. In a way I felt as if I'd come home after a long journey full of wrong turns and roads leading nowhere—but I'd arrived too late. My home would soon belong to someone else.

I finished up the paperwork in the office, made a call to get an estimate on the papier-mâché box, and then ran it all by Rachel, who gave me her stamp of approval—or the equivalent: a freshly baked snickerdoodle. The parlor required a quick vacuum, and then I was bounding up to my room, where I unpinned my name tag from my blouse and set it on the sill beside the potted pansy from Adam. I didn't take time to change. I would do that later, since I was anxious to get back to him.

On my way out I passed Rachel and Nana in front of the TV, a bowl of popcorn between them, watching *Serpico*. Must have been Nana's turn to pick the flick. "Where's Evan?" I asked.

"Taking out the trash," mumbled Nana through a mouth full of popcorn.

"Now that's the perfect Godfather impersonation." When I asked if I could borrow a car for later that evening, Rachel said Dad was out on the first of two removals. "The van's at the body shop for repairs, so he had to take the hearse," she added.

I'd have to walk to meet Devlin.

Adam would be starving by now, so I packed a few leftovers, nabbed a carton of chocolate milk I'd kept hidden at the back of the refrigerator just for him, and hustled out into the fading twilight.

The cottage was dark. I let myself in and flicked on the light.

Adam's bed was empty.

I checked the pass-through and Nana's workshop. He was nowhere. I felt a surge of panic until I realized his things were still where he'd left them. So where was he?

And then I remembered him telling me about a promise to Zmira to trim his front hedges. That had to be it. *Idiot! What is he thinking? He's in no shape for yard work.*

At least he hadn't left me for good, but the sun was setting. He should have been back by now, and I worried that Zmira had conned him into more chores. Looked like it was up to me to keep Adam from doing himself in.

My meeting with Devlin was in a little over an hour— assuming he showed. I rushed out the back gate, thinking the alley was the quickest path to Zmira's, and ran into Evan. "Where you off to?" he asked, slamming down the lid on the garbage can.

"To stop Adam from digging himself into an early grave."

"What?"

"No time to explain."

With an indifferent shrug, Evan went back to the house, locking the gate behind him.

I'd gone six houses when an engine rumbled to life, its cough and sputter hard to miss. I glanced back and saw an old clunker creeping along. The way it prowled the empty alley reminded me of a certain SUV in a beach parking lot and sent a shiver coursing through me. Had the ex-feds switched cars? If it was them, I needed to warn Adam, but I also couldn't risk leading them to him in the process.

The clunker was getting closer. I slipped into the shadows of a nearby dumpster, my heart pounding in my chest. The old heap slowed, stalled, and revved back to life to resume it's hunt. I leaned against the fence to my back, doing my best to keep out of sight, and felt one of the boards give. I lifted it free, slipped into the yard, and replaced it.

With my eye to a knothole further along the fence, I watched to see what the car would do, hoping I was imagining things. I wasn't. The clunker came to a stop beside the dumpster, the engine still coughing like it was on its last piston. I was certain now that I was being followed.

At last the car rumbled away in a cloud of oily smoke. I didn't get a good a look at the driver, but a peeling sticker on the rear bumper read Rent-a-Wreck.

I turned back down the alley. Whoever was behind the wheel of the Rent-a-Wreck was going to be disappointed if they thought I would take them to Adam.

I knew a shortcut.

RULE #36
THE CLOTHES MAKE THE CORPSE.

The only way through was over.

I stripped off my work shoes, hitched up my skirt, and scaled the chain-link fencing circling the decrepit old elementary school. I cut straight through the yard and to the other side, again scaling the fence to exit the property. This time, though, the hem of my skirt snagged. That was my best skirt, too. Oh well. If I couldn't stop the sale of the mortuary, I wouldn't be needing it anyway.

My slow limp across the parking lot brought me to Sluice Street a little after nine. After walking a couple more blocks, I faced Sal Zmira's house. My shortcut had taken me much longer than I'd planned, but to my relief the Rent-a-Wreck was nowhere in sight.

Adam said he'd promised to trim the front hedges, but there was no sound of clippers or voices, only a thin ribbon of cigarette smoke rising from behind the overgrown shrubs. Sal Zmira. So where was Adam? There was no way the Rent-a-Wreck could have beat me here. Maybe I was overreacting.

I started across the street, the tingling and itching already racing up my arms.

The yapping mop dog blazed out from behind the hedge and circled my feet, snapping and foaming at the mouth.

"Mr. Puddles, you goddamn mutt, get back here," ordered Zmira. A stream of profanity befitting a trucker followed, but he cut short when he caught sight of me. "Oh, Lily, it's you. I thought Puddles was after that white cat, the one that marks my mailbox post."

Specter was the only white cat in the neighborhood, but now didn't seem the time to bring that up. "Hello, Mr. Zmira. Have you seen—"

The mop dog caught hold of my dangling hem and started to tug at it. I tried to twist away, but that only made him snarl louder and pull with more determination. Zmira clamped the butt of his smoldering cigarette between his teeth and swiped at Mr. Puddles, but the mop dog was too fast for him. He sprang out of reach. There was a ripping noise, and a piece of my skirt, now slathered in doggy drool, hung from Mr. Puddles's mouth. The mop dog vaulted over the curb and raced through the open side gate.

Zmira started making a fuss. "It's all right," I insisted. "It was already torn. By the way, have you seen—"

"No, no, no. I need to pay you for that. Come on inside." He ground out his cigarette on the side of his mailbox and led me in through the front door. "Oh, and I've got something for Jo I want to give you. I meant to run it by this morning but didn't get the chance."

I hovered in the entry. "My Nana Jo?"

"Is there another Jo?"

There was a loud *bang* from outside. I leaped half out of my skin. "Was that a gunshot?"

"Nothin' but a car backfiring." He squinted at me in that way teachers do when they think you're hiding something. "You sure are jumpy tonight. You and that boy in some kind of trouble or something?"

"No, no, everything's fine," I lied.

"Right." Zmira set two twenties on his dining-room table. "That should be enough to cover the cost of your skirt. Now, where'd I set that flyer?"

"Mr. Zmira, I need to find—"

He disappeared down the hall. I could hear him rummaging around in one of the back rooms, and then mop dog wanted out to do his business. Zmira spent another five minutes trying to wrangle the mutt back into the house before resuming his search for the flyer. My patience was wearing thin and the dread lodged in the pit of my stomach was mounting. I had a terrible feeling I knew where Adam was.

"Oh, here it is!" Zmira announced from the kitchen. He appeared a moment later and placed a piece of paper firmly into my hand. "The convention center is hosting the Scottish Highland Games next weekend. Lots of dancing, traditional sporting events, and exhibits. I thought Jo might like to go with me."

"Are you asking my nana out?"

"S'pose I am. It was Adam's idea." He laughed, then noticed I didn't. "That a problem?"

"No, no, it's great. So Adam was here?"

"Nope. To be honest, I'm disappointed in that boy. He said he would trim the front hedges for me today."

"He wasn't feeling well. He's supposed to be resting," I said, imagining the worst. "I gotta go."

"Wait, you forgot your money—"

"Keep it," I shouted, slamming the door behind me.

It took a minute for my eyes to adjust. There were no street-lights in this part of town—no lights at all, in fact, except for two. One was the light shining through Zmira's kitchen window. The other? A distant glow emanating from a hole in the ground next door.

RULE #37
GRAVES—WHEN IN DOUBT, DIG DEEPER.

As usual, I was late to the party. The Rent-a-Wreck was parked at the end of the Lassiter driveway with no one in sight. It must have snuck by me when I was inside Zmira's house. Not good. I suspected where I'd find Adam and the occupants of the car—at the source of the light.

I crept across the broken ground toward where the fallout shelter's gaping hatch emitted a dull glow from between two mounds of dirt. A rust-tinted smear glistened on the rim of the open hatch. "Dammit, Adam," I hissed through gritted teeth. There could be only one reason he would risk going back into the shelter: to retrieve Neil Lassiter's research, with the intention to either sell it or destroy it. And from the look of things, he had company.

I peered into the hole. The single bulb still shone from the sagging ceiling, which was riddled with fresh fissures. The slightest tremor could collapse the shelter, but Adam's life, my future, and, perhaps, evidence of the true origins of life on Earth were all at stake.

I loosened the terror that gripped me and took that first dreadful step down into the narrow stairwell. My ears strained to pick up a voice, a footfall, anything that might hint at what waited below. I heard only the rattle of the loose railing beneath my hand.

At last the stairs leveled out into near-total darkness. Why the lights in this part of the tunnel were turned off, I could only guess, but I didn't dare turn them on for fear of alerting whoever was down here. So I groped my way along the passage, hand over hand, until my shoulder grazed the cold steel door of the small utility room— the halfway point. Inside, the feeble generator clanked and wheezed, sounding as if it would give up and die at any moment. I considered calling Evan, but realized in my rush I'd left my phone at home and there was no time to retrieve it. I needed to warn Adam, assuming I wasn't already too late.

I turned the next corner and froze. A weak light shone through the entrance to the lab, allowing me to make out the faint outline of two men sitting on the ground at either side of the entrance, each with chin to chest. If they were supposed to be on watch, they were doing a lousy job. They were both asleep—or so I thought until I caught a whiff of a familiar metallic odor.

I approached cautiously. Still no movement. On tiptoes, I jiggled the bulb overhead. It flickered, and a brief halo of light illuminated the end of the corridor before the bulb blinked out. But that brief flash of light was enough to confirm my suspicion. The two ex-feds from the train, the same two who attacked Adam at the beach, were slumped against the walls, a bloodied brick on the ground between them. Judging from the dark smears on the walls and their vacant stares, there was no question: they were dead. To be absolutely sure, I checked each man's wrist for a pulse. Zilch.

I turned away. It was like something out of those golem tales. But this was real. Bracing myself against the wall, I wretched.

Christ, Adam, what have you done? When has revenge ever been the answer?

From the far side of the shelter came the squeal of a heavy door resisting its hinges, then a thud, followed by what sounded like something or someone being dragged across the gritty floor. "At last," exclaimed a grating voice.

Miles Devlin. I was supposed to meet him near the old post office on Fifth in about twenty minutes. Had Adam changed the plans?

I forced myself to look at the men at my feet. Only a monster could have done such a thing, but who was the monster? Devlin? Or Adam? They each had their reasons. I recalled the golem of Prague and its murderous rampage. I feared I had my answer and knew it was up to me to stop Adam. The Seed of Life Project had already cost too many lives—Neil, possibly his fellow researcher, and now these two in the hall.

Stepping carefully over the dead men's sprawled legs, I snuck toward the partly open door and peered into the lab. The star charts had been ripped back from the wall to expose what appeared to be an open vault the size of a large storage closet. Inside the walls were flanked by floor-to-ceiling shelves crammed with binders, all stamped on their spines with the Seed of Life symbol. Stacks of boxes crowded the floor, but it was the two or three large, plastic zipper bags—body bags by the look of them—that lay neatly folded on a crate that stole away my breath.

Just inside the vault door Devlin cradled a thick binder in his hands. He was examining it as though it were some lost relic. Not five feet away, Adam lurked behind the copper behemoth, a spade from our garden shed tightly gripped in his hands.

Adam raised the spade over his head and silently stalked closer to his target. Before I could holler a warning, he brought down the blade as if to split Devlin's skull in two. At the last possible second, Devlin turned. Adam twisted and struck a stack of binders, missing Devlin's head by a fraction of an inch. Papers flew up like a flock of frightened doves.

"What the hell are you doing?" shouted Devlin, leaping to the right of the door.

Adam had him trapped. He raised the spade again and held it like a battle-ax. "You killed Neil and those two men in the hall. Are you planning to kill me, too? Then what?" Adam gestured with the spade toward the stacked boxes and binders lining the vault. "Sell all of this to the highest bidder? Sell *me* to the highest bidder?"

"You're the one who called me to change the time and place. When I got here, the hatch was open and they were already dead," shouted Devlin. "And I'm not the one holding the shovel or the vault key."

One of Adam's hands drifted to his pants pocket, an unconscious reaction to Miles's words. I'd thought the key in the lockbox was a spare, but was it actually the key to this vault? To his father's research? Was that why he'd been so desperate to find the lockbox? *Good god am I stupid.*

"If what you say is true, if you really came here intending to keep your word, then prove it. I want to see the money."

Devlin snorted. "I'm not fool enough to have it on me. Not that it matters—as soon as you have what you want, you plan to kill me. Isn't that right?"

"It's what you deserve. You—killed—Neil—Lassiter! You left him for dead, then leveled our home to cover up your crime."

"It was an accident, I swear," insisted Devlin, but shame was written all over his weathered face.

"*Istum mendacium est!* That is a lie! I read your letter to Veronica. She warned Neil that you were coming for him." Adam's voice thundered through the chamber, causing flakes of ceiling to drift down all around us. He hardly seemed to notice.

"It's true," admitted Devlin. "I did confront Neil. The fool left out his pistol, and I threatened to kill him with it if he didn't turn over the research. He grabbed for the gun, and it went off. I never meant to kill him, and I had nothing to do with the explosion."

Then who did?

Devlin shook his head and sighed. "Every minute of every day I've had to live with what I did, so go ahead and kill me. You'd be doing me a favor, but it won't change anything, and you'll just end up ruining your own life like I ruined mine."

Adam swayed. He was growing weaker by the minute, but Devlin showed no signs of noticing. Even if Devlin had, he was probably too ill himself to take him. "Adam. We want the same thing, don't you see?"

"Don't you dare compare us. You can't possibly know what I want."

"Maybe you are like your father after all. I could never make Neil understand that some knowledge is dangerous and should never be sold—not for any price. He called me a man of little vision and said only *he* appreciated the full value of what we discovered. He had a prototype to prove it."

"Prototype?" Adam made a face like the word left a bad taste in his mouth.

"Neil boasted that he created life from clay. It was unimaginable."

"Well, meet the unimaginable." Adam lifted his hoodie and T-shirt and ripped the blood-soaked bandages from his chest, exposing the characters etched into his flesh. *Emet.* Truth.

Devlin went pale and shifted away from Adam and out of view. "I don't believe it!" I heard him exclaim. "We actually did it. After all those years of testing, all the failures—and yet here you are, living, breathing proof that life from clay is possible."

Adam reached for the door jam, the slender handle of the spade no longer enough to support him. His body was failing him. I saw it. Adam knew it. But Devlin had yet to realize that the very life he and Neil created was draining before his eyes.

I leaned farther into the chamber from the doorway. From behind me I heard the quick scrabble of heavy feet. Evan must have followed me. Damn him. Before I could turn to give him a piece of my mind, I felt cold, hard steel press against the back of my head—a gun.

"Make a sound," threatened a voice beside my ear, "and you'll be joining those two on the floor."

RULE #38
DON'T FEAR THE DEAD.
FEAR THE LIVING.

"Move," the man behind me ordered, and he shoved me through the lab door, prodding my back with the barrel of his pistol. He must have been hiding in the utility room, watching and waiting for the right moment to catch me unaware.

I inched forward, attempting to stall as I searched for a way to warn Devlin and Adam, who had disappeared into the vault. My brain could only focus on one problem at time, though, and most pressing was the bullet a trigger pull away. As I angled sideways to fit between two tables, my elbow knocked a pair of forceps into a beaker. *Clink.* Bless my clumsy nature.

Adam emerged from the vault, the spade still clutched in his grip. "Lily, how did you—?"

The man behind my back stepped into view. "Hello, Adam."

"Neil?" Adam faltered. "Is . . . is that really you?"

Rewind. Did he say *Neil?* It couldn't be. Neil Lassiter was dead. They found his body in the ashes.

"That's far enough, son. Drop it." The gun's muzzle shifted to my temple. Adam hesitated, then let the spade slip from his hand. "Miles, you come out, too."

Devlin stepped into view. "Hello, Neil."

I twisted my head slightly, only now catching up to speed. "*You* killed those two men in the passageway."

"Those double-crossing sons of bitches left me no choice," said Neil, his scarred fingers adjusting their hold on the pistol. "Adam, I'm sorry, but I had to protect you from them, and from him." He tipped his head at Devlin.

"Protect me?" Adam glared. "The same way you protected me by leaving me trapped down here to die?"

"I always intended to come back for you, but by the time it was safe, you were gone. At first I thought you were dead."

"I nearly was, no thanks to you."

I inched away from Neil. "Don't even think about it," he hissed, leveling the gun at my back.

"So how'd you pull it off, Neil?" goaded Devlin. "I saw you drop to the floor, saw the blood."

"All an illusion, my friend. Kevlar vest and stage blood. The explosion sealed the deal. I figured if you thought you killed me, you'd leave the country to avoid going to prison on an involuntary manslaughter charge."

"I should have known you'd find a way to cheat death. You've cheated in every other way."

"You're just bitter that Veronica chose me over you."

"I'd have given her a good life. What did you ever give her?"

The corner of Neil's mouth curled. "A son."

Adam had stopped blinking altogether. "What about the body? All this time I thought it was you."

"It was manufactured as part of an earlier experiment," explained Neil.

Adam flinched at the word *manufactured*. "You stole it from the morgue, didn't you?"

"I could hardly allow it to be autopsied."

Maybe that's what I saw Neil Lassiter hauling to the shed that day so long ago. No wonder he reacted the way he did. "Were there others?"

"Three, to be exact. Of all of them, Adam, you've survived the longest. You see, Miles, I was right. The secret to prolonged reanimation of clay is the incorporation of human remains—the dust of ash and bone."

Human ash and bone? I got a sick feeling in my gut as I flashed back to Adam's memories of us in the orchard, of his mother, of the day I fell. I didn't want to accept what it might mean. "Where did you get the cremains? From the cemetery?"

Neil lifted his chin as though offended by the very notion. "I'm no grave robber. What kind of monster do you think I am?"

The most horrific kind, I wanted to say. From the look on Devlin's face, he agreed. Adam appeared dumbstruck.

"Eternal Memorial provided what I needed," Neil clarified.

I couldn't believe what I was hearing. "EMS sold you cremains?"

"They were indigents. Eternal Memorial has a contract with the county."

"That doesn't make it right!" I argued. "They're people, too!"

"Not anymore," said Neil, like it was the cleverest joke ever.

My hands balled into fists, my nails digging into my palms. *Forget the gun. I'm gonna—*

"Lily, don't," warned Adam.

The muzzle of the pistol pressed more firmly into my flesh, a forceful reminder that I needed to calm down or face the consequences.

"So what do you plan to do with us?" asked Devlin.

"Nothing. You wanted all this." He gestured around the room, at the vault and the lab. "It's yours."

"You're going to lock us down here?" asked Adam.

"Not you. *Them.* Adam, you're young. In time you'll see this is all for the best. We'll rebuild, and, if you want, we can make you an Eve with her ashes."

"You can't do that. She saved my life!" Adam protested. "If not for me, neither of them would even be here."

"You should have thought of that before you led them here. I've worked too hard and sacrificed too much to lose it all now. Their deaths will be on your conscience, not mine." Neil nudged me forward and pointed at a spool of copper wire near Adam's feet. "Bind their wrists and feet," he ordered Adam. "Try anything and I'll shoot her."

Adam met my eyes but made no move to obey.

"I'm your father!" Neil thundered.

"I know what I am, and *et ego filius tuus non sum.* I'm not your son."

"You may think you know what you are," said Neil, with a wave of the pistol. "But there are things I never told you. Five years ago I sealed up the conversion chamber and initiated the first phase, unaware that you'd crawled into the capsule while I was away. By the time I discovered what happened, it was too late."

I could see the marred interior surface of the copper vessel's porthole out of the corner of my eye. I shuddered at the scene it conjured in my mind—a fifteen-year-old Adam, pounding and clawing at the porthole to make his presence known.

The pistol, which was no longer pointed at my head, trembled in Neil's hand. Was this a sign of hesitation? Remorse? "You can't imagine the guilt. I thought I'd done everything to keep you safe, and then to lose you like that? I couldn't work. Your mother left me. The orchard withered to a wasteland. My life lost all meaning and purpose. Then one day, as I stared at the urn containing your ashes, I knew what I had to do."

"You used your son's ashes?" asked Devlin.

My mind reeled. "What about the grave in the orchard?"

"Found that, did you?" Neil shrugged. "We placed a handful of remains there so his mother would have a place to grieve. The rest, well . . . Adam, I was desperate to have you back, but my impatience . . . Rather than build a new capsule, I used the one in which you died. The stresses were more than it could handle, and I was forced to shut it down prematurely—it was that or risk losing you forever. At first you barely clung to life. I cared for you day and night and watched you grow stronger. I taught you how to better manage your temper, and with some . . . modifications, your body became like any normal boy's."

"Normal?" raged Adam. "You call this normal? You had no right."

"I had every right. You are *my* son. I created you once; it was my *right* to do it again, so don't give me any self-righteousness. If not for me, you'd still be dead."

It all made sense now, in a warped sort of way. "Adam, that's how you remember the day in the orchard. You—or a part of you, your spirit—*were* there. You really are Adam."

"I—*am*—Adam," he said, as if trying on a new suit to see if it fit. He met his father's eyes. "I deserved the truth."

"Perhaps, but fathers make mistakes. They're not perfect. They're human."

"Unlike me," said Adam.

"That's not true," I argued. "Adam, it's not flesh and blood that makes us human. It's heart." I knew it now like I knew my own heart and how it felt about him.

"She's right," said Devlin. "Something magical happened in that capsule the day you were created. Some part of the Adam who died remained and became a part of you."

"You have his soul," I said, now sure of it.

"Magic? Souls?" Neil's voice reverberated throughout the chamber. "Her I can understand, but you, Miles? You're a man of science. Surely you can appreciate that Adam is a product of observation, reason, and deduction."

"He is a product of grief," said Devlin.

Neil shook his head. "Miles, what do you know of grief?"

Devlin had no answer, but *I* knew it had the power to knock even the most stoic of people to their knees.

Neil pinned my elbows to my sides with his free arm and dug

the gun muzzle back into my skull. "Enough of this. Adam, tie them up."

Adam glanced from Devlin to Neil to the weapon. "No," he said. "I won't let you kill them."

"It's not your decision."

Adam straightened; he nearly towered over Neil. He began speaking in a firm voice, his language shifting to something more archaic. *"What profit is there in my blood, when I go down to the pit?"* With a pang of recognition, I realized it was a verse—the verse I'd found marked in the Bible on the day I discovered Adam. *"Shall the dust praise thee? Shall it declare thy truth?"* His resolve seemed to strengthen. "The truth is you are not a god. You don't get to decide who lives and who dies. If they die, then so do I."

Neil's expression was not so different than the one that appeared on my father's face when he first learned I had no intention of taking over the business. At least in time Dad had accepted that I needed to make my own decisions. Unfortunately it took a heart attack and losing our livelihood, but he got there.

Neil had yet to figure it out. I could tell it had never occurred to him that his creation might have a mind—a heart—of his own.

Neil shifted the gun away from my temple and aimed directly at Adam's chest. "You forget I can build you again."

"No!" I shouted, and swung at Neil's arm, knocking it upward. The pistol went off, the sound like the firing of a cannon at close range. With my ears ringing, I watched in horror as the entire chamber shuddered. There was an eerie moment when the world seemed suspended in time and space—followed by the inevitable chain reaction we all sensed was coming.

Supports rumbled and groaned. With a loud, splintering *crack*, a steel beam set into the ceiling tore away from its moorings. Suspended by a cluster of cables and secured by only one brace, it swung perilously over our heads. It wouldn't hold for long.

"Run!" Devlin shouted. Neil shifted his aim at his ex-partner and fired just as Devlin dove to the side. The bullet grazed Devlin's scalp and ricocheted, striking an electrical panel. Sparks flew. Ducting and soil tumbled to the floor, filling the entire laboratory with billowing clouds of dust. Another shot rang out.

With a thunderous groan the vault's ceiling began to collapse under the unsupported weight of the earth above. Shelves splintered like matchsticks. The single illuminated lightbulb exploded in a shower of glass. In seconds Neil's precious research lay underneath a mountain of rubble.

Other side rooms soon followed suit. Devlin scrambled toward the exit on all fours, Adam yelling, "Go! Go! Go!" I stumbled through the main laboratory and from behind me heard what could only be the last remaining brace shearing away from the ceiling—ending in an agonizing scream. I spun around. Squinting against the fallout, I made out the contorted shapes of toppled beams, twisted ducting—and Neil, pinned to the concrete slab beneath the wreckage. The pistol had flown from his hand and skittered through trails of earthy minerals.

Adam fought his way to his father's side through the downpour of debris.

"Adam!" I screamed, scrambling back to them. With one hand over my mouth and nose and the other protecting my head, I fell to my knees beside them.

"Leave me," gasped Neil.

"I can't. I'm not like you," said Adam.

He directed me to the other end of the main beam pinning Neil, and together we heaved. Neil groaned in agony, but the massive post wouldn't budge.

"Again!" shouted Adam. We straightened our knees and strained against the weight. I pulled until my arms were ready to give out, but Adam kept at it.

"Stop! It's no use," I cried.

"Listen to her." Neil coughed, and a trickle of crimson oozed from his mouth. Adam started to argue, but his father lifted a bloody hand to stop him. "You need to go!"

At that moment a light fixture slammed onto the table next to me, barely missing my head. Near-blinded by the deluge of dust and debris, I looked in the direction of the door, searching for the way out. I lost sight of Adam for a moment in the chaos, but a second later he was at my side, panting and shoving me toward the exit leading into the corridor.

Racing barefoot through the narrow passage—when did I lose my shoes?—I ran into Devlin at the bottom of the stairwell. I waited for Adam to appear, but he didn't. "I don't understand. He was right behind me!"

"Climb!" shouted Devlin. The sound of the fallout shelter collapsing was growing into a deafening roar.

"No—I have to go back!"

Devlin gripped my arm and started dragging me up the stairs—

A shot rang out.

"No! No! No!" I screamed. I ripped free of Devlin's grasp and raced back down the corridor. I reached the utility room just as Adam appeared out of the churning dust, hunched over and carrying a body on his back.

"Thank god you're alive!" I gasped, my sides heaving. "I heard the shot and—" That's when I realized the body Adam was carrying was not Neil. It was one of the murdered ex-feds.

One look at Adam's grim face told me enough. I knew what had happened before he could say the words.

Neil was dead.

RULE #39
LEARN TO ACCEPT THAT SOME BODILY DAMAGE IS BEYOND FIXING.

Adam shifted the weight of the lifeless body higher onto his back as an avalanche of debris plunged to the ground, blocking the passageway behind us. How could I have ever thought he had killed those two men? I tugged his sleeve. "Adam, you have to leave him. You're too weak—we'll never make it out in time."

Reluctantly he let the body slide to the floor.

Together we hobbled toward the stairs, the sounds of Armageddon all around us. Each time Adam slowed, I turned back to urge him on. I wasn't leaving here without him.

When we reached the stairs he insisted I go first. Coughing and heaving, we climbed toward the exit. I emerged from the hatch, and, to my relief, Adam's head cleared it a moment later.

"Don't stop!" shouted Devlin, frantically waving us forward.

The ground buckled beneath our feet and began to sink. Adam grabbed me under both arms and hurled our bodies clear. The earth belched up a foul-smelling cloud, then slumped back down. There was nothing left but a pit to mark what was now a grave.

I lay stunned in the dirt. Slowly I sat up, testing to see if anything was broken. Everything ached, but otherwise I was in one piece. Beside me, Adam stared blankly ahead into the dark. "Neil?" I asked him, dreading the answer.

"He begged me for a quick death. I picked up his pistol but couldn't pull the trigger, so I gave him a choice. He chose the gun."

"It was the humane thing to do."

He'd lost his father all over again, but this time I imagined it was so much worse. Neil Lassiter's death stood in the face of all the man had done to give Adam life.

The moon had risen while we were below. Huffing and wheezing, Devlin sagged to the ground beside a tree stump. His long shadow sagged with him. "I never meant for Neil to die—not the night I confronted him in the house, not now. I only wanted to ensure that his research stayed out of the wrong hands."

"I know," I said. "He didn't leave us much choice, did he? But you accomplished what you set out to do—although probably not in the way you intended. At least now you know you're not a murderer."

Devlin sighed and, with a frail hand, lifted a corner of his shirt to wipe the grime from the hollows of his cheeks. "Small consolation when all my years of work and sacrifice are buried, along with every shred of the evidence of what we accomplished." He tipped his head toward Adam. "Well, almost every shred. But it's better this way. Greed tends to bring out the worst in people." He reached into his front shirt pocket and produced a creased slip of paper. "Fortunately for you, though, not all people are beholden to greed. Here."

I took the paper from his hand and unfolded it. "A check."

"You did fulfill your end of the bargain, after all."

Adam's eyes narrowed. "I thought you said you didn't bring the money."

Devlin shrugged. "Shoot me. I lied."

That piece of paper, with its many zeroes, represented all my hopes for saving the family business. Even so, I passed it back. "It isn't—"

Devlin held up a hand. "Don't worry. That's not all of it, but it'll get you by for now."

"No. It's not that. It's more than enough—generous, in fact. It's—"

"Please." Devlin's eyes shone dull in the moonlight. "I want you to have it."

It didn't feel right to take it, not even my share. I thrust the check at Adam. "You take it. It rightly belongs to you, and who knows how long it will take to settle your father's affairs? You need the money for a fresh start."

"It's too late for that."

Too late? A lump formed in my throat at what that might mean.

"I came here tonight for reasons," Adam began, casting a glance at Devlin, "I'm not proud of, but I always meant for you to have the money. Use it to get the mortuary out of debt, if that's what you decide you want to do. But, no matter what you choose, for once, Lily, do it because it's what *you* want and not because it's what's expected of you." Adam turned to Devlin. "Tell her she has to accept it, Miles. Tell her it's the only way."

Devlin rubbed his chin. "Lily, let me tell you a story. You like stories, don't you?"

I nodded. For me, working with the dead had always been

about the stories. It doesn't matter how destitute, cantankerous, or loathsome a person might be; everyone leaves behind a tale when they go. I'd never seen otherwise.

Maybe Miles Devlin knew me better than I thought.

"My mother abandoned me at the local five-and-dime when I was six years old. A neighbor—a widow—took me in, raised me as her own. She was the dearest woman you'd ever hope to meet. Gave me my bike. But she was also tough. Growing up I needed that, too." Devlin beamed as he recalled his memories of her.

"She stood by me throughout the trial when no one else would," he continued more slowly now, "and she was perhaps the only person who ever believed in my innocence. I lost contact with her in prison. Word reached me that she'd lost her house and was livin' on the streets, but by the time I knew about her circumstances, she'd died. I didn't make it to her viewing. But I heard about a young woman who worked at the funeral home, a young woman who went out of her way to honor dear Helen in my absence. That girl was you."

"Me? Wait. Helen? What was her full name, the woman who raised you?"

"Helen Delaney."

It clicked. The scrappy little kid in her photos—that was Devlin. Funny, I hadn't noticed the resemblance until now. I smiled. Caribbean Coral and a string of pearls. "She was a great listener."

"Yes, she was," agreed Devlin, with a smile all his own.

"Thanks, Helen," I said, and patted the earth beside me because it was all one and the same. "And you too, Miles." He nodded his approval. Convinced at last that I was deserving, I slipped the check into my back pocket.

With the aid of the tree stump, Devlin rose to his feet, so thin that a sudden gust of wind might blow him away. "I'd best be going. I suggest you two do the same. Neighbors are sure to call in a disturbance if they haven't already." He retrieved his battered bike from where it lay in the weeds that had sprouted over the summer, strapped on his helmet, and pedaled off into the night.

"I wonder if we'll ever see him again." Adam mused, getting to his feet. It seemed to take much more effort than it should have. "We better be going, too."

I stood and brushed myself off. "Not yet. There's something I have to say first."

"It can wait."

I took his hands in mine. "We've both said that before, and both times it cost us dearly. Some things shouldn't wait. If I've learned anything these past two months, it's that keeping things to myself is as risky as speaking my mind—maybe more so."

Time to throw out the rulebook and wing it. I took a deep breath.

"Adam, I love you."

If we'd been playing Name That Expression right then, I'd forfeit; I couldn't read his face at all. But I'd already laid my heart on the table, so I figured I might as well go on. "I admit, in the beginning I was obsessed with the idea of you—the boy who saved me that day in the orchard, the boy at the heart of you—but today, this night, I love you for who you are now."

"How could you possibly love a thing like me?"

"Because I don't see the monster you claim to be. I see a man."

He stared into my eyes as if measuring the depth of my sincerity, but I could not have meant it more.

"*Ego te amo*," he said. "With all my heart and—" He couldn't finish it, couldn't make himself say the word, but I heard it in the silence.

Soul.

"Adam, are you crying?" I touched the bridge of his nose, which was miraculously moist. It was another first, one among many since he'd come back into my life.

"No," he lied, his eyes blurry.

"That's what I thought," I said, wondering again how he could so easily defy the word etched into his flesh.

A far-off whine of sirens rose above the sporadic moans of settling earth.

"Come on," I said. "We need to get you home."

"Yeah. Home," he repeated, sounding like he hadn't understood its meaning before now.

We made for the street beyond the fallen gates. Adam's feet dragged through the dust. I let him lean against me, but each of his steps came slower than the one before. I saw red lights flash in the distance; the police were close now.

We shambled onto the sidewalk, but it was clear Adam couldn't go on. He gestured toward the lawn behind Zmira's hedge. We stumbled over to it, and Adam sank to his knees, taking me down with him.

"It's your wound, isn't it?" I said.

He nodded, his face pale and ashen in the light streaming from Zmira's kitchen window.

"We'll get help back at the house."

"I'm not going to make it."

"Sure you will," I said. "I'll help you."

"Lily, it's okay. I've known since that day you found me sitting by the apple tree that my time was running out.

Heartwood and the dying tree. That's what that was all about. "Why didn't you tell me?"

"I didn't want you to stop me from seeking my revenge for Neil's death. But I couldn't do it. I couldn't take a life, not when mine had meant so much to . . . my father." He paused to take a labored breath. "Besides, I still had a promise to keep, and now with the check from Devlin you can save the mortuary or choose another profession." He smiled.

I'd been waiting all this time for him to crack so much as a grin, and he picked *now* to smile? Panic welled up in me. I understood what he'd done. He knew his body was failing, so he changed the plan in order to confront Devlin. But by sparing him, he not only proved his humanity, he'd ensured that I could have the freedom to choose my own path.

Well, I wanted to walk the path with him.

"Dammit. I won't let you do this. Get up, Adam. Get up!" I seized him by the arm and pulled. "You may be ready to throw your life away, but I'm not."

But he had neither the strength nor will to rise.

How was this happening? The wound on his chest was deep but not *that* deep and with no signs of infection, so it was not a fatal injury. There was something I'd overlooked . . .

The tattoo.

Emet meant truth, but hadn't he just lied to me about crying? I wracked my brain, thinking back to the story of Judah Loew ben Bezalel. What happened to the golem at the end? The rabbi . . . he destroyed the golem when it was no longer needed. He removed the first character of the word *emet*, which left just *met*—

Oh Christ. That's what Adam had been trying to tell me when he woke from his delirium. "*Met* means death. That's it, isn't it?"

Adam blinked. Yes.

Instantly my eyes started to sting. Damn reflex. This was no time for tears. "Tell me what to do, Adam. More bandages? A doctor? I'll call an ambulance." I reached for my phone, forgetting that in my rush to find Adam I'd left it at home.

"Make it *emet*," he mumbled.

"What? I can't embroider skin. You're not a pillow. I've never— not on a living person. I mean, Tony let me . . . with a needle on a cadaver once, but that was . . . that was completely, completely different."

"Not so different."

"You want me to—on Zmira's front lawn? There's no way!"

A shadow passed in front of the kitchen window. Adam tried to lift his arm to point, but even that was too much effort. "Trust him."

"What if I fail?"

"You won't."

"But if I do?"

"*Moriar.*"

I will die.

RULE #40
EACH DEATH HELPS
TO MAKE US MORE HUMAN.

I pounded on the front door, hoping Zmira could hear me over his blaring television. The sounds of explosions and rapid gunfire were silenced but quickly replaced with muffled dog yaps and Zmira's shout of "Don't you people know what time it is?" The porch lamp flicked on. A second later the dead bolt unlatched and Zmira's face appeared in the crack of the door. "Lily? What in the name of—"

"Mr. Zmira. Adam's hurt. I need your help."

He unfastened the chain, poked out his balding head, and spotted Adam slouched beside the hedge. "Let's bring him inside."

Together we dragged Adam into the house, where we laid him out on the sofa. Adam was babbling in unfiltered English and broken Latin, calling for Neil. Zmira flipped on the nearest table lamp. Its dusty, incandescent bulb barely cast a shadow from my hand as I placed it over Adam's forehead.

He was as cold as a tombstone in January.

Mr. Puddles stretched up to lick Adam's chin. Adam smiled ever so slightly.

Zmira scooped up the mop dog. "So what happened?"

"We were next door. There was an accident. If I can't stop the bleeding, he'll die."

"I'm calling 911."

"No!" I shouted, louder than I intended. "They can't help him."

Zmira looked confused. "Well, if they can't, how can you?"

"I just . . . can," I answered, less than confident. "You'll have to take my word for it."

I waited for Zmira to lug the mop dog into another room before unzipping Adam's hoodie the rest of the way. His T-shirt underneath was soaked through. I grabbed hold of the hem and ripped it to the neck.

It was worse than I imagined. The wound gaped, as raw and deep as it had been the day the rusty barbed-wire fence tore into his flesh.

Zmira peered over my shoulder. "Is that what I think it is?"

"Yes, blood."

"I may be colorblind, but I can see *that*. I meant the tattoo."

"A birthday present from his father," I explained, not bothering to hide my disgust.

"His father tattooed him with the Hebrew word for 'truth'? Well, I'll be damned. You know, most Jews don't think too favorably of tattoos."

"His family isn't Jewish. Hold on—you can read that?"

"Four years of Hebrew school. That tattoo is straight out of a golem story. He told me his father had a thing for ancient texts, but if you ask me, that's taking it to the extreme."

"You have no idea. Here, I need you to apply pressure."

"I don't do well with blood." He retreated several steps as if to prove it.

"Fine. I'll do it." I did my best to slow the bleeding, but it was the damage to the inked lettering that concerned me most. The first character has been sliced down the middle.

"I still say you should get him to a doctor. That boy needs stitches."

"I can do it, but I need a needle and some thread."

"Think I can rustle up a sewing needle, but the only thing I've got close to thread is fishing line."

"That'll do. The finer the better."

Zmira headed for a back room.

"Hang on," I told Adam. He blinked. Good. He was still with me, but for how much longer?

The oven clock ticked off the minutes. In the time it took Zmira to find what I needed, Adam's eyes began to drift and his pulse weakened further.

"Mr. Zmira, any luck?"

"Got it!" he yelled. A moment later he was back at my side, needle and line in hand.

The bleeding had slowed significantly, but with each twitch came a gush of syrupy orange ooze. "Try not to move, Adam." I coached.

I can do this became my silent mantra as my quaking hands attempted to thread the needle in the lamp's dim light. I didn't want Adam to see my nervousnes, but staying calm isn't easy when you're pumped up on adrenaline.

Finally the needle was threaded, the line knotted at the end. "This is going to hurt," I warned him. "I'm sorry." He inhaled sharply at the first prick of his flesh. Inflicting pain had never been a concern for me until now, and it rattled my confidence. But there was no other way, so I slid the needle deeper and drew the fishing line through to make the first stitch. One down. Many more to go. Each time, the tug and pull caused the bleeding to worsen. "I can't see what I'm doing. There's too much blood. I need a towel."

"Keep sewing. I'm on it," said Zmira. Doing his best not to look, he blotted up the blood, no questions this time.

I worked more steadily now, pulling together the flesh, meticulously matching up the edges. It had to be perfect. Finally I tied off the last suture and sighed. I'd done it. Each tiny stitch was exact, the tattoo fully restored. Now, with Zmira huddled over my shoulder, all I could do was wait for some sign that we'd been successful in saving him.

Adam's eyes remained shut, and he lay so still. Too still.

"Adam? Adam, can you hear me?"

"I am Adam," he mumbled mechanically.

"I am."

"I."

Blink.

I placed my ear to his chest. His heartbeat was barely audible. "I don't understand. It should work. It's supposed to work."

"Give him some time. The boy's been traumatized." Zmira checked the clock.

Ten agonizing minutes went by before Zmira picked up his phone. "I'm calling 911."

"No, one more minute, please. I'm missing something." I wrung my hands and scanned the room for an answer, a clue, anything that would guide me. Again and again my eyes were drawn to a framed needlepoint propped in the middle of a crowded bookshelf. It was an odd piece, adorned in symbols like the ones comprising Adam's tattoo. One character in particular seemed strangely familiar. Then I remembered Christian Tomopolo's pendant.

What if I'm wrong? I can't afford a mistake.

"Mr. Zmira, can you bring me that needlework? The framed one with all the symbols?" He brought it over. "What's that one mean, right there?"

"The *chai*?"

"Yes, that one."

"It means 'life.'"

I compared it to the arched symbol on Adam's chest. One of the characters was nearly identical. "That's it!" I said. "*Truth* won't save him." I didn't bother explaining. "Quick. I need permanent ink and a clean razor blade."

"I have an old bottle of India ink in my den, but a clean razor blade? I don't think I have one. How about an electric razor?"

"What? No. A sharp pair of scissors then. Hurry!"

I turned back to Adam. "Blink if you can hear me."

Nothing.

"Here, found them—and the ink," said Zmira, once more at my side. "Not sure how sharp they are. They were my mother's sewing scissors."

"They'll have to do."

With two fingers to Adam's wrist, I felt for a pulse that was no longer there.

I began to cut.

RULE #41
THE LAST AND MOST IMPORTANT RULE: RULES ARE MADE TO BE BROKEN.

Three months have come and gone since the shelter collapsed. That night was the last time I spoke to Miles Devlin—until today.

I flipped over the news tabloid lying on my dresser with a certain satisfaction. There was Jim Sturbridge's startled mug, plastered front and center. Behind him was the Eternal Memorial Services, Inc., facade with its emblem of a setting sun, a symbol that's taken on double meaning now that charges have been filed. Seems an anonymous tip to a certain reporter named Mae Wu prompted an investigation into EMS concerning the illegal processing and sale of cremains to Neil Lassiter. The resulting storm of bad press derailed Sturbridge's political ambitions, shut the doors on EMS, and sent more business our way than we'd handled in years. I couldn't hold back a smug smile.

I guess speaking up has its benefits after all.

It was funny, thinking back to the day I said goodbye to Helen Delaney. I'd thought it was the end of an end. Instead it was the start of a whole new beginning—but not for everyone. Today was another goodbye.

I slipped into my finest black dress and slingbacks, then stood before my new full-length mirror. The dress would do. My bedroom door creaked open; Evan's polished black shoes preceded him. "Tony says he's ready, but Mom and Dad thought you might like a minute alone with him before the service. And Lily?"

"Yeah?"

"Don't talk his ear off. People are waiting."

I lobbed my embroidery hoop at him as he dodged out the door. With a swipe of Midnight Madness mascara, a brush of Royal Ruby lip color, and a pat of powder to set it all in place, I was ready. Rachel still wasn't over the fact that I'd put a streak of aqua through my hair. When she asked me why, I told her I wanted to try something different for a change and that I was already considering deep magenta for next time. She dutifully rolled her eyes, but secretly I saw her smile.

Propped on my desk was a manila envelope. I tucked it into my handbag and headed out.

Downstairs, Sinatra's "My Way" was already wafting across the yard from the chapel. I choked up—I always did—but today there would be no tears. There were none left to shed. I retreated to the prep room and its welcome serenity.

He lay in the center of the room, enveloped in tufts of white satin. A silk pillow embroidered with a simple chain stitch supported his head. I'd taken extra care with this one. It was the least I could do after all he'd done for me. The casket's cherry wood complemented his skin tone; I was glad I went with the Rose Hue foundation instead of Beige Wonder like I'd originally planned.

I let out a long sigh and relaxed my hunched shoulders. My only consolation, if there was one, was that his passing had finally ended a long suffering. I straightened his tie and adjusted the rosebud in his lapel, a soft pink one I'd picked special from the garden, courtesy of 'Queen Elizabeth'. The tie was ridiculously old-fashioned. I'd told Rachel not to go cheap on this one, but she couldn't help herself. Not after all those lean months.

"I tried," I told him. "Rachel isn't in the habit of taking my suggestions yet, but we're getting there. Be glad we were able to rehire Tony. He's the best, but I intend to give him a run for his money as soon as I complete my mortician certification."

Mallory rapped on the door. "It's time, Lily." She'd given up the idea of joining the cheer squad. No time for it, not after I begged her to come work for us. Now she handled the billing—under Dad's tutelage, of course. She still avoided the back end of the house where the prep and cold rooms were located, but we were working on that.

Mal and I were good now. I'd promised to confide in her more if she promised to listen. And she and Evan did decide to test out the whole relationship thing in the end, thanks partly to me. I explained to my brother that he'd be a fool not to give her a chance. Unlike some people—namely Dana—Mal calls 'em like she sees 'em. Not such a bad thing. They didn't get to see each other much with Evan off at college, but they were on the phone constantly. Perhaps distance does make the heart grow fonder. Of course, she was thrilled he made it home this weekend.

"Shall I escort you to your waiting audience?" I asked my client. I unlocked the wheels and lowered the casket lid. "I'm going to apologize in advance for hitting the wall. The new gurney is on back order—"

My apology was interrupted by the sound of someone entering the code into the prep-room keypad. I didn't need to turn around. I knew who it was—as did my heart, which was on autopilot and beating wildly.

"You'll never guess who's here." Adam's voice was as playful then as it was those afternoons we spent in the orchard together.

I turned to face him. "Who?"

"Veronica."

"She read your letter?"

"She did, but she's still getting used to the idea that I'm her son, at least in part. It will take time. The important thing is she came."

He moved to hold the door for me.

"Wait. Before we go, I have something for you." I handed him the manila envelope from my purse.

He weighed it in his hand. "What's this?"

"A gift. Open it."

Adam undid the clasp, withdrew the single sheet tucked inside with a piece of sturdy cardboard, and read. "A birth certificate?"

"Better late than never," I said.

"But I thought all my records were destroyed. How . . . ?"

"When we found out about EMS's shady dealings, I had a hunch that someone over at the County Recorder's Office has been fudging documents. I bluffed them into thinking I knew more than I did, and my hunch proved right. I got them to draw this up on the condition I keep quiet. As you know better than anyone, that's my superpower."

"One of many," Adam interjected. He grinned, and I couldn't help but be equally amused by the boyish humor that lit his dark, gold-flecked eyes. "So I officially exist now," he said with a wave of the certificate. "That reminds me, I have something for you, too." He set the document and envelope aside and reached inside his front vest pocket to pull out a simple square black box tied with a red ribbon. "I was going to give this to you later, but—"

"What's that on your neck?" I said, distracted by a small round bandage.

He blushed. "If you can believe it, I cut myself shaving this morning."

I closely examined the Scooby-Doo bandage. A bright red spot of blood had seeped through the pad. In its own way, that spot *was* the gift. Adam was human now—as human in body as he was in soul.

The gift box was featherlight in my hand. "Open it," he urged, more like the boy I remembered high up in a tree than the young man he was now.

Lately he'd made a habit of giving me small trinkets, so I untied the bow and lifted the lid, expecting another packet of seeds or a particularly pretty pebble. Instead I found a porcelain sand dollar pendant on a silver chain. The charm was as round and milky white as the moon under which we found the sand dollar Adam broke. I shook it and, to my delight, heard distinct tinkles from inside. "How did you . . . ?"

"That company you found that makes custom urns? I asked them to make it special. Turn it over. There's an inscription on the back."

"*Amplae vitae simul,*" I read. "Latin?"

"Of course."

"Translation?"

"To a long life together."

"A proposal, then?" I teased.

"Not a proposal. A promise—for now," he said, quite seriously. "*Te amo etiam.*"

No translation needed there. "You love me."

"I think I always have."

"Since that day I found you in the fallout shelter?"

He shook his head.

"No?"

"No. Since that first time I saw you running through the orchard."

"When you pulled me into our tree to save me from those kids?"

"Yes. But one day you climbed higher than ever before."

"And I fell."

"Like a rock."

"I was as good as gone. But you brought me back. Want to try again?"

"Seems risky."

"I'll take my chances."

Adam beamed. "I like this new, adventurous you." His warm hands cupped my face, and my body trembled with anticipation as he brought his lips to mine. His kiss was tender but filled with such earnestness, such depth of emotion, that there was no doubt every human cell in that perfect "prototype" body of his was behind it.

I pressed my mouth more firmly to his, and his arms circled my waist, lifting me into the air. It was like that county fair Spinout ride all over again, turning and turning with the floor dropping away, leaving me breathless.

Only I didn't ever want this ride to end. Not if I could ride it with him.

But all things come to an end, especially in that room. Slowly he lowered me back to earth, but instead of falling, I felt as if I'd been resuscitated all over again, minus all the broken bones. For the first time since that fall, I was whole again.

I traced the welts beneath Adam's starched white shirt. They marked where, using a scissor blade, I'd cut through the first two letters of the word that once spelled *emet*. Only the last character had remained, and I had altered and added to it to form *chai*. Life.

"That right there is probably some of my best cosmetology work." I kissed the air over the spot, grateful that my hunch worked. Who knows how? What I did know was that Neil was wrong; not everything can be explained by science. Call it magic, call it a miracle, call it faith. Whatever you call it, something happened when that last drop of ink entered Adam's flesh. There was no other way to explain the red oxygen-rich blood that now flowed through his veins.

He placed both hands over mine, drew me in, and said gravely, "I still say you've made a poor career choice."

I pulled back. "What? You don't think I can manage a mortuary?"

"It's not that." He patted his chest with his hand. "It's that I wonder if you would've made a better surgeon or tattoo artist."

"Thanks, but I think I can do more good here, although Mr. Zmira might not agree. It's not every day you have someone reanimated on your living-room couch."

"I'll be at work in his yard to pay off the reupholstering for months. I still don't think he's fully accepted what I am—correction, was. But the sooner he can forget the entire episode, the better. Did I tell you he connected me with a landscaper yesterday?"

"No. That's great, Adam! That's what you wanted, isn't it?"

"Yes, but I'm going to have to learn the business from the ground up."

I was slow on the uptake, but then—"Oh my god, did you just make a joke?"

He shrugged with embarrassment and cracked his largest smile yet. "Come on. The mourners will be here soon. Can I give you a hand?"

"I'd like that. I think he would, too. Wouldn't you, Miles?" I gave his casket a gentle caress. "Besides, I just had the walls patched and repainted."

Adam laughed, something he did often now. It had become my favorite sound.

"After the service Rachel and Dad are off to check out a possible location for their bakery, so I'll be driving Miles to the crematorium. You want to come?"

"Sure, as long as the hearse has airbags."

"Very funny. Two jokes in one day. You're *way* over your quota."

He held the door to let Miles and me through and then joined me at my side. I smiled to see the dirt under his nails. Some things never change.

Together we pushed the gurney down the hall. We bumped the chair rail only once.

ACKNOWLEDGMENTS

A few years ago, I began a creation story about a girl who was more comfortable with the dead than the living. Without the assistance of some extremely knowledgeable, talented, and generous souls, that seed of an idea might never have sprouted to life.

First, I have to thank my steadfast agent, Abigail Samoun at Red Fox Literary, for her undying faith in me and the tale I wanted to tell. With patience and reassurance, she challenged me to take the story beyond what I thought possible and sent it out into the world.

By the grace of the goddess Fortuna, I landed in the capable and nurturing hands of my editor, Ardi Alspach—a match made in heaven! I cannot thank her enough for her enthusiasm and gentle guidance. There are not enough deep pink roses in all the world to express my gratitude.

Not even a pandemic could stop the superheroes of Team Sterling. They went above and beyond in making this book the very best it could be and with a cover to match. Team members include Irene Vandervoort, Elizabeth Lindy, Julie Robine, Kevin Iwano, Renee Yewdaev, Kayla Overbey, Blanca Oliviery, and Kathy Brock.

I'm also extremely grateful to the Society of Children's Book Writers and Illustrators (SCBWI), especially Lin Oliver and Stephen Mooser, for the grant that enabled me to work with the amazing Deborah Halverson, editorial wizard extraordinaire. Deborah helped me to navigate a major rewrite and to see my story's potential. She is a gift to all in the field of children's books.

Special mention goes to the experts who answered my endless questions: Claire Simmons and Anthony Hernandez at the Reardon Simi Valley Funeral Home. Claire cheered me on even before there was a story, and I can still feel the goose bumps of our first encounter when we discussed a certain Adam. Chuck and Linda Goolden offered me their insights gleaned from years of experience. I will forever be grateful. (Keep the anecdotes coming, and I'll see you on the ski slopes or the steps of JUMP!) And the brilliant Karen Wadley from the Department of World Languages at Boise State University not only verified and refined all of my Latin but enlightened me as to the language's nuances and made me laugh out loud in the process.

So many people read early versions of this book over the twelve years it took me to write it that it is difficult to remember them all, but some will never be forgotten. Eternal thanks to Lori Cook and Sally Rogan, who willingly endured countless revisions and never complained—at least not so I could hear. I will always love and cherish them both for their friendship, honesty, and unwavering encouragement. Every Batman needs a Robin, and for me that person is Rebecca Langston-George. Her humor and mad organizational skills helped me stay the course. And an extra-special thank-you goes to my critique partners and fellow sister-writers

Naomi Howland, Nancy Hayashi, (pod-sister) Lisze Bechtold, Anita McLaughlin, Marla Frazee, Barbara Bietz, Anne-Marie Saunders, Alexis O'Neill, Julie Frankel-Koch, and Joan Bransfield Graham. Additional thanks to my CenCal pals Toni Guy, Charlie Perryess, and Gwen Dandridge for their helpful insights and to Erin Wilcox and Jillian Bietz.

And last but not least, I could not have written a word if not for the love and support of my family. Ian, Alex, and Brett, you inspire me every day to make you proud. To my mother, who said I could do anything I set my mind to. And to Todd—you are my Adam. *Te amo etiam.*

It's been a long road, but the company has been stellar!

ABOUT THE AUTHOR

Mary Ann Fraser enjoys getting lost—in the wilderness, in the wilds of a book, or in a world of her own creation. This is her YA debut, but she writes and illustrates for children of all ages, with over seventy books to her credit. Mary Ann is a proud member of the Society of Children's Book Writers and Illustrators and a founding member of the Children's Authors Network. When she is not lost in a story, she is hiking and skiing the trails of Idaho, digging in the garden, or playing her hammered dulcimer and djembe drum (thankfully not at the same time). To learn more, visit www.maryannfraser.com.